MW01644367

Dangerous Influence

To Christina & Tom
Thanks for your support.
Bill

Dangerous Influence

William F. Amato

Cover design by Nancy Angeline.

Library of Congress Number:		00-191614
ISBN #:	Hardcover	0-7388-2989-7
	Softcover	0-7388-2990-0

This is a work of fiction. Names, characters, places and incidents either are the product of the author's imagination or are used fictitiously, and any resemblance to any actual persons, living or dead, events, or locales is entirely coincidental.

This book was printed in the United States of America.

To order additional copies of this book, contact:
Xlibris Corporation
1-888-7-XLIBRIS
www.Xlibris.com
Orders@Xlibris.com

PROLOGUE

RICHARD J. CASPER, the Commissioner of Streets and Sanitation for the City of Chicago, staggered down the concrete steps leading from upper Wacker Drive to the lower level of Wacker Drive which ran below Chicago's famous downtown Loop. He let go of the handrail, pulled up the collar of his suit coat and wrapped the lapels around his neck. A gust of wind rushed through the stairwell, nearly knocking him off his feet. He grabbed the rail and held on tightly to regain his balance before resuming his descent.

Casper wasn't a big man, but he wasn't small either. He stood about five-ten and weighed about one-sixty. He had a square face and dark gray eyes. His most impressive physical feature was his hair. He wasn't quite fifty, yet his hair was totally white. Even his eyebrows and facial hair were devoid of any color at all.

He looked at his watch; it was after midnight and unusually cold for late summer. Like many Chicagoans, he'd learned to ignore the weather, knowing that at any minute it might change, from hot to cold, rain to snow, windy to calm. He felt good nevertheless. Patting the left side of his suit coat he felt a bulge and heard the crinkling sound of paper as the envelope in his breast pocket and the contents within compressed and expanded under the pressure of his hand. He stopped again and took a deep breath. He'd had too much to drink. He should have quit after two martinis, but it was a celebration. There was no way he could refuse to participate, especially since the leasing company executive was picking up the tab for him and several of his political cronies including the Superintendent of Police. After all, it was one of the benefits that came with his job.

Among other things, it was his job to let out contracts. So what if he let them out to insiders? Insiders knew how to show their appreciation in the form of envelopes containing campaign contributions in cold hard cash. There was no harm in it. The city *did* need a new fleet of trucks. With winter coming, the streets had to be kept clean, the snow had to be plowed, and thousands of tons of salt had to be spread to prevent the roadways from icing.

Providing safe driving conditions for the city's motorists was a big responsibility. Why shouldn't he take advantage of the perks offered by those seeking to provide the material and equipment necessary to make it all possible? Why should he be any different than his predecessors? For well over a century, Chicago politicians had used their positions to enrich themselves. Why should things change now? Just because the turn of a *new* century was only a decade away.

Casper reached the bottom of the stairs and scanned the cars parked diagonally along the curb, each space protected by a meter standing at attention like a palace guard. The average citizen had better make sure he kept the meter fed with quarters unless he chose to nourish the city's coffers by paying a fifty dollar parking meter fine. Casper, of course, need not be concerned with such things. He had connections; he had clout. He didn't pay fines; he levied them and collected them.

Casper glanced around, suddenly sensing that he was not alone, but saw no one.

Casper took in another deep breath of crisp cold air, hoping it would clear his head of the fog clouding his brain and the low pitched hum sounding in his inner ear causing his pupils to vibrate, making it impossible for him to focus on anything.

He continued to feel as though someone were watching him, but after looking around again, and again seeing no one he dismissed his feelings and continued searching for his car.

Casper squinted his gray eyes and tried again to distinguish his car from the several other vehicles lined up along the curb. That's when he noticed it. At first he thought it was just a shadow. He squinted his eyes even tighter and put his hand to his forehead like an Indian brave to shield his eyes from the glare of the overhead lighting. Seeing was still difficult, but he could now make out the figure of a man, a man in a dark suit, and he was holding something in his hands.

"Hey, I know you," Casper said, as he stepped toward the man. "You're the . . ."

He heard a click and then a whooshing sound and then nothing. The dark figure took six quick steps then knelt beside the still remains of the late city commissioner. He removed the envelope from his pocket and disappeared into the darkness.

* * *

Patrick Grogan, Alderman of the 61st Ward of the City of Chicago, sat with his chin in his palms. His eyes were glued to the headline on the front page of the Chicago Courier . . . COMMISSIONER CASPER MURDERED. The news story described the violent death of Grogan's old friend and associate as being caused by an arrow, the kind shot from a mechanical cross bow. Grogan grimaced when he read that the wound was to the head. A perfect shot, right between the eyes.

Another old friend paced the floor in front of Grogan's desk: John McLaughlin, the Commander of the 35th Precinct of the Chicago Police Department. The three had been lifelong friends since kindergarten and had remained close for over forty years.

They went to the same schools, they had the same friends, they even screwed the same girls, and they did it all in the same ward that Grogan now controlled. The same ward that was now slipping away from them, where a new element was beginning to threaten their power. A new element that was slowly, but surely, taking over what had been theirs for decades.

Grogan looked up from his newspaper and focused on his friend.

"Pat, this is our neighborhood," McLaughlin said as he paced the floor in front of Grogan's desk. "Our parents and grandparents made this neighborhood what it is. This has always been the best neighborhood in the city. Hell, even the mayor is from this ward, and the two mayors before him. This has been the most influential, the most important ward in the city for the last forty-five years and look what's happened to it. Those fuckin' spics are everywhere. For all we know, it was one of them who killed Richie. After all . . . they do have Indian blood in them."

Grogan smiled. McLauglin continued to pace with his head bowed and his hands behind his back.

"This used to be the cleanest neighborhood in town." The commander lifted his head. He stopped pacing, then turned to face Grogan. "Look at the neighborhood now: beer cans and booze bottles litter the streets and sidewalks. You gotta be careful where you walk or you'll step in piss or vomit. Everything it took our people generations to build, these fuckin' Mexicans tore down in just a few short years. Now they're threatening to take our political power away from us."

McLauglin resumed his pacing.

"Taking Richie out may be only the beginning; who knows, maybe one of us will be next. Imagine that, a bunch of drunken, illiterate, wife-beating junkies are on the verge of wiping us out."

Patrick Grogan listened to his old friend rant and rave about Casper's murder, the neighborhood, their parents and grandparents, and how the spics were ruining the ward. He knew McLaughlin was deeply moved by the loss of an old friend, but he also knew he didn't really care about the neighborhood any more than *he* did. He knew McLaughlin was leading up to something, and he wished he'd get to the point.

"Well, fuck them," McLaughlin continued, "let's see who wipes out who."

"John, please," Grogan interrupted. "I can't take it any more. What are you driving at?"

McLaughlin stopped his pacing, turned and placed his beefy palms on the desk, his large frame casting a shadow over his old friend. Grogan felt a chill as he looked up at McLaughlin standing stiff-armed, his long thick fingers spread out on the desk top, his eyes glaring at him. "Money! That's what I'm driving at."

"Okay, John, now you have my undivided attention, I guarantee it. Please sit down, relax, tell me about it."

Grogan shifted in his chair and leaned back; he locked his hands behind his graying head of hair and smiled, revealing a large gap between his two front teeth.

McLaughlin remained standing. "Do you have any idea how many junkies we have in our ward? Better yet, do you have any idea how many dope dealers we have in our ward?"

Grogan sat silently, his mind already anticipating where McLaughlin's words were headed. "Are you suggesting we join forces with the drug dealers and therefore remove ourselves from this hit list you think we're on?" Grogan asked, becoming a little impatient.

"Join forces? We don't have to join forces. We simply take over . . . by force. You almost got your ass kicked in the last election, right? Even with all the votes we were able to steal, you still came close to losing. We have three and a half years till the next election . . . if you live that long. Can you guarantee you're going to win? I don't think so, but I can guarantee that I'll get kicked out on my ass along with Tommy O'Mara if you lose."

"You say we simply take over by force. If it's so simple, why hasn't law enforcement done it a long time ago?"

"Come on, Pat. You know law enforcement has to follow the rules. As a cop, my authority is so restricted I have to get permission to wipe my own ass, but as a man I can do as I please. I can deal with these lice on my terms."

"And what are your terms?" Grogan interrupted.

"My officers are arresting twenty to thirty Mexican junkies every night. Each one of these guys has at least a hundred-dollar-a-day habit. That means two to three thousand dollars minimum passes through our precinct every day. We're only talking about the junkies we pinch; there are hundreds more we don't."

McLaughlin stopped for a moment and studied Grogan's pockmarked face. Grogan smiled. McLaughlin knew his friend liked what he was hearing. It was obvious by his expression.

"I'm listening," Grogan said, taking advantage of an opportunity to get a word in.

"A man in my command busted one of these street level dealers the other day. He's been busted before, and he's done time for dealing once already. The officer who busted him is one of my best and most loyal men, Jack Bronkowski. You know who he is. He's the guy I call the 'Littlest Polock' because he's the shortest man in my command."

"He may be short," Grogan added, "but if he's the same Bronkowski I'm thinking of, he's pretty tough, and smart, too."

"That's him. He's very smart. Instead of recording what this dealer told him and including it in the arrest report, he came to me with it."

"What's the kid's name, and what exactly did he tell Jack?" Grogan asked.

"His name is Jose Herrera, and he told Bronkowski he wanted to make a deal. He offered the name of every major drug supplier in our area. That's when Jack came to me."

"What happened next?" Grogan asked, shoving the newspaper aside.

"I told Jack to bring the kid to my office where I wouldn't have to worry about anybody accidentally overhearing what we were about to learn. The kid was a wealth of information. It turns out there are six major suppliers. Our local vendors, so to speak, purchase drugs from them for resale on the street. These major suppliers have representatives in our ward who deal directly with guys like Jose Herrera. Herrera says he alone buys twenty-five thousand dollars worth of goods every week, and that's at his cost . . . and he's small potatoes."

"Okay, I think I know where you're going," Grogan said. "Please continue, I want to hear you tell it."

"All right, here's my plan," McLaughlin whispered, as he finally accepted Grogan's invitation to sit down and relax. "We let Herrera lead us to his suppliers, only instead of buying the goods, we guarantee them protection as payment. It's perfect; in the next three years, we could make millions. Of course, we can't actually peddle the stuff ourselves, so that's where our spic partner comes in. As long as they keep Herrera supplied with merchandise at no cost." McLaughlin leaned back in his chair and grinned proudly.

"What about all the rest of the dealers in the ward?"

"I can push my men to keep as many small-time dealers off the street as possible, therefore cutting Herrera's competition substantially. Of course, we'll have to provide protection for Herrera. That'll be Jack Bronkowski's job. He'll be like Herrera's shadow, for two reasons: number one, he'll have to be sure Jose operates unmolested, but more important, it will be his job to make sure our profits aren't molested."

"How do you intend to divide these profits?" Grogan asked. "And how do you know we can trust this junkie Herrera?"

McLaughlin held his hands up in front of himself. "Jack will handle the junkie. I'm not worried about him. Bronkowski knows how to handle that end, and Herrera knows he'll be watching. As far as the profits are concerned, Herrera will be satisfied with enough to maintain his habit, and our guarantee to keep him out of jail, plus a couple of grand a week for spending money. Considering the amount of business I expect we'll be doing, that calculates to be about ten percent of our total take. I figure we can split the rest three ways between you, me and Jack."

"Four ways," Grogan broke in. "I want Tommy O'Mara to share equally. Don't worry, we'll find enough work for him to make it worth our while."

McLaughlin's eyes flashed as he jumped to his feet. "Does that mean you go for my idea?"

"Whatda you think?"

"Okay, four ways, twenty-two and a half percent each," McLaughlin retorted. He stopped for a moment to marvel at how quickly he did the math in his head. "That should translate into at least seven or eight grand a week for each of us."

Just then, a buzzer sounded, signaling someone was entering the outer office. Seconds later, there was a knock on the door.

"Come in," Grogan answered.

The door swung open and Tommy O'Mara swaggered in. Though only five feet six inches tall, he had the ego of a giant. His light brown hair was heavily shellacked to hold his style in place. His manicured finger nails sparkled like the diamond pinkie ring he wore on his right hand. He wore a tailor-made suit with no tie, his shirt collar was open and his cuffs were exposed just enough to display his monogrammed initials. His brown eyes were concealed by the dark glasses he wore. Tommy O'Mara was in every way your stereotype, two bit, Chicago politician.

"What's happening, Patrick? Hey if it isn't our gallant protector in blue. How you doing Johnny?"

O'Mara may have had the ego of a giant, but McLaughlin, at six feet, four inches tall, looked like one next to him.

"How you doin' Tommy," McLaughlin greeted with a wave, flopping his large frame back in the chair.

Tommy O'Mara stopped in the middle of the room, shifting his eyes from Grogan to McLaughlin.

"What the hell's going on here? You two guys look like you just got caught in the act of something nasty. Oh man, if you could see the images in my mind right now." Tommy began to laugh almost uncontrollably.

Grogan and McLaughlin just sat, waiting. After several seconds, it was obvious that Tommy realized he was the only one who saw the humor in his remarks.

"Are you through?" Grogan asked. "Do you want to sit down and listen to what we've been talking about?"

Tommy stood motionless for a second, then, without saying a word, he sat down in the chair opposite Commander McLaughlin.

"What's up?" Tommy asked in a calm, concerned voice.

For the next thirty minutes, Grogan and the Commander brought Tommy up to date on Jose Herrera and their plans for the future.

* * *

Tommy listened without saying a word, without interrupting once. Even though his mind was flooded with questions, he resisted the impulse to ask them. He didn't want to seem skeptical or suspicious. He didn't want to seem concerned or frightened. He *was* frightened, he *was* concerned, but the money, the money chased the fear from his gut. The money made the risk seem acceptable.

The more his cronies revealed the details of their scheme, the more acceptable the risk became. The more they discussed the potential profits, the less concerned he felt. Grogan's final words on the subject would remain embedded in O'Mara's brain for the rest of his life.

"Come on Tommy, help us out with this. You won't be sorry, I guarantee it."

"Okay, I'll go along, but we have to be careful, very careful. You both know that half-breed Dago-Jew bastard has been on our asses for months now. He'd been riding Richie Casper's ass—God have mercy on his soul—even longer. If he *ever* gets wind of a scheme like this, we won't have to worry about the Mexicans wiping us out."

Grogan slammed his palms on his desktop and rose from his chair. "Fuck him and the radio waves he rode in on. If 'Mr. Radio Talk Show Host' continues to fuck with us, we'll start fucking with him. I've got plans for that big mouth. I'm going to shut him up for good, I guarantee it."

CHAPTER 1

"I heard them today. I heard what they said about the one man who has the guts to stand up to them. They want to silence him. They want to run him out of town. Well let them try it. Do they really think they could get away with something like that? Who do they think they are? Don't they know the power they possess is not really theirs? It was granted to them by the people. They weren't born with it, it's on loan. It's supposed to be used in the service of the people. Not to service themselves."

MARCO FISCHER SMOOTHED his thinning brown hair back and put his headset in place. He waited for his producer's cue to begin his afternoon talk show. Marco wiped his palms on his blue jeans and pulled at the open collar of his cotton shirt. Unlike his producer, he never wore a tie to work; the studio was so stuffy, he often removed his shirt and worked in his undershirt.

Marco enjoyed his work immensely. He often wondered how many forty-year-old men were as happy and content with their jobs as he was. He listened as the disclaimer and the taped introduction prepared the waiting audience. He focused his brown eyes on the outstretched arm and index finger of his producer, Tony Ruskin, pointing in his direction.

"Good afternoon, ladies and gentlemen and children of all ages. This is your favorite Jew-Wop, Marco Fischer. Welcome to another session of Marco's Morgue, where we expose abuse and corruption by crooked politicians and their lackeys, our so-called protectors, the Chicago Police Department. Now don't misunderstand me, I'm not saying all politicians and police are corrupt, but many, far too many of them are, and it is our intention, here on Marco's Morgue, to embalm them and bury them forever."

Marco unbuttoned his shirt down to his waistline.

"For those of you who may be listening for the first time, let me explain something about myself, my values and beliefs.

"I consider myself to be a true American, a traditional American if you will. One who stands up for his principles and when he gets pushed, pushes back. I'm not a tough guy by any stretch, but I'm proud of my heritage. I'm proud to identify with those who made this country what it is today, many of whom gave their lives in the process. Lives that were sacrificed so those of us who survived would not have to be afraid to speak our minds."

Marco paused for a moment to adjust his headset.

"We owe those who died to preserve our rights. How do we pay them back? By standing up to anyone who would try to take those rights away from us. As an American, I believe we have an obligation, a responsibility to all other Americans to resist, to complain, to proclaim out loud whenever anyone, especially our government, attempts to control or silence us."

He stopped to wipe away the perspiration beginning to form on his forehead, pulled out his shirt tails and continued.

"To accept what government deems without question is un-American. If we have learned anything from history, it is that we must question government. If we do not, government will become totalitarian. Once that happens, we no longer have the right to question.

"You can call me a fanatic if you like. You can call me a right wing radical, please do. You can turn your back, walk away and disassociate yourself from me. But, remember, if the day ever comes when your rights are being denied and trampled upon, it will be me and those like me that you will come to for protection.

I pray that day never comes. If it does, however, you can depend on me, even if I couldn't depend on you."

Marco shifted in his seat as he organized his notes.

"Okay, let's get down to business," he said.

"Today I want to talk about two young men. One who was recently found in his cell with a towel tied around his neck. The police say his death by strangulation was self-inflicted. I ask you, how is that possible? Have any of you ever tried to strangle yourself with a towel? Is this an insult to our intelligence, or what? And yet they expect us to believe it. To just accept their word, without question. Well, not me and I hope, not you. Jose Herrera was accused of stabbing to death a police officer named Jack Bronkowski. A policeman who, I might add, was under investigation for shaking down drug dealers. Yes, Jose Herrera was a convicted drug dealer and an addict himself, but he was still entitled to a fair trial before being executed."

He turned to the next page of his hand written script.

"The second young man, however, was not a drug dealer or even an addict. He was an honor student and a credit to the Hispanic community, but he, too, is dead, supposedly as a result of his own actions. This boy, Louis Zappata, according to the police report, was shot and killed by an officer who claimed Zappata pulled a gun on him. There's only one problem with the cop's story, no gun has ever been found."

Marco paused again to give his audience a chance to digest what he had just said and prepare themselves for what was coming next.

"The cop says one of the dead boy's accomplices ran away with the gun, but I say, because of the crowd that gathered around the body immediately after the shooting, the cop didn't have time to plant a gun on his victim. Oh, I almost forgot . . . there's one more problem. Young Louis was shot in the back . . . three times. Again, ladies and gentlemen and all you children out there, are we supposed to believe this just because a cop said so?

"This kind of out-of-control behavior by the police has to

stop, but how can we ever stop it when two-bit politicians continue to protect and make excuses for their lackeys. I am outraged by the actions of the police department in this city, and I know you folks out there are just as fed up as I am. So, let's talk about it. The lines are open. We'll take a commercial break for two minutes, then I want to hear what you have to say."

* * *

After the break, Marco took his first call. "Line four, you're on. I see this caller doesn't want to be identified. Okay, that's your prerogative," Marco said as he pushed the button opening the line. There was silence for two or three seconds. "Hello caller, you're on the air."

"I just wanted to say I'm with you," the caller said.

Marco listened to the unusual sound of the caller's voice. It had a strange quality, a hissing quality. It made Marco uncomfortable and a little nervous.

"I support everything you say," the caller continued. "I know you have a lot of people who call you and say that, but I really mean it. Someday soon you'll find out I'm not just talking on the radio."

"Could you be more specific? What exactly do you mean by that comment?" Marco interrupted.

"You'll see. You'll see soon enough that you're not alone. You have a friend who backs up his words and *yours* with action."

CLICK. The mysterious caller hung up, leaving Marco a bit confused and curious.

Marco took several more calls and seemed to get over his initial shock from the first caller.

Marco heard Tony's voice come through his headset. "Time for a break."

Then Marco said. "We'll take a break, then I'll be back with more of Marco's Morgue."

* * *

Marco removed his headset to again wipe the perspiration from his brow. He looked up when he heard a tapping on the thick plate glass widow separating him from the technician's booth. His producer was pointing to the telephone receiver in his hand and mouthing the words "line 3". Marco got the message and pushed the button opening the line, hoping it wasn't the hissing caller again. "Marco Fischer," he announced.

"I don't know anything about the Zappata kid, but I can tell you a lot about Herrera."

"Who is this?" Marco questioned, as he wondered how many cigarettes it had taken to make the man's voice sound as it did.

"This is someone who's had it, just like you. I can tell you a lot, but it has to be confidential and not on the phone."

"How do I know this isn't some kind of prank?" Marco asked.

"How do I know what you preach on your show is really what you believe and not just a lot of show biz bullshit?" the caller shot back in a raspy growl.

"All right, I'll think about meeting with you, but I'm ready to go back on the air in just a few seconds. Call me after the show. I'll try to have an answer for you by then. If I decide to meet with you, we'll set up a time and place then."

For the next three hours, Marco tried to listen to the complaints and concerns of his callers, but two callers in particular preoccupied him. He couldn't get the hissing sound of his first caller's voice out of his mind. And then there was the one with the raspy voice.

He had received many calls over the years from people who claimed to have important inside information, but he could always detect phonies by the sound of their voices. The raspy-voiced caller was no phony, he was for real. The man's voice held an unmistakable sound of truth. The hissing voice was still on his mind, but he hadn't made a judgment about it yet. He needed to think about it a little while longer.

* * *

Alderman Patrick Grogan sat at his desk listening to the radio as his personal assistant, Tommy O'Mara, poured another shot of scotch into his waiting glass. "That son-of-a-bitch," O'Mara growled. "He's rabble-rousing again. Something has to be done about this guy. If he ever latches on to something solid, he could bring us all down."

"Forget it," Grogan said. "He's an entertainer, an actor, it's all fluff and no guff. He's gonna clean up corruption. Yeah, sure! If he did, he'd be out of a job and he knows it. Without us, he can't make a living. Besides, I told you. I have plans for him. He won't be around much longer, I guarantee it."

"Whatever you say, Pat," Tommy said as he poured another round. "But he burns my ass, anyway."

"He's all talk,"Grogan assured. "Don't worry, soon we're going to burn his ass, good. I guarantee it."

* * *

Hoffman Estates is a far western suburb about thirty-five miles from Marco Fischer's broadcast studio. It was a long drive, but Marco knew it wouldn't take more than an hour. He had made the drive many times when he lived in Schaumburg, the suburb adjoining Hoffman Estates.

Marco felt fine traveling the Kennedy Expressway from downtown Chicago to Cumberland Avenue. He was actually pretty excited about meeting the raspy-voiced caller. As he approached the toll way entrance, he reached into his pocket, hoping to find enough change to throw into the toll basket.

Fucking leaches, he thought, separating the coins in his right hand with his thumb, remembering the promises made decades earlier. *Thirty years ago, the scum bag politicians told us we would only have to pay the toll until they recouped the costs for building the highway. Yeah, sure*, he thought, snickering under his breath.

The toll was only a nickel then, and there were far fewer cars on the roads. Now it's forty cents, and they have a new excuse for ripping off the people. They need the money for maintenance. Oh yeah, road repairs, one of the most favored methods of politicians for picking up a few extra bucks, kickbacks from road construction companies.

Suddenly, Maryanne's face appeared in his thoughts. Memories flooded his brain; he couldn't ignore them. He tried to push them out of his mind, but they were relentless, like huge waves rushing, pounding against the shoreline of Lake Michigan. Just as the earth eventually gives way, Marco also gave in, he surrendered. Tears filled his eyes and clouded his vision. His arms stiffened, pushing his back against the leather seat of his late model Cadillac. He tightened his grip on the steering wheel, restricting the blood flow to his hands.

The vision of two mangled cars, twisted, smashed beyond recognition flashed before him. The windshield of his car became a screen, his mind projecting the pictures like a torturous slide show.

"Maryanne. Maryanne," Marco whispered, bowing his head momentarily, tears dropping from his eyes onto his lap, soaking into the heavy denim material of his blue jeans. He thanked God that she had died instantly.

Six years had passed since her death. Six years since Maryanne and another motorist, who didn't realize the traffic light wasn't working, collided in the middle of an intersection. It was a terrible accident, which resulted in the death of both drivers, but it was avoidable. It should have never happened.

Two policemen were at the scene. Instead of taking control of a dangerous situation, instead of placing flares in the intersection to alert drivers and direct traffic, they remained in their car because it was raining.

"Why? Why? Why did you let her die? You lousy mother fuckers" Marco cried out pounding his fist on the steering wheel, but the frustration continued to build up inside him. He let the tears come now, drowning himself in self pity, as memories of that horrible night saturated his thoughts.

It wasn't a heavy rain, just a slight drizzle, but it was enough to keep the cops from performing their sworn duty to "serve and protect." Two people died because of the arrogance of two cops who forgot, or maybe never knew or cared, that they had a responsibility to people who entrusted their safety and welfare to them. And why not? Were they punished for their negligence? Were they penalized for dereliction of their duty? Were they even reprimanded for failing to take two simple measures that would have prevented the deaths of two innocent people?

"*No! No! No*!" Marco's brain shouted; *No . . . no . . . no . . .* ," his heart sobbed.

The officers, according to their supervisors, had no responsibility to leave their vehicle and physically direct traffic. Their only responsibility was to notify the proper authorities of the malfunctioning traffic light, which is what they did.

The cops returned to their usual daily lives, but Marco Fischer's life would never be usual again. He had gone from a happily married man with a stay-at-home wife and ten-year-old daughter to a broken and bitter man with a heart filled with rage and vengeance. Had it not been for his daughter, Sarah, and her repeated pleas for him to let his anger go, he probably would have driven himself mad.

Marco smiled, remembering how it was Sarah who gave him the idea to change the format of his radio program from a home improvement show, where through his experience as a building contractor, he answered questions about construction and remodeling and advised his listeners on their do-it-yourself projects, to a program dealing with incompetence and corruption in politics and police matters.

The new format became the perfect outlet for his anger and frustration, not only for him, but for his many listeners who felt the same helplessness and alienation. In a matter of a few short weeks, Marco's Morgue, as his new show became known, found itself at the top of the ratings and became the biggest moneymaker his station, WHLP, ever had.

In time, Marco was able to deal with his grief by helping others deal with theirs. Sarah continued to encourage her dad, and she, too, learned to cope with her grief by helping him. Marco sold his home in Schaumburg, and he and Sarah moved to a spacious three-bedroom condo on Chicago's famous Lake Shore Drive, just a few short blocks from the radio station. The change helped Marco greatly, eliminating the constant reminders of Maryanne, enabling him to work through the unbearable anguish he was suffering. The emotional breakdowns became less frequent, making it possible to conceal them from Sarah.

After Sarah graduated grammar school Marco enrolled her in the city's prestigious Astor School, where only the most motivated students were welcome.

Life had become very good for Marco. His fame and popularity grew to the point where he was the most influential radio personality in town. Sarah continued to work hard and remained at the top of her class. As a junior in high school, Sarah was beginning to look forward to college and, later, a career in broadcasting. She hoped to follow in her father's footsteps.

The thought of what a beautiful intelligent young lady his little girl turned out to be brought a smile to Marco's face and helped him stop the tears. It also brought his thoughts back to the present just in time. Looking up, he saw the road sign indicating Roselle Road as the next exit. Marco exited and turned left toward Golf Road, then turned right on Golf and continued west for about a mile and a half to Walnut Lane.

* * *

The Covered Bridge Family Style Restaurant was located on the southwest corner of Golf and Walnut. Marco parked his Sedan DeVille on the opposite side of the entrance and cautiously entered.

A very pretty young brunette carrying a leather-bound menu approached him. "Just one for dinner?"

"I'm meeting someone," Marco answered. "I'm sure he's here." Marco scanned the sparsely occupied dining room. The dinner crowd was long gone; most of the tables and booths were empty. Only a spattering of patrons remained.

"The party's name?" The hostess inquired.

Marco had to stop and think for a second; the code name he was to use momentarily slipped his mind . . . "Oh yes. Mr. Caller," Marco stammered.

"Yes! This way," the young lady said as she turned to lead Marco into the smoking section. Marco followed the hostess to the north wall of the room and last booth in a long line of booths with burgundy upholstered seats and backrests, trimmed in natural oak.

Seated facing the entrance was a middle-aged man. He was unshaven and in need of a haircut. He was dressed in a black woolen crew-neck sweater and a pair of faded blue jeans. He was much older than Marco imagined judging by the sound of his voice on the telephone. When he heard the man speak there was no doubt, it was the same voice. "Mr. Fischer?" the man said as he died out his cigarette and offered his hand. "It's a pleasure to finally meet you."

Marco accepted the man's hand and searched his dark eyes as he felt his firm handshake. "The pleasure is mine, I hope," Marco chided. "Please call me Marco."

"Okay, Marco," he said, lighting up another smoke.

"What can I call *you*?"

"For now, Mr. Caller will have to do," he said as smoke flowed through his nostrils. "Please understand, if you knew exactly what kind of people we're dealing with, you'd know I can't be too careful." Mr. Caller warily darted his eyes from side to side.

"What kind of people *are* we dealing with?" Marco asked, sliding into the booth, wanting to get down to business as quickly as possible.

"No small talk?" the man asked in a large cloud of blue smoke.

"No small talk, Mr. Caller. You said you could tell me a lot. That's why I agreed to meet you. Let's not waste any time, if you don't mind."

"Okay, Mr. Fisch . . . I mean Marco, we won't waste any time. You're right, Herrera didn't strangle himself, he was murdered. It's *why* he was murdered that I think will interest you."

"I'm interested," Marco said as he leaned back and prepared himself for what he hoped would be the story he'd waited years for.

"Jose Herrera was a junkie and a dope dealer. You already know that, but what you don't know is that he was working for Pat Grogan."

"Pat Grogan, the alderman?"

"Not so loud, I told you I can't be too careful. For all I know, we're being watched right now."

"Okay! Okay! But did I hear you right? Did you say Alderman Patrick Grogan?" Marco asked in a hushed voice.

"Yes, that's exactly what I said."

"That dirt bag, slime ball, son-of-a-bitch. I knew it! I knew that scum bag was involved in something. Tell me! Tell me now," Marco demanded, slamming his palms on the table. "All of it, everything. Give me something I can use to hang the bastard with, and I promise you I'll have him dangling in no time."

"If you don't lower your voice, *I'll* be the one dangling," the man growled through his clenched tobacco-stained teeth.

Marco hunched his shoulders and looked around the room. Confident that no one could actually hear what was being said, he turned his attention back to his mysterious new friend. "Excuse me please, but I've been trying to get something on that asshole for years. I guess I'm getting a little excited. Tell me more. I promise I won't interrupt."

The man lit another cigarette and took a long deep drag before continuing. "As you know, Grogan's ward has become more and more Hispanic in recent years. In the last two elections, Latino opponents came darn close to defeating him. It doesn't take a genius to figure Grogan's days as alderman are numbered, and as I'm sure you know, Grogan is no genius."

There was a slight pause. Marco kept his mouth shut. It was difficult, but he'd promised. Then Mr. Caller began speaking again.

"Grogan's always been a thief, but he spent it as fast or faster than he could steal it. Fixing tickets, shaking down small businessmen, taking kickbacks on construction projects; they were all money-makers, but as I said, not enough. Then one day, the biggest money-maker of them all just fell into his lap."

Marco's eyes almost bulged out of his head. It was all he could do to prevent shouting out what he knew he was about to hear.

"Dope," Mr. Caller said. "Drugs, all kinds; from pot to cocaine, crack to heroin. Drugs of all shapes and forms, and they were pure profit. Unlike other dealers who had to buy their goods, Grogan's supply was free. It was 'no charge' and it came in an uninterrupted flow from the safest source in town."

There was another pause. Marco wanted desperately to shout, "Who? Who?", but he remained silent. He waited patiently for a very long time. To be exact, about ten seconds.

"The cops," Mr. Caller said, nodding his head slowly. "How much safer can you get?"

"Wait a minute," Marco said, holding the palms of his hands up as if to physically stop the man in his tracks. "Are you about to tell me there's more to the killing of that cop Bronkowski than meets the eye?"

"You're a very adept mathematician, Marco; you're beginning to put two and two together. Yes, there's much more. It was a killing, but it wasn't murder. It was self defense," the man said, blowing another huge cloud of smoke into the atmosphere.

"Self defense?" Marco repeated.

"That's right. Bronkowski was sent out to silence Herrera, who was about to upset the cart and expose all the rotten apples.

Bronkowski made one fatal mistake. He tried to take Herrera out with a knife. He forgot Herrera grew up on the streets of Tijuana, Mexico, where knife fighting is the favorite sport. By the time Bronkowski reached for his service revolver, it was too late. Herrera's mini machete had already done it's job. Bronkowski was found with his stomach sliced open and gutted like a pig in a slaughterhouse."

"That's a detail the news reports failed to reveal," Marco pointed out suspiciously. "How is it that you came upon information the police have obviously withheld from the media?"

"One day I may tell you how, or maybe you'll eventually figure it out for yourself. For now, you'll just have to take my word for it."

Marco looked directly into his informant's eyes. "What about Herrera?" Marco asked. "Who killed him?"

Mr. Caller waved off the waitress who approached with her order pad in hand.

"Exactly who, I don't know," he said. "But it was definitely someone in the Cook County Sheriff's Department. As you know, the County Jail is manned by county employees. I don't have to tell you that Grogan is closely associated with the County Sheriff, Morgan Connelly. I'm sure you realize Connelly is just babysitting the office for the ex-sheriff, Sean O'Bannion, until he gets out of the federal pen some time next month." He leaned back in his seat and took another deep pull from his cigarette.

"Where else but Chicago and Cook County could shit like this be going on?" Marco sighed as he closed his eyes and held his head in his hands. "Do you think it's possible that O'Bannion thinks he can be re-elected sheriff after being convicted in federal court of bribery and racketeering charges?"

Lighting another cigarette, the man remarked, "In this town, anything can happen. Nothing would surprise me. A Chicago politician's greed is surpassed only by his arrogance. I put nothing past them." Mr. Caller looked at his watch. "I must go now, we'll talk again. I'll call the next time I can get away. And don't try to follow me after I leave, or you will surely never hear from me again." Mr. Caller began to extricate himself from the booth.

Marco slid his six foot frame out of the seat and blocked Mr. Caller, who stood as tall as Marco, but heavier and more muscular.

"Wait a minute," Marco said, grabbing the man's sleeve. "What am I supposed to do now? I can't keep this to myself. I want to tell your story on my show. My listeners will go crazy when they hear this."

"Go ahead, use it. Why do you think I want to remain anonymous?" The man started to walk away, then turned to face Marco again. "Tell me something. Why do you call yourself a Jew-Wop?"

"You don't know?" Marco laughed. "I'm half Jewish and half Italian. Jew-Wop. Get it?"

The man looked at Marco without expression for a second or two then lit another cigarette and walked out. As he did, Marco noticed a slight bulge around his waist as the man pulled his sweater down.

This guy must really be scared, Marco thought. Scared enough to carry a gun for protection.

* * *

It was almost eleven o'clock by the time Marco walked into his apartment. "Hey! Where have you been? I was beginning to get worried." Marco's sixteen year old daughter Sarah stood hands on her hips looking like the spitting image of her mother. Sarah had her light brown hair pulled back in a pony tail. Her brown eyes had the same sparkle as her mom's. Her complexion was clear and unblemished, unusual for a girl her age. At five-foot-six, she already had the body of a grown woman. She wore a short sleeve red and white gingham blouse and a pair of jeans. She padded toward her father, her feet covered in white cotton socks.

Marco took his little girl into his arms. "Thank you, Sweetheart," he said, as he held her close to him.

"Thanks for what?" She asked as she kissed his cheek.

"Thanks for being worried about your old man and thanks . . . for just being you."

Sarah took a step back and looked into her father's eyes. "What's going on, Dad? Is everything all right?" she asked. She always knew when something new or unusual was happening in her father's life. Whatever his mood, whatever he was feeling was always revealed in his eyes.

"Don't tell me," she giggled. "You met someone. Is she pretty, is she rich? I can tell something is going on. You're excited about something. What is it?"

"Something is going on, but it's not a woman," Marco said, shaking his finger at her.

"Well, I wish it were, Dad. You've been alone too long. I wish you'd meet a nice lady. You need someone to share your life with. I'll be going away to college soon, and I hate the thought of you being all alone with no one to nag you and get on your nerves."

"I don't need a woman for that, I have Tony Ruskin. He's a worse nag than any woman, and he gets on my nerves even more than you do." Marco said with a smile.

"And how is your producer? He hasn't been around for quite awhile."

"Well, as a matter of fact, he's the one who met a woman. She's been running him ragged. It seems he has no time for anything but her."

"Is she pretty?" Sarah asked, as she wrapped her arm around his waist and looked up at him.

"Not as pretty as you."

"No, really. Is she pretty?

"Well, he thinks she is, but she's a little too skinny for my taste."

Sarah hugged her dad and squeezed as hard as she could.

"Come on Dad, tell me what happened tonight. What are you so excited about?"

"I'm not excited," Marco insisted.

"Yes you are. I can see it in your eyes."

"Okay, okay! I'll tell you, but you have to promise not to talk to anyone about it."

"Okay, I promise," Sarah said, as she took Marco by the hand and led him toward the couch. For the next hour, Sarah sat wide-eyed as her father brought her up to date on the day's events.

CHAPTER 2

"I can't let him stand up to those bastards alone. I must do something to help. But, what?"

TONY RUSKIN GREETED Marco as he entered the studio in his usual obnoxious, but lovable fashion. "Where have you been?" Tony bellowed, his brown eyes flashing while waving his arms wildly over his head of thick, bushy, brown hair. "I have a million things to go over with you before air time."

At thirty-one, Tony was a bit high strung, but he did an excellent job as Marco's producer. More than that, however, he was a good and loyal friend, which made it easy for Marco to tolerate his occasional emotional out-bursts.

"Don't worry, we have plenty of time," Marco assured.

"Plenty of time? You call forty-five minutes plenty of time? We have to review the latest news reports. We have to check the headline stories in the papers, and we have to decide how we're going to follow-up on yesterday's broadcast."

"Forget about all that. I know exactly what today's show is going to be," Marco said as he entered his office.

"What are you talking about?" Tony Ruskin bellowed as he followed close behind. "How can you know if I don't know? Did you forget I'm your producer? I'm supposed to know what's going on at all times. How am I supposed to do my job if I don't know what the hell is going on?"

"Take it easy, you'll find out," Marco said as he shuffled through his briefcase looking for his notes from the night before.

Tony flopped his slim frame into the chair in front of Marco's desk and began fidgeting with his tie. "Okay, tell me about it. What are we doing today?"

"Not now," Marco said with an impish look on his face. "We don't have time."

"That's what I've been trying to tell you!" Ruskin roared, as he jumped back to his feet. "I can't take this anymore. You're going to give me a nervous breakdown."

"Relax, will you?" Marco said, taking Tony by the arm. "Just go to your desk and find something to occupy yourself with until air time. I have to organize my thoughts and prepare myself for the broadcast. I know how you feel, but you'll find out what I'm planning soon enough. Right now, I need peace and quiet." Marco stopped to check his watch. "I'll see you in the booth in half an hour."

Marco sat down behind his desk and looked around his small office with pride. The walls were adorned with plaques and awards celebrating the success of the most talked about radio show in Chicago. The bookshelves over the credenza were crowded with trophies, recognizing the accomplishments of his ten years in the radio business.

He looked down at his notes from the night before. *Is this it?* He asked himself. *Is this a new beginning for Marco's Morgue?*

* * *

Marco watched the big clock on the wall as the second hand swept its face. He could hear the recorded announcement introducing the start of what promised to be the most controversial session of Marco's Morgue to date.

* * *

"Good afternoon, ladies and gentlemen and children of all ages. Welcome to Marco's Morgue. Get your shovels ready. Today we begin to dig the graves of one of Chicago's slimiest slime ball politicians and two of his scum-bag lackeys."

Tony Ruskin, for the first time in his life, was speechless. In the six years he'd worked with Marco Fischer, he'd learned to never be surprised at anything he said. He'd become accustomed to the outrageous charges and accusations made by the most inflammatory radio personality in Chicago, perhaps in the entire country, maybe in the world. What he was hearing tonight, however, was more than just inflammatory, it was dangerous and on the verge of being insanely irresponsible.

For four solid hours, Marco continued his tirade. The telephone lines were on fire. Calls came in from every corner of the city, but the most important calls came in from the 61st ward. Calls describing all sorts of police misconduct, from soliciting bribes to extreme physical brutality. The most pertinent came from several anonymous callers who claimed to be drug dealers who had been shaken down by police officers including the murdered cop, Jack Bronkowski.

"Ah, Yes. The murdered cop," Marco quipped. "Jack Bronkowski. OOPS! Excuse me, but he wasn't murdered at all. According to my source, the accused murderer and now dead Jose Herrera acted in self-defense. That's right folks, self-defense. Let's go back a few weeks to when a certain drug dealer, who was really an undercover DEA operative, was approached and threatened with death unless he turned over his supply of illegal drugs. He was threatened with death, ladies and gentlemen, not arrest. Since when did it become *you're under the threat of death instead of you're under arrest?*"

Marco ran his fingers through his hair, which was now saturated with perspiration.

"Should there have been any question of this officer's intentions? Only if you're a Chicago politician or another cop could there be another explanation for his actions. Shake down, out and out abuse of authority and malicious disregard for his sworn duty to 'serve and protect'. Was he suspended while the investigation into his actions that night was conducted? Nooo! He was allowed to continue stinking up the streets of Chicago. But, it all turned out for the best because if he had been suspended he'd still be alive today."

Marco put his hand to his mouth thinking perhaps his last comment might have been a little too strong. He decided it *was*, but continued in the same vein nevertheless.

"The furor caused by his death and the subsequent death of Jose Herrera is what started the sequence of events that brought us to where we are today. So I say, thank you, to all those two-bit politicians who came to the defense of yet another dishonest cop. This time your actions are going to come back to bite you where it really hurts. Let's take a commercial break. When we return, I'll have my final comments."

As Marco began gathering his notes to prepare for the close of his broadcast, he heard the studio door open. He looked up to see Jerry Kaplan, the station manager, standing over him, impeccably dressed in an expensive wool shark skin suit and highly polished Italian loafers. At forty-eight he still looked pretty good, but he didn't look very happy. Small beads of perspiration were visible on his freckled brow. His red hair matched the color of his face.

"What are you doing here?" Marco asked, surprised to see him. "I thought you had some kind of luncheon with the network people today."

"I did," Kaplan said, sounding very concerned. "But my secretary called me on my cell phone to tell me my office phone has been ringing off the hook with calls from everyone from the Mayor's office to the Superintendent of Police, not to mention every newspaper in town. What the hell are you trying to do, have our license revoked?"

Kaplan was not a big man, as a matter of fact he was only average in weight and height, but he had a forceful personality and a hot temper. Marco remained calm. Refusing to be intimidated by his boss, he held his ground.

"You want ratings, don't you?" Marco shot back. "Before I'm finished this station will have the highest numbers in the country."

"We already have the highest numbers in the country, but if you can't back up these statements, ratings won't mean a thing. This place will be a real morgue and your career will be dead. Before you leave, I want to see you in my office." Kaplan turned and stormed out of the studio.

After Marco made his closing remarks, he invited his audience to tune in next time for another session of Marco's Morgue. As he removed his headphones and turned off his mike, he suddenly felt a surge of fear and apprehension. He was emotionally spent. The fury he felt at the start of his show had been released. Now, for the first time, he began to feel concerned about what he had done.

What if he never heard from the mysterious Mr. Caller again? What if what he'd been told was a lot of bullshit? Did he act too impulsively? Maybe he should have waited to discuss his plans with Tony Ruskin and Jerry Kaplan before he shot his mouth off. Again, he felt the presence of someone standing over him. He looked up; this time it was his producer, Tony Ruskin. Marco prepared himself for another tirade, another ass chewing, but to his surprise Tony was calmer than he'd been in a long time.

"Great show, Marco," Tony said as he squatted down to Marco's seated frame. "I've never seen you in better form. The phones were hotter than I've ever seen them. I thought they were going to burst into flame. I only hope you know what you're doing, but I want you to know I'm with you. I'm behind you a hundred percent. What did Kaplan have to say? He didn't look very happy."

"He wants to see me in his office," Marco said. "And you're right, he was very upset."

"When?" Tony asked.

"Now," Marco replied, still wondering if he'd done the right thing.

"You need back up?" Tony asked in a quiet voice.

"No. I don't want to drag you into this. I'll make sure he understands you didn't know what I was doing. I'll take full responsibility for everything. If my ass is on the line, it's all my doing. But thanks, Tony, I'm grateful for your support."

Tony stood up to allow Marco to exit the booth. As he did, he noticed line three on Marco's private phone flashing. "Hey Marco, wait a minute. Your line is flashing. Maybe you better see who it is."

Marco's sullen expression suddenly changed. He snatched the phone from it's cradle. "Marco Fischer," he answered.

"I'm convinced," the raspy voice said. "You're not a lot of show business bullshit. I'm not so sure you're in complete possession of your faculties, but now I know for sure that I can trust you."

Marco recognized the voice immediately. "I'm happy for you," Marco answered. "But I want you to know my balls are on the chopping block and my boss is waiting for me in his office with an ax in his hand. If I can't back up these charges, he's going to turn me into a soprano. When can we meet again?"

"Whenever you're ready."

"I'm ready. How about this evening, same time, same place?" Marco said excitedly.

"I'll be there. See you then."

"Wait a minute," Marco said. "My boss has to be convinced I'm not off my rocker. I want to bring him along. You can remain anonymous, but I want him to know that you're not just a figment of my imagination." Marco glanced up at Tony Ruskin to see him pointing to himself mouthing the words *me too, me too.* "And my producer, too," Marco added before Mr. Caller had a chance to respond.

"Look, I *told* you . . ."

"I know," Marco broke in. "You can't be too careful, and I appreciate that, but you're still anonymous. I don't even know who you really are. I've gone public with this and everybody knows who I am. I assure you, I give you my word, these men can be trusted. Your identity will be protected, but please understand I need the confidence of these people if I'm going to be able to continue."

"Okay," Mr. Caller said. "I understand. I'll consent to meeting your boss and producer if you can promise me that by doing so we will be able to continue and complete what we've started."

"No problem," Marco assured. "Everyone concerned wants this to continue, even if it's for different reasons. We know what our reasons are, and I think my producer is in line with us. My boss, he's interested in ratings and ratings mean money for this station and even more for his career. If we can convince him, . . . we're in. Nothing short of some unforeseen catastrophe will stand in our way."

Marco hung up the phone and turned to face his friend Tony Ruskin. "The situation has changed, Tony boy. Maybe you should join me in Mr. Kaplan's office after all. We have some convincing to do."

* * *

As Marco waited for traffic to clear, he scanned the parking lot of the Covered Bridge Restaurant. He considered jotting down the license numbers of all the parked cars, but let the thought go. Mr. Caller had honored his request to include Tony and Jerry in on their meeting; the least he could do was honor his request to remain anonymous, at least for the time being.

"This better not turn out to be a wild goose chase," Kaplan threatened as he climbed out of the back seat.

"He's here," Marco said, as he activated the power door locks.

"How do you know?" Tony asked curiously.

"To quote Alderman Patrick Grogan, 'I guarantee it'." Marco said, as he slammed his door shut.

The mysterious Mr. Caller was waiting in the same booth. The ashtray in the center of the table already overflowing with cigarette butts. Mr. Caller remained seated as Marco introduced his two companions. As in their first meeting, Marco suggested they get right to the point.

"No small talk?" Mr. Caller said, as he died out his cigarette.

Before Marco could say a word, Jerry Kaplan began with a question of his own. "How can I be sure you're not just playing some kind of game here? Do you realize my station could get sued for what Marco did today? Do you realize our license to broadcast could be in jeopardy if these charges can't be substantiated?"

"How do I know you can be trusted?" Mr. Caller retorted. "Do *you* realize we already have a dead cop and a dead junkie? If you fuck up and expose my identity, *my* life could be in jeopardy. Listen, the fact that I'm here right now, the fact that I've agreed to meet two additional people I don't know from a bucket of shit should convince you that I'm sincere." Mr. Caller lit up another cigarette.

"Look, I want to nail these guys, but I can't nail them alone. We need to do this together. We need to get the people in this town riled up. We need to shake them up. We need to make them understand they're not as helpless as they think, but they need a leader. They need a spokesman, someone who's crazy enough to say the things our friend Marco said today."

"But why not just go to the police if you have the information you claim to have?" Kaplan asked.

Mr. Caller sat silently for almost a full thirty seconds. During that time, he reached for his package of cigarettes to discover it was empty.

"Do you want me to call the waitress and ask her to bring you some cigarettes?" Marco offered.

"No, that's okay," Mr. Caller said as he retrieved another pack from his shirt pocket. Then he turned toward Kaplan, who was still waiting for a response to his question.

"Where the fuck are your brains?" Mr. Caller snarled. "The cops are the bad guys. They're the ones we're trying to expose, for God's sake. I don't know how long you've been living in this town, but I've lived here all my life. There's one thing I know for sure: the cops, the politicians, the mob, the junkies and dope dealers, they're all the same. Take away their badges, cheap cigars and pinkie rings and they all look alike. You can't tell them apart."

Mr. Caller paused for a moment to compose himself.

"The only hope I have to expose these bastards is to trust the media, and frankly, I have my doubts about them. For the most part, they can't be trusted, either. The only loyalty they have is to themselves. They'd turn on their own grandmother for a story. I took a chance with Marco because somehow I sensed something genuine in him. In the beginning, I wasn't totally convinced, I admit, but after today, I know my instincts were right. I can only hope his instincts are right about you two." Mr. Caller said shifting his eyes from Kaplan to Ruskin.

"Okay! You win," Kaplan said placing the palms of his hands flat on the table. "I'll go along with this thing, but sooner or later you'll have to identify yourself. You can't expect us to take the heat forever. The day will come when we'll be forced to produce solid evidence to back up our claims. That's when you'll have to come forward."

"By that time, we'll have the people and the media demanding the cleansing of our political system in this town once and for all. When that time comes, you won't have to look for me. Now let's get down to the real reason why we're here," Mr. Caller suggested, as he died out his cigarette and reached for yet another.

* * *

On the drive back to the studio, the excitement the three men were feeling became impossible to contain. Tony was the first to break the silence.

"I can't believe the arrogance of these guys. I know, I know this is Chicago, but don't forget, I only came to this city eight years ago. It's still hard to believe these kinds of things go on here."

"Eight years? I came here from Cleveland almost six years ago. Remember?" Kaplan recalled. "You and Marco had been doing Marco's Morgue for only about six months when I took over. I thought I knew all about crooked politicians, but this town is the Mecca of corruption and greed."

"Gentlemen," Marco chimed in, "I've lived in Chicago all my life. Don't forget, I was a building contractor for ten years before I got into this crazy business. With the amount of graft that goes on in the building department, it's a miracle every building in town hasn't collapsed a long time ago. What we heard tonight, however, is even hard for me to believe."

"A million dollars," Tony said, slapping his cheek. "Even split three ways, it's still a lot of money. What do they do with all that money? Why are they never satisfied?"

"It's like Mr. Caller said," Marco reminded. "They spend it faster than they can steal it."

"Listen guys, let's make use of the time it takes to drive back downtown," Jerry suggested. "We have to discuss just how we intend to reveal what we heard tonight on tomorrow afternoon's show."

"This afternoon I was a madman, remember?" Marco said. "I was going to cost the station its license. Now that you've met Mr. Caller, you're just as caught up in this thing as I am." Marco wasn't going to let Kaplan forget how he chewed his ass out.

"Tony," Marco continued. "Get your notepad ready. Let's list what Mr. Caller told us tonight item by item:

1. Grogan owns a security company, but because most of its business comes through city government contacts, Grogan put his flunky Tommy O'Mara in as president and CEO.
2. O'Mara, being the incompetent goof ball he is, has poorly managed the business.

3. The company is over eighteen months behind in payroll taxes, amounting to over a million dollars, including interest and penalties.
4. The Feds have been putting great pressure on Tommy to pay up.
5. Grogan goes to the 35th precinct Commander, John P. McLaughlin's son-in-law, who owns a small trucking company specializing in hauling construction materials and debris to and from job sites.
6. Grogan, through his contacts in city government, arranges for the son-in-law to secure twenty million dollars in city contracts.
7. Grogan takes the son-in-law to the South Chicago National Bank, where coincidentally, his cousin is president, and arranges a two million dollar loan for the son-in-law on the strength of the signed contracts.
8. The son-in-law "loans" Grogan's security company two million dollars to pay the overdue payroll taxes and provide a bonus for Grogan, O'Mara and McLaughlin. The loan is really a kick back; there is no intention of ever paying it back. Do I have it right?" Marco asked. "Did I forget anything?"

"You got it," Tony said, still writing, not looking up from his notepad.

"Do you agree?" Marco asked tilting his head toward the rear seat, where Kaplan sat contemplating Marco's summary of the information their source had provided.

"I think you covered everything, except I didn't hear you mention the name of the security company Grogan owns or the names of the son-in-law or his trucking company or the name of the bank president."

"We can fill in those details during the broadcast tomorrow," Marco answered.

"Marco and I will prepare a detailed script before show time," Tony assured. "Don't worry, Mr. Kaplan, we won't leave anything out."

"Tony," Kaplan said placing his hand on Ruskin's shoulder. "From now on, call me Jerry, okay? After tonight, our relationship is no longer at arm's length."

"Thanks, Jerry," Tony said, detecting a slight smile on Marco's face.

"By the way, Tony," Marco added. "You can continue to refer to me as Your Majesty."

For the remainder of the drive, the conversation continued in a lighter, more jovial vein, except for the time when Kaplan suggested they make an attempt to ascertain the true identity of Mr. Caller. However, the strange new team of crusaders agreed to go along with Marco's decision to honor Mr. Caller's request to remain anonymous for the time being. They felt good about themselves. They felt excited about embarking on a dangerous, but what promised to be a very rewarding and profitable, adventure. What they didn't know was that for one of them, the danger was far greater than they ever imagined, and it was about to manifest itself very soon.

* * *

"The lines are jammed, the main trunk line is overloaded," Tony Ruskin informed, even more excited than usual. "The show has been over for five minutes and the calls keep coming. What should we do, Marco? Should we continue to take calls or what?"

"We can't Tony, we'll never get out of here. The show is over; our listeners know we can't go over our allotted time. Let's go to my place. Sarah's cooking dinner tonight, and you know what a good cook she is. After we eat, we can prepare for tomorrow's show. What do you say, want to join us?"

"I don't know. I'm supposed to meet Karen for dinner," Tony whined.

"Bring her along. Sarah wants to meet her anyway."

"Well, I guess so," Tony said. "I'll pick up Karen and meet you at your place, let's say eight-thirty."

"Eight-thirty it is," Marco agreed. "I'll call Sarah and tell her we're having guests for dinner."

* * *

"Oh great!" Sarah said when she heard the news. "I love cooking for company, but I don't have anything special for desert. Will you do me a big favor, Daddy?"

"You bet, Honey. What do you want me to do?"

"Will you drive to the west side and pick up some cannolis from Belmonti's Bakery?"

"Sure, Honey, I'll leave now. By the time I drive there and back, it'll be time for dinner. Call Belmonti's and tell them to hold some cannolis just in case. See you by eight-thirty or a little after. Bye, Sweetheart."

"Bye, Daddy, hurry home, and get one for yourself, too. Tonight we'll make an exception."

It was seven-twenty by the time Marco left the studio. He ran for the elevator and pressed the U button. The elevator arrived a minute later and Marco stepped inside. The doors closed and Marco placed his life in the hands of fate. Every time he rode an elevator, he wondered what he'd do if the cables suddenly broke and sent the little box, with him in it, into oblivion. When the elevator safely reached its destination, the underground parking lot, the doors opened and Marco exhaled a sigh of relief.

He stepped out of the car and was momentarily startled by a man standing slightly to the right of the elevator doors. Their eyes met for only a split second, then the man turned away. Marco noticed a red mark on the man's neck.

I wonder who he is? he asked himself as he walked past the man. *Maybe I should say something to the lot attendant on the*

-AMAT

way out. But by the time Marco reached his car, he'd forgotten all about the man at the elevator.

He backed his car out of his designated space and headed for the expressway. He needed about an hour to complete the round trip barring any unforeseen contingencies. *An hour should be just enough time*. Marco thought, as he entered the west bound lanes of the Eisenhower expressway and switched on his cruise control. He pushed the button which engages the mechanism, but nothing happened. He tried again, and again nothing happened. Then he noticed the little green light that indicates the cruise control is engaged was not lit.

Oh shit, Marco said to himself. *I'll have to stop at Stan's on the way home and have him check this out. I need to fill up anyway, I'm driving on fumes now.*

After picking up dessert Marco drove to Stan's Service Station a block north of the radio station. "Stanley, I'm glad you're still here," Marco said, as he entered the front service area.

"What's the problem, Marco, did you find a bomb in your car?"

"Very funny, Stan, I'd laugh, but I don't have time right now. My daughter has dinner waiting. Please take a look at my cruise control. It suddenly stopped working," Marco said, handing Stan his car keys. "And fill it up with premium, the tank is empty."

Marco browsed through the magazine rack while Stan fiddled under the hood and dashboard of his Sedan DeVille.

* * *

"It's no big deal," Stan said coming through the door, wiping grease off his hands. "Two of your fuses are burnt out."

"Fuses?" Marco sighed. "Can you fix it right away? I'm late for dinner."

"Can't do it tonight," Stan said. "I'm all out of that AMP fuse. I'll send my helper to the supply house in the morning. Come back when you get off work tomorrow. It'll only take five minutes."

"Okay. I guess I can go one more day without cruise control," Marco said.

"You'll have to do without your cigarette lighter and horn, too," Stan added. "They're not working either."

"It's a good thing I quit smoking," Marco said, as he opened his car door.

"Yeah, but did you quit honking at the pretty girls?" Stan quipped, as Marco drove off.

* * *

After dinner, Marco and Tony went into Marco's office to plan their follow-up show for the next day. Karen, Tony's twenty-nine year old girlfriend cleared off the dining room table, while Sarah put coffee on and prepared dessert.

Karen Hovey was not exactly a raving beauty. Her hair was a kind of dull blond color and she was awfully skinny and flat-chested. She was tall, however, with very long shapely legs, and Tony liked that about her. She was crazy about Tony, and Tony, though reluctantly, was falling in love with her.

"Coffee's ready," Sarah said, as she opened Marco's office door and poked her head inside.

"I could use a cup of coffee," Tony said closing his briefcase.

"Me, too," Marco agreed.

As Marco leaned forward to lift himself out of his chair, his desk phone rang.

"Tony, you go sit down. I'll see who this is. Tell the girls I'll be right there. Marco picked up the receiver. "Hello?"

"Is this Marco Fischer?" the voice whispered.

"Yes, who's calling?"

"A friend. I have information I know you'd be interested in."

"What kind of information?" Marco asked, slowly lowering himself back into his chair.

"The same kind you've been talking about on your show."

"Okay, let's hear what you have to say."

"Not on the phone," the voice insisted.

Not again. Marco thought. "Okay, where and when would you like to meet?"

"Tomorrow, late morning. Let's say ten-thirty. I'll be waiting at 3536 South Halsted. Just pull your car up to the curb and I'll get in."

"Ten-thirty, 3536 South Halsted," Marco repeated as he jotted down the information. "I'll be driving a. . . ."

"I know, you drive a Caddy. Just be there."

Before Marco could say anything else, he heard the click signaling a broken connection and then the dial tone.

* * *

"Oh, oh! What was that call about Dad?" Sarah inquired. "It was something important, I can see it in your eyes."

"It's another mysterious informant," Marco revealed.

"Another one? You mean a different one?" Tony asked.

"Yes, different, but somehow not as convincing as the first," Marco said rubbing his cheeks and chin with his right hand.

"What exactly did he say, Dad?"

"He really didn't say anything except that I should meet him tomorrow morning at . . ." Marco looked down at the note in his hand, then continued, "At 3536 South Halsted."

"Thirty-fifth and Halsted," Tony repeated. "That's in the heart of Pat Grogan's ward."

"I know," Marco said. "And that's exactly why I have to go. This guy just might be someone close to Grogan who, because of Mr. Caller coming forward, found the courage to come out himself."

"Sounds reasonable," Tony said.

"I know this doesn't concern me," Karen broke in. "Of all of us, I have the least right to express an opinion, but shouldn't you trust your gut instinct?" she asked, looking directly at Marco. "After all, you did say he didn't sound convincing."

"I said, not *as* convincing," Marco retorted. "But you're right, Karen," he conceded. "I should be concerned about this guy. I guess I am, but I can't just ignore him. I have to go tomorrow. If he turns out to be a phony, I'll just dump him and all I did was waste a couple hours."

"If it is a prank, he probably won't even show up," Tony said. "Maybe I should go with you, just in case."

"No," Marco argued. "If this guy is for real and he sees you in the car, for sure he won't show up."

"Yeah, I guess you're right. Well, be careful anyway," Tony cautioned.

"Who wants a cannoli?" Sarah asked, getting back to the business at hand.

Everyone sat down and devoured the cannoli. Marco tried not to show it, but he was concerned about who his new mysterious friend might turn out to be. He was successful in concealing his true feelings to everyone. Everyone, except Sarah. She watched his eyes for the rest of the evening. She didn't like what she saw.

CHAPTER 3

"Where is he? A stranger is sitting in for him today. Why, is something wrong? Have they figured out a way to silence him?"

"UP KIND OF early this morning, weren't you Dad?" Sarah asked as she joined her father at the kitchen table. "I know you're not exactly comfortable about this meeting, Daddy. Why don't you just forget it? You can apologize on the air during your show. This guy will probably be listening."

"I can't do that, Honey," Marco said pouring himself a cup a coffee. "What if this guy is who he says he is? This could turn out to be one heck of a story. Don't forget sweetheart, your dad has a radio show that thrives on this kind of thing. It's how I make my living. It's worth the gamble. What can happen anyway? What have I really got to lose?"

"I don't know, Dad, I guess you're right, but I'm worried anyway."

"Thanks, Sweetheart, but your old man can take care of himself," Marco said, looking at the clock on the wall. "Wow! It's almost eight o'clock. You better get ready for school honey. I'll drive you so you're not late."

"I have plenty of time, Dad. My first class today isn't until ten o'clock."

"Good, I'll drop you off anyway. If we get to your school by nine-forty-five, that'll leave me forty-five minutes to get to my meeting. That should be just about what I'll need."

Marco poured himself another cup of coffee. Sarah prepared herself a breakfast of cereal and fresh fruit as she continued to watch her father's eyes.

* * *

Winter's coming. Marco said to himself, as he started up his engine and turned the climate control to 74°. He'd arrived at his destination about ten minutes early. Traffic was much lighter than he had expected it to be. As Marco sat in his Caddy with the engine running, he heard a tapping on his passenger side window. Marco was startled for just a split second at the sight of a very strange looking woman. The woman tapped again.

"What do you want?" Marco asked.

The woman motioned for him to lower the window. Marco reached down and activated the power window button. He fingered the button just long enough to crack the window about three inches.

"What do you want?" he repeated.

The woman said nothing.

"PUT YOUR HANDS WHERE I CAN SEE THEM! . . . NOW!"

The voice was loud and menacing. It was coming from Marco's left. He turned to see what was going on."

"PUT YOUR HANDS WHERE I CAN SEE THEM! . . . NOW!"

He saw a man standing just outside his car. He had a gun pointed at his head.

"Now, now!" the man repeated.

It took a few seconds for Marco to realize the man was speaking to him. Marco glanced to his right looking for the woman. She was gone. She had vanished.

"Open the door!" he heard the man say, as he yanked on Marco's door handle with his left hand, holding his revolver with his right.

"Open the door and get out of the car."

Several seconds had gone by, and Marco was beginning to recover from the initial shock of the situation. Suddenly he knew, he understood exactly what was going on. He fingered the auto-lock button, the door locks snapped open. Marco got out of his car holding his hands out in front of his body.

"Turn around. Face the car, spread your legs and put your hands on the roof."

Marco did as he was told. As he turned, he could see two more men. He knew they were police officers. Marco could feel the officer kicking his feet, forcing him to spread his legs further apart. He could feel the officer's hand on his back, pushing his upper body down and closer to the car. The officer began his search. Marco felt a sick feeling coming over him. He felt humiliated, violated and helpless to do anything to defend himself.

"Ah, what's this?" he heard the cop say. "Don't you know it's illegal to carry a gun in this state?"

Marco heard the words, but they were all mixed up and didn't register in his brain.

"Did you hear what I said, mister?"

Slowly, Marco's brain sorted out the cops words and arranged them in their proper order. Suddenly Marco knew he was in a lot of trouble, and he knew he was being victimized by the oldest cop ploy in the book.

"I don't know what you're talking about," Marco answered.

"Well, how about this? You're under arrest. You have the right to remain silent . . ."

As Marco listened to the cop's recitation, he bowed his head and thought about Sarah's words earlier that morning.

I'm worried about you Dad. Why don't you just forget it?

Oh, Sarah. Why didn't I listen to you, Marco thought as he felt the handcuffs tighten around his wrists.

After reading him his rights and grabbing Marco by the back of his shirt collar, the cop snarled, "Do you know what I'm talking about now, pervert?"

"No, I don't," Marco snapped back. "You planted that gun on me and you know it."

"Oh yeah? And did I tell you to solicit that transvestite, too?" the cop mocked, as he pushed Marco into the back seat of his unmarked squad car.

"What?" Marco screamed. "You son-of-a-bitch! You can't do that!"

"I can't? Let me tell you what else I'm going to do. I'm going to impound your car and lock you up, you degenerate bastard."

Marco wanted to fight back. He wanted to break free and run for his life, but he was helpless. He realized the best thing he could do was shut up and think. He had to think of a way to get himself out of the biggest mess of his life.

* * *

Upon arriving at the 35th precinct police station, Marco was escorted into a small interrogation room. After cuffing him to a steel bar fastened to the wall, the arresting officer turned toward the door. As he opened it to leave, he said, "Don't go away now, somebody wants to talk to you."

Marco stood leaning against the bar he was cuffed to.

Somebody wants to talk to me? he asked himself. *Who?* he wondered.

It wouldn't be long before he found out.

* * *

Several minutes had gone by since Marco had been locked in the room. There was a table and four chairs, but his restraint wouldn't allow him to get close enough to sit down. He looked around the room. Loose, cracked and missing tiles revealed the black mastic that once adhered them to the floor. The grooves left by the installers trowel were still visible though flattened by years of foot traffic. The walls were plaster, not drywall, indicating the age of the building, and were in pretty bad shape, too, with dents, scuffs and gouges everywhere. A good paint job was certainly in order.

A two-foot by four-foot light fixture hung from a ceiling stained with the film left by a million cigarettes; light bulbs flickered through a cracked plastic lens that had also seen better days. The light provided was not nearly enough to defuse the dinginess of the tiny cubicle. He was dead tired, all his energy had been drained by his ordeal. It was all he could do to remain on his feet. Suddenly, the door flew open. A large, uniformed figure loomed over him. Marco recognized him at once.

"What are you trying to pull here, McLaughlin?" Marco growled, trying to conceal his fear. "You know this is a set up. You'll never get away with this."

McLaughlin placed his size twelve shoe on one of the chairs and gave it a shove. Marco had to side step, barely in enough time to avoid being pinned against the wall.

"Sit down, asshole," McLaughlin said, as he half leaned and half sat on the edge of the table.

Marco turned the chair with his free hand and sat down. He waited silently.

"Just in case you haven't figured it out for yourself, let me explain where you stand. You're in deep shit, Mr. Radio Talk Show Host. Your mouth has finally gotten your ass in a lot of trouble. You're under arrest for soliciting sex from a transvestite prostitute, and during a routine search at the crime scene, a loaded .25 caliber semi-automatic pistol was found in your pocket. The soliciting charge is a misdemeanor, but the weapons charge in this state is a felony, punishable by a mandatory one year jail sentence. However, no reports have been made yet, there is nothing in writing regarding these charges and there never has to be. Do you get my drift?"

"Yeah, I get your drift," Marco said, looking McLaughlin straight in the eyes. "You're telling me this farce you pulled off is just that. A farce, a set up, a frame."

"Call it whatever you like, Fischer, but remember, I'm calling the shots. If this gets out, if the media learns what happened today, you're through in this town. You're through in any town. Your career is over. You'll have to go back to pounding nails for a living."

"Fuck you. You don't scare me," Marco spat through clenched teeth. "I'll fight you all the way. I'll expose you and this whole conspiracy, you'll never get me to shut up. You can play your dirty games, but in the end, I'll beat you, no matter how you hurt me now."

"Okay, suit yourself, but I'd think about my daughter if I were you . . . What's her name? Oh yes, Sarah. I wonder how she'll feel when she finds out her father is a pervert, a degenerate. One who goes around picking up drag queens and . . . oh well, we'll let her imagine what her father does with them. I'm sure she'll be able to conjure up some pretty interesting pictures in her mind."

Marco jumped to his feet and leaped toward his tormentor, only to be yanked backward by his restraint.

"You son of a bitch! Leave my daughter out of this," Marco was yelling at the top of his lungs, jerking his cuffed hand as though it were possible to break the cold steel chain connecting the clamps at either end.

McLaughlin, knowing he was in no danger, remained in his half sitting, half leaning position, smirking at the furious but helpless figure before him.

"Let it out," McLaughlin laughed as he got up to leave. "I'll give you an hour to think about it. Don't be a fool, Marco, you can't win. We hold all the cards in this game. Do the smart thing, quit while you still have a bankroll."

Marco watched as McLaughlin closed the door behind him. His mind was racing. His thoughts were exploding in his head like aerial bombs at Sox park after a Frank Thomas home run. After several minutes of mental mayhem, he began to take control of his faculties. He was finally able to think clearly, to step away emotionally and survey his predicament and consider his options and possible solutions. One thought, one image, however, continued to overshadow all else. *Sarah, how will this affect my Sarah?* He thought.

What would Sarah want me to do? Marco asked himself. *Would she want me to abandon my principles, my integrity, my honor? Would she still respect me if I forsake all I've preached for the last six years? Would she still love me if she thought I was a coward?* No! No! No! I can't, I can't. Without realizing it Marco's thoughts escaped the confines of his brain and leaped to freedom through his mouth.

"What the fuck are you yelling about?" McLaughlin shouted, as he reentered the room.

"No! No! You mother fucker. No deal. Go ahead, charge me. Call the media. I swear, I'll make you pay. Whatever I suffer, you'll suffer ten times more. Whatever I lose, you'll lose a hundred times more."

McLaughlin opened the door and shouted, "Jerkowski get in here."

"Yes, sir." Jerkowski said, as he entered the room trying to catch his breath after running the length of the police station.

"Throw this piece of shit in a cell. I want him mugged and printed. I want him transferred to the county jail and processed on a felony charge."

McLaughlin turned to face Marco.

"You asked for it, dog shit. This is the first day of the end of your life. Get him out of here," McLaughlin roared, as he shoved his way past Officer Jerkowski.

"Don't I get a phone call?" Marco demanded.

"Shhh," Jerkowski cautioned. "Take it easy, let the commander get out of ear shot. I'll make sure you get to make a call before you're transferred. For now, try to remain calm."

Officer Walter Jerkowski closed the door and walked to the bar Marco was attached to. He removed a key from his pocket and opened the cuff. "Let me help you, Marco, let me try to make what's coming as easy on you as possible."

Marco looked at the cop suspiciously. He tried to determine what kind of a man he was dealing with by examining his physical characteristics, but there was no way he could do that. The man was average in every way. Five-foot-nine, give or take an inch. Dark brown hair, combed to one side. Brown eyes housed in a pleasant looking round face. Marco figured the man's age to be around forty-five to fifty. There was nothing ascertainable from his looks alone.

"What do you mean, what's coming?" Marco asked.

"Look, you're going to the County Jail, don't you know what that means?"

"Not exactly," Marco admitted.

"Listen to me," Jerkowski said, "When you get to the County, you're going to be made to take a complete physical exam, including a chest x-ray. When you get to that point of the process, tell the guards you're sick. If you have to, pretend to faint, do whatever you have to do to convince them you need special attention."

"What if I tell them I'm diabetic?" Marco asked.

"That's perfect," Jerkowski answered. "But can you back it up?"

"Sure I can back it up," Marco said, as he pulled up his right shirt sleeve.

"What's that?" Jerkowski queried, pointing at the bracelet on Marco's arm.

"That's my ID bracelet identifying me as a diabetic in case I'm ever in an accident or go into a diabetic shock or something."

"Do you take insulin?" Jerkowski asked, slightly shocked.

"Yes I do." Marco replied.

"Perfect," Jerkowski said happily. "Oh no . . . I mean, it's not perfect . . . I mean I'm sorry you're diabetic, but believe it or not, the fact that you are may have saved your life."

"I don't get it. What do you mean, saved my life?"

"The County Jail is hell on earth; there are nothing but animals in that joint. There's no telling what would happen to a guy like you in a place like that. Listen, when you get there make sure you tell them you're diabetic. Tell every guard you come into contact with. Tell them you need your medication, your insulin. By the way, when are you due for your next injection?"

"Not till later this evening," Marco answered.

"I'll make sure the desk sergeant and the guy in charge of the lock up know your medical history. You'll have to be taken to the hospital tonight for your shot. You probably won't be transferred to the County till five or six in the morning."

Jerkowski walked to the door, opened it and peered out into

the hall. "Sit down, rest a while longer. Can I get you anything, a Coke, some coffee maybe?"

"Why are you doing this?" Marco asked. "Am I being set up again? What is this, the good cop, bad cop routine?"

Officer Jerkowski looked forlornly at Marco, shaking his head slowly.

"Look, we're not all assholes. No matter what you think. Some of us really do take our oath seriously. Some of us actually joined the police department to 'serve and protect.' There are a few of us here at the 35th who refuse to go along with the program."

"I'm sorry," Marco said, recognizing a true sincerity in the man's voice. "I hope you understand I'm grateful for all you've done for me. It's just that after what I've been through . . ."

"I do understand, there's no need to explain . . . Listen, I have to take you to the lock up now, you have to be processed. It shouldn't take more than an hour, then I'll get you to a phone. You got a lawyer?"

"I have a lawyer, but he's not a criminal lawyer. He helps me with contract negotiations and stuff like that."

"You don't need Perry Mason at this point. All you need is someone to get you through the bond hearing, which will be sometime tomorrow afternoon. Even a half-assed lawyer should be able to have you back on the street by nine or ten tomorrow night."

"Nine or ten o'clock tomorrow night? That's over thirty hours from now. Why can't someone bail me out now?" Marco asked.

"You're charged with a felony. You can't get a bond hearing until you've been processed, that's how the system works. If you do as I told you and exploit your illness, you'll save yourself a lot of grief. Instead of locking you up in the general population, they'll send you to the medical lock up. It's a lot less dangerous there, but don't get careless, it's still dangerous."

Marco just sat there looking at his new friend. He put his head in his hands and said in a voice loud enough for Jerkowski to hear, "What the fuck did I get myself into? Sarah, Sarah, now you really do have reason to worry about your old man."

"Come on."

Marco looked up to see officer Jerkowski standing over him.

"Come on, let's get you processed so you can make your call."

Marco got up from his chair and placed his hands behind his back. Officer Walter Jerkowski put the cuffs back on.

CHAPTER 4

"They did it, the rotten bastards framed him. I can't stand by and do nothing any longer. I must do something. Maybe this is an omen. Maybe the spirits are sending me a message. Maybe now is the time to pick up where I left off and put my plan into action."

IT WAS ALMOST three o'clock, and Tony still hadn't seen or heard from Marco.

Something's gone wrong, he thought. *I better get hold of Jerry and let him know we might not have a show today.*

* * *

"What?" Jerry Kaplan roared. "Where is he?"

"I don't know, he had a meeting with another informant at ten-thirty this morning. He should have been here a long time ago."

"Well, my friend," Kaplan bellowed. "It looks like this is your lucky day. Prepare yourself; you're going on for Marco."

"Me?"

"Yes, you. You're the only one who knows what he knows. You're going to have to pacify his listeners until I can find him."

Kaplan's secretary Sally interrupted the conversation. "Excuse me, sir, there's an urgent phone call for Mr. Ruskin. Line two."

Jerry Kaplan picked up the receiver of his desk phone and pressed line two. Handing the instrument to Tony, he said, "Maybe it's Marco."

"Hello," Tony said tentatively.

"Tony, it's Marco."

Tony let out a sigh of relief.

"I'm in trouble. I need a lawyer."

Tony gasped, took in a deep breath and held it.

"Get hold of Marvin Levin, tell him to call the 35th precinct and ask for Officer Walter Jerkowski. I have to go now, I'm only allowed a couple of minutes."

"Wait a minute," Tony yelled into the phone. "What's going on? You can't just leave me hanging like this, your show is about to go on in about ten minutes. What am I supposed to do? Jerry says I have to go on in your place."

"You can do it, this is your big chance. Who knows? Maybe you'll end up with a show of your own. Oh, wait, I almost forgot. Please call Sarah, tell her I won't be home tonight. Tell her I'll explain when I get out, hopefully tomorrow night, and call Marvin."

"Get out? Get out of what . . . where?"

"Tell him to talk to Jerkowski, no one else. He'll tell him what needs to be done. Oh, one more thing, start asking around, I need a list of the best criminal lawyers in town."

"Criminal lawyers? Does this have anything to do with your meeting this morning?"

"I hate to admit it, but you guys were right. I should have trusted my gut feeling as Karen suggested. Gotta go now. Call Marvin, then call Sarah. Thanks, Tony."

* * *

In a sort of daze, Tony handed the receiver back to Kaplan, then as though he'd been zapped by a cattle prod, he turned with a jerk and ran out of the office.

"Hey, where are you going?" Kaplan yelled, as he jumped out of his chair and chased after him.

"I have to look up Marvin Levin's number," Tony yelled back, as he ran down the hall. Tony made his way to Marco's office. By the time Jerry caught up to him, he was going through Marco's Rolodex. "Yes, here it is," Tony said, as he picked up the phone.

"Are you going to tell me what's happening?" Kaplan coughed, trying to catch his breath.

Tony held up his free hand. "Wait a minute," he said, dialing Levin's number.

Kaplan waited, not very patiently, and listened to the one-sided conversation.

"Is Mr. Levin in please? This is Tony Ruskin, Mr. Marco Fischer's producer . . . Mr. Levin? This is Tony Ruskin. Yes, that's right, Tony Ruskin . . . I'm fine . . . please excuse me, sir . . . please listen, sir, we have an emergency. Marco has been arrested . . . yes that's right arrested. He needs your help . . . Yes I know you're not a criminal lawyer, but you're the only lawyer he knows . . . Please, sir, I have to go on the air in two minutes . . . He wants you to call Officer Walter Jerkowski at the 35th precinct police station . . . Yes, now, right now . . . Yes, I'll be here. I'd appreciate it, if you'd keep me informed . . . Thank you very much, I must go now."

Tony hung up the phone and ran out of the office toward the broadcast studio.

"Hey where are you going now?" Jerry whined.

"I have a show to do. Did you forget?" Tony reminded him, as he tried to set a new record for the forty-yard dash.

* * *

"Good afternoon, ladies and gentlemen, this is Tony Ruskin. I'll be sitting in for Marco Fischer today. Marco has been unavoidably detained and won't be joining us tonight. I assure you, however, he will be back Monday afternoon with a full report explaining his absence. I promise I'll try to keep you entertained for the next four hours. The lines are open, so please call. Let's talk."

* * *

During commercial breaks, Tony brought Jerry up to date as much as he was able to. After the show, they sat in Marco's office, waiting.

"Did you tell Sally to contact us here when Marvin calls?" Tony asked.

"Yes, she knows what to do," Kaplan said. "By the way, you did a great job. The callers seemed to like you, but I wish you hadn't told them Marco would explain his absence on Monday."

"Well, I had to say something. Besides, something tells me that by Monday, everyone is going to know anyway."

"What do you mean by that?" Kaplan asked with a quiver in his voice.

"I don't know," Tony said. "I just have a feeling Marco's really done it this time."

"I just hope whatever he's done, he did to himself," Kaplan said angrily.

"Listen, Jerry, Marco's in trouble. I don't know how serious it is, but I know he's in trouble. Maybe we should be thinking about how we can help him instead of covering our own asses. Please, Jerry, let's hold off making any judgments until we know all the facts. I understand your concern, but we owe Marco a chance to tell his side."

"You're awfully loyal to Marco, aren't you?" Kaplan remarked. "That kind of loyalty is unusual in this business."

"I haven't been in this business as long as you have, Jerry, but it doesn't take very long to realize you have to watch your back if you don't want a knife stuck in it. You never have to watch your back with Marco. He's always the same, no matter which way you're facing. He's the only man I truly trust. Yeah, I guess I am loyal to him, but not just as his producer. I'm his friend, too. Come to think of it, Marco's the only real friend I have."

Jerry and Tony sat silently in Marco's office for a long time. Tony, reflecting on his words. Kaplan, feeling a little ashamed and envious. Then the phone rang, startling both of them.

"Hello," Tony answered.

"Is this Tony Ruskin?" Marvin Levin asked.

"Yes, this is Tony."

"Is Jerry Kaplan with you?"

"Yeah, he's right here."

"Good. I want you both to wait till I get there. Prepare yourselves, I have one hell of a story to tell you."

* * *

"Wake up!"

Marco was at the kitchen table with Sarah when he heard the gruff voice.

"Wake up, it's time to go."

Marco opened his eyes. He looked around. *What happened to Sarah*? He thought. *What happened. Where am I*? The dream was comforting while it lasted, but reality now surrounded him.

"Let's go, get up."

Now fully awake, Marco groaned as he rose from the bare steel bunk, his back and neck stiff and aching. He heard the clanking, squeaking sounds echoing through the dimly lit cell block as the guard unlocked the outer door and approached his cell. "Here," the cop said, handing Marco a Styrofoam cup filled with strong black coffee. "You'll be leaving in just a few minutes for the County."

Remembering what Officer Jerkowski told him, he said. "I'm diabetic; I need my insulin shot."

"Your condition is noted in your paperwork," the cop said, waving a large brown envelope over his head. "You got your shot last night, didn't you? So shut up and drink your coffee."

Marco looked at his watch; it was five o'clock in the morning."I need another injection no later than nine o'clock. How long will it take to get there?"

The cop didn't answer. He didn't even look up from his labor of filling out transfer forms for Marco and several other prisoners.

"Hey, did you hear me?" Marco said in a louder voice. "How long will it take to get there?"

"Don't hey me, asshole. Can't you see I'm busy? Shut the fuck up, don't bother me. You'll get there when you get there."

"I could go into diabetic shock if I don't get my shot," Marco shouted.

"That's your problem." the cop mocked.

Marco glared at the insensitive scum bag. He knew what he wanted to say to this so-called public servant, but he decided not to complicate his situation. He knew his day would come. For now, it would be best to keep his mouth shut.

* * *

With his right hand cuffed to the left hand of another prisoner, Marco and his cuff mate climbed into a large step van followed by several similarly restrained pairs. It was almost five-thirty.

Marco realized a large black man dressed in raggedy clothing and shoes falling apart at the seams hadn't taken his droopy eyes off him since they entered the vehicle. He was sitting directly across the aisle. Suddenly Jerkowski's words replayed in his mind. *Don't get careless.* The man's eyes widened, the muscles of his unshaven face produced a smile exposing four gold capped teeth, each with a cut out in the shape of the different suites of a deck of playing cards. Spades. Hearts. Diamonds. Clubs. Marco couldn't help smiling.

"Say man, is dat really you? Day say you bees da man on da radio."

"Yeah, that's me," Marco replied, wondering if he should have lied.

"I'd shake yo hand if I was able to," the black man smiled. "I likes da way you stays on da poe-leece ass. You got some balls, I likes dat."

"Shut up back there! No talking," One of the officers in the cab hollered, as he pounded on the metal partition separating the prisoners from the cops.

The van stopped at three other precincts to pick up more transferees before arriving at the County Jail on 26th Street just west of California Avenue. It was seven-fifteen when Marco climbed out of the van.

"All right you low lives, up the ramp and through the double doors. No talking," the swaggering Cook County Sheriff's deputy ordered in a high pitched voice. He was trying to sound tough, but he wasn't making it. The pudgy deputy shifted his beady little eyes from one prisoner to another, trying his best to look intimidating.

"Line up facing the wall on your right. Your right, you stupid son of a bitch," the deputy screeched, as he yanked a helpless drunk, turning him around to face the wall. "Are there any more assholes here who don't know left from right?" The deputy was beginning to sound more and more like Mayberry's Barney Fife.

One by one, the cuffs were removed while the prisoners faced the wall. "Eyes straight ahead, "the deputy said, as he keyed the locks.

Joined by another deputy, "Barney" continued to yelp out orders still trying to make them sound like the growls of a vicious police dog.

"Empty your pockets and pull them inside out. Take off your shoes, hold them upside down and shake them."

Over and over, the prisoners were put through humiliating searches, shuffled from one holding cell to another. The ritual of picture taking and fingerprinting was repeated. All the while, the prisoners were treated with contempt. The slightest hint of human kindness or compassion was nowhere to be found.

Marco had no idea what time it was because his watch and other personal belongings had been taken from him and placed in a large brown envelope shortly after he arrived. The guards ignored him, refusing to acknowledge his questions in any way.

No wonder prisoners are so filled with hate, Marco thought. *These guards are animals, they're worse than the criminals. What about me? There must be a lot of guys like me in here. Guys who crossed the wrong cop or rubbed some two bit politician the wrong way and found themselves set up just like me. Oh wait you rotten bastards, wait till I get out of here. I'll expose all of you, I'll let the world know how you treat people.* "This is the 'U.S. of A', you're supposed to be innocent until proven guilty. What happened to common, ordinary, human respect for your fellow man?"

"Hey you, no talking."

Marco looked up to see a deputy glaring at him. He realized his thoughts had escaped again.

"Did you hear me? No talking," the guard was now yelling louder than before.

Suddenly, Jerkowski's words came back to him. Closing his eyes, Marco allowed himself to fall backwards. The prisoners standing behind him broke his fall and Marco hit the concrete floor with very little force. The guard smirked as Marco went down. "You fuckin' faggot," he growled. "What's the matter, can't take getting your ass chewed, so you faint like a little girl?"

Marco heard every word, but he just laid there and let his body relax. It felt good, he hadn't felt that good since being arrested.

"Get this guy out of here," the guard roared at the two guards hurrying to the site. "Take him to area four; let them deal with him."

Area four was where the physical exams took place; chest x-rays, blood tests and general health checks.

"Hey, Marco," he heard a voice say. "Hey, Marco, it's okay now, open your eyes."

Fuck you, Marco thought.

Marco sensed the man's body coming closer. Then he felt his hot breath on his ear.

"It's okay. Walter Jerkowski is a friend of mine. He told me to expect you coming in this way."

Marco opened his eyes slowly. He saw a short, fat man in his middle forties, dressed in blue scrubs standing over him. He had black hair and what looked like an Afro hairdo and a round face badly in need of a shave. "It's okay, Marco. My name is Stewart Garabaldi. I'm an old friend of Walt's. He called me last night and told me the whole story. Don't worry, I'm pulling you out of the regular processing procedure and sending you upstairs to the hospital."

"What time is it?" Marco asked.

"It's almost ten o'clock. I know you're due for your shot. Give me two more minutes to find your paperwork then we'll get you upstairs. I'll stay with you and make sure you get your injection."

Stewart Garabaldi walked out leaving Marco lying on the gurney he was rolled in on.

"I'll never take my bed at home for granted again," Marco said out loud.

"Okay, all set. We can go upstairs," Garabaldi said upon re-entering the room.

Stewart wrapped his chubby fists around the chrome plated steel tube framing of the mobile stretcher and began pushing.

"Thanks, Stewart," Marco said as he reached up to pat Stewart's hand. "When you talk to Walt Jerkowski, tell him I said thanks again."

"That's okay. We half breeds have to stick together," Stewart said looking down at Marco.

"Half breeds?" Marco asked.

"Yeah, we have something in common. We're both half Jewish and half Italian."

"Nice to meet you, *Cumbare*," Marco said, raising his hand.

"My pleasure, *Chaver*," Stewart said, as he took Marco's hand in his.

They were both still laughing and kidding each other when the elevator stopped on the sixth floor.

"Okay, compose yourself," Stewart said. "We have to look serious. Remember, you're supposed to be sick."

"I have somebody here who needs an insulin shot," Stewart announced as he rolled Marco up to the nurses station. He handed the nurse the envelope. She was a very pretty black woman in her middle thirties, dressed in a white nurse's uniform.

"Okay, I'll get a wheel chair and you can take the gurney back down with you," the nurse said.

"We can switch him to a chair, but I have to stay with him till he gets his shot," Stewart said.

"That won't be necessary," the nurse insisted as she examined Marco's papers.

"Look, those are my orders," Stewart shot back.

The nurse stopped what she was doing and looked up at him. "Who gave you such orders?" she asked.

"Who do you think?" Stewart snapped with a confident look on his face.

The nurse shrugged her shoulders and said, "okay, what do I care anyway?" She turned away. "I'll be right back, I have to go to the pharmacy for his insulin."

Marco looked up at Stewart when the nurse was out of hearing range. "What would you have said if she pressed you for a name?" Marco asked.

"I would have given her one," Stewart said. "Look, nobody here knows or even gives a shit what's going on. Everybody is just going through the motions. These are all political patronage jobs. Even me, I'm a nurse, an LPN on paper, but in reality I'd never make it in the real world. I never wanted to work that hard; here, it's all bullshit. You come to work every day, put your time in and after twenty years, you retire with a pension. No grief, no aggravation, no pressure to succeed, because on this job, how hard you work means nothing. It's who you know that counts. If your ambitious, if you want to get ahead through hard work, go get a job in the private sector."

* * *

"Okay, here you are," the nurse said, walking back toward Marco and Stewart. "Do you want me to administer the injection or do you want to do it yourself?"

"That's okay, I'll do it," Marco said, as the nurse handed him the necessary items to complete the task.

Marco opened the packet containing the alcohol swab, and after removing the plastic shield on the needle, he cleansed the instrument before disinfecting the skin on his thigh where he injected himself.

"Ah!" Marco said as he plunged the needle into his leg. "Thanks, I needed that."

"Well, my job is done," Stewart said. "I hope you enjoy the remainder of your stay; please feel free to contact me if I can be of any further service."

"I'll be sure to do that," Marco said, smiling as he watched his new friend head for the elevator. "Ciao," Marco said, waving good bye.

"Shalom," Stewart said as the elevator doors opened.

CHAPTER 5

"Don't give up, hang in there. They're trying to destroy you, but I won't let them. I'll help you. I just need a little more time, then we'll make them pay. We'll make them sorry. We'll make them curse the day they were born."

TONY RUSKIN AND Jerry Kaplan couldn't believe what they were hearing. Marvin Levin wasn't exaggerating when he promised a hell of a story.

"You say he's charged with soliciting a prostitute for sex and possession of a loaded firearm?" Tony asked. "That's crazy. Sure, I know Marco never supported the gun laws in this state, but I've never known him to actually carry a gun in defiance of them."

"Do you think he decided to take a gun with him, just in case?" Kaplan asked. "After all, you did say he wasn't exactly comfortable with the guy he was meeting."

"Yeah, but I don't think he feared a physical or life threatening situation. Besides, I don't think he owns a gun. Owning a gun in the city of Chicago is illegal. One of his basic beliefs is, if you disagree with the law, you should obey it, until you can legally change it."

"I've heard him say that a million times on the air," Kaplan remembered. "Well, what's the next step? What do we do now?" he asked looking at Marvin.

The fifty-eight year old attorney sat silently for a few seconds, smoothing the few strands of hair bridging a wide gap, on his balding scalp. About average height and a little stocky, he looked like your typical LaSalle Street lawyer, dressed in his blue pin-stripped suit, white shirt and yellow tie peppered with little blue judge's gavels.

"Right now we can't do anything, but tomorrow I'll go to the bond hearing. I'm sure I can have him out by tomorrow night. But after that he'll need a lawyer, a criminal lawyer. Carrying a concealed weapon is a serious crime. A lot of people don't realize it, but it's a felony in the state of Illinois. Efforts are being made to change the law, but for now, it remains a felony."

"What about the solicitation charge?" Tony asked.

"That's a misdemeanor and will probably be dropped anyway. They'll go for the felony conviction; that's where the real damage can be done."

"How much damage?" Kaplan asked.

"He could go to jail if he's convicted. That's why I'm telling you he needs a good lawyer, someone who knows his way around the criminal courthouse, if you know what I mean."

"Wait a minute!" Tony said. "Let's talk plain English. I don't want to have to guess at what you're trying to tell us. I want you to tell me straight out. What exactly do you mean when you say the lawyer has to know his way around? Are you suggesting a payoff or bribe may be necessary to get Marco out of this mess?"

"That's one way, but not the only way."

"You say it's not the only way. But is it the route you suggest we take?"

"No, all I'm saying is that you need a lawyer who knows how to navigate in dirty water."

"Do you have any suggestions?" Tony asked.

"There are several who have waded through the swamps of the Cook County court system and have allowed the leeches to suck their blood because it was the only chance they had of winning their case. There is one, however, who knows all the crooked games and corrupt players, and has remained above it all and, to my knowledge, has never lost a case."

"What's his name?" Kaplan asked removing a pen from his shirt pocket.

"Christopher Musso," Levin answered.

"Musso. He's the biggest mob lawyer in Chicago!" Tony cried out. "I thought you said he's remained above all the corruption?"

"He has," Levin answered.

"Then how do you explain his getting all these mob guys off?"

"Simple," Levin calmly answered. "He's the best. He doesn't need to fix cases. He wins them fair and square. I've watched him work a couple of times. He has an uncanny ability to sway the jury; even judges are intimidated by him. He has a charisma reminiscent of Clarence Darrow. His power of persuasion is legendary."

"That may be, but we'll have to find somebody else. I don't like the mob connection. It might reflect unfavorably on the station," Kaplan said, scratching out Musso's name in his notepad.

"There you go," Tony said angrily. "Thinking only about yourself again. Well, maybe you should think about how it would reflect on the station if your highest paid host goes to jail."

The three sat silently, then the phone rang.

Tony, who was sitting at Marco's desk, picked it up, "Hello. Oh! Hi, Sarah."

"Have you heard from my dad?"

"No, there hasn't been any word from your dad, but Marvin Levin's here and he has everything under control. He's sure he'll have your dad out on bond by about nine or ten tomorrow night."

"Tony, my dad needs his insulin."

"We know that, honey, Marvin has been assured that your dad's condition is known and his insulin injections are being provided."

"Tony, I'm worried. What's going to happen to my father?"

"Don't worry, sweetheart, your dad is a tough guy. He knows how to take care of himself."

"I know," Sarah said, remembering her father words that fateful morning. "That's what he told me just before he left for that meeting." Sarah started to cry.

"Please don't cry, Sarah. I promise everything will be okay."

There was a knock on the door. "Come in," Kaplan said.

* * *

Sally Quinn, Kaplan's secretary entered Marco's office; all eyes shifted in her direction at once. Her flaming red hair, bright green eyes and confident air always attracted much attention. It was difficult for any man not to notice her slim, firm five-foot-six inch frame, perfectly proportioned from head to toe. At thirty-six Sally Quinn had the body of a nineteen year old; she was a beauty and she knew it. She understood the effect she had on men, but there was only one man she hoped to attract.

Tony said good bye to Sarah and hung up the phone without taking his eyes off the sexy secretary.

Sally was carrying the latest editions of all three of Chicago's major newspapers.

"I thought you'd want to see these," Sally said as she dropped them onto her boss' lap. "And, by the way, there are about two hundred messages from every newspaper in town, not to mention the radio and TV news reporters. I knew you wouldn't want to talk to them, so I left the messages on your desk."

Jerry Kaplan looked at this watch. "Thanks, Sal. It's almost ten-thirty, why don't you go home now. I'll see you Monday morning."

"I don't mind staying, Mr. Kaplan. My ex-husband has the kids for the weekend. I don't have anything to do anyway."

"In that case, I'll take you out to dinner. What do you say?" Kaplan said.

Yes, yes. Sally said, but not out loud. Acting coy, she answered, "Oh, that would be very nice, Mr. Kaplan. Thank you very much."

Kaplan looked at Tony and Marvin with an inquiring look on his face.

"It's okay with me," Marvin said. "I have to go."

"I'm picking up Karen," Tony said. "We're going to keep Sarah company."

Tony and Marvin started to get out of their chairs.

"Excuse me, gentlemen," Sally interrupted. "I brought these papers in here for a reason. Take a look at the headlines before you go."

* * *

Kaplan turned the paper on the top of the pile over to reveal the headline of the Chicago Courier.

"Oh no!" Kaplan said as he read. "MARCO FISCHER ARRESTED ON SEX CHARGES."

Handing the Courier over to Tony Ruskin, Kaplan picked up the Daily Messenger.

"Dear God, give me a break," Jerry Kaplan cried.

"TALK SHOW HOST THREATENS COP WITH GUN."

"I'm afraid to look at the Guardian's front page," Kaplan said, as he covered his eyes with his hand and gradually spread his fingers to reveal the big black letters. "TALK SHOW HOST AND TRANSVESTITE LOVER ARRESTED ON GUN CHARGE."

"Oy vey." Kaplan cried out, remembering a phrase he used to hear his grandfather say.

* * *

Marco sat on his bed surveying his surroundings. Except for the uniformed guard seated at a small table next to the entrance, the place looked very much like your average hospital ward. The only other exception was that nobody looked sick. A couple of guys didn't look exactly normal, but they didn't look sick.

"Fischer, Marco Fischer."

Marco's head jerked to attention when he heard his name. A guard stood in the doorway reading from a list attached to a clipboard.

"Fischer, Marco Fischer."

"Here," Marco called out rising to his feet and holding his left arm out at the same time.

"Follow me," the guard ordered. The guard walked just outside the entrance and stepped aside, allowing Marco to pass.

"Get in line and face forward, no talking, no laughing, no whistling. I want total silence."

Marco did as he was told. It was almost four-thirty in the afternoon. He knew he was about to get his bond hearing, and he didn't want to do anything to screw up his chances for release. After all the prisoners scheduled for a hearing were gathered, they were taken to the first floor and herded into a holding room where they waited to be called. Marco didn't have to wait long. For some unknown reason, his name was the first to be called.

"Fischer, Marco Fischer."

Marco jumped to his feet.

"This way," a guard said, pushing Marco ahead.

Hey watch who you're pushing, asshole, Marco said, but only in his mind. He knew it was only a matter of a few hours before he could say it out loud. For now, he said it only to himself.

The guard reached out and pushed the heavy steel door open. Marco walked into a small but crowded courtroom. He could see Marvin Levin standing in front of a large table. The Judge, dressed in a black robe, was seated behind the table. Uniformed deputy sheriffs were busy on either side of him stacking, arranging and stapling legal paper work, reports and who knows what else. Marco felt himself being shoved again.

Watch who you're shoving, you piece of shit. Marco said, again only in his mind.

Marvin was standing with a file folder in his right hand and his left hand held flat against his side. Patting his left hand against his leg, he motioned for Marco to join him.

"Come here," Marvin whispered. "Stand next to me."

"Is this your client, Mr. Levin?" the judge bellowed.

"Yes, your honor."

Judge Arthur P. Brickhouse, sat hunched over the table holding his right fist in his left hand. He was a big man, about sixty with graying hair. He leaned further over the table and said in a loud voice, "Your client is charged with a felony, Counselor. Can you give me a good reason why I should let him back on the street?"

"Your Honor, my client has no previous arrest record. He owns a home and is a professional person who has worked for the same employer for over ten years. Your Honor my client also has a teenage daughter who is solely dependent on him, as her mother, my client's wife, is deceased. I assure the court that my client has much more to lose by fleeing than facing the charges against him, charges, I might add, we are confident he will successfully defend himself against."

The judge turned his head and looked at the young Assistant States Attorney standing at Marvin's right. He was a very tall, skinny young man. His fingernails were bitten so short, dried blood could be seen on his fingertips. His straight black hair was much too long, and his colorless complexion made him look sickly. He was standing with his shoulders slouched and his mouth wide open, looking as though he didn't quite understand what was going on.

"Counselor," the judge said. "Counselor!" the judge repeated impatiently. "Hey," the judge scolded loudly.

"Oh, excuse me Your Honor," the young man said, adjusting his round wire rimmed eye glasses, then pulling at his shirt collar, which was at least two sizes too big.

"Well, do the people have any objection to the defendant being freed on bail?"

"Oh, yes sir, Your Honor. The people feel the charges against the defendant and the defendant's past criminal record are sufficient reason to deny bail, . . . sir . . . Your Honor, . . . sir."

"I see no evidence of any past criminal record," the judge stated, as he reviewed the documents before him, growing more and more impatient.

"Oh, I'm sorry, Your Honor. I must be looking at the wrong file. Let me get the right one."

"Don't bother, young man. I'm setting bail at fifteen hundred dollars." Looking at Marvin Levin, he said, "I'm sure you know what to do, Counselor."

"Yes, Your Honor, thank you. Excuse me, Judge, one more thing. May I have a few minutes alone with my client?"

"Bailiff," the judge roared. "Show Counselor Levin to a private room where he may consult with his client."

"Next!" the judge said, as Marco and Marvin followed the bailiff to a small room behind the judge's table.

"I'll have you out of here in a few more hours," Marvin assured. "I just wanted to let you know everything is under control. Tony and his girlfriend are with your daughter at your place. I'll call them and let them know things went well here. Just sit tight. I'll start the process and wait here until your release."

"What about my car?" Marco asked.

"We'll worry about your car after the probable cause hearing Monday morning."

"Probable cause hearing?" Marco repeated.

"That's where you go before a judge. He hears the case against you and decides whether or not there's enough evidence to justify a trial."

"You mean it's possible this could be over Monday morning?" Marco asked, surprised.

"No way," Marvin said without hesitation. "Not in this case. You'll have to go to trial, there's no question about that. But please, don't worry about that now. First things first. Let's get you out of here."

* * *

Marco could not believe the mob of reporters and photographers waiting outside the County Jail, even though Marvin had tried to prepare him.

"Marco, is it true you tried to pick up a transvestite prostitute?"

"The police say you were carrying a loaded gun. Is that true?"

"Is it true you've had a long standing relationship with the transvestite prostitute in question?"

Questions were being shouted from all sides as the reporters pushed toward Marco and Marvin all the way to their waiting car. The car door swung open, and Marco dove into the back seat, with Marvin close behind. After picking himself up off the floor, Marco brushed the dirt and dust off his clothing.

"Hey, Marco, good to see you safe and sound."

Marco turned to the sound of Jerry Kaplan's voice.

"Good to see you, too, Jerry."

"I'll bet you never thought you'd hear yourself saying that," Kaplan said with a laugh.

*   *   *

Thirty minutes later in Marco's Lake Shore Drive condo, Marco, Marvin, Kaplan, Tony, his girlfriend Karen and, of course, Sarah gathered around the dining room table. Marco related his experiences of the previous thirty-six hours and answered the many questions his friends had for him.

"I can't believe it," Tony said. "What balls . . . oh, excuse me Sarah, what nerve these guys have to actually set someone up like that."

"How could you be surprised after learning what we have over the past few days?" Marco asked.

"Excuse me," Marvin broke in. "It's almost one o'clock I have to get some sleep. I'll be here to pick you up at eight o'clock Monday morning, we have to be at court by nine. After the hearing, we'll go to the auto pound and pick up your car. Make sure you bring your checkbook; you'll have fees and charges to pay."

"I'm going, too," Kaplan said. "I'm getting too old for this kind of excitement."

Marvin and Jerry got up to leave. Sarah retrieved their coats from the foyer closet and saw them to the door. Suddenly, Marvin turned and walked back into the dining room.

"Forget something?" Marco asked.

"Yes," Marvin said. "We never talked about getting you a lawyer. After Monday, I'm at my limit. I know nothing about criminal law beyond the most fundamental aspects."

"It was my intention to go over that with Marco tomorrow morning at breakfast," Tony said.

"Breakfast?" Marco asked, shocked.

"Yes, Daddy," Sarah broke in. "Tony and Karen are coming back in the morning for breakfast."

"Let's make it brunch, okay?" Marco suggested. "I need a good night's sleep."

"Okay," Tony said. "Karen and I will see you at eleven tomorrow morning."

By one-thirty, Marco and Sarah found themselves alone in the kitchen, loading the dishwasher.

"I'm so sorry, Honey." Marco said, as he poured soap into the dispenser.

"Sorry for what?" Sarah asked.

"For putting you through all this. I should have listened to you in the first place."

"Don't be sorry, Dad. I'm proud of you."

"Proud of me?"

"Yes, proud. You stood up for your principles. You refused to take the easy way out. You're a brave man, Dad. I'm proud to be your daughter."

"Thanks, Sweetheart, but you've seen the headlines. I'm afraid you're in the minority."

"Not for long, Daddy. When you get back on the air Monday, you'll have a chance to tell your side of the story."

"But will anybody believe me?"

"I believe you. I can see it in your eyes. I know your listeners will hear it in your voice."

Marco gazed at his daughter. She was no longer a little girl. Over the past few days, she had become a woman.

"I hope so, Honey," Marco said. "I certainly hope so."

CHAPTER 6

"I see you have chosen a lawyer to represent you. I can't say I'm very pleased with your choice, but you may be right. Maybe it's time to fight fire with fire."

SARAH ROSE EARLY Sunday morning and rushed out to the grocery store. She bought fresh fruit, orange juice, eggs, bacon, pork sausage, potatoes, milk and a variety of breakfast cereals. Today, she would allow her father to gorge himself on all the foods she would normally forbid him to eat. Sarah would make this a very special day for a very special dad.

* * *

"Wow, I haven't eaten like this in I don't know how long," Marco said, patting his stomach.

"I'll say," Tony agreed.

"Yeah, sure," Karen kidded. "You eat like this at every meal."

"Very funny, but I can't laugh right now. Marco and I have some very important business to discuss." Tony put his arm around Marco's shoulder and walked him toward the third bedroom, which had been converted to an office.

"I assume you have a list of possible lawyers for me to look at," Marco said.

"Not exactly," Tony said.

"You mean you haven't prepared a list?"

"Well yes, I have a list, but there's only one name on it."

Marco was about to say something when he was interrupted by the ringing phone.

"Hello."

"Do you recognize my voice?"

"Yes, I do."

"I'm sorry Marco. I feel responsible for what happened. I want to help you if you'll let me."

"Are you a lawyer?" Marco quipped.

"No, but I can recommend one."

"Who?" Marco asked.

Tony watched as Marco wrote something on a notepad.

"What makes this guy so good?" Marco asked.

"Simple, he's the best."

"So you think I should call this guy?" Marco asked thoughtfully.

"Only if you want to win," Mr. Caller responded.

"Okay, I'll call him tomorrow afternoon after court and after I get my car out of hock."

"You won't be sorry. Let me say again, that I'm really sorry for getting you into this."

"It's not your fault; I should have known better. I'll look up this lawyer tomorrow, and please stay in touch," Marco said, then hung up the phone.

"Was that who I think it was?" Tony asked.

"If you think it was Mr. Caller, you're right."

"I wonder how he got your home number?" Tony asked.

"Hmm, I don't know. Probably the same way the guy who set me up got it, I guess," Marco answered. Suddenly the image of Mr. Caller pulling his sweater over the bulge on his waist line flashed back to him. "Hmmm, I wonder," Marco muttered.

"What did you say?" Tony said.

"Oh. Ah, I was saying, Mr. Caller gave me the number of a lawyer; he says he's the best."

"That's what Marvin says about this guy," Tony said as he handed Marco his "list."

"Very interesting," Marco said, as he handed Tony the notepad from his desk.

"Hey, it's the same guy!" Tony said, surprised.

"That's right, Christopher Musso," Marco said.

"Did Mr. Caller give you any background on Mr. Musso?" Tony asked.

"Only that if I wanted to win, he's my man."

"Well, maybe I should warn you, this guy Musso is reputed to be a mob lawyer, a mouthpiece, if you will."

"Yes, I thought I recognized the name," Marco said."Chris Musso; he successfully defended the Bianco brothers in a federal racketeering charge last year, and in a Las Vegas casino skimming charge, where the star witness suddenly disappeared without a trace."

"That's right, and you don't get any bigger than Ralph and Billy Bianco," Tony added.

"Didn't the Feds go back and reopen murder cases where the victim was killed by three bullet wounds in the head and try to pin them all on Ralph Bianco?" Marco recalled.

"Yes, they claimed it was his trademark, but Musso went back even further and produced files of unsolved murders dating back to before Ralph was born. They had all died from three gun shots to the head."

"Well, I guess that does it. If he's good enough for the Bianco brothers, he's good enough for me," Marco said, as he started for the door.

"Where are you going?" Tony asked.

"Our work is finished. We've decided on a lawyer. So let's go see a movie."

* * *

The front, rear and side entrances of Marco's building were packed with reporters hoping to corner Marco for a statement. So Tony sneaked him out through the underground parking lot. After a couple blocks, Tony let Marco out of his trunk.

"Next time buy a bigger car," Marco kidded.

"Can't afford a Caddy like some people I know," Tony kidded back.

Marco climbed into the back seat and joined his daughter Sarah.

"By the way," Marco said, "Jerry tells me you did a very good job sitting in for me. Thanks, I always knew you could do it. Jerry and I agree, Tony; you should be my regular replacement from now on, you know vacation, holidays; whenever I can't do the show, you'll be sitting in for me. Jerry and I have already discussed it, it's a done deal."

"Aren't you afraid I'll pull a Joan Rivers and go into competition with you?"

"It wouldn't bother me," Marco said. "Kaplan, however, would have you shot."

* * *

The probable cause hearing went exactly the way Marvin said it would. After the arresting officer testified that he witnessed the solicitation and found a loaded firearm on Marco when he searched him at the scene, it was all over. The presiding judge agreed with the prosecutor that there was enough evidence to warrant a trial. Within forty-five minutes, Marco and Marvin were battling the same bunch of reporters coming out of the courthouse as they had going in.

"When will these leaches back off?" Marco sighed.

"Let's hope they're not waiting for us at the auto pound," Marvin said, as he handed Marco a file folder. "Give this to Chris

Musso when you see him. It contains everything he'll need to understand what's happened so far."

"Do you think he'll take my case?" Marco asked.

"I can't say for sure," Marvin said. "But if he can find a way to expose a conspiracy between corrupt politicians and the police to frame an innocent person of a crime he didn't commit, it would be great for his reputation. I think he'd jump at the chance. It's the kind of case that could bring him a lot of positive publicity."

"Do you think there's still a chance he won't defend me?"

"There's always that chance, but if you lay on the old Marco Fischer charm, and more important, convince him that you're an honest, honorable man, you'll win him over. If you do, he'll win the judge over."

"The judge, no jury?" Marco asked.

"I told you, I'm no criminal lawyer, but I think he'll recommend a bench trial."

"Why?" Marco asked.

"I don't want to tell you any more. Let him tell you what he thinks is best for you. Please do as he says."

* * *

The Chicago Police Department auto pound was deserted, except for what seemed to be a million cars. Cars of every make and model, new and old. Compact cars, expensive luxury cars; there were even a couple of motorcycles. Marco and Marvin walked into a trailer that served as an office. A uniformed cop greeted them. After paying the fine and towing and storage charges of almost thirteen hundred dollars, Marco's car was released.

"Inspect your car thoroughly," Marvin warned. "Make a list of any damaged and/or missing articles."

Marco slowly walked around his vehicle, inspecting it carefully.

"Hey, where's my front license plate?" Marco moaned.

"Write it down," Marvin ordered.

"Look at this scratch," Marco cried. "My hood emblem is missing."

"Write it down," Marvin repeated.

By the time Marco drove out of the pound, he had a list of fifteen items of damaged or missing property.

* * *

"They even stole the flashlight I kept in my glove compartment," Marco complained into his cell phone as he traveled the Dan Ryan expressway on his way to meet Tony at Chris Musso's office.

"Marco, take it easy," Tony said. "All things considered, your flashlight is the least of your worries right now. Get back downtown as fast as you can. I'll meet you at Musso's office at one o'clock."

Marco entered the express lanes. The traffic was unusually light. He switched on his cruse control and pushed the button to engage. Nothing happened.

"Oh, shit," Marco cursed out loud. "I forgot my cruise control isn't working. Maybe I'll have time to stop at Stan's before I go to see Musso."

It was twelve-thirty when Marco drove into Stan's service station. Stan came running out of the office when he saw Marco's Coupe DeVille.

"Marco, say it isn't so," Stan said grinning like a clown.

"Please change those fuses and let me get out of here. I have to be on LaSalle Street by one o'clock."

In less than five minutes the new fuses were installed and Marco was on his way. As he drove out of the driveway, he looked at his receipt one more time before folding it neatly and putting it into his pocket. Later, when he got to the office, he would file it in his auto maintenance and repairs file.

"Eight dollars for two lousy fuses," Marco complained, as he turned onto LaSalle Street. "That fucking Stanley ought to be prosecuted for highway robbery."

* * *

Tony looked up from his magazine and checked his wrist watch. "Cutting it close, as usual," he scolded.

"Had to stop for gas or I would have never made it here," Marco said in self defense, as he picked up something to read and sat down next to Tony.

Just then, the door leading to the inner offices swung open. An imposing figure appeared. The man stood only about five nine, but he was built like a rhino. He was dressed in an expensive gray silk suit, but it couldn't disguise the massive chest, arms and legs it caressed. Tony nudged Marco with his elbow as the man passed them. The man turned and caught Marco's eye when he lifted his head. Marco felt a chill.

There was something strangely intriguing about the man. He had a strong, handsome face and a full head of chestnut hair, graying only slightly at the temples. His deep brown eyes were cold, but not necessarily fearsome; though piercing, they were not threatening, at least not at the moment. The man slowed his pace and nodded without changing his expression. Marco smiled and nodded back.

At that moment, the door opened again. A young woman poked her head into the waiting room and announced. "Mr. Musso will see you now, gentlemen.

Marco had turned at the sound of the secretary's voice. When he turned back, the man was gone.

* * *

"Very pleased to meet you, Mr. Fischer. I've been a fan of yours for a long time."

"Thank you, Mr. Musso, but the pleasure is mine. Allow me to introduce my good friend and associate, Mr. Tony Ruskin. Tony is my producer."

Everyone shook hands.

"Please sit down, gentlemen," Musso, a man in his late thirties said, motioning toward the chairs in front of his desk.

"Excuse me," Marco said, as he took a chair and crossed his legs. "The man who left your office a minute ago, he looked familiar."

Musso did not respond; instead, he smiled knowingly, but ignored Marco's comment.

* * *

Christopher Musso was not your typical looking lawyer; there was something almost theatrical in his appearance, not gaudy or over done, but classy and well polished. He was not especially tall, but with his dark curly hair and tanned skin wrapped in a beautiful custom-made Italian silk suit, he made a very statuesque impression.

Chris Musso sat down and reached for a yellow legal pad and said, "From the beginning, Mr. Fischer. Take your time, concentrate on the facts leading up to your arrest. Minor details at this point are not important, but may be later. You may start whenever you're ready."

Chris Musso reached over and turned on a tape recorder. For the next thirty minutes, he listened as Marco described his ordeal.

* * *

"Someone else might call that an unbelievable story, Mr. Fischer, but I believe every word of it."

"Perhaps bringing Tony along to collaborate my story was a good idea," Marco said.

"Well, it was helpful, but your story was backed up by another person as well," Musso said, as he leafed through his legal pad. "You see, I interviewed your Mr. Caller earlier this morning. Frankly, for reasons I can't divulge, he was even more convincing than you."

"I knew it. You two know each other, don't you?" Marco asked excitedly.

"If I expect you to be honest with me, I'm going to have to be honest with you, Mr. Fischer."

"Please, call me Marco."

"Okay, Marco, you're right. I do know Mr. Caller, but please understand I cannot reveal his identity, at least not yet."

"You said we should be honest with each other. Does that mean you've decided to take my case?"

"I made that decision this morning. Yes, I have every intention of taking your case. If you'll have me." Chris said leaning back in his chair.

"Wait, I must be sure of something first," Marco said. "I'm told that if I retain you as my lawyer, there is no way I can lose this case. But I want to win. I don't want a fix. I don't want any payoffs. I want to win because I'm not guilty, not because I have a connected lawyer."

Marco took a chance. If Chris Musso was the man Marco thought he was, he'd understand why Marco had to say what he had. If Musso was offended by Marco's words, then he was the wrong man for the job.

"Wow, you are being honest," Musso remarked.

"I hope I haven't offended you."

"Not at all, I understand and I don't blame you. Let me respond to your concerns." Musso leaned forward, placed his elbows on his desk top and rested his chin on his hands."It's true, I have represented many organized crime figures, including Ralph and Billy Bianco. It is also true that I have never failed to successfully defend any client, but never, never have I found it necessary to fix a case. Not that I couldn't if I wanted to, but because I never needed to." Chris Musso leaned back in his chair again and looked directly into Marco's eyes. "I want you to know one more thing. If it were not for the Bianco brothers, I probably wouldn't be here talking to you now."

Chris Musso paused for a moment to switch off the tape recorder.

"It was their generosity, their encouragement, their influence that brought me to my senses. As a young man, I was on the verge of wasting my life, never realizing my true potential. As a favor to my parents, who were neighbors of the Biancos, they took me under their wings, so to speak. They gave me a job and kept me away from the dangerous influences that were about to destroy my life. That's right, Marco. The Bianco brothers turned out to be the most positive influences in my life."

Musso rocked back and forth a couple times in his plush leather chair, then continued.

"There is good and bad in all of us. There are those who would say *you* are a dangerous influence; to some you may very well be. Your reason for being here today is evidence of that. To many, however, I'm sure you are a very positive influence. It will be my job to demonstrate that when we go to court."

"Please accept my apologies, Mr. Musso."

"No need to apologize. I told you, I understand, and please, from now on, call me Chris." Musso tugged at his sleeve and checked his solid gold wrist watch. "It's almost two-thirty; I know you have to get to the studio. I'll call you after I've had a chance to study your file".

* * *

After Marco and Tony left, Chris got up from behind his desk and walked to the door, opening it just enough to poke his head into the outer office. "I don't want to be disturbed for the rest of the day," he said, startling his secretary, causing her to jerk her head up as she worked at the word processor. Chris closed the door and locked it. He walked over to the solid oak bar, built into a wall of custom built bookcases filled with volumes of leather-bound legal books. He poured himself a cup of coffee and returned to his desk to begin formulating his closing argument.

For many years, this had been his routine whenever he decided to accept a case. He believed that the closing argument was the most important part of his defense strategy. Before he would begin, he would have to review all the facts again. The evidence the prosecution planned to produce, the anticipated testimony of the witnesses on both sides and the results of his own investigation. He reached for the large brown envelope which contained the material he would have to study for the next several hours.

Newspaper accounts of the events surrounding his clients arrest. Police reports and photographs of the crime scene, if any. Statements by witnesses and of course the indictment itself. But most of all, it was his own account of what he considered to be the true facts of the case that would guide him. Not until all the facts and information were consumed and thoroughly digested would he begin to write what would be his final plea to the jury, even though the trial had not yet begun and not one word of testimony had been offered. Chris Musso had no idea of knowing that a closing argument, no matter how convincing, would never be heard.

CHAPTER 7

"I like that, it fits. From now on that's what I'll call myself. Why not? He was the hero, the defender of his people. Yes, I like it. That's who I'll be from now on."

"THREE, TWO, ONE." Tony signaled as he cued Marco to begin his show.

"Good afternoon, ladies and gentlemen and children of all ages. Welcome to another session of Marco's Morgue. We usually do the burying, but today I need your help to exhume someone who was buried last week. That someone is me. I know you've heard the news reports and read the headlines. Now I hope you'll give me a chance to tell *my* side of the story."

For the first hour of the broadcast, Marco poured his heart out to his faithful audience. The next three hours were the best of his life. Caller after caller expressed support and encouragement. One caller informed Marco's fans that a defense fund had been set up to help him with his legal expenses. Two calls stood out from all the rest. One was especially gratifying, the other was strangely disturbing. The first was from Marco's daughter, Sarah.

"Hello, this is Marco Fischer."

"Hi, Daddy. I wanted to call and thank all the wonderful people who have expressed their support. I'm proud that my dad is loved and respected by so many people. I also want you to know, I'm still your biggest fan."

The second caller remained anonymous. His voice had a strange sound to it, a hissing quality, like that of a snake. Marco recognized the sound; he'd heard it before.

"I want everybody out there to know that it's time to fight back. Big government and big business are conspiring to take over our lives."

"Excuse me, caller. What exactly do you mean when you say take over our lives?" Marco asked.

"They want to control us. They want to tell us what to do, when to do it, how to do it and where to do it. They already make us wear seat belts. They tell us how fast we can drive our cars, where and when we can turn a corner and under what circumstances. They control how much money we can withdraw or deposit in our bank accounts. If it's over a certain amount, we have to fill out all kinds of forms and answer all kinds of questions."

Marco adjusted his headset, which had slipped slightly off kilter. He didn't want to miss anything this caller had to say.

The caller continued. "Why? Why do they have to know these things? I'll tell you why, it's because they want to know how much money we have. They're afraid we might get away with a few bucks that haven't been taxed. You can't even get on a plane anymore without showing your picture ID. Sure, they say it's for our own protection, but that's not the real reason. It's because they want us to become accustomed to producing our 'papers' everywhere we go. There's another reason too. This is where big business, in this case the airlines, and big government conspire to rip off the American people."

"So you think the government is conspiring with the airlines?" Marco asked, rolling his eyes, tapping his temple with his index finger.

"You think it's a joke?" The caller responded, "I'll give you an example. It used to be that as long as you had a ticket, you were allowed to get on the plane, which meant, if you bought a fare and gave the ticket to me, you would get the travel miles credited to your account. This is no longer possible, because by federal law, the name on the ticket must match the name on the picture ID. The airlines are savings millions every year. That is the real reason for the new law. It has nothing to do with 'our own protection,' as they would like for us to believe."

This call was running on a little longer than usual, but Marco decided to let the caller continue.

"Here's another farce being perpetrated on the American people. Baggage X-raying and metal detectors. They tell us they're checking for bombs and weapons, again for 'our own protection.' If they're so worried about explosives, why don't they X-ray the baggage we check with the sky caps or at the front counter? I'll tell you why, because it's not our safety they're interested in, it's our compliance with another oppressive and invasive regulation. It's another way of controlling us."

Marco leaned back in his seat and put his hands behind his head.

"We are being regulated to death in this country. They even tell us how much water we can have in our toilet bowl tanks. Every day it gets worse, and it won't stop until we do something about it, but it won't be easy. Look what happened to you, Marco. You tried to expose corruption, and you were attacked by the very same people who are supposed to be protecting you. We the people gave the power to these guys. And what do they do? They use it to intimidate us. Don't think this is the end, Marco. They're not through with you. They're out to get you, and they will, unless you get them first. You must destroy them."

"What exactly do you mean, destroy them?" Marco interrupted.

"Don't you know what destroy means? Annihilate, wipe out, kill."

"Kill?" Marco asked, thinking perhaps he let this caller go on too long after all.

"Yes, kill. The penalty for betraying the public trust should be death."

"Whoa," Marco said. "Isn't that a bit extreme?"

"Extreme? You're the one who says we should embalm them and bury them forever. Don't you think we should at least make sure they're dead first? Remember Richard Casper? He betrayed the public trust."

Suddenly, Marco became frightened. Not so much by what the caller was saying, but by what Chris Musso had said earlier that day. Like a bolt of lightning, Musso's words flashed in his mind. *Some say you are a dangerous influence*. Could it be? Is it possible that his words could incite people? Could it be that he *is* a dangerous influence? Could he really affect the way people think and act?

"Shouldn't we?"

Marco was shaken back to reality by the caller's words.

"Well, shouldn't we?"

"Shouldn't . . . we . . . what?" Marco asked, trying to compose himself.

"Shouldn't we make sure they're dead first?"

"Caller, you're taking what I say literally. I never meant we should really embalm and bury people, much less actually kill them."

"Maybe you don't think so, but I do."

Marco heard a clicking sound indicating the connection had been broken.

* * *

Later that evening, Marco and his daughter sat at the kitchen table reflecting on the day's events.

"What did you think of Chris Musso?" Sarah asked, pouring herself a glass of milk.

"I like him," Marco answered. "I admit I had reservations at first, but after meeting him, they were all expelled." Marco got up and opened a kitchen cabinet. He lifted a glass off the shelf and placed it on the kitchen table, "pour me half a glass, sweetheart."

Sarah poured the milk from a plastic jug. "Is it true what they say about him?" Sarah asked.

"You mean that he's a mob lawyer? I asked him about that, and he admits being associated with the Biancos. That doesn't necessarily make him a mobster. I'm sure the Biancos retained him for the same reasons I did. They wanted to win, and so do I."

"Yeah, but you really are innocent, Dad."

"That's all the more reason why I need Chris Musso to defend me."

Changing the subject Sarah asked, "What was with that caller who wanted to kill people. He sounded weird, didn't he?"

"I guess you could say that, but what worried me was that he might have been influenced by things I've said on the show. I should be more careful about the things I say and how I say them."

"You don't make the news, Dad, you only comment on it."

"That's true, honey, but after listening to that guy today, I realized my words have a much greater affect than I ever thought. At least on some people."

"There will always be some people who are not exactly all there, if you know what I mean. You can't be responsible for them."

"Perhaps I'm not responsible, but I should be aware of them. I'd hate for my words to incite some nut into doing something horrible."

"I guess you're right, Dad. I hadn't thought of it that way."

* * *

"I've decided a bench trial would be our best bet," Chris said, as he leafed through Marco's file. "Unless you want to prolong this thing and intensify the media frenzy."

"No, no," Marco said. "I want this thing to be over as soon as possible."

Marco sat in front of Musso's desk in blue jeans, powder blue linen shirt and brown leather aviator jacket. Chris wore a charcoal gray wool, double-breasted suit, white shirt and multi-colored silk tie.

"Okay," Chris said. "In two weeks, we have our preliminary hearing at 26th and California. At that time, we'll find out who our judge will be. Now, listen carefully, if we don't like the judge assigned to our case, we'll have an opportunity to request another one, but I hope it doesn't come to that."

"Why not?" Marco asked.

"Simple," Chris answered. "Once we request a second judge, we're stuck with him. If he turns out to be worse than the first, it's too bad, we can't ask for a third."

"When do you think the actual trial will take place?" Marco asked.

"Probably about thirty days or so after the preliminary hearing."

"What should I be doing between then and now?"

"Nothing," Chris said. "Just go about your business as usual. See you in two weeks."

Marco left Musso's office feeling pretty good. Chris' attitude and confidence were infectious.

* * *

"Ladies and gentlemen, the rumor persists. What rumor, you ask? The rumor that our old friend Sean O'Bannion, 'The Sheriff of Nottingham' is considering another run for the office of Sheriff of Cook County. Can you believe it? As a matter of fact, my sources tell me that a fund-raiser disguised as a welcome home party is being planned for early next month. You would think that any self respecting, honest, honorable politician wouldn't want to be seen within ten miles of that slime ball. Not in this town." Marco looked up to see Tony smiling behind the plate glass window.

"The way I hear it, The Sheriff of Nottingham is expecting a full house. All his scum bag cronies will be there. Think about it, folks. A convicted felon is treated like nobility, while the people who voted for these meatballs are neglected. When will we smarten up? Where's Robin Hood when we need him? The lines are open. I'll be taking calls after a commercial break."

* * *

For the remainder of the program, Marco listened to his callers express their disappointment, disgust, shock and disbelief. One caller, however, though disgusted, felt no shock and certainly no disbelief.

"I've been listening to your callers whine and cry about those nasty politicians, but I haven't heard one of them say what he was going to do about it. Oh sure, I heard one or two say he wouldn't vote for anyone who shows up at the party. I even heard a few say they weren't going to vote altogether. Big deal! What good does that really do?"

"What do you suggest?" Marco prodded, recognizing the voice.

"Hang em! Hang em all. Line them up against the wall and shoot 'em," the caller hissed.

"Hold on, please," Marco broke in. "That's not the way we do things in America. What you're suggesting is vigilantism, anarchy. In a civilized society, that cannot be tolerated."

"Civilized? Do you call what these bastards are doing to us civilized? I say we give them what they've been giving us. The shaft, right through the heart."

With that the caller hung up.

"Ladies and gentlemen, and especially my most recent caller, I understand the frustration some of you must be feeling. I understand how helpless you must feel. However, what our anonymous caller suggests is not the solution. Getting involved is what we have to do. Taking part in the political system and changing it from within. Vote! That's how you change things, but vote intelligently.

"Don't vote for someone if you don't know and agree with what he stands for. Don't vote for someone just because your friend voted for him; maybe your friend is an idiot. Vote, that's what I say you should do. However, if you are not going to vote intelligently, it's better that you don't vote at all."

CHAPTER 8

"My plan will soon be implemented. You will no longer have to fight these bastards alone. Soon these treasonous sons-of-bitches will have a new enemy, one who fights with more than just words."

TWO WEEKS FLEW by, and Marco's trial date drew closer. At the preliminary hearing, it was learned that the Honorable Judge Rolando J. Rios would be in charge of the proceedings.

"What do you think of the judge?" Marco asked, as he and Chris headed toward the parking lot.

"He's good," Chris said. "I've tried cases in his courtroom before. He's fair and he knows the law. Most of all, he's Hispanic."

"What does that have to do with anything?" Marco asked.

"You're a strange paradox, Marco," Chris explained. "You're considered a conservative by many, and yet those who are usually aligned with the liberal element think very highly of you. The Blacks and Hispanics for instance, you're very popular in their neighborhoods. You have a reputation for sticking up for the underdog, the under-privileged. You have often come to the defense of those who cannot defend themselves. Everybody in this town knows who you are. I assure you, the judge knows who you are, too".

"Is it fair for us to exploit that?" Marco asked.

"We didn't ask for this judge. We had nothing to do with his appointment to our case." Chris pointed out. "It's my duty to put up the best defense I possibly can. It's fair for me to take advantage of every opportunity and every advantage allowed by the law."

As always, whenever Marco was with Chris, he became infected with his confidence. That afternoon, Marco felt exhilarated when he went on the air.

* * *

"Ladies and gentlemen and children of all ages, welcome to Marco's Morgue. Today I had my preliminary hearing. My trial date is set for thirty-two days from today in Judge Rolando J. Rios' courtroom. We feel . . . that is my attorney Mr. Christopher Musso and I, feel confident that Judge Rios will see to it that I receive a fair trial. Enough about me. Let's talk about the latest developments involving our old friend, 'The Sheriff of Nottingham,' Sean O'Bannion.

"O'Bannion has been seen carousing on the Near North Side. My sources tell me he's been sipping martinis at Denny's Den on Division Street. I've also had reports that he's been slurping spaghetti at Angelo's on Rush Street. Now, you may be wondering, what's wrong with that? Normally nothing, but the sheriff was supposed to be sound asleep in his room at the halfway house on Monroe Street, not cabareting with his buddies Prince John and Sir Guy Gisbourne, otherwise known as Alderman Patrick Grogan and his flunky Tommy O'Mara. After a commercial break, we'll talk about it."

As usual, the phone lines on Marco's Morgue were hot with callers. And as usual, the callers were outraged by what they were hearing. One caller who had become a regular fixture on Marco's Morgue was more than outraged.

"Where were his guards? How can this guy who is technically still a prisoner in the federal corrections system come and go as he pleases? These guards are paid by the taxpayers. This is another example of how we are being betrayed by the very people who depend on the taxpayer for their livelihood. As I have said before, it's time to do something about these crooks, these deceivers, these double-crossers, these enemies of the people."

Again, before Marco had a chance to respond directly to the hissing caller, the call was abruptly disconnected. Again, Marco was forced to rebut the caller by directing his comments to the general audience.

"Something *is* being done. By exposing these 'enemies of the people' as you call them, we educate the people. The more educated we are, the more informed we are when we enter the voting booth. That's how we change things. That's how we regain the power we relinquished to those who have used it to enrich themselves. Caller, whoever you are, your concerns are shared by many of us, including yours truly, but your way is the wrong way."

Marco softened his tone, trying to sound as though he was speaking one-on-one to the caller.

"Caller, listen to me carefully, this program is meant to inspire people, not incite them. I'm flattered that you've placed such importance on my words, but you have misconstrued their meaning. You have totally misunderstood the message I'm trying to convey. I am grateful for your loyalty to this program. If I have misled you, I assure you it was unintentional; please accept my apologies. My intention, my hope is that I can be a positive influence on my listeners, not a negative one."

* * *

Chris Musso was just about to call it a day when his secretary buzzed him on the intercom.

"Yes?" he answered.

"There's a call for you on line four."

"Hello, this is Chris Musso."

"Do you recognize my voice?"

"Yes, I do," Chris said.

"Have you heard, the prosecutor assigned to Marco's case has been replaced?"

"No, I haven't," Chris said. "I'm not surprised; I've been expecting something like that to happen. Do you know who the new man is?"

"An old friend of yours, . . . Richard Testa. He's bad news. He's as dirty as they come, but you already know that."

"As you know, I'm very familiar with Testa. I know what he's capable of, and I know he's been out to get even with me ever since I kicked his ass in the Bianco case. Thanks for the warning, but I can handle Testa. He plays dirty because he's not a very good lawyer. It's for that reason he's going to get his ass kicked a second time. Thanks again, stay in touch." Chris hung up the phone and buzzed his secretary.

"Yes sir?" the secretary answered.

"Call Mr. Fischer, ask him to meet me tonight at eight-thirty for dinner, . . . on me. Ask him to bring his daughter Sarah. I'd like to meet her. Call Cosmo's and make reservations for four. I'm going home to pick up my wife."

* * *

Ever since his arrest, Marco felt self conscious whenever he entered a public place. The second he entered the lavishly decorated, art deco-styled restaurant through its ornately carved oak doors he felt as though all eyes were watching his every move. As he and Sarah were led to a table where Chris and his wife Gail were waiting, Marco scanned the room. Eyes were indeed following him, but only two. They were the bluest, most beautiful eyes he'd ever seen.

Chris introduced Gail, but Marco couldn't pull his eyes away from the gorgeous blond seated just two tables away.

"Daddy," Sarah said, nudging her father with her elbow.

"Oh, excuse me. Very pleased to meet you, Mrs. Musso," Marco said. "This is my little . . . I mean, my daughter Sarah; she's sixteen."

"A pleasure to meet you," Sarah said, bowing slightly as she offered her hand.

"A very firm handshake, young lady," Chris observed.

"Thank you, Mr. Musso. I inherited it from my dad."

Sarah looked at her father. He was looking at the blond. The woman was seated with her elbows on the table top, her chin resting on her folded slender hands. Meticulously manicured nails adorned the tips of her long fingers. Every few seconds, her eyes would shift in Marco's direction. He felt a thrill every time their eyes met. Although seated, she seemed rather tall, perhaps five-eight, Marco estimated.

She was dressed in a plain, tight fitting, light blue dress with rope-like shoulder straps.

The dress accentuated her slender well-toned body perfectly. Her breasts were not large, but they were firm and extremely sensuous. Marco had never liked large breasts anyway. It was her legs, however, that his eyes were glued to. She had long legs, slender, but shapely. Her right leg was crossed over her left with one shoe dangling, half on, half off.

Occasionally she would turn her head and look directly at Marco. He had never seen such a beautiful face. Her naturally long eyelashes and flawless complexion made makeup totally unnecessary, though there was some evidence of a small amount of eye makeup, just enough to highlight her stunning blue eyes.

"Marco, *Marco*."

Marco felt a hard, stabbing jolt to his ribs. "Ow," he uttered turning to his right. It was Sarah, no longer just nudging. "Daddy, Mr. Musso is talking to you."

"Oh, excuse me, Chris. Something caught my eye. I was distracted for a moment. What were you saying?"

"I was about to say, I thought it would be a good idea to go over your case in a more casual atmosphere. I want you to consider me your friend, Marco, not just your lawyer."

"Thank you, Chris, I appreciate that. I do consider you my friend."

"I want you to know I talked to our *mutual* friend today," Chris said. "He informed me of a very interesting development. It seems we're going to have a new prosecutor, Assistant State's Attorney Richard Testa."

"Is that good or bad?" Sarah asked.

"Normally, I wouldn't pay much attention to that kind of move. In this case, however, I get the feeling there's more to it than meets the eye."

"Why would they change prosecutors?" Marco asked.

"Testa is tough. A lot tougher than their first choice. Perhaps it's for that reason. I don't know. In any event, in the end it won't make any difference. It's how good a lawyer he is that matters . . . and on that count we have him beat. We're going to win."

"How can you be so sure. After all, isn't it true that judges tend to believe the police when it's their word against yours?" Marco asked.

"This isn't the movies or TV where the cops are always heroes. In reality, cops are liars. Every criminal defense lawyer knows it, and believe me, the judges know it, too."

"But don't you have to prove it?" Marco asked.

"All I have to do is create a reasonable doubt, but that's only if we actually go to trial."

"I thought that was what we were doing," Marco asked, shocked and confused.

"Not exactly," Chris said. "The judge will hear my motion to suppress first."

"Motion to suppress?" Sarah asked.

"Yes. You see, the cop claims to have found a loaded pistol in your father's pocket after he arrested him on a misdemeanor charge. The misdemeanor is what gave the officer the right to search your dad in the first place. If we can prove, however, that the misdemeanor never took place, then the search was made illegally. If the search was illegal, whatever came as a result of it is not admissible in a court of law."

"Is that what they mean when they say 'he got off on a technicality?'

"Very good, Sarah. Technically speaking, that's exactly what they mean."

"Wait a minute Chris. Getting off on a technicality isn't good enough. I have to be vindicated, totally, without question. We have to expose the set up, the conspiracy."

"My first duty is to clear you of the criminal charges. After that, we can worry about the rest of it."

Marco let out a long sigh. "I'll leave it in your hands, Chris. I'm through trying to understand what's going on."

"Thanks, Marco. I won't let you down, you'll see. What do you say we order dinner?" Chris looked around for the waiter, while Marco looked around for the blond. Her table was empty, the bus boys were busily resetting it. She was gone. "Shit," Marco said under his breath, wondering if he would ever see her again.

The waiter took everyone's order and reached for the menus. As he did, he placed a small, folded slip of paper in front of Marco. Marco picked up the paper, unfolded it and read what the hand-written note revealed.

> *Please call me. Am very anxious to meet you.*
> *Days (312)555-8900*
> *Nights (312)555-2643. Hope to hear from you soon.*
> *Donna Michaels.*

The waiter returned with the drinks, set them on the table and walked away without a word to anyone. Marco got up and followed him.

"Excuse me," Marco said, tugging the waiter's sleeve. "That note you gave me-who gave it to you?"

"The young lady seated at the second table on your left."

"The blond?" Marco asked.

"Yes, sir, and she had striking blue eyes, too."

"Yes . . . and those legs," Marco said under his breath.

"Pardon me, sir?"

"Oh . . . nothing . . . just thinking out loud." Marco removed a ten dollar bill from his wallet, handed it to the waiter and returned to his seat.

"Where did you go, Daddy?" Sarah scolded. "I thought you followed that pretty girl out."

"No, honey, I didn't, but I should have." Marco handed Sarah the note.

"Wow! Cool! "Sarah said after reading it.

Chris and Gail looked up startled.

"Excuse me," Sarah said.

The Mussos looked at Marco. Marco just closed his eyes, smiled and shrugged his shoulders.

* * *

The following morning, Sarah found her dad seated at the kitchen table studying the note from Donna Michaels.

"How many times are you going to read it, Dad? Why don't you just call her?"

"Why would a beautiful girl like her want me to call her?" Marco wondered out loud.

"Mom was as pretty as she is. She fell in love with you, didn't she?"

Marco smiled. "Yeah, but that was twenty years ago. I was younger and better looking then. And I had all my hair." Marco said smoothing his hair back with his hand.

"I think you're more handsome now and more distinguished looking."

"You mean . . . extinguished, don't you?"

"Don't be silly, Dad. Just call her."

"This day time number is obviously her work or office. I'll wait till after nine o'clock to call her. Okay?"

"Okay," Sarah said. "I have an early class this morning, gotta go. I'll see you tonight. You can tell me all about it then. Bye."

Marco said goodbye to his daughter and poured himself another cup of coffee. It was eight twenty-five. He looked at the note and read it again. He drank three more cups of coffee and read the note six more times. He checked his wrist watch again; it was finally nine o'clock . He went to the phone and dialed the number.

"Good morning, WNUZ."

"Sorry, I must have the wrong number," Marco lied. "Shit," he cursed, slamming the phone down. "I knew it was too good to be true."

Marco whisked the note from the table, crumpled it in his fist and threw it toward the waste basket. The wad of paper rolled around the rim like a golf ball then fell to the floor. As Marco leaned over to pick it up, he heard the phone ring.

"Hello."

"Mr. Fischer?" a female voice asked.

There was a moment of silence.

"Mr. Fischer, are you there?"

"Yes . . . Who is this?"

"My name is Donna Michaels. We sort of met last night, at Cosmo's."

There was another moment of silence.

"Mr. Fischer?"

"Oh, yes. The blond, right? The one with the note."

"I hope you'll forgive me for that, but I was sitting with another reporter who didn't recognize you. I didn't want to introduce myself at the time for fear he wouldn't respect your privacy. Knowing how he is, I knew he'd disrupt your dinner."

"Oh, how very thoughtful of you," Marco said in a very sarcastic tone. "Since when does a reporter, especially a TV reporter, worry about disrupting someone?"

"Please believe me, I don't mean to intrude or invade your privacy in any way. I just want to hear your side of the story. If you could set some time aside for me, I'm sure you'll find my intentions to be honorable."

"Does three o'clock this afternoon sound okay?" Marco asked.

"Yes, that would be fine." Ms. Michaels suddenly stopped in her tracks. "Wait a minute, don't you start your show at three o'clock?"

"That's right. Every day, Monday through Friday. If you want my side of the story, just tune in."

"Mr. Fischer, please, you can trust me. I assure you my intentions are good and honorable. I only want to help you."

"Help me or help yourself?" Marco knew he should have just hung up on her, but he couldn't. He loved the sound of her voice, even if he hated the topic of conversation. "You know . . . I've refused every reporter in town an interview. If I granted you one, it would be quite a feather in your cap . . . Wouldn't it? By the way, why is it that I never heard of you before? I know every reporter in Chicago."

"I'm new in town. I just joined the staff at WNUZ a few days ago."

"And you want to make a name for yourself by slicing me up in little pieces."

"No, I promise it's not you I want to slice up, it's Grogan and his buddies I'm after. The reason I got this job in Chicago is because back home in Middletown, Ohio, I was an investigative reporter specializing in exposing corrupt politics."

"Corrupt politics in Middletown, Ohio?" Marco said with a laugh.

"Don't laugh," Ms. Michaels pouted. "I made a name for myself there. My work was very highly respected. I want to show my new boss I can do just as well here."

"Please forgive me, I'm sure you worked very hard and I'm sure you did an excellent job, but this is *Chicago*, the womb of crooked politics."

"Mr. Fischer, please help me. I know your reputation. I'm familiar with the work you've done. We're very much alike, you and I. We can work together, sort of like a partnership, unofficial, of course."

"Okay, if you want to interview me, you can. Do you think your boss will like that?"

"Will he like it? He'll love it. I'm afraid to tell him, he might have a heart attack. Thank you, thank you so much. I don't know how I can ever express my thanks."

"Have dinner with me."

"Uh, . . . I mean. When?"

"Tonight. I'll call Cosmo's and make reservations for eight o'clock, is that okay?" Marco softened his tone recalling her face. Picturing those legs in his mind. "You know, I called you only a minute ago, but I hung up when I realized I was calling a TV station. I felt kind of foolish, but I'm over it now."

"Why did you feel foolish?"

"Well, when I received your note, I thought it was me you were interested in, not my story. You are very beautiful, you know."

"Thank you, Mr. Fischer. I wouldn't flirt that way, after all, I know you're married."

"Please, call me Marco, and I'm not married, I'm a widower."

Maryanne's face flashed before him. He felt a tinge of guilt, but then remembered Sarah's words. *You've been alone too long.*

"Oh no, I'm sorry. How could I have missed that?"

"It's okay. I never talk about my marital status. Most people assume I'm married because I talk about my daughter often on my program."

"That was your daughter you were with last night?"

"Yes, Sarah, she's sixteen. She was ten when her Mom died."

"She's very pretty, she looks a lot older than sixteen. I hope I can meet her someday."

"She'd like to meet you, too."

"I'm looking forward to dinner tonight, Marco, and incidentally, I think you're very good looking yourself."

"I bet you say that to all the Jew-Wops."

"Do you always make jokes when a girl flirts with you?"

"I thought you weren't flirting with me."

"I said I wouldn't flirt with a married man."

Marco was feeling an excitement he hadn't felt since he was a teenager. He couldn't stop the words that blurted out. "What are you doing for lunch, Donna?"

"Nothing, Marco."

"I'll pick you up at noon in front of your building."

* * *

Marco pulled up to the curb and powered his door locks open. Donna was waiting. As soon as the Caddy made a complete stop, she opened the passenger side door and slid into the front seat.

"Where are we going for lunch?" she asked.

"You like Italian?" Marco asked.

"Pasta?"

"No, beef, unless you like sausage better."

"Beef? Sausage?"

"Yeah, Italian beef and sausage, Chicago style. We're going to Nick's Beef Stand on the West Side."

"Okay, whatever you say."

* * *

Donna let her eyes wander around the small establishment while Marco stood at a long counter which separated the customers from the food preparation area. Nick's was a typical Chicago-style Italian beef joint. The charcoal grill covered with sausage links skewered on long stainless steel rods sizzled, filling the air with a delicious aroma. Wire baskets submerged in boiling oil overflowed with fresh cut French fries.

A young man stood at a steam table filling stainless steel trays with thinly sliced Italian-style roast beef and steamed, green sweet peppers cut into large pieces. He stopped what he was doing and wiped the solid maple cutting board lining the front of the steam table with a damp cloth. He turned and ambled toward the counter. His eyes lit up when he recognized his favorite radio personality standing before him.

"Marco. Good to see you. What'll you have? You name it, its on the house."

"Good to see you too, Pete. I'll have the usual, an Italian sausage, juicy, sweet and hot peppers and one beef, plain."

"Any fries?" Pete asked, yanking a loaf of fresh French bread from a long brown paper bag, chopping it into sandwich size buns.

Marco turned; Donna was shaking her head. "No fries," he said, "but we'll have two diet Cokes."

"Large?" Pete asked, approaching the counter with the sandwiches wrapped in aluminum foil.

"Small," Marco answered.

A drink dispenser was attached to the front counter next to the cash register. Under the counter, an ice making machine. After placing the sandwiches on a plastic serving tray, Pete scooped ice into two soft drink cups and filled them to the brim. "Enjoy," he said, placing the drinks on the tray.

Donna had taken a seat at a long counter that hung on the wall under a window looking out onto the sidewalk. Hurried diners would belly up to this snack bar, down their sandwich and rush out the door, but Marco was in no hurry.

As he turned away from the counter, Marco motioned with his chin toward one of several Formica covered tables surrounded by metal folding chairs. "Sit down here," he said, dropping the tray on the table top.

Donna unwrapped her sandwich and took a large bite. "Wow! This is delicious," she said with a mouth full.

"Wait till you try the sausage," Marco bragged.

"Next time," Donna said, sipping her diet Coke. "I'm sure I'll be full after this."

"Will there be a next time?" Marco asked.

"I hope so," Donna answered, her deep blue eyes looking directly into his anxious browns. Marco felt a tingling on the back of his neck and shoulders.

"Is Pete the owner?" Donna asked.

"No, he just works here. I hear this place is owned by the Outfit."

"Outfit?" Donna asked, lifting her head to look quizzically at Marco.

Just then, a small bell attached to the door tinkled, a distinguished, but menacing looking figure entered nodding at Pete as he crossed the dining area. Pete reached under the counter. A buzzer sounded. The man let himself through a door marked "private" accessing the area behind the counter. He then disappeared into what Marco assumed was a storage room or office.

"Speaking of the devil," Marco said, raising his eyebrows.

"Hmm?" Donna remarked a little confused. "What do you mean?"

"In Chicago the organized crime syndicate is known as the Outfit, and judging by his looks, I'd say he's a member." Marco said in a whisper, shifting his eyes toward the door.

"You can teach me a lot about this town."

Marco took a sip from his Coke. "Chicago's a big city. Like New York or LA, its a mixture of good and bad. Before you learn about its bad side, I'd like to show you some of the good. Do you have to go back to the office right away?"

"No, I told my boss I was meeting with you. He told me to take all the time I needed."

For the next two hours Marco guided Donna on a tour of his home town. With Lake Michigan on their left they traveled south on Lake Shore Drive passing the Shedd Aquarium and the Adler Planetarium. They exited at 55th Street and drove through Hyde Park, home of the University of Chicago and its world renowned medical center. On the way back to the Drive, they passed the

Museum of Science and Industry, beautifully located on the shores of Lake Michigan.

Donna marveled at what she was seeing. "I never realized Chicago was so big. There's so much to see and the lake front, it looks more like the ocean."

Marco turned onto Lake Shore Drive and headed north back toward Chicago's famous "Loop". They passed the Field Museum on the edge of Grant Park, then turned west to Michigan Avenue, then north again. Marco pointed out the Fine Arts Building, Chicago's Art Institute and the East Randolph Street peninsula supporting fabulous high rise condos with Lake Point Tower at its tip, jetting out into the lake.

"The beauty of this city is grossly unrecognized." Donna remarked in a hushed voice.

Marco continued north on Michigan showing off Chicago's Magnificent Mile lined with grommet restaurants of every kind, elegant shops, small, exclusive boutiques, large department stores, as well as luxurious high rise condos, the John Hancock Building, once the tallest building in town, but now dwarfed by the Sears Tower which was located a few blocks south and west.

"You like shopping?" Marco smiled, as he passed a massive structure which housed Water Tower Place, a combination of luxury condominium apartments and indoor mall. "You can live a lifetime there and never leave the building."

Marco stayed in the right lane which blended with the north bound lanes of Lake Shore Drive. They continued north to Sheridan Road passing more high rise apartments and condos and the beautiful campus of Loyola University lined up along the shore of Lake Michigan. A little further north on Sheridan, they reached the city limits and crossed over into Evanston, one of Chicago's most exclusive suburbs and the home of Northwestern University.

Donna was enthralled by the skyline of her new home town as Marco cruised along Lake Shore Drive on their way back toward downtown Chicago.

"The architecture of this city is amazing, these buildings along the Drive are really gorgeous."

"Many of them date back to the early nineteen hundreds," Marco pointed out. "That's where I live," he said, drawing her attention to a relatively modern structure.

"What a beautiful building," Donna said. "I'd like to see your apartment some time."

"If you like, I'll take you to see it after dinner tonight."

"Can I trust you not to take advantage of me?"

"No, you can't, but my daughter, Sarah, will be home, so you'll be safe."

"Maybe you can tell her to go see a movie or something," Donna teased.

"Cut it out, or I will."

Donna didn't respond, she just smiled and watched Marco as he turned off the Drive and headed toward her office building.

"Thanks Marco. I really enjoyed this." Donna said, as Marco pulled up to the curb.

"We've only scratched the surface. There's a hell of a lot more to this city. A lot more than I can show you in one day. I hope we can do this again some time."

"Why not. We can talk about it at dinner tonight. Maybe this weekend."

* * *

Donna Michaels didn't start out to be a political reporter; her ambition was to be an actress. After leaving college with a degree in dramatics, she took a job as the morning weather person at a local television station in her home town of Middletown, Ohio. This job was supposed to be temporary, something to do while she prepared herself for an acting career. As luck would have it, however, she found herself in a situation that would set her on a new path, one that would change her life forever.

She was having lunch one day with her best friend, Susan

Drake. Susan, a very pretty brunette with reddish brown eyes who had recently married a young man who dealt in real estate development, didn't look as happy as a young bride should. Her new husband's father had been in the business for many years and was getting ready to turn it all over to his son.

"Randy is becoming very difficult to live with," Susan complained in her cute, high-pitched voice.

"I thought Randy was doing well in his business," Donna remarked.

"He is and he isn't," Susan said. "This new development he's planning could make us a lot of money, but he's having trouble getting it off the ground."

"Is it money problems?" Donna asked.

"Yes and no," Susan answered.

"Susan, I'd like to help you, but you have to be more specific. Is he or isn't he doing well? Is he or isn't he having money problems?"

Susan looked at Donna very seriously. "Okay. I'll tell you, but you have to promise to keep it to yourself," she insisted.

"I promise," Donna agreed as she settled into her chair, not knowing what to expect.

Susan gathered her thoughts and began telling her story. "There's another developer interested in a parcel of land Randy and his father own. They invested every penny we had and all they could borrow to purchase it. The other developer has been trying to get them to sell it to him for months now, but they keep turning him down."

"So, why should that be a problem if they own it?" Donna asked.

"Owning it is one thing. Being able to develop it is something else," Susan said. "For months now, Randy has been trying to get approval from the building department to begin construction, but he's run into one problem after another. First it was zoning, then it was environmental regulations, then it was water retention. Each time Randy and his father would satisfy a demand, the city would create another obstacle. In the meantime, the interest on the loan, property taxes and legal fees keep mounting."

"What does the other developer have to do with this?" Donna asked.

"Everything," Susan said angrily. "Randy found out last week that the other developer is the son-in-law of Jasper Swensen."

"The councilman?" Donna asked excitedly.

"Yes," Susan said. "His name is Donald Landis. Until the other day, Randy only knew the corporate name he's been operating under, Mid States Properties. The lawyer who represents the corporation never divulged the name of the individuals who owned the company."

"How did Randy find out about this?" Donna asked.

"Randy's lawyer became suspicious and decided to do some research on Mid States; that's when it all came out."

Donna looked her friend in the eye and said. "Susan, I know I promised to keep this to myself, but hear me out. Maybe I can help you, but I'll have to talk to my boss at the station first."

Donna told Susan what she was thinking. Later that evening, Donna met with Susan again; this time Randy and his father were present. Donna's plan was daring, maybe even a little dangerous. Everyone, however, agreed it was worth a shot. If it worked, tens of thousands of dollars would be saved in legal fees and other expenses. If it didn't, their future in the real estate business could be destroyed forever. If they couldn't solve the problem, they would probably be wiped out anyway.

The following morning, after her weather report, Donna met with her boss in his office. Harvey Klein, an old pro in the news business, sat quietly, listening to her story. The sleeves of his white dress shirt were rolled half way up his forearms, his tie hung loosely around his open collar. At sixty, he had been in the news business for almost forty years. Donna sat, legs crossed, nervously tapping her foot.

Harvey tapped his thick lips with the eraser end of a pencil; occasionally, he'd put the pencil down and fidget with the wrist watch he wore on his hairy arm. The hair on his arms was the same color as the hair on his head, white, almost pure white. Harvey removed the eye glasses from his oval face. His brown eyes looked directly into Donna's anxious blue eyes.

"I want you to check out all the facts," Harvey instructed, rubbing his hand over the white stubble on his face. "Talk to their lawyer. I want you to personally look at all the documents regarding this case, and I want you to see the results of his investigation into the corporation. Then I want you to make a thorough investigation of your own. When you've done that, we'll sit down again and decide how you'll handle reporting the story."

"You want me to investigate and report the story?" Donna said shocked and excited.

"That's right. I want you to do it," Harvey said. "Allen Gold is leaving our employ and accepting an offer with the network in New York. I've already begun a search to replace him, and I've decided to replace him with a woman. If you handle this the way I think you can, my search will be over."

Donna Michaels, the would-be actress, had become Donna Michaels, the investigative reporter. Harvey Klein became her mentor and teacher. The instincts that served him so well over the years proved to be as keen as ever. His latest discovery attacked her new responsibilities with enthusiasm and dedication beyond what anyone could have expected. Anyone, except Harvey Klein.

Donna's expose' of corruption and abuse of power in Randy Drake's case was only the beginning. Soon, reports of other abuses began to pour into the station. For the next four years, Donna cultivated her natural ability for investigating and uncovering illegal and unethical activities by politicians and appointed government officials. Before long, she had built a reputation for being fearless and unrelenting for her crusade against those who would betray the public trust. No one was surprised when the offer to join WNUZ in Chicago came. At twenty eight years old, Donna Michaels had come a long way.

"What should I do, Harvey?" Donna asked sadly.

"What should you do? Take it. This is what you've worked for. This is the greatest opportunity of your life. Chicago is the best market in the country. With your talent, there's no telling how far you can go in this business."

"I hate to leave you, Harvey. You've been so much help, such a good friend," Donna said tearfully.

"I'll always be your friend, and if you need help, I'll always be here. Just pick up the phone."

* * *

Two weeks later, Donna was on her way. After packing everything she owned into her little Honda Civic, she set out on her six-hour drive to Chicago, but not before stopping one last time to say goodbye to her dear friend, Harvey Klein. After a tearful embrace and a tender loving kiss on the cheek, she embarked on a new adventure. She wondered, as she traveled the highway, where it would take her. She wondered what new experiences lay ahead. She had no idea of the dangers awaiting her.

CHAPTER 9

"Watch out, be careful. I hope this lawyer you chose knows what he's doing. I know they're planning to stack the deck against you."

COSMO'S WAS JAMMED, as usual. Fortunately, Marco had made reservations.

"Good evening, Ms. Michaels and Mr. Fischer. Nice to see you again," the waiter said, sneaking a wink at Marco when Donna looked away.

"Very nice to see you again, too," Marco said. "By the way, what's your name?"

"My name is Charles, but you may call me Chuck, my friends do."

"Okay, Chuck," Marco said.

"If you don't mind, I like Charles better," Donna said, patting him on the elbow.

"You, Ms. Michaels, may call me anything you like."

After ordering something to drink, Marco looked at Donna and asked, "Were you serious about working out some kind of a partnership?"

"Absolutely," Donna said instantly.

"I've been thinking about it, maybe we could work something out along those lines," Marco said thoughtfully. "It would mean we would have to share all our leads and informants."

"I haven't developed any leads or informants yet, but I'm sure I will. When I do we can cultivate them together," Donna offered.

"Let's give each other some time to think about it, okay?" Marco said.

After dinner, Marco called Sarah to make sure she was still up.

"Are you kidding? Of course I'm still up. When are you coming home?"

"We'll be there in fifteen minutes."

"Good. That gives me time to make coffee and slice the cake. Bye, see you soon."

Marco hurriedly paid the bill and tipped Chuck very handsomely.

"Let's go," Marco said. "We don't want to be late. Sarah will never let us live it down."

* * *

"Wow," Donna said as she entered the mirrored foyer."What a beautiful apartment! And the windows, the whole wall is glass," Donna marveled, as she raced to inspect the view. "The lake seems to go on forever!"

"Please, let me take your coat." Marco said, looking in all directions for Sarah.

"Hi, Dad," Sarah said, poking her head out from the kitchen.

"Donna Michaels," Marco said, as he outstretched his arm. "This is my daughter, Sarah."

"Pleased to meet you," Sarah greeted, as she took Donna's hand in hers."Very firm handshake, Ms. Michaels, my dad likes that in a woman."

"You do?" Donna said, smiling at Marco.

Marco did not respond.

* * *

While Marco and Donna were enjoying their dinner at Cosmo's, Patrick Grogan and company were gathered around a table at the Pacific Islands restaurant in Chicago's famous Chinatown.

"I want that mother fucker out of this town forever," Grogan growled.

"Don't worry about it, Pat. His Honor Judge Rios knows what to do if he wants to remain a judge," O'Mara said.

"My men know what to do, too," McLaughlin smiled.

"What about the faggot?" Grogan asked. "He's the weakest link in our chain. You guys better make sure he doesn't fuck up."

"He won't," McLaughlin assured.

"If he does, it's your ass," Grogan threatened. "I guarantee it."

"The judge is with us. What could go wrong?" O'Mara assured. "One week from now, that fuckin 'Jew-Wop' will be sitting in the county jail."

* * *

Marco and Donna continued to meet for lunch and dinner until the night before the trial, when Marco met with Chris Musso in his office.

"How long do you think the trial will last?" Marco asked.

"It's not a trial. We will make the motion to suppress. If we win, there will be no trial," Chris said. "I'm going to call on you to testify tomorrow. Just tell your story the same way you always have, don't change anything. I'm going to try to trap the prosecution's witnesses into contradicting each other.

"How will you do that?" Marco asked.

"They're lying, we know that. All I have to do is trip one of them up. The witnesses are not allowed to hear another's testimony. During cross examination, I should be able to expose inconsistencies in their stories."

"What inconsistencies?"

"I won't know that until I get them on the stand."

"I must tell you, Chris, my confidence is beginning to fade."

"We're going to win," Chris said assuredly. "Go home, get a good night's sleep. I'll see you in the morning."

CHAPTER 10

"Good luck, my friend, you'll need it. You're up against the scum of the earth."

AT SEVEN-THIRTY on the morning of his trial, Marco and Sarah sat at the kitchen table as they had hundreds of times before.

"Don't worry, Dad, you have the best lawyer in town."

"I'm not exactly worried," Marco said, sipping his coffee. "It's just that I'm out of my element; I feel helpless. I don't like having to depend on someone else to defend me. I've always been able to take care of myself."

Sarah sprinkled a small amount of sugar on her cereal and poured some milk over it.

"We all need to depend on someone else from time to time, Dad. I've depended on you all my life, you've never let me down. Chris won't let *you* down."

At eight o'clock, Marco called Donna at her apartment.

"Hello."

"Good morning," Marco said, trying to sound cheerful.

"How are you feeling?" Donna inquired.

"Just wanted to talk to you before I left for court. Hope I didn't wake you."

"You didn't, and I wouldn't have minded if you did. To tell you the truth, I was sitting here wondering if I should call *you*."

"Really, are you worried about me?"

"Not really, I just wanted to tell *you* not to worry."

"Everybody tells me not to worry, Sarah, Tony, Jerry and Chris, of course. Though I'm not exactly worried, I still don't feel comfortable."

"It's natural to feel a little jittery at a time like this, but it'll be okay. You'll see. Call me when you get back home; I'll be waiting."

Marco decided to take a cab rather than drive himself. He avoided the mob of reporters outside his building by letting the cab enter the underground parking lot and lying down in the back seat. The cabby's cooperation earned him an extra ten dollars. Marco entered court room #109 at nine forty-five, fifteen minutes early. Chris Musso was already seated at the defense table.

"Good morning, Marco," Chris said, as Marco took the seat to his left."Good morning, Chris," Marco said, unenthusiastically.

The prosecution arrived about five minutes later. Assistant States Attorney Richard Testa was a relatively tall man in his middle thirties with hawk-like features. He was dressed in an expensive brown striped suit, white shirt and brown tie, which matched his brown hair and pencil thin mustache. He looked to his left and nodded confidently at Chris Musso. Chris acknowledged his greeting with an impish wink.

At ten o'clock sharp, Judge Rolando J. Rios entered his courtroom. Judge Rios, who was in his early sixties, had been a judge for almost twenty years. During that time, the tightly curled hair on his small round head turned from pitch black to salt and pepper.

"All rise!" The bailiff ordered.

Judge Rios pulled his black robe up so not to step on it's hem and ascended the three steps leading to his throne behind the bench. He surveyed his courtroom, which in the two minutes before he appeared had filled with spectators, mostly reporters. Marco looked around, too.

Every reporter in town is here to watch me get humiliated, except Donna. Marco thought.

The judge, projecting his voice like a baritone in an Italian opera, made the standard speech regarding order in his courtroom, addressing most of his comments to the mob of reporters crowded into the small seating area. After a short conference between the judge and his clerk, the Honorable Rolando J. Rios turned and directed his attention to the defense table. Picking up his eye glasses and slipping them onto his head, he said, "Mr. Fischer, I have been tendered a jury waiver by your attorney. Is this your signature?"

The judge handed the waiver to the clerk, who then showed it to Marco.

"Yes, your honor," Marco answered.

"You understand when you sign it, you're giving up your right to a jury trial and asking that I hear the evidence and make the determination of whether you are guilty or not guilty?"

"Judge," Testa broke in, "are we proceeding on the motion first?"

"Your honor," Chris joined in, "I'm prepared to call Mr. Fischer as my first witness. I thought we could do the motion first, then stipulate everything for the trial."

"If the people have no objection, it's fine with me," the judge agreed.

Chris called his witness. The clerk swore Marco in and said, "Have a seat, please." Marco stepped up on the witness stand and sat down.

Chris asked the usual opening questions; name and proper spelling, marital status, number of children, if any, and then, "Sir, what do you do for a living?"

"I host a radio talk show on WHLP."

"Can you describe what you do on your radio show?"

"I comment on current events, mainly political and police matters and issues. I also discuss these issues with my audience by telephone."

"And how long have you been doing this?"

"I've been doing radio for over ten years. I've been doing this particular format for over six years."

"During these six years, would you say you've made some enemies?"

"I would say so."

"On the date in question, were you working?"

"Yes, I was."

"Do you often find it necessary to leave your office or studio to conduct your business?"

"Yes, I do."

"At ten-thirty on the morning in question, were you parked at 3536 South Halsted?"

"Yes, I was."

"And what brought you to this address?"

Marco told the court about the phone call from the anonymous informant.

"Did that person show up for the meeting?"

"No, he did not."

Chris asked several more questions about what time Marco arrived and where he parked his car, then said, "Tell the court what happened at about ten-thirty that morning."

"A woman tapped on my window, the passenger side. I opened it slightly and asked her what she wanted. The next thing I knew, I was surrounded by police."

"How many police officers were there?"

"Three."

"Did you say anything else to the woman other than asking her what she wanted?"

"No, I did not."

"Did she, or you, for that matter, broach upon any subject regarding sex for money?"

"No, we did not."

"Tell us what happened next."

Marco went on to tell the judge how he was pulled out of his car, searched and cuffed.

"Did you have a gun in your right rear pocket?"

"No, I did not."

"Are you right-handed or left-handed?"

"I'm left handed."

"Have you ever been convicted of a felony?"

"No."

Richard Testa raised his hand.

"Objection, Judge, that's not relevant for the motion or the trial. I ask that the question and answer be stricken."

"All right," The judge said. "That question and answer may be stricken. You may continue, Mr. Musso."

"Nothing further, Judge."

"Alright," the judge said. "The people may cross."

Richard Testa rose from his seat and addressed the defendant. "You testified you had an appointment with someone at 3536 South Halsted. Is that correct?"

"Yes, it is."

"What address were you at previously?"

"I was at home . . . excuse me . . . I was at my daughter's school."

"What direction was your car going when the police officers stopped you?"

"It wasn't going in any direction. It was stopped. Parked."

"In what direction was it facing?"

"South."

Marco felt relieved, the prosecutor who was supposed to be so tough, was not so tough, after all. His questions were very routine, almost a carbon copy of Chris', until; "Tell the court about the gun."

"What gun?"

"Please answer my question."

"I object, Your Honor." Chris broke in. "The prosecution didn't ask a question. He gave an order."

"Over-ruled, answer the question," the judge ordered.

"I can't Your Honor. I don't know anything about a gun."

"The gun you had in your pocket!" Testa shouted.

"I didn't have a gun in my pocket!" Marco shouted back.

"Objection. The prosecution is badgering the witness!" Chris was on his feet, pounding his fist on the table.

"Sit down, Mr. Musso, you're over-reacting a bit, aren't you? Over-ruled!"

Chris felt his face begin to flush. *Something's going on here.* he thought.

"Isn't it true, sir, that you offered a prostitute money for sex?"

"No."

"Isn't it true that after being detained at the scene for questioning, the officer noticed a gun in your pocket?"

"Objection Your Honor." Chris jumped to his feet again. "The witness has already answered the question."

"Sit down, Mr. Musso, you're out of order. I don't want to have to tell you again. Over- ruled!"

Marco looked at Chris for help. Chris nodded his head slightly.

"Don't look at your lawyer, he can't help you now," Testa yelled. "Look at me and answer the question."

"I had no gun in my pocket. I don't even own a gun."

"Tell me, Mr. Fischer. What kind of a gun was it?"

"Objection, Judge the witness . . ."

Judge Rios held up his hand. "I'm glad you didn't find it necessary to jump to your feet and get all dramatic, Mr. Musso. Over-ruled!"

Looking at Chris and again seeing the slight nod, Marco answered. "I don't know. I never saw a gun."

"You never saw your own gun?"

"Objection Your Honor."

The judge glared at Chris.

"For the record, Your Honor," Chris said calmly.

"Answer the question," Testa ordered.

"I DON'T OWN A GUN," Marco said, enunciating each word very carefully.

"How much money did you offer the prostitute?"

"I didn't offer anybody any money."

"How much money did you have with you that day?"

"I think I had a couple hundred dollars in my pocket."

Testa picked up a file folder from his table and opened it. "According to police records, you had two hundred thirty-seven dollars and sixty-three cents on your person the day you were arrested. Does that sound about right?"

"That's about right."

"No more questions," Testa said as he turned and walked back to his table.

"Is there any re-direct?" the judge asked.

"No Judge." Chris answered disgustedly. "We rest as to the motion."

"All right, Mr. Fischer you may be seated next to counsel," the judge said.

Marco got up and stepped down from the stand. Chris looked very upset as he joined him at the defense table.

"Are you still confident?" Marco whispered.

"I knew Testa was dirty, and I knew the cops were lying, but I didn't think the judge was in on it," Chris was speaking like a ventriloquist, barely moving his lips.

"What?" Marco asked, trying to keep his voice low.

"Shh," Chris held up his palm. "It's not over yet. They're bound to make a mistake. When they do, not even the judge will be able to help them."

"State," the judge said directing his comments to the prosecution.

"Judge, the people call Officer Carl Ruck."

Officer Ruck entered the courtroom from a side door. He was a short man who looked to be in his early forties. His hair was a light brown color. He had a large head, with small round brown eyes. He was dressed in blue jeans and a V-neck sweater over a denim shirt and knit tie.

After being properly sworn in and answering the routine preliminary questions, Officer Ruck settled into his seat, waiting for Testa to get down to business.

"Officer Ruck, were you working on the date and time in question?"

"Yes, I was."

"Were you working between the hours of nine that morning and five-thirty that afternoon?"

"Yes, I was."

"Who were you working with at that time?"

"Two other members of the 35th Precinct tactical team, Officer Handleman and Officer Dayton."

"What were your specific duties on that day?"

"We had received many complaints from citizens and local business people that prostitutes were working along Halsted Street between 31st and 42nd Streets. We had been ordered to patrol the area and arrest known prostitutes if we observed them in the act of soliciting."

"Did you happen to observe such an act on the date and time in question?"

"Yes, I did."

"Would you explain to the court what exactly the circumstances were and what took place?"

"My partners and I were parked at 3527 South Halsted Street, observing a known prostitute. She was standing on the northwest corner of 35th and Halsted."

"Excuse me, Officer. Were you and your partners in an unmarked squad car?"

"Yes, sir."

"How did you know the person was a prostitute?"

"I have personally arrested her . . . or should I say him . . . several times."

"Did you say *him*?"

"Well . . . yes, you see the person is actually a transvestite prostitute."

"What exactly do you mean by that, Officer?"

"A transvestite prostitute is actually a male homosexual who dresses as a woman and engages in deviant sex acts with men who go for that sort of thing."

There was some mumbling and giggling in the gallery. Judge Rios looked up and glared at the spectators. The disturbance stopped immediately.

"Please continue Officer. You said you observed the transvestite prostitute standing on the corner of 35th and Halsted. What happened next?"

"As we were observing her, we saw a late model Cadillac pass where she was standing. As the car passed, the driver blew his horn to attract her attention."

"Did he attract her attention?"

"Yes, he did."

"How do you know?"

"I know, because she . . . I mean he . . ."

"Excuse me Your Honor," Testa interrupted. "Your Honor, would it be all right if we referred to the prostitute simply as the 'prostitute' from this point on?"

"Any objections from the defense?" the judge asked.

"Yes, Your Honor. The defendant had no idea that the person was a prostitute, therefore, it would be self-incriminating to agree to such a notion," Chris said.

"Over-ruled!"

Assistant States Attorney Richard Testa continued. "Officer Ruck, how did you know the defendant was successful in attracting the prostitute's attention?"

"She . . . he looked at him as he drove by. When he pulled over to the curb she . . . he followed him to where he was parked."

"What happened next?"

"We continued to observe the defendant and the prostitute for a few seconds. Then we saw the defendant reach into his pocket and remove a wad of money."

"And then?" Testa asked.

"At that point, we got out of our squad car and ran across the street. I ordered the defendant out of his vehicle while my partners detained the prostitute."

"Did you act as you did because, in your experience, the defendant's actions were typical of one who was soliciting for sex?"

"Objection, Your Honor. The prosecution is leading the witness."

"Over-ruled!"

"Excuse me, Your Honor," Chris argued. "If we're going to allow Mr. Testa to ask his questions in that manner, what do we need a witness for? We might as well let Mr. Testa provide the answers as well."

"Don't tell me how to run my courtroom, Mr. Musso. If you don't like it here, perhaps you should extricate yourself from these proceedings. I'll be happy to allow your client ample time to retain another lawyer."

Chris could not believe his ears. Then it finally dawned on him. The judge was deliberately trying to cause a mistrial, or at least give Chris all he needed to file for, and be granted, a reversal. The judge's position was beginning to become clear. On the surface, he looked very hostile, very unfriendly to the defense; underneath, however, he was anything but. Chris felt a new surge of confidence. He turned and winked at Marco, as he had to Testa, with the same impish smile.

"Did you place the defendant under arrest at that point?" Testa continued.

"No, not immediately. I asked to see his identification and vehicle registration."

"When did you place him under arrest?"

"When my partners told me the prostitute told them he solicited her . . . I mean him."

"Then what did you do?"

"I conducted a custodial search, which revealed a .25 caliber semi-automatic pistol, which I found in his right rear pocket."

"Would you recognize that person again if you saw him?"

"Yes."

"Do you see that person in this room today? If you do, would you point him out for the court, please?"

Officer Ruck stood up and pointed at Marco. "That's him," he said.

"After you recovered the gun, what did you do?"

"I proceeded to the 35th precinct to process the defendant."

"Where were the other officers when you found the gun?"

"They were arresting the prostitute."

"Did they witness you finding the gun in the defendant's pocket?"

"Officer Handleman did; Officer Dayton was facing in the opposite direction."

"The gun you recovered from the defendant, was it loaded or unloaded?"

"It was loaded. Eight rounds of live ammunition."

Testa turned to face the judge. "No further questions, Your Honor," he said.

Judge Rios looked at Chris Musso. "Your witness," he said.

"Sir, are you left-handed or right-handed?" Chris asked.

"Objection, not relevant," Testa interrupted.

"Sustained," the judge agreed.

Chris continued. "When you ordered the defendant out of his car, were you holding your gun on him?"

"Yes, I was."

"Will you show me exactly how you did that?"

"Objection, not relevant," Testa interrupted again.

"Sustained," the judge agreed again.

Pointing to the empty holster on the officer's right side, Chris asked. "Is that your holster?"

The officer looked down. "Yes, it is."

"Why do you carry your gun on your right side?"

"Objection, not relevant," Testa said with a cocky smile.

"Sustained," the judge said.

"Officer, you testified you knew the so-called prostitute was definitely a prostitute because you had arrested her several times yourself. Is that correct?"

"That's right."

Chris walked back to the defense table and picked up a sheet of paper.

"I request that this be marked as defense exhibit number one," Chris said as he handed the paper to the judge.

As the judge inspected the document, Chris handed another copy to Testa.

"Proceed," the judge said, handing the paper back to Chris.

Chris looked at the judge and said, "Your Honor, may I approach the witness?"

The judge waved his arm.

Holding exhibit number one in his hand, Chris said, "This, Officer Ruck, is the arrest record of one Julio Mendoza, the so-called prostitute." Chris handed the document to Officer Ruck.

"Objection, not relevant," Testa said, confidently.

The look of confidence, however, swiftly left Testa's face when he heard the judge say, "I'll allow it."

Chris quickly turned to look at Testa. He could see the judge's words had a visual affect on him.

Chris noted a slight change in the judge's demeanor after seeing the report. He continued feeling more confident. "Not one arrest for prostitution, by you or anyone else. Plenty of other arrests. Possession, shop lifting, disorderly conduct, resisting arrest, but not one for prostitution. How do you explain that, Officer Ruck?"

"She's . . . he's . . . a prostitute, everyone knows it."

"Everyone? The police department doesn't know it. If it did, it would be in the record. Don't you agree Officer Ruck? One more thing, Officer Ruck. You testified that you arrested Mr. Mendoza several times. Can you tell the court why that is not reflected in the official police department records?"

"Well, I guess I never actually arrested her, but I shagged her off the street many times."

"Is shagging the same as arresting?"

Testa rose from his seat. "Objection, Your Honor he's . . ."

Before Testa could finish what he was about to say, Chris broke in. "I withdraw the question Your Honor." Chris turned to face the judge again; this time he had a somber, pleading look on his face. "Your Honor, I think I have demonstrated that this officer's recollection of certain pertinent facts is rather faulty. Therefore, I ask that you grant me a minimum amount of latitude regarding the officer's behavior and habits concerning the use of his weapon."

The judge's expression relaxed as he looked Chris in the eye. Since the admission of the police report, it was obvious that Chris Musso had done his homework and was about to turn things around.

Judge Rios had agreed to allow the prosecution as much margin as possible. After realizing, however, that the defendant was being railroaded, he gave the defense a clear path to an appeal. Both actions, however, reflected negatively on him. His reputation was in jeopardy, but it wasn't too late to recover and join the turning tide.

"All right Counsel, I'll allow you some latitude," the judge said, settling in his seat.

"Objection," Testa yelled.

Judge Rios glared at Testa. Testa slowly lowered himself back into his chair.

"OVER-RULED," the judge said, still glaring.

"Officer Ruck," Chris continued. "are you right-handed or left-handed?"

"I'm right-handed."

"If you were going to put a gun in one of your back pockets, which one would it be?"

Officer Ruck looked at his right hand, moving it to his right, searching for his rear pocket.

"I guess I'd put it in my right pocket."

"Why is that Officer?"

"It would be easier . . . more comfortable if I needed to pull it out."

Chris continued. "You testified that the defendant had a gun in his right rear pocket, isn't that correct?"

"I don't remember," Ruck blurted out nervously.

"I do, and so does the court," Chris said, pointing at the court reporter who was busily taking down every word of testimony.

Chris looked up at the judge. "No more questions, Your Honor."

"Any redirect from the people?" the judge asked, looking at the Assistant State's Attorney.

Testa started to get up from his seat to say something, then decided to leave well enough alone. "No Judge," he said.

"All right then, you may call your next witness."

"The state calls officer Roger Handleman."

Officer Roger Handleman entered the courtroom from a side door opening into a small passageway leading to the witness room on the left and the main corridor on the right. Officer Handleman was even shorter than his partner and looked to be about the same age. He had his eyeglasses propped on his head, resting in his curly brown hair. He was wearing blue jeans, a powder blue linen shirt, a multicolored paisley tie and western style boots. Several cigars were visible in the breast pocket of his tweed sport coat. Handleman and Ruck nodded as they passed each other.

After being sworn in and answering all the routine questions, Officer Handleman sat confidently, waiting for his shot at Marco Fischer.

Testa was careful not to lead Handleman into any areas where he might be tripped up by Chris Musso in his cross-examination.

"Officer Handleman, did you witness Officer Ruck finding a loaded handgun in the defendant's pocket?"

"Yes, I did."

"Did you witness the defendant offer a known prostitute money?"

"Yes, I did."

"No more questions, Judge." Testa turned and walked back the his table.

The judge looked at Chris. "Your witness."

Chris got up and walked toward the witness. "Thank you Judge," he said.

"Officer Handleman, which pocket did your partner find the gun in?" Chris asked casually.

Though seated, Officer Handleman came as close to standing at attention as possible. "In his right rear pocket," he said loud and clear, in a tone that exuded pride and confidence.

"Officer Handleman, prior to the arrest, when did you first see the defendant?"

"I saw him pass the corner where the hooker was standing."

"And then what did you see?" Chris asked.

"He pulled over to the curb and the hooker walked over to where he was parked."

"So, the defendant didn't do anything to invite the hooker, to use your term, to the car?"

"Oh yeah, he blew his horn when he passed her."

"How did you know the person you call the hooker was a prostitute?"

"Everybody knows."

"Did you just assume the defendant knew?"

"Yeah, I guess so," the cop answered.

"Officer Handleman, did you actually see the defendant give the prostitute money?"

"Yes, I did."

"How much money did you see him give her?"

"I couldn't tell."

"You couldn't tell? Then how did you know it was money?"

"He put his hand in his pocket and took something out," the officer said, rather irritated.

"Then you just assumed it was money, is that correct.?"

"Yeah, I guess so."

"Is that what you're supposed to do as a policeman? Guess? Or are you supposed to gather facts and evidence before you arrest people?"

"He had the gun in his pocket, that's a fact."

"Please answer the question. Is it your job to guess?"

"I guess not."

"No further questions, Your Honor," Chris said.

"Redirect?" the judge asked, looking at Testa.

"No Judge," Testa said, shaking his head.

"All right then, you can call your next witness."

"The state calls Julio Mendoza."

The witness was shown in and properly identified for the record. Marco sat dumfounded. The person on the witness stand looked nothing like the woman who had tapped on his window.

It was obvious to Chris that Mendoza was gay. He was a young man in his early twenties with dark skin. He had delicate features and long slender hands; his fingernails were long and well groomed. He wore a gold chain around his neck and another around his wrist.

"On the date and time in question, were you standing on the corner of 35th Street and Halsted?" Testa asked.

"Yes, I was," The witness said with a lisp, in a meek, high-pitched voice.

"As you were standing there, did you see the defendant?" Testa asked pointing at Marco.

"Yes, I did."

"What made you notice the defendant?"

"He blew his horn and waved at me." With very feminine mannerisms, Mendoza waved his arm in an attempt to demonstrate his testimony.

"Then what did he do?"

"Pulled over and parked."

Chris was sitting at the defense table, watching the witness very closely, listening to every word. His concentration was broken, however, when he felt a nudge. He looked to his left. It was Marco, sliding a small folded piece of paper in front of him.

"Read it," Marco said in a whisper.

"Not now," Chris said, pushing the note back toward Marco.

Marco pushed the paper back toward Chris. "Read it, now," Marco said, looking up at the judge, hoping he wasn't speaking too loudly.

Chris picked up the piece of paper, unfolded it and read its contents.

"Your witness, Mr. Musso," the judge said.

Chris was still engrossed with what he'd been reading.

"Your witness, Mr. Musso," the judge said again in a louder voice.

Chris was startled back to the business before him. He stood and said, "Your Honor, it is almost twelve o'clock. My client is diabetic and must eat regularly. If it pleases the court, may we adjourn now for lunch?"

"Does the state have a problem with that?" the judge asked.

"No, Your Honor." Testa said, grateful for the break.

"Very well," the judge said. "We will adjourn and reconvene at one o'clock."

Chris turned to Marco. "Why didn't you tell me about this a long time ago?"

"Who knew?" Marco said. "I didn't know what their testimony was going to be. Besides, I just remembered. I forgot all about it until just now."

"Can you prove this?" Chris asked.

"Yes, I can," Marco said, getting up from his chair.

"How?" Chris said, following Marco out of the courtroom.

"Let's get to a phone. I have to call Tony Ruskin. I hope he's at the station."

* * *

"Tony? It's Marco. I need your help. Please, don't ask any questions. Listen and do as I say. We only have an hour."

Chris tried to listen as Marco hastily told Tony what he wanted him to do.

"Tony, you have to find it and get it here by one o'clock; I'm depending on you."

Marco hung up the phone and removed his wallet from his back pocket. He hastily fumbled through a collection of business cards and pieces of paper with names and phone numbers on them. "Ah! Here it is," Marco said, as he began to dial the number on the card.

"Hello, where's the boss? It's Marco Fischer, I must talk to him. It's *very* important."

* * *

At one o'clock sharp, Judge Rolando J. Rios entered his courtroom. The look on Chris Musso's face was enough to tell him something very interesting was about to happen.

"Counsel, are you ready for your cross?"

"Yes I am, Your Honor. Thank you very much," Chris said, as he stood up and walked toward the witness.

The judge removed his eyeglasses and looked down at Mendoza. "Need I remind you you're still under oath?"

"I understand, Your Honor." Mendoza said, looking sheepishly at the judge.

Chris stood as close to the witness as he was allowed. "Mr. Mendoza, you testified that you were standing on the corner of 35th and Halsted when the defendant passed your position in his car. Is that correct?"

"Yes."

"You also testified that the defendant blew his horn and waved to attract your attention. Is that correct?"

"Yes."

"Tell the court, Mr. Mendoza. Did he blow his horn first then wave? Or was it the other way around?"

"Objection. What difference does it make?" Testa protested rising to his feet.

"Sit down Mr. Testa. . . ."

"Your Honor. . . ."

"Sit down . . . Mr. Testa . . . OVERRULED."

"So, which way was it? Mr. Mendoza. Horn first? Wave first? WHICH WAY WAS IT? MR. MENDOZA. Chris asked firmly. Raising his voice. Startling the witness.

"I . . . I . . . don't remember."

"YOU DON'T REMEMBER?"

"I . . . I'm sorry . . . I'm sorry . . . I don't remember."

"But you're sure he waved. Do I have that right? Are you absolutely sure he waved?"

"Yes."

"Then you're just as sure about him blowing his horn. Or is there any chance that you may be mistaken about that? Is it possible that you may be mistaken about the horn part? Are you as sure about that as you are about the waving part?"

"No. No."

"No? Allow me to clarify that. When you say no. Are you saying that it is impossible for you to be mistaken about the wave and the horn? Except of course for the order of their occurrence."

"That . . . that's right."

"You're ab . . . so . . . lutely sure he blew his horn."

Mendoza shifted in his seat. He leaned to his right and craned his neck. Chris stepped to his left, blocking Mendoza's view. Preventing him from communicating in any way with the prosecutor.

"Please, Mr. Mendoza . . . ANSWER THE QUESTION."

"Yes . . . yes. Absolutely."

Chris turned on his heel and walked back to the defense table. He picked up two pieces of paper. "I offer this receipt as defense exhibit number two," he said, as he handed one copy to the clerk, who in turn, handed it to the judge, and the other to Richard Testa, who accepted it with a trembling hand.

Judge Rios examined the document through his bifocals and handed it back to the clerk, who gave it back to Chris.

After asking permission to approach the witness, Chris handed the paper to Mendoza and said, "This is a document properly submitted, and accepted into evidence. Will you read what is described in the document please?"

Mendoza studied the document he held in his hand. Suddenly the 8X10 piece of paper began to quiver. He looked up at Chris, then at the judge. He stretched his neck again to look at the State's Attorney. This time, Chris didn't stand in his way.

"It . . . it says . . . re . . . replace two fifteen amp fuses for cruise control . . . horn and cigarette lighter."

"OBJECTION," Testa yelled. "This receipt is dated three days after the arrest took place."

"Your Honor," Chris pleaded. "We are aware of the date stamped on the receipt. I have an expert witness who will testify that the defendant's horn was not working on the day of the arrest. He will also testify that the repairs were not possible until the date stamped on the receipt. That witness is here in the witness room waiting to testify. I will produce that witness to rebut the State's witness as soon as the prosecution rests it's case."

Judge Rios looked at the State's Attorney. Small beads of perspiration were visible on Testa's forehead.

"OBJECTION . . . OVER RULED," the judge said loud and clear.

Chris turned and glared at Testa, then turned back to the witness and continued. "Mr. Mendoza, do you understand what that receipt indicates?" Chris said, motioning toward the sheet of paper Mendoza held in his hand.

"Yes . . . I think so."

"You think so? Perhaps you should read it again and again if necessary. Until you are sure you understand what it means."

"OBJECTION!" Testa protested.

Judge Rios slowly lifted his head and looked at Testa, who was now standing, waiting for a ruling on his objection.

"Sit down," Rios said, turning his attention back to the witness.

"Your Honor, I respectfully insist on your ruling."

The Judge turned toward Testa and glared at him over the top of his eyeglasses.

"I withdraw my objection, Your Honor," Testa said, flopping into his chair.

Chris turned back to his witness. "We have a choice, Mr. Mendoza. I can excuse you now and recall you after my expert witness has testified, or, you can save us all a lot of time and trouble by telling the truth now. Which will it be, sir? By the way, perjury is a serious crime and punishment can be very severe."

"OBJECTION!" Testa was on his feet again, perspiration running down his face. "He's badgering and threatening the witness, Your Honor, I object."

"I disagree," the judge growled. "Over-ruled," Rios said disgustedly, whisking his hand in a disregarding motion.

"Mr. Mendoza, your fate is now entirely in *your* hands. This is your opportunity to correct a terrible wrong you have helped to perpetrate on my client."

Julio Mendoza put his face in his hands. "Oh no, God forgive me," he said.

Judge Rios leaned closer to the witness stand; as he did so, he raised his eyebrows and gave Chris an inquiring look.

"I'm sure God will forgive you, Mr. Mendoza. This court, however, will not be so quick to forgive if you don't start telling the truth, NOW," Chris said firmly.

"I object," Testa said, pounding his fist on the table.

"OVER-RULED!" the judge said pounding *his* fist.

Chris looked at the witness compassionately, "Are you asking God to forgive you because you've broken one of commandments?"

Mendoza looked up at Chris. Tears were streaming from his eyes now. His whole body seemed to be trembling. He closed his eyes and clenched his teeth. His body stiffened as he raised his head up, his eyes squeezed tight. His right fist was clenched, he began pounding it into his left hand again and again. "YES!" he cried out. "Yes, but it wasn't my fault!"

Chris came to attention with his hands clasped behind him. He leaned slightly toward the witness. "Could it be that the commandment you broke is, THOU SHALT NOT BARE FALSE WITNESS AGAINST THY NEIGHBOR?"

There was total silence in the courtroom. Every eye was on the witness.

Mendoza, still holding his fist in his hand, raised his bowed head. "Yes," he said in a soft, barely audible voice.

"Please, Mr. Mendoza, the court can't hear you," Chris said in a soft voice.

"Yes," Mendoza said again, not much louder than the first time, but loud enough.

Chris turned and glared at his opponent. Richard Testa looked down, then away. He wouldn't meet Chris' eyes.

Once again, Chris turned his attention to the witness. "Mr. Mendoza, why did you testify as you did?"

Mendoza seemed more relaxed now, his eyes were still glassy, but the trembling disappeared and he no longer sat stiffly in his seat. His expression was blank.

"Mr. Mendoza," Chris said kindly, "you have nothing to fear. I promise you that I and this court will prevent any harm from coming to you. Please tell the court why you testified the way you did."

"They threatened me," he said. "They said they'd lock me up with those animals in the County Jail." Mendoza's voice seemed deeper and more resonant.

"They?" Chris asked. "Who exactly are they?"

"The cops; Ruck and his partners." Mendoza said, feeling more relaxed and confident.

Chris turned again and glared at Testa, then his features softened as he smiled and once again winked that same impish wink. He turned to face the witness, who had a slight smile on his face, as if he were anxious to reveal something he knew would send a shock wave through the entire courtroom.

"Cops don't have the power to lock people up. They can arrest you, sometimes they can even detain you, but they can't sentence you to jail. They don't have the authority to do that," Chris said, looking up at the judge who was leaning even closer than before.

"Maybe they don't, but *he* does," Mendoza said standing up, pointing toward the prosecution table.

Suddenly the courtroom erupted with the sound of voices and shoe leather slapping the tiled floor of the gallery as reporters jumped to their feet, some holding recorders in their outstretched hands, others writing frantically in long hand or short hand, trying to record the events as dramatically as they occurred.

Judge Rios repeatedly slammed his gavel on his oak desk top. He glared at his bailiff and pointed toward the throng of reporters. "Get those recorders out of here," he ordered, then banged his gavel again. "ORDER, ORDER!" he shouted.

The spectators and news people settled down, and at last the courtroom was quiet again.

Chris Musso resumed his questioning. "Would you please repeat . . ."

"THAT'S ENOUGH, MR. MUSSO," the judge snarled. Motioning Chris to stand back, the judge growled, "I have one question for the witness." Judge Rios looked around his courtroom, then at the Assistant State's Attorney, then at Mendoza. Judge Rios stood up, leaned over the bench and looked the witness directly in the eyes. "Mr. Mendoza, are you telling me that the arresting officers and the State's Attorney told you to lie, to falsely testify against the defendant in these proceedings?"

"Yes, . . . Your Honor."

Judge Rolando J. Rios stood straight up. With his arm outstretched toward the witness room, he ordered, "Bailiff, I want the two officers who testified brought back here immediately. Mr. Testa, you are not to leave this courtroom until I say so. Mr. Musso, I'm dismissing the case against your client and dropping all charges against him as of right now."

* * *

Standing at the pay phone outside the courtroom, Marco searched through his wallet looking for his calling card.

"Need change?"

Marco looked up to see Donna standing in front of him, her palm stretched out, overflowing with coins.

"What are you doing here?" Marco asked, surprised, but happy to see her.

"Sorry, I just couldn't wait," she said. "I got here just in time to see my colleagues trampling over one another as they rushed out of the courtroom. I stopped one long enough to get the news. I'm happy for you, Marco. I never had any doubt about your innocence. I never dreamed your vindication would be so complete, however. To actually expose the conspiracy and all the participants is more than we could have ever hoped for."

"Not all the participants," Chris said as he approached the couple and wrapped his arm around Marco. "The cops and Testa were acting on behalf of or on the orders of others, there's no doubt about that." Chris looked at Donna. "Excuse me, I don't think I've had the pleasure, though you do look familiar."

"Donna Michaels, my attorney and, after today, my very good friend, Christopher Musso," Marco said, making the introduction.

"Very pleased to meet you," Donna said, shaking Chris' hand. "I want to thank you, Mr. Musso, for saving my friend's reputation and his career."

"I'd like to take the credit, but I'm afraid it was our friend who saved himself."

"Cut it out, Chris, there was no doubt you would have won. You created a reasonable doubt with the arrest report and the fact that I'm left-handed."

"Yes, I would have won, but we could never have nailed the cops and the State's Attorney without that repair bill, and that was your doing, Marco," Chris reminded. "It's lucky for all of us that you remembered it when you did."

Chris started for the elevator. "Gotta get back to the office," he said, waving his arm. "Call you tonight."

Marco turned to pick up the phone, but a man was using it. "Excuse me. Will you be finished soon?"

The man turned, still holding the phone in his hand. He looked at Marco, but he didn't say anything. When he turned back, Marco noticed a large red birth mark on the back of the man's neck. The shape of it resembled the head of a dog or a wolf. *No.* Marco thought. *It looks like a fox. Where have I seen this person before*? He thought.

"Here, use my cell phone," Donna offered, handing the phone to Marco.

"Thanks. Sarah is waiting for my call. I can't wait to tell her the good news. Oh, Donna, I need a ride home. Would you mind?"

"Not at all, but shouldn't you be getting to the station? Your show goes on the air in half an hour."

"Tony agreed to cover for me until I got there. That reminds me, I have to find a way to thank Tony for finding that receipt and getting it here in time."

"What's with this receipt you guys have been talking about?"

"I'll tell you about it later," Marco said, as he dialed his home phone number on Donna's cell phone.

"Hi, Sarah, it's Dad . . . yes, everything went fine. I'll be there soon. Donna's here with me; she's going to drive me home." Marco handed Donna's phone back. "I have to get home and hug my little girl," he said, as he hurried down the hall.

"Hey, what about me?" Donna said. "Don't I get a hug?"

Marco stopped, turned around and waited for Donna to catch up. He wrapped her in his arms and squeezed her tight.

"I planned on giving Sarah a big kiss, too," he said, as he pressed her even closer.

Donna raised her head and looked into Marco's face. She closed her eyes. She felt Marco's lips on hers. They kissed for a long time.

"I wondered how long it would take you to do that. I was running out of hints. Do I have to wait for you to get arrested again before I get another kiss?"

Marco kissed her again and again and again.

CHAPTER 11

"You did it. I'm impressed. I must say, I didn't expect such a spectacular conclusion. Good job. What you've done will make what's coming that much more awesome."

"THANK YOU, TONY, for sitting in for me while I went home to give my daughter a big hug and kiss. And thank you, ladies and gentlemen and all you children out there for keeping the faith. Thank you for your support, and thank you for giving me the courage to stand up against those slime balls who tried to silence me. And thank you, Mr. Christopher Musso, for having the courage to take my side and defend me against a stacked deck. A stacked deck that would have surely destroyed me, had it not been for your skill in the courtroom.

"And thank you, Judge Rolando J. Rios, for making sure I got a fair trial. Four down and four to go. That's right folks, it's not over yet. The scum bags we exposed today are just flunkies. The real culprits, the brains, for lack of a more appropriate word, behind the attempted assassination of yours truly are still on the loose.

"A certain two bit-politician and a couple more of his lackeys are shaking in their boots, because they know their buddies are spilling their guts to the authorities as we speak. Oh yes, let's not forget 'The Sheriff of Nottingham.' You're next. I'm sure your name will come up while your friends are spilling the beans to the federal investigators. Is there any doubt that they're singing like canaries in order to save their own necks?"

* * *

It didn't take long. After less than twenty four hours, the dam broke. Commander John P. McLaughlin was the first to break. After McLaughlin, Handleman made a full confession, naming officers Ruck and Daryl Dayton as co-conspirators. Ruck implicated Assistant State's Attorney Richard Testa as the one who helped in setting up their victim.

Two weeks later, McLaughlin made a deal with federal authorities to testify as the prosecution's star witness against Alderman Patrick Grogan and his special assistant Tommy O'Mara in exchange for immunity from prosecution. Only Testa remained uncooperative, refusing to talk to police, refusing to confirm or deny any of the confessions made by his codefendants.

He remained silent, hoping to buy enough time to devise a defense strategy that would successfully refute the testimony of his fellow conspirators. His experience as a prosecutor taught him that a suspect who refused to incriminate himself was always the most difficult to convict. It was all over just as Marco had promised McLaughlin months earlier. In the end, he hurt them much more than they hurt him.

* * *

Cosmo's was jammed, as usual. Almost every table and booth were filled. The oval-shaped bar and floral carpeted waiting area were occupied beyond their legal capacity. When Marco Fischer came through the solid oak front entrance doors with his two favorite girls, one on each arm, not a single complaint was heard when he was escorted to the only empty table in the house. Making his way through the crowd, Marco stopped to shake hands with fans and well-wishers as Sarah and Donna smiled politely.

"I see we're the first ones here," Sarah said, taking her seat, glancing up at the elegant chandelier that bathed the diners in a warm, inviting glow.

"Mr. Musso called a few minutes ago and said he'd be a little late," Charles said, handing Marco the wine list.

"What about Tony and Karen?" Donna asked. "Tony's never late."

"Here we are," Tony said, weaving his way through the crowded dining room, followed by Karen, Jerry Kaplan and Kaplan's secretary, Sally Quinn.

Five minutes later, Chris and Gail Musso appeared, accompanied by a third person, a man in a police lieutenant's uniform. Marco, Tony and Jerry stood when they recognized him.

"Mr. Caller," Marco announced.

"Excuse me, folks," Chris said. "If I may have the honor, let me introduce the man who started it all." Chris Musso stood at the head of the crowded table with his arm around his surprise guest. "Lieutenant Mike Nicoletti of the Chicago Police Department."

"I should have known," Marco said. "And a lieutenant, no less."

"Retired lieutenant as of Monday morning," Nicoletti said, a cigarette dangling from his lips. "You did a hell of a job, Marco. I'm proud of you."

"Couldn't have done it without you."

"All I did was start something; that is the easy part. You finished it," Nicoletti said, lighting another cigarette with the tiny butt he held in his fingertips.

"Yeah, and he almost finished himself in the process," Jerry added, lifting his water glass into the air. "I'd like to propose a toast." He waited for everyone else to join him. "To Marco Fischer, the only man in Chicago to go against Patrick Grogan, or should I say Prince John and Sir Guy Gisbourne, and live to tell about it."

"Here, here," Tony said, as he lifted his glass even higher.

"Well, things will seem a little dull around here from now on," Jerry said. "Looks like you'll have to find another bad guy."

"Marco shouldn't have any trouble doing that in this town," Chris said with a laugh.

"What about 'The Sheriff of Nottingham?" Donna suggested.

"After what happened to his buddies, don't you think he'll be afraid to show his face?" Tony asked.

"I don't think so," Nicolleti spoke up. "His only chance for a future is to get back into politics. It's all he knows."

"We'll just have to wait and see," Marco said. "As far as I'm concerned, I hope he doesn't back off. I'd like nothing more than to see him get what he deserves."

"Here, here," Tony said lifting his glass again.

"Here, here," everyone said, joining him in another toast.

"Excuse me."

Everyone looked up. It was Charles the waiter. "I don't mean to interrupt, but shall I bring some champagne, or do you prefer to toast with water all night?"

"Good idea," Chris agreed. "Make it the best in the house."

"Wait a minute," Marco interrupted. "Is this going on my bill?"

Chris held out his arms. "It's your party, isn't it?"

It was a joyous evening. All the friends, new and old, ate, drank and made merry till the wee small hours.

* * *

Patrick Grogan cursed the evening news reports. Out on bond, he more or less placed himself under self-imposed house arrest. Unwilling to expose himself to the harassment levied upon him by his constituents, he refused to leave his home. His only contact with the outside world was through his television set. He had thrown his radio out the window so as not to be reminded of Marco Fischer. The TV, however, seemed to be obsessed with his arrest and the story surrounding Marco's trial, therefore a constant reminder of his predicament.

Unable to cope any longer, he decided to take a chance and leave the confines of his residence and venture outdoors for some fresh air. As he stepped out onto his front porch, the alderman was distracted for a moment by the sound of leaves being rustled. He turned his head and stood silently for a few seconds, then reached into his pocket and came out with his key chain.

Grogan reminded himself that he still had a lot of friends and many beholden to him for one reason or another. He heard the rustling sound again. He turned his head from side to side, but he didn't see anything out of the ordinary.

The sons-of-bitches they have me hearing things. Pretty soon I'll be seeing things, he thought, as he pulled the door closed behind him. He pushed his key into the lock and began to make a mental list of all those who owed him. He heard a strange noise as he twisted the key; it made him turn his head to his right. Patrick Grogan never identified the noise; he couldn't. His hearing, his eyesight, as a matter of fact all of his senses suddenly stopped functioning. Patrick Grogan no longer existed.

CHAPTER 12

"How do you like it? Couldn't happen to a nicer guy. Don't you agree? This is only the beginning. You are no longer alone. ROBIN HOOD has come to save the day."

MARCO OPENED HIS front door and found his Sunday newspaper lying in the middle of the corridor. Still half asleep and a little hung over from the night before, he picked up the paper, folded it and tucked it under his arm. A muffled ringing sounded in his head.

"Daddy," he heard Sarah calling. "Telephone. It's Donna."

Feeling a surge at the sound of her name, Marco picked up his pace and hurried into the kitchen. "Please make some coffee," he pleaded, as he took the phone from Sarah's hand.

"Had a little too much?" Sarah kidded.

"Hi, Donna. What are you doing up so early?"

"Have you seen the morning news?"

"What news?"

"The morning news shows?"

"I hate television, you know that. I'm a radio man. Did you forget?"

"Marco, Grogan was murdered last night."

"Murdered?" Marco repeated, as he snatched the paper from under his arm.

"Yes, murdered," Donna said.

"I'm looking at the front page now," Marco said. "I can't believe it. What does it say? He was killed with an arrow?"

"Yes," Donna said. "An arrow, the kind you shoot with one of those cross bow things, you know, the kind you sort of shoot like a rifle."

"Through the head?" Marco said, as he listened to Donna and continued to read at the same time.

"Yes, right through the head; he died instantly, according to the coroner."

"I see here it says they have no suspects," Marco said, becoming more engrossed in what he was reading.

"Marco, can I come over? I'll stop and pick up some bacon and eggs on the way."

"Just come on over. I have everything we need. Hurry up. Coffee's almost ready." Marco hung up the phone without taking his eyes off the newspaper.

Donna made it in fifteen minutes. Marco was on his second cup of coffee and had WHLP tuned in on his radio.

"Any new developments?" Donna asked, as she poured herself a cup of coffee.

"No, nothing new. No leads, no clues, no suspects, no nothing. Except that Casper was killed the same way. There has to be a connection."

If Marco hated anyone, it was Grogan. Yet the news of his death hit him hard, very hard. He felt as though an old friend had died. He couldn't shake the empty feeling, the sensation of loss. Marco sat silently trying to understand the emotions churning inside him.

"What's the matter, Honey?" Donna asked, as she stood up, wrapped her arm around his head and pressed it against her.

"It's hard to explain, but I actually feel sorry for the bum. Even after what he tried to do to me, I still feel bad."

"That's because you're a good man, Marco, you care about people. That's why you have the following you have. People sense that about you."

"Hey, what's going on in here?" Sarah said, walking back into the kitchen.

"Where have you been?" Donna asked.

"Whenever I want to watch TV, I have to go to my room. My dad won't allow television anywhere else. The reports on Grogan's murder are on every channel. It's as if these TV news people wish for this sort of thing to happen. They seem to enjoy telling us about the tragedies and misfortunes of others. Oh, I'm sorry, Donna," Sarah said, holding her hand to her mouth. "I forgot, you're a TV news reporter."

"That's okay, Sarah, you're right, only I wouldn't say they enjoy it, at least not generally. You see, the news is their livelihood. Without murder, mayhem, disaster and, as you say, the tragedies and misfortunes of others, they're out of a job. It's a fact I've struggled with ever since I became a reporter. I've considered going into some other line of work, but reporting is what I do, it's what I am. It's all I know how to do. That's why I've tried to specialize in political reporting. Chasing ambulances and fire trucks never appealed to me."

"Well, don't blame Sarah," Marco said. "She's been hanging around me too long. I've always hated the news-mongers, especially the ones on TV. I'm afraid I've been a bad influence on my little girl."

"I'm afraid you've been a bad influence on me, too. I'm beginning to feel resentful of my own colleagues," Donna said, smiling and shaking her finger at Marco. "I hope you don't hate me, too."

"You are the one exception," Marco said, rising from his chair, placing his hand under Donna's chin and kissing her tenderly. "You are the one beautiful exception." Marco kissed Donna again and said. "Let's go out for breakfast. Let's get away from all this bad news. Come on, I'm buying.

* * *

Sarah couldn't believe her eyes. Not since her mother had she seen her father act this way. *Go for it Dad*, she said to herself, smiling.

For the first time in a very long time, Sarah felt like she and her dad were a real family again. Donna made them feel complete, and she loved it. She knew her father loved it, too, even if he was reluctant to say so. She could see it in his eyes.

* * *

Tony Ruskin queued Marco for the beginning of Monday afternoon's show. The topic, of course, would be what had been on virtually everyone's mind since Saturday night. Marco kept his opening comments brief to allow maximum time for his callers to express their opinions and concerns.

"I think he was killed by his own people, someone who was afraid he was going to make a deal," one caller said.

"Are you suggesting Grogan was just a puppet while a hierarchy of corrupt politicians pulled the strings?" Marco asked.

"That's exactly what I'm suggesting."

"Thank you, caller. Let's go to Louise on line two."

"I agree. Grogan was killed because he had to be silenced."

"Thank you. Let's see what Steve on line three has to say."

"No way," the caller said. "It was suicide. Grogan stuck the arrow through his own head just to throw us off the track. The investigation into his activities was about to expose the real brains behind his organization."

"And who might that be?" Marco asked, bracing himself.

"Elvis, who else?"

"Elvis? There has never been an Elvis sighting in Chicago, as far as I know," Marco played along.

"That's right. Elvis was about to be exposed. Grogan killed himself in order to throw the Feds off track."

"Okay, Caller, I'm sure my audience will give your theory

serious consideration. Now, let's go to line four." Marco removed his headphones for just a moment to wipe away the perspiration that formed around his ears.

TAP, TAP, TAP.

Marco looked up. Tony was tapping on the glass. "Line five," he mouthed. "Line five."

Working with Tony was becoming a lesson in lip reading. Marco thought, as he said, "Line four, please continue to be patient. I'll get to you after I take this call. Okay line five, you're on the air."

"Hi, Marco." The snake-like voice hissed.

"It sounds like our old friend, Mr. Anonymous. I wondered when we'd hear from you again," Marco answered.

"From now on, you can call me Robin Hood," the caller said. "I heard you ask one time where Robin Hood was when you needed him. Well, here I am."

"Okay, Robin. What are your comments on the Grogan murder?"

"It wasn't a murder."

"Oh, don't tell me you think it was suicide, too," Marco chuckled.

"It wasn't suicide, either." There was a hint of impatience in the caller's voice.

"Okay, tell us what it was then."

"It was the first execution brought about by Marco's Morgue. The execution of Prince Philip."

Marco heard a click. The caller hung up. Marco suddenly felt dizzy and light-headed. For the first time in years, he searched his empty shirt pocket for a cigarette. Tony watched Marco through the glass; he looked faint, the color in his face drained, beads of perspiration formed on his forehead. Tony rushed into the broadcast booth and removed Marco's headset. Speaking into the microphone he said, "Marco will be back after these commercial messages."

"Marco, are you all right?"

"Yeah, yeah, I'm all right. I don't know what happened. I felt funny for a minute." Marco looked up at Tony. "Do you think it's possible?"

"What do you mean?" Tony asked, puzzled.

"Do you think it's because of me that Grogan is dead?"

"Don't be silly," Tony assured. "The guy's a kook. He's just exploiting a situation. He's having some fun at your expense."

"I don't think so," Marco disagreed. "The guy's for real, I can hear it in his voice."

"Marco, listen to me. The guy's a nut, a screwball. We'll never hear from him again."

"I hope you're right, but I don't think so."

* * *

Marco finished his show and immediately called Donna at her apartment.

"Were you listening?" Marco asked, anxiously.

"Yes, I was."

"Then you heard Robin Hood? You heard what he said?"

"Yes, I did, but . . ."

"I have to see you. Meet me at Cosmo's. We'll have dinner."

"We already have a dinner date, at my place. Did you forget?" Donna scolded.

"Oh, yes, I'm sorry. I forgot. This Robin Hood thing knocked me for a loop."

"Do you want to talk about it?"

"Yes, but not now. I'll see you in a little while."

"I'll be waiting. Please don't be late."

"Alright I'll see you at your place. I just want to call Sarah and remind her that I'll be coming home late tonight. See you soon."

"Why don't you tell her you won't be home at all tonight," Donna said, before Marco had a chance to hang up.

"Five minutes ago, I felt rotten, like my world was coming to an end. After talking to you for thirty seconds, I feel wonderfully exhilarated. I'm so happy you've come into my life. I never thought I'd ever feel this way again. Thank you."

"Please hurry, I want you here with me." Donna hung up the phone and ran around her apartment shutting off all the lights, except two, the one on the end table next to her couch and the one on the night stand next to her bed.

* * *

The next morning, just before seven o'clock, Marco sneaked into his apartment. As he quietly closed his bedroom door, he heard Sarah's alarm clock ring. Minutes later, he heard Sarah tiptoe through the hall on her way to the bathroom. Her footsteps stopped outside his door. Marco heard her say, "Next time, let's try to get home at a more reasonable hour, young man."

Marco heard the bathroom door close and rushed to his phone.

"Hello."

"I told you, she knows."

"Who, what?" Donna said sleepily.

"Sarah. She knows where I was and what we were doing," Marco whispered.

"Yes, and you do it very well, too."

"Stop that; you're going to get me in more trouble."

"Marco, she's your daughter, not your wife. Besides, she's a big girl and she knows her dad is a big boy."

"I know, I know. I guess I'm having a hard time getting used to it."

"I know. My father still thinks I'm a virgin, too."

"Don't talk like that. I *know* Sarah is."

"Marco, go to sleep. I'll call you before you go to the studio."

CHAPTER 13

"I told you it was only the beginning. I told you that you were no longer alone. But why do I detect rejection in your voice and attitude? Don't you know that I'm your friend? Don't you understand that I have chosen you to be my spokesman? Don't you know that I have chosen you to help me begin the new revolution?"

ALMOST TWO WEEKS had passed since the death of Patrick Grogan. Marco was in his office going through his mail. A large envelope with no return address caught his eye. He opened it and found a copy of an invitation sent by an unidentified informant, an invitation to a welcome home party for a certain ex-con, Sean O'Bannion, AKA "The Sheriff of Nottingham."

* * *

"It's true ladies and gentlemen, the fund raiser disguised as a welcome home dinner party will be taking place at seven o'clock, cocktails at six-thirty, of course, in the Grand Ballroom of the Sherwood Hotel this coming Saturday night. All things considered, they did a good job of keeping this a secret. An invitation, however, fell into the wrong hands . . . mine. Now, I'm not making any threats, but if I were the ex-sheriff, I'd be ex-pecting some unexpected guests."

For the rest of the week, Marco opened every show with comments concerning O'Bannion's fund raiser and his plans to re-enter Chicago politics. By the weekend, Marco's followers had been stirred into a frenzy.

"Well, ladies and gentlemen and children of all ages, tomorrow night is the night we've been waiting for. Let's see who shows up to pay respect to one of Chicago's slimiest slime ball politicians ever. Let's see how many low-life politicians have the guts to show their faces tomorrow night. Let's see how many of you show up to stand up and protest against this kind of blatant disrespect for the honest, hardworking people of this great city. I'll be there at six o'clock along with Tony Ruskin, my producer. See you then."

Marco closed his show and gathered his notes. Donna was waiting in his office.

"Hungry?"

"You know," Marco said, "I've gained five pounds since I met you."

"That's because you're so much more content than you were before you met me."

"Oh? I thought it was because we were always eating."

"Shut up," Donna said, grabbing Marco's hand. "Let's go, I'm starving."

"How about a beef?" Marco said.

"Only if you promise to give me a half Italian and half Jewish sausage later," Donna kidded.

"You know, people say *I'm* a bad influence," Marco said, reaching to pinch Donna's butt.

Donna jerked away and ran toward the elevator with Marco close behind. As she reached the door, it opened. Marco scooped her into his arms and carried her into the compartment. With Donna still in his arms, he kissed her. Donna reached over and pushed the "L" button. By the time the doors opened again, she had forgotten about her hunger for food. She had a different kind of hunger, one that had to be satisfied, NOW!

* * *

Later that evening in Donna's apartment, the lovers lay in bed.

"Marco, I'm really starving now," Donna said.

"Sex and food. That's all you think about," Marco kidded.

"Marco," Donna said seriously.

"I'm only kidding, honey."

"Oh, I know that. I was just thinking about tomorrow night. May I come along? Would you mind?"

"Sure, why not. We're partners, aren't we? Bring your camera crew." Marco took Donna into his arms. He whispered something in her ear.

"Yes," she responded. "But afterwards, can we go *out* for something to eat?"

* * *

Marco, Donna, Tony and a three-man film crew were overwhelmed by the crowd in front of the Sherwood Hotel on Chicago's famous Michigan Avenue. Three, maybe four hundred people had shown up, many with picket signs.

"This is really exciting," Donna said. "Just think, Marco, you made it all happen."

Inside the Grand Ballroom, the attendance was not quite what was expected, but large nevertheless. After drinks, dinner and a few boring speeches, the guests awaited the appearance of the man they all had come to honor, the former sheriff of Cook County, Sean O'Bannion.

"Thank you. Thank all of you for coming and making this such a wonderful evening. I want to take this opportunity to . . ."

Sean O'Bannion felt a blow to his midsection. He looked down to see something protruding from his chest. The crowd gasped as O'Bannion collapsed on the stage.

* * *

Marco and Donna were busy interviewing protesters while Tony directed the film crew. Suddenly, a woman came running through the main entrance doors of the hotel.

"He's dead! He's dead! O'Bannion is dead. He's been murdered!"

Marco looked up to see the frantic woman running toward him and Donna.

"Excuse me, Miss," Marco said, motioning to Tony to bring the cameras closer. "Did you say O'Bannion has been murdered?"

"Yes," The woman said, trying to catch her breath.

"How did it happen, was he shot?"

"Yes . . . no . . . well not exactly. He was shot, but not with a gun."

Marco turned and looked wide eyed at Donna. She knew instantly what he was thinking.

"Was he shot with an arrow?" Marco asked the woman, knowing what her answer would be.

"Yes, it came out of nowhere."

Marco could now hear the sirens coming from all directions.

"Are you sure he's dead?"

"The arrow went right through the center of his chest."

"Thank you, Miss," Marco said, putting his arm around Donna's shoulders. "Let's go to my place," he said, handing Donna his keys. "You drive. I don't think I'm able."

"Marco, Marco. Where're you going?" Tony called out, running to catch up.

"I have to go home, Tony, I can't stay here." Turning to face Donna, he said, "You were right, I made it all happen."

"Don't start blaming yourself again," Tony said.

Marco put his right hand on his forehead and extended his left. "Look, Tony, don't try to deny it. You know O'Bannion was killed by the same guy who murdered Grogan and Casper, and you know who that guy is."

"I agree it looks that way, but that doesn't mean it's the same guy who's been calling the show," Tony reasoned.

"We both know who the killer is," Marco said.

"You can't jump to that conclusion. You don't know for sure. The caller could still be some nut having fun with you."

"So far, that nut has killed three people, and don't tell me it's not him. It *is* him, and he actually thinks he's Robin Hood, and I'm the one who put that idea in his head."

"Do you really think it's him?" Donna asked.

"There's no doubt in my mind, no doubt whatsoever."

"What should we do?" Donna was trembling; she was very frightened.

Marco stopped and faced his two best friends. Putting an arm around each of their shoulders, he said, "I created this monster. I'll have to be the one who destroys it."

* * *

Monday morning, Marco and Sarah had their usual chat over breakfast, except Marco wasn't his usual self.

"Are you still worried about that Robin Hood guy?" Sarah asked.

"Yes, honey, I'm very worried about him."

"But Dad, you don't even know for sure that he's the real killer."

"I know. I've talked to this guy several times, believe me, it's him. *I know.*"

"Do you think he'll call again?"

"I know he'll call again. As a matter of fact, I'm going to invite him to call again today. I'm going to ask my audience to refrain from calling between three-thirty and four o'clock so he won't have any difficulty getting through."

"What are you going to say?"

"I'm only going to say enough to get him talking. Maybe he'll say something incriminating. If I can convince the police that this guy is the murderer, it should be no problem getting clearance to trace his number. All I have to do is think of a way to keep him talking. Sooner or later, he'll make a mistake."

"Be careful, Daddy, right now he thinks you're his friend, or at least his ally. He calls your show and he thinks you agree with him. If he ever gets the idea that you're trying to expose him, he may decide to come after you."

"I've thought about that, and that may be the only way."

"You can't do that," Sarah exclaimed. "You can't make him come after you. He's too dangerous."

"Don't worry, honey. I won't do anything stupid. I'm going to call Mike Nicoletti and ask him to help me set a trap."

* * *

Mike Nicoletti was sitting alone in his den reading when his phone interrupted him.

"Hello." Nicoletti said, searching his breast pocket for a cigarette.

"Is this the mysterious Mr. Caller?"

"Marco, how you doing?" Nicoletti relaxed at the sound of Marco's voice.

"How you doing?" Marco asked.

"Since I quit smoking, I get a little jittery now and then; otherwise I'm fine."

Marco's tone became more serious. "Mike, I think I know who killed Grogan and O'Bannion . . . and Casper."

"Are you kidding?"

"No, and I want you to help me set a trap for him."

"Is there some reason you don't just call the police?"

Marco went on to give Nicoletti the whole story about the caller who calls himself Robin Hood and why he suspected him.

"Sounds reasonable," Nicoletti said. "I agree, you can't call in the police at this point. Let me think about it for awhile. I'll listen to your program today. I want to hear what this guy has to say, if he calls."

"He'll call," Marco said. "When he hears me say I'm holding all other calls for thirty minutes just for him, he won't be able to resist. He'll be the center of attraction. My entire audience will be waiting to hear him speak. Believe me, Mike, he'll call."

"I think you have this guy pegged. What he wants is recognition. He has a philosophy, and he needs a platform from which to preach his beliefs. If you offer him the opportunity to use your show for that purpose, he'll grab it. Then all we have to do is let him talk. Eventually he'll make a mistake."

"Mike, my old friend, that's exactly what I hoped you'd say."

Mike Nicoletti placed the receiver back into it's cradle. "Thank you, God," he said.

Mike had been retired just a few weeks, but he was already beginning to regret the decision to take his pension. After thirty years on the police department, his new life was a little boring, not to mention the loneliness that was beginning to overcome him. Marco's call couldn't have come at a more welcome time. The loneliness is what bothered him more than anything. Though his wife, Joanne, had been dead for almost eighteen years, he still missed her terribly.

The responsibilities of his job helped greatly in coping with his loss. He would bury himself in his work, putting in many hours of overtime. At day's end, physically and mentally exhausted, sleep would come easily.

He'd enjoyed a few short-lived relationships with other women over the years, but his dedication to his work took it's toll on them as well. However, it was no loss because he knew he would always remain faithful to the only woman he could ever really love. Mike picked up his book to resume reading, but he couldn't. Instead, he closed his eyes, settled back in his recliner and let his thoughts take him on a mental journey back in time.

* * *

It was springtime. He had gone to his neighborhood book store to stock up on the latest best sellers. He was having a hard time finding one book in particular. A young woman wearing an orange smock was busily stocking shelves, crouched just a few feet away.

"Excuse me," he said as he approached her.

She looked up at him. "May I help you?" she asked.

He was speechless. He had never seen a face so angelically beautiful. Her deep blue eyes expressed a gentleness, a tenderness he'd never seen before. Her hair was light, but not quite blond, and pulled back in a pony tail. Her skin was smooth and clear with a kind of luster that made her face glow. When she smiled at him, she exposed her perfectly aligned white teeth.

She stood up and asked again, "May I help you?"

He tried to speak calmly, but his heart was beating so rapidly, he became short of breath.

"Ah, . . . well I'm looking for a certain book, . . . but I can't seem to find it," he said, dry-mouthed, hoping he didn't sound like a fool.

He couldn't take his eyes off hers, yet he could see her whole body at the same time. She was tall and thin. When she reached up to adjust her eye glasses, he marveled at her slender hands and long fingers with perfectly manicured, unpolished nails.

"What's the title?" she asked, with a slight smile, one that told him she understood his awkwardness.

"Now. . . . And . . . Forever," he stammered.

"Oh, yes, It's right here," she said, reaching for the book just inches away from his shoulder.

She came so close, he could smell her. A clean pure smell, undiluted by perfume or other artificial scents. He felt something, a feeling he couldn't describe, a wonderful, exciting feeling.

"Here you are," she said, handing him the book. "Is there anything else I can help you with?"

YES, YES! he wanted to say. But instead, he just stood there, looking at her.

"Well, please let me know if I can be of any further assistance."

"Thank you," he said, making a mental note of the name displayed on the tag pinned to her smock. On the drive back to his tiny apartment, he repeated the name over and over again in his mind. *Joanne, Joanne.* He burned it into his brain. It was a name he would never forget.

Going to the bookstore became an almost daily ritual. Finally, after several weeks and the realization that it would take years to read all the books he'd purchased, he built up enough courage to ask Joanne out on a date. When she said yes, he almost broke out in tears. From that day on, he knew what his future would be. The courtship lasted just over a year.

On an unusually cool August day, they made their vows to love, honor and obey. Mike prayed it would be a good omen. One foretelling a long, happy, prosperous life together.

Though their time together was happy and prosperous, it wasn't long. After only five years, Joanne was diagnosed with cancer. Over the next five years, there were times when it looked as though she would survive, but it was not to be.

On an unusually cool August day, their tenth anniversary, Joanne died. Even with five years to prepare, her death was still a devastating blow to Mike Nicoletti. True to his nature, however, he refused to become bitter or delve into self pity. Instead, he gave thanks for the years of happiness he was able to share with Joanne. He also vowed to do good in his life to justify the blessing he had enjoyed.

This vow was the reason he set out to uncover and expose corruption, even if it meant jeopardizing his own security. Even if he would have to operate secretly. Even if his actions would be considered traitorous by many of his peers. For almost twenty years, Mike carried out his mission without ever coming close to being exposed. He felt proud of his participation in ridding his city of many corrupt police officers and officials and the occasional politician who got caught up in the investigations.

He knew his decision to retire brought a breath of relief to many who suspected him as a traitor, an informer, but he also knew he'd done the right thing, even if his contribution would never be known by the general public. He never did what he did for praise or recognition. He did it because it was his duty, his responsibility; because he took an oath to do it.

Mike opened his eyes and looked around his den. He wondered if he had fallen asleep, then he noticed the clock on the fireplace mantle. Which read two forty-five. He went into the kitchen, tuned his radio to WHLP and waited for Marco Fischer to begin his show.

CHAPTER 14

"Why, why have you betrayed me? How could you go against me, the only real friend you have? I see you have even recruited others to help you in your betrayal. Did you think I didn't know? Did you think you could fool ROBIN HOOD?"

DONNA SAT NERVOUSLY in the technician's booth with Tony Ruskin, listening to Marco make his announcement to the caller named Robin Hood.

"That's right, Mr. Robin Hood, I'm holding thirty minutes open just for you. I want to hear your comments concerning the events of the past few days, especially the murder of the ex-sheriff, Sean O'Bannion."

Marco looked at Donna and Tony. From the corner of his eye, he saw one of his lines light up. He watched as Tony looked down at his console in the booth. Tony pushed the button and began to speak to the caller. Marco could not hear, but he could see the look on Tony's face. He knew who the caller was. Tony's voice came through Marco's headphones.

"It's him," he said.

"And now, on line one, we have our most outspoken caller," Marco said.

"And how are you today, Mr. Robin Hood?"

"You can drop the Mister, just call me Robin Hood."

"Okay, Robin Hood. Whatever you say."

"You want to hear my comments on the death of O"Bannion? Okay, you got it. Number one, he wasn't murdered. He was executed the same way Grogan was. They got back what they have been giving all these years-the shaft. Grogan got it through the head, and O'Bannion got it through the heart, assuming he had one."

Marco knew Robin Hood was the murderer, but he wanted to dispel any doubts anyone else might still be harboring. His next question would accomplish that.

"Tell me Robin, was Casper executed, too?"

"He was the first."

Marco looked up at Donna. Tony was standing next to her, shaking his clasped hands over his head.

"Do you think it's right to murder . . . or execute people who you think are guilty of something without giving them their day in court?"

"They don't deserve a day in court. They deserve just what they got. Every day these bastards betray the trust of the people; and if their actions ever do become known, they look at us and say; 'what are you going to do about it?' Then go right back and do it again. What happens to them? Nothing. And what can we do about it? Can we go to the police? No. Can we go to another politician? Of course not. Can we go to the media?"

Marco remained silent, allowing Robin Hood to speak as long as he wanted to.

"The newspapers don't even bother to report the things they know are going on, and television news is more interested in a fire on the south side of town, or an automobile accident on the Dan Ryan Expressway, who won the ball game or what rock and roll group is playing in Grant Park. Who cares? Compared to the thievery that goes on in this town every day, how important can who won the game be?"

Marco leaned back in his chair. *Keep talking*, he said to himself.

"More time is wasted reporting sports in this town than how our tax money is being squandered irresponsibly or how much of it is being outright stolen. They had their day in court when they promised they would honestly represent us if we voted for them. So we vote for them. And what do they do? They get into office and they thumb their noses at us. If we should try to do something about it, they use the power and authority we gave them against us. Did you forget already what they did to you?"

There was a pause. Marco suspected that Robin Hood expected a response, but he remained silent. Then Robin Hood continued.

"They tried to destroy an honest man and they used the police to do it. The police are paid by the taxpayer. They are sworn to serve and protect us. But who do they protect, who do they serve? Politicians, crooked, scum bag politicians. The police violated your civil rights, falsely accused you of a crime and tried to lock you up. Why? Because they were ordered to. Why? To shut you up, because you were putting pressure on a corrupt politician, because you were doing your duty as a loyal citizen of the United States of America."

Robin Hood paused again. Again, Marco did not respond.

"Well, my friend this is America, and America is born of revolution. Revolution against political tyranny and oppressive government. It is our right, our heritage, our responsibility to stand up against those who would take our freedom away from us."

Marco could no longer remain silent.

"Excuse me, Mist . . . I mean Robin Hood. Is it our right to break the law because we disagree with it?"

"It is not only our *right* to break the law, it is our *responsibility* to break the law when it is unjust. When the law is created to control us instead of serve us, when the law is created to prevent us from questioning the authority we the people are supposed to control, it is our obligation to break the law and fight against those who would prevent us from doing just that."

Keep talking. Keep talking. Marco prayed.

"Do you think politicians want to take our guns away from us to protect us from killing each other? If you do, you're a nit wit. They want our guns because they want to protect themselves.

They're afraid the American people will rise up one day and take their government back. That's why they want to disarm the American people, to make us helpless to fight them.

"We must always have the courage to question those who seek to govern us. If we do not question, we give up the freedom to decide our own destiny and give others the power to control our lives. Once we give up that power, it is very difficult to get it back. One day we wake up and find ourselves in a position where we no longer have the power to question, even if we possess the courage to do so."

Marco was surprisingly moved by the man's words. He tried to think of a rebuttal to what he'd just heard.

"Robin, I must admit I can't really find a whole lot to disagree with you about, but killing is wrong. That's the one thing I find impossible to justify. Even if we disagree with man's law, didn't God tell us it was wrong to kill?"

"Was it wrong for Samson to kill the enemies of his people? He killed hundreds, perhaps thousands. Was it wrong for David to kill the giant, Goliath? Was it wrong for Moses to bring death and destruction upon the Egyptians in order to bring about the freedom of his people?"

Marco interrupted, "These people were being oppressed by outsiders, by foreigners if you will, not their own government."

"The government we have today is not the government our founding fathers foresaw. Thomas Jefferson warned us to be wary of government when he said, 'Some say we can't trust man to govern himself. If so, how can we trust man to govern others?' It's not government per se, however, that is our enemy. It's ourselves. It is our own ignorance and apathy that has allowed our government to become so self-centered. We have allowed ourselves to be alienated."

Marco once again tried to think of a rebuttal, but he couldn't. He allowed Robin Hood to continue his lecture.

"*We* are supposed to be the government. Instead, we find ourselves on the outside looking in. That's what's happened to us. Now we have to fight our way back inside, just as we did in 1776. The American people today, however, are no different than they were over two hundred years ago. Most of them are afraid to fight. It will be left up to us who have the courage, the love of freedom, the pride in our heritage. You say the Biblical Jews were fighting outsiders. Do you call Grogan, O'Bannion and other corrupt politicians Americans? Do Americans take freedom away from others? No. Americans put their lives on the line so others can be free."

Marco heard a click. The call was over.

* * *

Later that evening, Marco, Sarah, Donna, Tony and Mike Nicoletti were gathered around the dining room table.

"How can you argue with this guy? He does have a point," Marco said, scratching his head. "He doesn't sound all that crazy. What he said made a lot of sense to me."

"Sure, he made sense," Mike said. "That doesn't mean, however, that he's not some kind of nut. There are a lot of people out there who make sense, but they have one little quirk that carries them just a little too far. In this guy's case, it's carried him over the brink."

"Are you saying that Robin Hood may be as normal as any of us except in this one area where he seems to be obsessed?" Donna asked.

"That's right," Mike answered. "In police work, you see it all the time. A guy could be just a guy, like everybody else, except when it comes to a particular subject. It could be anything. I've seen guys get into fist fights over a baseball game. When I first started out on the police force, we'd get a call to break up a fight among family members; when we'd get there, someone would be dead. Often, the witnesses couldn't even remember what started it all.

"There's one thing you learn as a cop, and that is that very few people are all bad. Most people are good people who sometimes do bad things. I believe this guy Robin Hood is probably, in most situations, a normal person. He has a problem, however, with political corruption. He's become frustrated to the point where he's snapped and lost control. He no longer thinks logically on the subject; he acts purely on instinct. What I fear is that one day he'll go over the edge and become a total nut. I've seen that happen, too."

"What if that happens?" Sarah asked.

"If it happens with this guy, I'm afraid we'll have a real serious problem on our hands. He won't be just any nut. He'll be an intelligent nut and a very cunning one at that."

Tony put his hand on Marco's arm. "You need protection. We have to get you a bodyguard."

"Protection? This guy's already proven that if he wants to kill someone he will," Marco argued. "What I have to do is keep him talking until we can set some kind of trap."

"Why can't we just trace his number and find out where he lives?" Sarah asked.

"We can't do that. We need a court order to do that. Right now, we don't have enough evidence that Robin Hood and the killer are one and the same."

"Even I can trace a call simply by installing a caller ID box on my telephone line," Sarah argued.

"That's different," Tony broke in. "This is your home. When he calls your dad, he's calling a radio station. If we did that, it would be an invasion of his privacy. That's why we allow callers to remain anonymous if they choose. Remember, by pushing a couple of buttons on your phone, you can render the caller ID box useless. That insures your right to privacy."

Mike Nicoletti interrupted, "Remember what I said earlier? This Robin Hood guy may be a nut, but he's an intelligent nut. Even if we traced his number this afternoon, I doubt very much if we'd have learned very much about his true identity. He's too smart to call from his home. He's probably calling from a pay phone or a place of business.

"He may be using some kind of a call forwarding system, or he may have one of those phones like the telephone repair men have. If he does, he could be calling from anywhere. With one of those phones, he could be calling from atop a telephone pole or from the basement of an apartment building. He could tap into any phone he wanted to. Our best bet is to get him to meet with Marco and grab him, but we can't even do that until we have enough evidence to justify it."

"Do you have any ideas how we can get him to meet with me?" Marco asked.

"Not yet," Mike said. "Just keep him talking. I'll think of something sooner or later. He'll say something to give us a clue to who he really is." Mike looked at Tony. "Is it possible to record his calls? I want to listen to them. There's something about his voice. It's been bugging me."

"I've already done that," Tony said. "I tape all of Marco's shows as a regular practice."

"Great!" Mike said. "Make me a copy of all his calls. I want to study them."

"I'll have them for you tomorrow," Tony said.

"Okay," Marco said. "Let's call it a night. Mike, if you like, you can come to the studio tomorrow and listen to Robin Hood live, if he calls."

Mike accepted Marco's invitation and bid everyone a good night. Shortly afterward, Tony did the same.

"Daddy, please be careful," Sarah said, as she got up and started for her bedroom.

"Don't worry, honey," Marco assured, as he got up to intercept his daughter. Wrapping his arms around her, he held her tight and kissed her forehead. "I won't do anything without Mike knowing about it. I won't be alone."

Donna walked over to where Sarah and her father were standing. Hugging both of them, she said, "When he's not with Mike, he'll be with me or both of us."

After Sarah went to bed, Marco and Donna sat quietly on the couch looking out onto Lake Michigan. "You were awfully quiet tonight," Marco said.

"I didn't have anything to say. I wanted to hear what Mike had to say."

"Did you learn anything?" Marco asked.

"Yeah, I learned that this Robin Hood is a lot smarter than I gave him credit for. I also learned that Sarah is really worried about you, and so am I."

"Well, then that makes three of us, because I'm as worried as you are. Please understand, Donna, this is something I must do. I have to stop this guy before he does any more damage."

* * *

For the next several days, there was no word from Robin Hood, despite Marco's repeated pleas over the air. Marco continued to keep the lines open between three-thirty and four o'clock, but to no avail. Hopes of trapping Robin Hood were beginning to wane. The weekend came and went, and except for the time Marco spent with Donna, it was uneventful. The following Monday morning, while Marco and Sarah were having breakfast, the phone rang. Marco recognized the ring; it was coming from the lobby.

"Hello," Marco said.

"Mr. Fischer, it's Andy the doorman."

"Yes, Andy, what's up?"

"There's someone here who says he has a package for you. Is it okay if I send him up?"

"What kind of package?"

"Wait, I'll ask."

About fifteen seconds went by. "He says it's a gift from one of your sponsors."

"A gift?" Marco wondered. "Okay, send him up." He hung up the phone realizing he should have asked what sponsor it was.

Marco opened his front door and stepped into the corridor, watching the elevator door until it opened. A young man stepped out carrying a small box.

"Mr. Fischer?" the young man asked.

"That's me."

The young man pulled something out from under the box and handed it to Marco. "Something for you, sir," he said, as he turned and walked back toward the elevator.

Caught by surprise, Marco accepted what were actually several sheets of paper stapled together and folded like a business letter. Marco unfolded the papers and discovered it was a summons. As he re-entered his apartment, he read the cover sheet.

"Sarah!" he called out. "What's this all about?"

* * *

Later that afternoon, Marco told his audience of his new dilemma.

"This morning, I was served with a summons, informing me that I am being sued. Now, guess who's suing me? Okay, you don't have to guess, I'll tell you. I'm being sued by Captain Robert M. Krosel of the Chicago Police Department. Now why, you ask, is that great big police captain suing little old me? Well, I could tell you, but I'll let my little girl, my lovely sixteen year old daughter, Sarah, tell you."

Marco pushed line #1 on his console. "Hi, sweetheart. Are you there?"

"Yes Daddy, I'm here."

"Will you please tell my listeners why your dad is being sued?"

"Okay. Well, it's like this. Captain Krosel's son, Timmy, goes to the same school as me. During the time when my dad was under indictment for a crime he didn't commit, Timmy would harass me every day. He would follow me around, taunting me about how my father was a pervert and a degenerate. He would call him names like faggot and queer. Well, anyway, one day after school, he followed me to the bus stop making dirty remarks about my father all the way.

"Up to that point, I ignored him. I never acknowledged him in any way. This time, however, he did more than talk. He came up behind me and pulled my pony tail and slapped me on the butt. I don't know what got into me that day, but when he did that, I turned around without thinking and punched him in the face. I knew I must have done some damage, because after he ran away crying, holding his hands to his face, I saw little drops of blood on the sidewalk. This happened on a Wednesday. He didn't come back to school until the following Monday. That's when I found out I had broken his nose."

"Excuse me, sweetheart," Marco interrupted. "Exactly how long ago did this confrontation take place?"

"I'd say about three months ago."

"Ladies and gentleman and all you children out there, do you know why it took so long for Captain Krosel to file this lawsuit? No, of course you don't, so I'll tell you. Little Timmy was ashamed to tell his father that it was a girl who broke his nose, that's why. How do I know that? I know it because my lawyer called the captain's lawyer and got the story from him.

"How the truth eventually became known is not exactly clear, but somehow the captain found out it was my sweet little sixteen year old girl who beat up his big tough son, Timmy. So, now he wants to sue me. Maybe I ought to send my daughter over to his house so she can bust his nose, too. Folks, what's this country coming to when a person cannot defend her honor without her father getting sued?

"I say we can settle this dispute the old fashioned way, without lawyers and judges. I challenge the Krosels, Timmy and his father, anytime, except during air time, of course. Let's see if they're men enough to let their fists do the talking. Of course, you realize that I get to beat up little Timmy; my daughter, Sarah, can handle the captain."

Marco paused for a second or two.

"Thank you, Sarah, for telling us how you gave the little punk what he deserved."

"Thank you, Daddy."

"Ladies and gentlemen, the lines are open. We're taking bets on the big fight."

Marco took calls from many listeners. The one he hoped for, however, never came. *What happened*? Marco wondered. *Did I scare him off? Is he just a prankster after all? Will I ever hear from Robin Hood again?*

* * *

The following morning, Sarah was greeted like a celebrity by her school mates, with the exception of one.

"You little bitch!" Timmy Krosel said. "When my dad gets through with you and your old man, you won't have a penny left to your names."

As before, Sarah did her best to ignore Timmy, but by the end of the day, she was at her wits' end.

"Listen here, you little twit. You better get away from me or I'll kick your ass again." Sarah could not believe the words coming out of her mouth.

"Go ahead, try it," Little Krosel dared. "Last time you sucker punched me when I wasn't looking. I'd like to see you try it again."

Sarah clenched her fists and went after him. Timmy's eyes almost bulged out of his head when he saw her coming. He instinctively covered his face with his forearms and went into a crouch as she bore down on him.

Sarah was almost on top of her tormentor when she felt someone grab her around the waist and say, "Wait a minute. Can't you see he's a coward? It's no fun beating up on a coward."

Sarah struggled to see who was holding her. She twisted her head almost a hundred and eighty degrees. Then she felt herself being lifted off the floor and carried away. It was a boy. She knew that for sure. He was strong and his arms felt good around her. The young man put Sarah down and faced her. Timmy could still be heard hurling insults, but he was not following her.

"You already beat him up once. Everybody in school knows

it. After yesterday, everybody in town knows it. You don't have anything to prove," the boy said, glancing over his shoulder, keeping an eye out for Timmy.

Suddenly, Sarah didn't even know what the boy was talking about. The near collision with Timmy Krosel, along with everything else, had been forgotten. All she could remember was the young man's arms around her and how it made her feel.

"Hey, you okay?" the boy asked, noticing the strange look in Sarah's eyes.

"What? I mean yeah, sure, I'm alright." Sarah stammered. She couldn't take her eyes off him. He was at least six feet tall. Her focus switched back and forth from his large expressive green eyes to his full, sensuous mouth. He had the reddest lips she had ever seen on a boy. He broke out in a brilliant smile. She took in every characteristic of his face. Noting everything from his smooth, dark complexion to his small narrow nose.

"Aren't you Ricardo Kelly?" she asked.

"Yeah, that's me. My friends call me Ricky."

"I'm Sarah Fischer."

"No need to introduce yourself. Everybody knows who you are."

For the first time in her life, someone other than her father made Sarah feel special. She had never placed much value on being a celebrity's daughter and never flaunted it. As a matter of fact, when people would ask what her father did, she would say he was a contractor. After all he *was* a contractor. When Ricky said everyone knew who she was, she knew it had nothing to do with her father. She had broken the nose of the biggest bully in school and had become a celebrity in her own rite.

"Could I buy you a Coke?" Ricky asked, still wondering about the strange look in Sarah's eyes.

"Where do you want to go?"

"If it's not too cold for you, we can walk down to Division Street, or if you like, we can drive to the West Side for some Italian lemonade."

"You have a car?" Sarah asked excitedly.

"Well, yeah."

"What kind?"

"A BMW."

"A new one?"

"It's three years old. It used to be my mom's. She gave it to me when my father bought her a new one."

"Is your father rich?"

"I guess you could say that. I know you won't hold it against me, because your father must be rich, too."

"Oh, no. My father could never be on Lifestyles of the Rich and Famous, because he qualifies in only one category. He's famous, that's for sure, but he's not rich."

"That makes us kind of even. My father is rich, but he's not famous."

Ricky put his arm around Sarah's shoulders. "Shall we go?" he asked.

Without even realizing it, Sarah snuggled up closer to him; as she did, he tightened his hold on her. "Yeah, let's go," Sarah said. "But I'll have to call my dad and let him know I'll be later than usual."

"That's okay. I have a phone in my car."

The school provided no parking for it's students. Being located in the Gold Coast district of Chicago, one of the most affluent neighborhoods in the country, property was definitely at a premium. Students who drove to school often had to park two or three blocks away. Sarah didn't mind the walk; Ricky's arm felt wonderful around her. She felt warm and secure. She was beginning to understand what it felt like to be a woman, and she liked it.

"Is it true that you're half Jewish and half Italian?"

"Actually, my father's father was German and happened to be of the Jewish faith. My grandmother was Italian and, of course, Catholic. My grandfather was never very religious so he didn't object to my grandmother raising my dad in her faith. Actually he's really not Jewish at all. He just uses that as part of his *schtick*, if you know what I mean.

"Now my mother, on the other hand, was one hundred percent Polish on both sides of her family and a very strict Catholic. When you throw in all the ingredients and boil it down, you end up with me, a true American, as my dad says. Half Polish, one quarter Italian and one quarter German. A Roman Catholic with ties to the Jewish faith. My dad calls me a crazy, mixed-up kid. How about you, how did you end up with a name like Ricardo Kelly?"

"Except for the religion part, our stories are similar. My mother is Puerto Rican and my father is Irish."

"I don't see the similarity," Sarah said.

"Don't you see? We're both crazy, mixed-up kids," Ricky said with a laugh. "You're a Jew-Wop and I'm an Spic-Mick."

Sarah could not remember laughing so hard with anyone except her dad, who made her laugh all the time. The young man, that she knew only as someone who attended the same school as she did, suddenly seemed like an old friend, someone she could relax with, have fun with. It was a new experience. Sarah thought she knew all about boys, but this was different. She didn't exactly know how to describe or interpret the feelings inside her, but she knew someone who would, and she couldn't wait to tell her.

CHAPTER 15

"Two more of your enemies will be eliminated; perhaps then you'll understand who your real friend is and who deserves your loyalty."

DONNA MICHAELS HAD become a very familiar face around the Fischer household, and a welcome one at that. Sarah had become very fond of Donna and felt comfortable confiding in her. Marco, of course, was grateful to Donna for filling a void in his daughter's life, not to mention the one in his. Sarah's discovery of her new feelings was being revealed to Donna in the privacy of her bedroom. Marco was in the kitchen, setting the table for dinner. The phone rang. By the sound of the ring, Sarah knew it was the lobby calling.

"What are you guys doing in there? Come on, the pizza's on the way up."

Donna and Sarah came bouncing into the kitchen like two school girls. "I can understand Sarah acting silly, she's a teenager, but you are a grown woman," Marco said, pointing his finger at Donna.

"We're not acting silly," Donna said, holding back her laughter. "We're discussing some very important business."

"Like what?" Marco said, stuffing a piece of pizza into his mouth.

"Sorry, it's strictly female. No men allowed," Donna said, bursting out in another fit of laughter.

Marco looked at Sarah. "Is this how you treat your old man, the one who's taken care of you all these years?"

"Sorry, Dad, but we girls have to stick together."

Marco felt good inside, seeing Sarah and Donna together, acting almost like mother and daughter.

Later that evening, Marco and Donna sat on the couch enjoying the view of Lake Michigan. They watched the waves as they gently rolled in and out, back and forth. Marco, who had his arm around Donna, would occasionally pull her close and kiss her temple or cheek. Sarah was in her room watching TV.

"So, what's the big secret?" Marco asked.

"I promised I wouldn't tell," Donna said.

"Uh, oh. It's a boy, right?"

"Shhh," Donna said. "She'll hear you."

Marco went back to gazing out at the lake. Suddenly, he saw a reflection in the glass, it was Sarah. Marco instantly knew something was wrong.

"Hey. What's wrong with you?" Marco asked, as he and Donna both turned to face Sarah.

"It's horrible," Sarah said, her voice quivering.

"What is it?" Donna asked, rushing to her side.

"Timmy's father, Captain Krosel—he's dead."

"What?" Marco cried out. "How do you know?"

"It was just on the television. There was a special news report."

"Don't tell me," Marco said, bringing his hands up to his face. "Was he shot with an arrow?"

"Yes, he was."

* * *

The following morning, Marco called Chris Musso.

"Don't worry about it, Marco. I agree it would be reasonable for the police to consider you a suspect, but they need evidence. Evidence putting you at the scene, or at least in the vicinity. Without some kind of evidence, they can't take any action against you."

"Okay, Chris, I won't worry about it."

"Not to change the subject, but I talked to Mike Nicoletti the other day. He tells me you and he have been working together on trying to identify that Robin Hood character. Be careful. If your suspicions are correct and your plan backfires, you may end up his next victim."

"You're not the first one who's warned me of that possibility."

"Stick with Mike," Chris said. "Don't make any moves without him and you'll cut your chances of making a fatal mistake."

Marco felt a little better after speaking to Chris, but not much. A lot of craziness had taken place over the last few months, and Marco had a feeling there was more to come.

* * *

That afternoon, Marco's phones at the studio were on fire again.

"The murderer listens to your show, that's for sure," one caller insisted.

"So far, everyone who got it deserved it," another caller added. "We ought to elect him mayor."

Marco heard from his regular caller, Steve. "I was wrong. Elvis doesn't have anything to do with these killings. The arrows are coming from outer space; they're being shot from UFOs."

"Thank you, Steve, for another one of your priceless contributions to Marco's Morgue." Marco looked down at his console. "Let's see, how about line two?" Pushing the button, he said,. "Welcome to Marco's Morgue. What is your name, caller?"

The voice was unmistakable.

"This is Robin Hood."

"Haven't heard from you in a while," Marco said, trying to sound casual.

"There hasn't been any reason to call until today."

"Your reason being the murder of Captain Krosel?"

"Murder? You mean execution, don't you? Krosel was a high ranking officer in one of the most corrupt precincts in the city. Dope, prostitution, gambling—you name it and it flourished in his district. Why? Because guys like Krosel provide a safe environment for unlawful activities and get rich in the process. What about the scandal involving four of his officers about a year ago?

"Two drug dealers testified that the officers beat them half to death. Not because they were breaking the law, but because they neglected to pay the protection money when Krosel's bag man made his rounds. What happened to those cops? Nothing. In the end, the Police Department claimed it couldn't come up with any evidence to back up the charges of the victims. They claimed the beatings came as a result of the suspect's own actions while resisting arrest."

"You seem to know an awful lot about Krosel and the other three victims . . . excuse me, I mean the executed."

"I make it my business to know who my enemies are."

"Have you been a victim of police brutality?"

"One doesn't have to do physical harm to me in order to be my enemy. A public servant who steals from you or abuses you directly does the same to me indirectly. If I stand by and allow him to hurt you, in effect, I'm allowing him to hurt me."

"Do you think the executioner is really doing a public service by ridding us of these people?" Marco asked.

"Absolutely."

"Do you think there will be more of these executions?"

"Well . . . of course, there's no way for me to know for sure, but if I had to guess, I would say yes."

"Would you hazard a guess as to who you think might be next?"

"I have a feeling you'll know soon enough."

CLICK.

Shit. Marco thought. *I almost had him. He almost admitted it. Maybe next time I can keep him talking longer.*

*   *   *

After the show, Marco went back to his office. He wasn't surprised to find Mike Nicoletti waiting.

"Sorry, Mike, I blew it."

"You did great, Marco," Mike disagreed. "You are too impatient. You have to bait this guy, then reel him in slowly, very slowly. So far, you're doing a great job."

"You really think so?"

"Just keep doing what you've been doing."

"You almost had him," Tony said, coming through the door.

"Don't you know how to knock?" Marco kidded.

Tony stopped in his tracks and turned around to look back at the way he came in. "What knock? The door was wide open." Tony threw an audio tape in Mike's direction. "Tonight's Robin Hood call," he said, as he watched Mike snatch it out of mid air. "Any leads yet?"

"Not yet," Mike said. "But, we're getting close. As you said, Marco almost had him tonight. It's only a matter of time. He'll make a mistake, and that's when we nab him."

"If he makes a mistake, he gets nabbed, and that's fine. If we make a mistake, somebody gets killed, and that's not so fine," Marco said.

"Listen, Marco," Mike said. "We are not responsible for this guy's actions. What he does, he does on his own. We have nothing to do with it. By blaming ourselves, we lose focus. We shift our attention away from what we're supposed to be doing. That's a mistake. Robin Hood must remain the center of our attention. We must keep him in the cross hairs. *He's* the target of our investigation, not ourselves."

"I'm sorry, Mike. We're very fortunate to have you working with us on this. Your approach is the correct one, the professional one. I hope you'll continue to be patient with us amateurs."

* * *

Richard Testa paced the floor of his living room. His wife Gloria was seated on the couch; she was crying.

"Please, Richard, you're fighting a war you can't win. McLaughlin's testimony alone will convict you, not to mention the three cops and the prostitute."

"But the whole thing was McLaughlin's idea. He's the one who ordered the cops to set up Fischer in the first place."

"You should have known better, Richard," Gloria said in a soft, defeated tone. "You have dealt with these people most of your life. You've witnessed them stab each other in the back a million times. How could you think they wouldn't do it to you? Please, Richard, change your plea. Offer your full cooperation. I'm sure the judge will be merciful if you do. Why go to trial and put yourself through all that grief and humiliation? What about the expense? Think about us, me and the children. We're already broke. Where would you get the money if you had to hire a lawyer and go to trial? You haven't had a pay check since you were arrested. Please think of your family. All we have left is the house. If you insist on going to trial, we won't even have that."

"You want me to become one of them?" Testa asked his sobbing wife.

"Face it, Richard, you *are* one of them. You conspired to convict an innocent man of a crime he didn't commit."

"How could I refuse? I owe everything I have to my political sponsors."

"You mean everything you *had*. All you have now is the possibility of spending the next twenty years in jail. You owe them that, too."

Richard Testa knew his wife was right. It was time to begin thinking of his family. They still had a future, even if he didn't.

"Okay. You win, I'll do it. I'll call my lawyer and tell him I want to cop a plea."

Testa went into his den, which was just off the living room. His wife let out a long sigh and leaned back on the couch, feeling exhausted and relieved at the same time. She closed her eyes and thanked God for answering her prayers. Suddenly, she was startled by the sound of breaking glass.

"Richard?" she called out. What was that?"

Gloria got up from the couch.

"Richard, did you hear me?" She asked, raising her voice. "Richard!" she screamed, as she ran toward the den.

CHAPTER 16

"Why do you continue to go against me? Why do you pretend not to understand what I am doing? Why do you refuse to recognize my accomplishments? Why do you insist on making excuses for those who tried to destroy you? WHY, WHY, WHY? You are trying my patience. Soon, I will no longer be able to make excuses for you."

MARCO, SARAH AND Donna stood in front of the TV in Sarah's bedroom. The image of Richard Testa's wife, Gloria, and her words were the glue holding their eyes fastened to the screen.

"Did you hear that?" Marco asked. "He was about to spill the beans."

"I don't understand, Dad. Spill the beans about what? McLaughlin already made a deal to expose the conspiracy and name all the participants."

"That's true, but Testa was about to name names and give information concerning other matters," Donna said. "What they did to your father was only the tip of the iceberg."

"Well, we'll never know now," Marco said. "Our friend Robin Hood acted a little too soon this time. If he had waited one more day before shooting an arrow through Testa's neck, he would have realized much of his goal. There's no telling how many scum bag politicians and cops would have been compromised by Testa's testimony."

"You have to point that out to him the next time he calls," Sarah said. "Maybe you can make him angry, angry enough to make him say something incriminating."

"Let's get Mike on the phone and see if he has any ideas on how we can go about doing just that," Marco said, as he headed for the kitchen.

* * *

The next day, Marco started his program as usual, taking calls for the first half hour, then reserving the segment between three-thirty and four o'clock for Robin Hood. At three thirty-seven line one lit up.

"Could this be Robin Hood?" Marco said. "Welcome to Marco's Morgue."

Marco recognized the strange hissing quality of the caller's voice. He knew it was Robin Hood.

"Marco, you're getting soft-hearted. I heard you say at the start of your show that you felt sorry for Testa's wife and kids."

"That's right, I do," Marco said. "They had nothing to do with his actions."

"Maybe his kids didn't, but his wife had to know how corrupt her husband was. Did you see the house Testa lived in? How could he afford a house like that in one of Chicago's most exclusive suburbs on the salary of an Assistant States Attorney? The phone in his den, the one he was calling on when he got it, it was gold plated. Need I say any more?"

"Look, you don't have to convince me that he was a slime ball. I know that better than anybody. I just said I felt sorry for his wife and kids."

There was no response.

"Hello," Marco said. "Hello, are you there?"

CLICK.

"Damn it!" Marco said. "He's gone."

After the show, Marco met Tony and Mike in his office. Holding an audio tape in his hand, Tony said. "This is the shortest Robin Hood tape yet. I doubt if it has any value. Here it is anyway."

Tony Ruskin handed the tape to Mike.

Mike took it from his hand with a big smile on his face. "It may be the shortest, but it is the most valuable."

"What do you mean?" Marco asked, startled.

"I mean he finally made the mistake we've been waiting for, when he mentioned the phone."

"The phone?" Tony asked. "The phone was mentioned in all the news reports."

"Yes, it was," Mike said, smiling broadly. "But, the police have witheld one very vital piece of information, and the media has cooperated in not revealing it in their reports."

"Okay, I give up," Marco said. "What is it?"

"The room Testa was in when he bought it. At no time has it been revealed that he was in his den." Nicoletti held the tape up. "On this tape, you'll hear him mention 'the phone in his den.' How did he know the phone was in his den?"

"That's right," Marco said, remembering the incriminating statement.

"Now what do we do?" Tony asked anxiously.

"We begin to set our trap," Mike said. "I hope we can snare him before he kills anyone else."

Nocoletti got up and started for the door. As he reached for the knob, a knock came from the opposite side. He opened the door. "Hey, what are you guys doing here?" he asked.

Two men stood in the doorway, holding their ID cards and detective badges in their hands.

"We're here to see Mr. Marco Fischer," one of them said.

"I'm Marco Fischer," Marco said, as he stood and offered his hand.

"Detective Robert Demos," the taller of the two said, as he accepted Marco's hand. "My partner, Detective Peter Calahan," he continued. "Mr. Fischer, we're here to ask you to accompany us to police haedquarters at 11th and State. You are not under arrest at this time and you may never be, however, our superiors would like to ask you some questions. We would appreciate your cooperation."

"Is this in regards to the recent murder of Richard Testa?" Marco asked.

"I'm not at liberty to say what it regards," Demos said.

"Then I'm sorry, I can't cooperate with your request."

"Mr. Fischer, I'm warning you . . ."

"Wait a minute," Mike Nicoletti broke in.

"Mike, you're retired now, you have no authority in this matter," Calahan shouted.

"Look, just hear me out," Mike pleaded.

"Okay, Mike, I'll listen to what you have to say," Demos said.

"If you think Marco has information regarding the murders, you're right."

"That clinches it," Calahan growled. "Let's arrest him now and take him downtown."

"Wait a minute!" Mike shouted again, holding the tape over his head. "This is it, but we didn't have it until just a few minutes ago. As long as you're here, we'll play it for you now."

Marco removed a small portable tape player from his desk drawer. Taking the tape from Mike he inserted it into the device and pressed the play button. Like Mike, the two detectives recognized the caller's mistake immediately.

CHAPTER 17

"My patience has run out. You have betrayed me for the last time."

SARAH AND RICKY had become almost inseparable. Sarah had accepted the fact that, for the first time, she was in love. Ricky was in love, too, but he tried to hide it. Not from Sarah, but from his friends, who constantly badgered him about how he prefered Sarah's company over theirs. Sarah knew about the teasing Ricky suffered everyday, and it made her love him even more. It had become a regular thing for Ricky to wait for Sarah outside her classroom door whenever possible. It had become something she looked forward to every day.

"Do you have to go home after school today?" Ricky asked, as she came hurrying out so as not to be late for her next class. "Do you want to go for a Coke or something?"

"Okay," Sarah said. "Meet you at the front entrance after my last class."

They always chose the front entrance as their regular meeting place after school because it was only crowded in the morning. When classes were over, the students left the building from the side exit. Sarah always knew where to find Ricky after school.

Ricky was sitting on the concrete stoop when Sarah came bouncing out of the door.

"Where do you want to go?" she asked.

Ricky didn't answer.

"Hey, did you hear me?"

"Sarah," Ricky said in a hushed voice. "Sit down."

"I thought we were going for a Coke."

"Sarah, sit down, please."

Sarah removed her backpack, which she had slung over her shoulder, and placed it on the cold concrete and sat on it. "What's the matter?" she asked.

"See that car over there?" he said, motioning toward a black Buick parked across the street about a quarter of a block south of the shool. "There's a man inside; he's been watching the entrance ever since I came out, and probably a long time before that."

"So maybe he's waiting for someone. Maybe he's someone's father or husband, or maybe your imagination is running away with you."

"Could be, but I got a funny feeling when I noticed him there."

"Come on, let's go," Sarah said.

"Okay, but I want to drive around the block and get a better look at this guy. Maybe we can get his license number, just in case."

"Okay, Sherlock," Sarah joked, as she took a pencil and notebook out of her backpack.

Sarah and Ricky walked two blocks to where he had parked his car that morning. He opened the passenger side door and said, "Hurry, get in. I want to see if that guy is still there."

Ricky slammed the door shut and ran around to the driver's side. As he pushed his key into the ignition switch, Sarah said, "You really are serious, aren't you?"

"I just want to see if he's still there, that's all."

Ricky pulled out of his space and headed north to the next corner. Turning left onto a one way street going west he turned left again at the next corner. He continued south for three blocks and turned left again. When he reached State Parkway, the street on which the school is located, he turned left again and slowly approached the spot where the Buick was parked.

"Shit, he's gone," Ricky spat. "I knew it."

"What do you mean, you knew it?" Sarah asked. "Do you think he was waiting for you?"

"I don't know. I just knew he'd be gone."

* * *

Daniel Castalano walked along the shore of the Chicago River between Dearborn and Clark Streets. During daylight hours, this area would be teaming with joggers, fishermen and office workers enjoying a leisurely outdoor lunch and tourists taking in the sights, but it was no longer daylight. The sun had set many hours earlier.

Daniel Castalano was a troubled man. He was in his fourth term as Cook County Collector, and for over twelve years, he had been successful in keeping his homosexuality a secret. Recent events, however, threatened to expose his true indentity and the fact that he had been embezzling from the taxpayers for years.

His live-in boyfriend had been arrested for driving under the influence. During the custodial search, three ounces of marijuana were found under the front seat of the car he was driving. The car was registered to Daniel Castalano. The boyfriend announced himself as a city worker hoping to receive a pass from the arresting officers. He even went so far as to offer them a bribe. To his shock and amazement, the cops refused and hauled him off to the police station.

The subsequent investigation revealed that, although the boyfriend was on the city payroll, no one at the collector's office had ever seen him on the job. This prompted an investigation of the office itself and its chief executive, Daniel Castalano. At that point, the Feds became involved and things got much worse. Federal auditors uncovered a two million dollar discrepancy in the collector's account of taxes paid by Cook County property owners. Daniel Castalano had been standing in front of the proverbial fan when the shit hit.

The thought of suicide weighed heavily on his mind. Suddenly, he was aware of a presence behind him. He turned. A man in a dark suit stood less than ten feet in front of him.

Daniel Castalano didn't cry out when the first arrow pierced his body. The next one rendered him helpless to do so.

* * *

Three days had gone by without a word from Robin Hood. All the concerned parties met in Jerry Kaplan's office: Kaplan, Marco, Tony, Mike, the two detectives and Chris Musso.

"I think he realized he screwed up. That's why he cut the call short," Marco said.

"You have to get him to call again," Detective Demos said.

"If Marco is right and Robin Hood knows he blew it, there's a good chance we may never hear from him again," Mike said.

"Right now, all we can do is wait," Kaplan said. "The trap is set if he calls again. We'll have a trace in a matter of seconds. Marco doesn't even have to keep him talking for a prolonged length of time."

There was a knock on Kaplan's office door.

"Yeah! We're busy in here," Kaplan yelled.

The door opened. It was Harry Silver from the news room. "It's important, Sir." he said, poking his head into the room.

"What is it?" Kaplan snapped impatiently.

Silver entered the room and quietly closed the door.

"Remember a guy named Castalano, Daniel Castalano?"

"You mean the Cook County Collector?" Marco asked. "How could anyone forget that goof ball? He's the guy who had his boyfriend on the payroll for sixty grand a year, but nobody ever saw him doing any work. He never even showed up at the office."

"Isn't he under indictment for ghost payrolling?" Tony said. "And isn't two million dollars he collected from the taxpayers still missing and unaccounted for?"

"He's the one," Silver said.

"Okay, so what?" Kaplan shouted.

"He's just been found floating in the Chicago River."

"Suicide?" Chris Musso asked.

"I don't think so," Silver said nervously. "He had a steel shaft in his groin and another in his left eye."

The two detectives got up and rushed out of the office, almost knocking Harry Silver down in the process.

"We don't have to worry about not hearing from Robin Hood any more. I'll bet he calls again today," Mike Nicoletti predicted. "I'm going home. I want to be alone for a while. Call me there if anything comes up."

"Will you be listening when I go on the air?" Marco asked.

"I'll be listening," Mike said, as he closed the door behind him.

Ten seconds later, the two detectives came back into the office.

"It's true," Calahan said. "We checked with headquarters."

"I go on the air in one hour," Marco said, getting up from his chair. "Mike thinks we're going to hear from Robin Hood today. Keep your finger on that button. Today might be the day we've been waiting for."

Marco went to his desk phone and called Donna at her office to see if she had any additional information.

"Sorry, we don't know any more than your people do," Donna said.

"If you get off before I go off the air, come here. If not, I'll see you at my place tonight. By the way, I've been thinking about telling you something."

"What's that?" Donna asked.

"I love you."

Marco waited to hear Donna's response; there was none. He pulled the phone away from his ear and looked at it, put it back to his ear and listened again. All he could hear was the dial tone. Marco dialed Donna's office number again.

"WNUZ," a voice answered.

"Ms. Michaels, please."

"Ah, I'm sorry, but Ms. Michaels just left. Would you care to leave a message?"

"No, that's all right." Marco hung up and scratched his head. *What the hell?* he thought.

Several minutes later, while working at his desk, Marco looked up when he heard a commotion in the outer office. He got up to see what was going on when his office door flew open.

"Donna," he said, startled by her entrance. She almost bowled him over as she threw her arms around his neck.

"Oh, Marco," she cried. "I love you, too. I've waited such a long time to hear you say those words." Donna was crying and kissing Marco all over his face.

"Donna, honey," Marco said, raising his arms to pull her's down. "Take it easy."

Exhausted and out of breath, Donna let herself drop like a rock into the leather chair in front of Marco's desk. She sat there trying to catch her breath.

"I had no idea you would react this way," Marco said, dropping to one knee.

"What did you expect? Do you think you can tell a girl you love her and for there to be any other kind of reaction?"

Marco stood up and pulled Donna to her feet. Taking her into his arms, he repeated the words, "I love you."

Donna burried her face in his chest and cried.

"Honey, I thought you'd be happy."

"I *am* happy," she said, crying even harder.

* * *

At three o'clock, Donna was sitting in the technician's booth with Tony. On the other side of the sound proof glass, Marco began his show.

"Good afternoon, ladies and gentlemen. And why aren't you children in school?"

The calls kept coming, hot and heavy, for three and a half hours. Then the hissing voice of Robin Hood brought everything to a screeching halt.

"Robin Hood. We haven't heard from you in a while."

"I wanted my next call to be timed perfectly so you would never forget it."

"Why is that?" Marco asked.

CLICK.

"Hello? Hello?"

The call was over.

"We'll be right back after these commercial messages," Marco said excitedly.

Marco yanked off his headset and rushed out of his studio into the adjoining studio, where the two detectives had set up their equipment.

"Did you get it?" Marco demanded.

Demos was writing something on a pad of paper. "We have an address and phone number."

Calahan had been on the phone since before Marco came barging into the room. Slamming the phone down, he said, "Come on, Bob, I have the address here, let's go. There's a car waiting downstairs." Demos threw the pad down, and the cops rushed out without saying another word to Marco.

Marco went back to his studio to finish the last twenty minutes of his program. After the show, Marco, Donna and Tony went back into the studio where the cops had been staked out.

"Look over there," Marco said pointing at the card table Demos had been standing at.

Donna got there first. "What am I looking for?"

"A small pad of paper," Marco said, as he caught up with her. "Here it is," he said, picking it up and turning on the small desk lamp on the table. Placing the pad under the light he read,

6213 West Torrence Avenue. Area code 773-555-9673, listed to M. Nicoletti. "Oh, no!" Marco cried out. "The son of a bitch was calling from Mike's house."

CHAPTER 18

"How do you like it, traitor? How do you like having to look over your shoulder everywhere you go? You know your time is coming, but you don't know exactly when; and you won't, until it happens."

CHRIS MUSSO AND his wife, Gail, stopped by Marco's place to join him and Donna in mourning the death of their mutual friend.

"I first met him way back, when he was a sergeant working out of the twelfth district," Chris reminisced. "A client of mine had been brutally beaten by a couple of greedy patrolmen who mistook him for a local drug dealer. After they realized their mistake, they proceeded to plant some dope on him and claimed he resisted arrest. Mike was as anxious to get rid of the cops as I was to help my client. Together, we were able to set up a situation were the cops could repeat their offense, only this time their victim was an undercover federal agent."

"Is that how he became a lieutenant?" Donna asked.

"Oh, no. Mike's part in that action was never known by the police department. As in the case with Marco, Mike always worked outside the department when exposing corruption. It was safer that way. I know he wasn't alone. I know he knew other cops who felt just as he did, but I never knew them."

"What a shame," Marco sighed. "A cop is someone we should be able to trust. Someone who, no matter what, will always be there to help you, to protect you. The truth is, not even a cop can trust the cops."

"There's something wrong in a society when the very elements that are supposed to be above reproach are the least trustworthy," Chris lamented. "It's no different in my profession. This is a nation built on laws, and lawyers are supposed to be the caretakers of the law. Instead, lawyers are the most maligned profession there is. Why? Greed, greed is the most corrupting thing there is, and it's not always greed for money. Sometimes it's power, but either way, it's greed that has destroyed the lives of many who have allowed it to consume them. Like hate and vengence, greed does the most harm to the one who is obsessed by it."

Everyone sat silently for a few seconds until Donna began to think out loud.

"A cop can't even trust the cops. Isn't that what you said, Marco?"

"What are you thinking, honey?"

"What if Robin Hood is a cop? A cop like Mike, but one who went over the edge and appointed himself judge, jury and executioner."

Marco looked up when he heard someone come in the front door.

"Hi, Dad. Hello, everybody," Sarah said. "I'm sorry to hear about Mr. Nicoletti. I liked him. He was a very nice man."

"Thanks, honey, he liked you, too," Marco said, as he got up and put his arm around his daughter to comfort her.

* * *

Later that evening, after Chris and Gail left and Sarah had gone to bed, Marco and Donna sat on the couch silently watching the waves on Lake Michigan.

"What do you think of my theory?" Donna asked, breaking the silence.

"What theory?"

"About Robin Hood being a cop."

"Oh, yeah," Marco said turning to face Donna. "We'll have to . . ." Marco stopped. Donna could see tears welling up in his eyes. "I was going to say we'll have to talk to Mike about that possibilty."

"I know," Donna said sadly. "It's hard to believe he's gone."

"We have to catch this guy, honey, but how are we going to do it without Mike?"

Suddenly, Marco jumped to his feet and stood before Donna.

"You're a genius," he shouted. "Of course he's a cop. How else could he have gotten to Mike? He *knew* Mike. The police said Mike must have let the killer into the house. There was no sign of forced entry, and Mike is the only victim who was not murdered with an arrow. He was shot with a gun. Of course Mike wouldn't let a guy carrying a cross bow into his house, but he'd let in a friend, or at least someone he knew."

"But why would he want to kill Mike?" Donna asked. "How could he know Mike was working with you?"

"The guy's a cop," Marco said, his mind racing. "He must have been watching me. He's probably seen Mike and me together. Maybe Mike even told him what we were doing. If he's another cop like Mike, Mike might have trusted him, not realizing he'd gone over the edge. Maybe that's why Mike wanted to go home and listen to the tapes alone. Maybe he heard something in the tapes. Maybe he heard something he recognized."

"Like his voice," Donna said excitedly.

"That's it," Marco said. "He knew it was only a matter of time before Mike recognized his voice."

"What do we do now?" Donna said. "Who do we go to with this?"

"I don't know." Marco said. "If he's a cop, we can't go to the police, that's for sure. I'll call Chris in the morning. I'll see if he has any ideas."

"Is there anyone else we can trust?" Donna asked.

"Only Tony," Marco said. "And you're not going home tonight. You're staying here from now on. I'm not taking any more chances. Robin Hood knows we're getting close to identifying him. I'm sorry, honey, but because of me, you might be in danger."

Marco turned and looked down the hallway leading to Sarah's bedroom.

"Sarah," Marco sighed.

"Oh, no Marco. Do you think he would try to hurt Sarah?"

"I wouldn't put anything past this bastard. He's capable of anything," Marco said, as he went to the hall closet and reached for a phone book.

"Who are you going to call?" Donna asked.

"I'm not calling anybody. I'm looking up the address of a gun shop. I'm buying a gun tomorrow and we're going to learn how to use it. All of us. You, me and Sarah."

* * *

The next morning, Marco called Chris and told him what he and Donna were thinking. Chris suggested they all meet at the station that evening at about ten o'clock.

* * *

"I agree," Chris said. "We can't go to the police, at least not now. In the meantime, however, you need protection."

"I went out today to buy a gun," Marco said disgustedly. "I couldn't get one because I don't have a FOID card."

"What's that?"" Donna asked.

"A firearm owners indentification card," Marco explained. "I filled out the form, but the guy at the gun shop said it might take a while to get it. I signed us up for lessons, anyway. By the time I get the card, you, me and Sarah will be expert shots."

"That's not the kind of protection I'm talking about," Chris said. "You need a bodyguard to be with you at all times until we can find someone in the police department we can trust."

"Do you really think we're all in danger?" Tony asked.

"I don't know, but we can't take any chances. Tony, do you live alone?"

"Well, my girlfriend moved in with me last week."

"I hate to have to tell you this, but that puts her in possible danger. Does she have family in town?"

"Yes, her mom and dad live out in the western suburbs."

"Tell her to move in with her parents until we get this situation under control. As far as you're concerned, be on the look out at all times. This goes for all of you. Don't drive to work anymore; take cabs. Don't let yourself get caught in a deserted parking lot or a dark street alone. Make the cab pick you up and drop you off in front of where you live or work. Never walk any further than you have to. Never open your door unless you know for sure who's on the other side. If you don't have a peep hole in your door, get one installed. Tony, of everyone here including me, you have the least to worry about, but be careful anyway. I'm going to call a friend of mine and ask him to help us."

"Who?" Marco asked.

Chris got up and started for the door, then stopped and turned to face his friends.

"Ralph Bianco," he said, as he walked out.

* * *

A full moon shone down on a cowering figure kneeling in the shadows of the Bianco brothers and their two companions. Ralph Bianco, a man in his late forties glared down on him.

"You brought a lot of heat on us, Freddie," he said, as he ran his fingers through his graying chestnut hair. "Me and my brother have Feds breathing down our necks, following us everywhere we go, because of you. It took us two hours to shake them tonight; for a while, I thought we'd miss our meeting with you. I hope you'll forgive us for keeping you waiting."

Freddie did not answer.

"Did you forget what happened to the last guy who talked to

the Feds?" Ralph looked to his right and smiled at his brother Billy, who was standing beside him. Then, without warning, he slammed his foot into Freddie's face, splattering blood and teeth in all directions. Freddie fell backward, stifling a painful cry by covering his bleeding mouth with his hands.

"Don't worry, Freddie, no one can hear you," Ralph said, as he kicked and stomped him again and again. He stopped only when he felt his brother's hand grasping his arm. Again, he turned toward him.

"Put him out of his misery, Ralph. Let's get out of here."

Billy Bianco, Ralph's younger brother had the same graying chestnut hair and a face almost identical to his older brother's. Ralph knew Billy never enjoyed violence or meting out punishment the same way he did. But Billy never shrank from violence when it was unavoidable, he accepted it as a necessary evil.

Grabbing Freddie by the hair, Ralph dragged him several feet to a hole in the desert floor.

Addio, Fredo were the last words Freddie would ever hear. Billy and his two most trusted lieutenants, Frank Spagnola and Tony Sansone, watched as Ralph removed a .9mm automatic, equipped with a silencer, from his coat pocket.

POP . . . POP . . . POP. The sound waves traveled for miles before finding something to bounce off of and by that time, the faint echo went unnoticed in the vast Nevada desert. Frank Spagnola turned and smiled at his companion as they shoveled sand into the hole.

"You know what Ralph always says," Frank said with a chuckle.

"Yeah" Tony said. "Three shots to the head does it every time."

* * *

Under the leadership of Ralph Bianco, with the help and advice of his brother, Billy, the Chicago Outfit prospered, not only financially, but in it's influence on organized crime throughout the country. Following the example of his predecessors, Albert DePaolo and his beloved teacher and mentor Giacomo "Jimmy A" Antonini, Ralph continued to build on the foundation they laid. One major building component Ralph was able to employ, that his predecessors were unable to, was education.

In the old days, success was dependent on muscle and violence. Only the lawyers who applied their talents and training to keeping their clients out of jail had the advantage of an education. The Bianco brothers, though uneducated themselves, realized that if they were going to continue the organization they inherited from the original "Big Al," Alphonse Capone, they would have to adapt to the world they now inhabited.

The young men they recruited had to be tough as always, but those who demonstrated an intellect and intelligence beyond the average were encouraged to educate themselves. Although gambling and other illegal vices would always be a major source of income for the Outfit, legitimate business was rapidly becoming a large part of the organization's profits. Coercion, threats and other methods of intimidation were still used in the infiltration of established enterprises, but not to the same degree as in days gone by.

Vast sums of money and trained businessmen were now the new tools used in expanding the interests of the Chicago Mob. Violence and murder, though occasionally necessary, were no longer the norm. The gangland slayings of Italian mobsters no longer dominated the headlines.

Bribery was still a favorite method for garnering favorable treatment from the authorities, but only at the highest levels. Greasing the palms of street cops was a thing of the past, for the most part. Albert DePaolo would be very proud of the young man he entrusted with his empire.

"Keep a low profile and stay out of the limelight," he had said, it was the most valuable advice he gave his young successor. Ralph followed that advice far beyond what Albert DePaolo ever dreamed.

The Chicago Outfit, for all intents and purposes, was no longer just an underground organization; it had actually blended into normal society.

CHAPTER 19

"Nicoletti couldn't protect you. What makes you think anyone can? Don't fret, my friend; it's not you I'm thinking about, right now. There is someone else I've been watching."

THE FAMILIAR FACE of Connie Bianco greeted Chris at the front door. Her firm slender body blocked the doorway just long enough to throw her arms around him and plant a loving kiss on his cheek. Her auburn hair, pulled back in a pony tail, made her look more like a teenager than a woman in her middle forties.

"Chris, it's so good to see you. How are Gail and the kids?" Connie Bianco looked as beautiful as ever. Chris and Connie had been friends for many years, since before she married Ralph. In some ways, she seemed even more beautiful than ever. Her marriage to Ralph was something that brought her great happiness, and it showed. Chris entered the sprawling River Forest mansion built by Albert DePaolo, the man who ruled the Chicago Outfit before turning over his throne to his sucessor, Ralph Bianco, the current Boss of Bosses.

"Come in Chris let me take your coat. Ralph's in his gym. I'll tell him you're here. He only arrived from Las Vegas a couple hours ago, but he's anxious to see you."

Ralph Bianco worked out every day; it was a habit he developed as a young man, while doing time in Statesville

Penitentiary. His daily regimen of strenuous exercise gave him a bull-like body with broad shoulders, a powerful chest and muscular arms. Though only five feet, nine niches tall, he was a majestic figure.

As Ralph entered the foyer, he removed his sweatshirt and used it to wipe the perspiration from his face. Scars, from the bullet wounds and subsequent surgery that saved his life after a failed assasination attempt years earlier, were still visible. He was almost fifty years old, but he acted like a man in his twenties.

"Chris," Ralph said, as he greeted his old friend. "Let's go in the kitchen. Connie just made some fresh coffee."

For the next hour, Chris brought Ralph up to date on what was happening.

"Marco Fischer," Ralph said. "You know, I've heard him on the radio; he's very entertaining. A little reckless, but he's fun to listen to. I heard about the jackpot he got himself into a while back. He's lucky he had you for his lawyer."

"He's a little crazy," Chris admitted. "But he's a good guy. His heart's in the right place, and he's an honorable man."

"That's good enough for me," Bianco said. "As matter of fact, I saw him in your office waiting room. It was a few days after he was arrested. I knew it was him because I'd seen his picture in the newspaper and because you had mentioned that he was coming in to see you that day."

"He recognized you, too," Chris said.

"Yes, I know. I could see it in his eyes. So, how can I help? Name it and it will be done."

"He's a decent guy, Ralph, and he's being threatened by a madman. The police can't really do anything to help at this point, and I'm helpless to provide what he needs."

"And what is that?" Ralph asked.

"Protection," Chris answered with a hopeful expression.

"Do you trust this man?"

"Yes."

Ralph reached for the telephone and dialed a number.

"Dominick? It's Ralph. Hold on, Chris has something he wants us to help him with." Ralph extended his arm motioning for Chris to take the phone. "Fill Dominick in on what you need."

* * *

Marco and Donna were at the kitchen table trying to figure out a reasonable explanation for why Donna slept in Marco's bed and not on the couch.

"Sarah's not a baby any more. We can tell her the truth," Donna insisted.

Marco was about to disagree when the phone rang. It was the doorman.

"Hello, Andy," Marco said.

"Mr. Fischer, there are four very large, very tough looking men down here who say they are friends of yours."

"Put one of them on the phone," Marco ordered.

"Is this Marco Fischer?" the voice asked. "Chris Musso sent us."

"Okay, let me talk to Andy again. I'll tell him to let you come up."

One minute later, there was a knock at the door.

"Come in, gentlemen. I'm Marco." Marco led the men into the kitchen. "This is my lady friend, Donna Michaels. I just made a fresh pot of coffee. Would you care for some?"

"Coffee would be fine," one of the men said.

Marco recognized the voice. It was the same man he'd spoken to on the phone. He was a fairly large man, about five foot eleven and very muscular. Marco estimated his age at somewhere around middle to late forties. At the ends of his short arms, two powerful looking hands hung at his sides. Marco didn't see any rings on his short round fingers, but a very expensive gold watch was visible on his right wrist when he extended his hand. There was something cat-like in the man's movements, but his eyes were his most impressive feature. His eyes were dark brown and piercing; they had an intensity the likes of which Marco had never seen before.

"My name is Dominick Cairo." The man said. Motioning toward the others, he said. "This is Larry Divizio."

Larry was an average height man in his middle forties with dark curly hair and a rather large nose and very thick glasses. He offered his hand. "How ya doin?" he said.

Dominick turned to a taller man about the same age as the others with sandy colored hair and a large square face and light complexion. "This is Howie Kendall."

Howie didn't say anything: he just nodded his head.

Dominick started to introduce the next man, but before he had a chance, the man extended his hand and said, "My name is Joe Saeli; my friends call me Joey."

Joey, though probably about the same age as the others, looked much younger. His skin was dark. He had brown eyes and his dark brown hair was cut very short, but not quite a crew cut. He stood about five foot ten, with broad shoulders and a small waist line. He was a powerful looking man, and yet there was a gentleness about him. Marco studied Joey's face. He had soft features, one might say he had a baby face, but that was not a suggestion Marco was about to make.

Dominick looked at Marco. "I understand you have a daughter who's still in school."

"That's right. She's getting ready for school now."

"Joey and Larry will stay with her. She'll never be alone. I don't want you to worry about your little girl; she'll be protected. Your lady, Miss Michaels, from now on she has two shadows. Howie will be with her at all times."

"And you," Dominick said, poking his finger in Marco's chest. "You are mine. I will be with you twenty-four hours a day. I hope your girlfriend isn't the jealous type."

"Hey, Dad, what's going on?" Sarah asked, coming into the kitchen, setting her backpack on the floor.

"These men are friends of Chris Musso's, honey. They're here to protect us. We each have full-time bodyguards. They'll be with us at all times, everywhere we go. I hope you don't mind, sweetheart."

"Mind. Why would I mind?" Sarah said grinning. "It's going to be fun. Which one is mine?"

"Well, actually, Joey and Larry will be your bodyguards," Dominick said.

"Wow, I get two?"

"It's only because we understand you're very special," Joey said, walking up to meet Sarah. "My name is Joey, and this is my friend Larry," he said, taking Larry by the arm and pulling him closer. "We'll try not to interfere with your activities or embarrass you with your friends, but please understand it's our job to protect you," Joey said, as he stroked Sarah's hair and patted her on the cheek.

"Will you be coming to class with me?"

"I don't think your teachers would like that," Larry said. "But we'll be close by. You might not see us, but we'll be watching."

"Cool," Sarah said.

* * *

At the studio that same day, Tony met Dominick as he escorted Marco into his office.

"Now I know how the president feels," Marco kidded. "By the way, has Chris called? I tried to reach him to say thanks, but he wasn't in."

"He called a few minutes ago. You'll get a chance to thank him after your show. He's coming here this afternoon."

Marco turned to Dominick. "Tony and I have to go to work now. You can wait here in my office, or if you like, you can sit in the studio, but you'll have to be quiet."

"I'll wait here," Dominick said.

* * *

After the show Marco found Chris seated at his desk when he and Tony entered the office. Chris and Dominick were reminiscing about the old days. Chris started to get up from Marco's chair.

"Sit down," Marco said, motioning with his left hand. "I've been sitting for four hours. By the way, Tony and I want to thank you for all you've done. We appreciate it, and so do Sarah and Donna."

"No problem," Chris said. "Mr. Bianco is a fan of yours."

Chris looked around the room as he opened his briefcase.

"Let's get down to business. I made some notes last night. I listed some facts as I know them. I wrote them down as they came to mind, not in any particular order. I'll go down the list. When I'm finished I'd like to hear your comments." Chris took a yellow legal pad from his briefcase and continued.

"Number one, we know the killer listens to your show."

"Number two, except for Casper, the murders didn't start until after your trial."

"Number three, we know the caller who calls himself Robin Hood is the same caller who called himself anonymous before the murders."

"Number four, the murderer is obviously an expert archer using a mechcanical type crossbow as his weapon."

"Number five, all his victims were killed with at least one arrow, except for Mike."

"Number six, again, except for Mike Nicoletti, all his victims were enemies of the people, to be sure. Victims two, three, four and five, however, were direct enemies of Marco's."

"Number seven, I believe it to be a fact that Mike Nicoletti knew his killer and unsuspectingly allowed his killer to enter his home."

"Number eight, the bullet removed from Mike's body was a .38 caliber, most likely fired from a Smith and Wesson snub nose revolver."

"Excuse me, Chris," Marco interrupted. "Where did you get that information?"

"I have a friend in the coroner's office."

"Number nine," Chris continued, "a .38 caliber Smith and Wesson snub nose revolver is missing from the evidence room at police headquarters."

"What?" Marco and Tony yelled at the same time.

"That's right," Chris smiled. "Through Ralph Bianco, I was able to contact an old friend." Chris looked at Dominick. "You know who he is, Dom. He used to be the Commander of the Twentieth Pricinct. He's retired now, but he still has a lot of clout. It was through his efforts that we found out about the missing gun. Tests made on the gun, however, are still in police files. A comparison of the bullet that killed Mike will be made to bullets already tested. If they match, we know for sure that Robin Hood is a cop."

"If he is a cop, that would explain why the police have not been able to find any physical evidence at any of the murder scenes. An experienced cop would know exactly how and what to do to cover himself," Marco said, pounding his fist in his palm.

"When will we know for sure?" Tony asked.

"We should know in a couple days."

"Mike was right, this guy is smart, and very shrewd, I might add. He's called the show many times and ripped the police to pieces. He sounded like the biggest cop hater in town, and all the while, he's one himself," Tony said shaking his head. "He sure had me fooled."

"He had us all fooled, until he mistakenly blurted out that he knew Testa was killed in his den," Marco said. "Then he made a bigger mistake, he killed Mike. Stealing the weapon from the evidence room was the biggest mistake of all. Before that, we only suspected he was a cop. Now we know for sure."

"But how does that help us?" Tony asked.

"Simple," Chris said. "Now we can focus all our attention in one area—the cops. We know he's desperate; he proved that when he killed Mike. Desperate people make mistakes. He's already made a couple big ones; he'll make more."

* * *

Donna and Sarah were preparing dinner when Marco and Dominick returned home. Joey and Larry were assisting.

"I've never cooked for so many people before," Sarah said, as she stirred a giant pot of spaghetti sauce. "Joey and Larry have been very helpful."

Joey and Larry looked up from their chore of rolling meatballs in their bare hands. Sarah caught their eyes.

"Well, I guess it's the other way around," Sarah confessed. "Donna and I have been helping them."

"Gee, I should have invited Tony for dinner," Marco said, looking around the kitchen. "Not so much to eat, but to help clean up. What a mess."

"We were planning on letting you clean up," Donna said with a laugh.

* * *

The next day, Ricky, who had been absent from school the day before, caught up with Sarah as she hurried to her next class.

"Hey, who were the two guys I saw you with this morning?"

"Oh, you mean those two rugged, yet handsome looking rouges?" Sarah asked with her nose in the air.

"Come on, cut the crap. You know who I mean."

"Those men, for your information, are my bodyguards."

"Bodyguards?"

"Shhh, not so loud. I'll explain at lunch, see you then," Sarah gave Ricky a quick kiss on the cheek and ran off, leaving him standing in the middle of the corridor looking slightly bewildered.

*   *   *

In the lunchroom later that afternoon, Sarah explained the presence of her bodyguards and why they were necessary. Ricky decided to tell Sarah about something he'd been keeping to himself for the last couple weeks.

"Remember that guy we saw in the Buick about two weeks ago?"

"What guy?"

"You know the guy who I thought looked suspicious?"

"Oh, yeah. I remember."

"Well, I've seen him since then, a few more times. I didn't say anything because I didn't want you to think I was being paranoid. After what you just told me, however, maybe . . ."

"Two weeks ago, I didn't know what I know now." Sarah interrupted. "If you see him again, we better tell Joey and Larry, just to be safe."

"Are they really gangsters?" Ricky whispered.

"They don't seem like gangsters, they're nice to me, but my dad told me they are two of Ralph Bianco's closest associates."

"Ralph Bianco? I've seen him on the news. He's the top boss of the syndicate, isn't he?"

"That's what they say."

"Your father knows him?"

"Chris Musso, my father's lawyer, knows him. My father never met him. I have to get to my next class. See you out front after school." Sarah got up and ran off.

Wow, Ricky thought. *This is getting exciting.*

*   *   *

As usual, Ricky was sitting on the concrete stoop outside the main entrance waiting for Sarah after school. He was trying not to stare at something that had caught his eye. Suddenly, he realized someone was standing over him. He slowly turned his head to see who it was.

"Excuse me, young man, I didn't mean to startle you. My name is Joe; I'm a friend of Sarah's."

"Oh, hi," Ricky said nervously. "My name is Ricky Kelly."

Sitting down next to Ricky, Joey put his arm around him and said, "I understand you're a friend of Sarah's."

"Yes, I am," Ricky said, avoiding Joey's eyes.

"You wouldn't want to see anything happen to Sarah would you?" Joey asked, tightening his arm around Ricky's neck, forcing his head to turn and face him.

"No, I wouldn't," Ricky said, now looking into Joey's deep brown eyes.

"Then you would tell me if you ever saw anything strange or unusal happening around her. Right?"

"You mean like if somebody was watching her? Like that guy in the Buick over there?"

"Who, where?" Joey said, looking around.

"That guy over there," Ricky said, as he motioned with his chin toward a black Buick as it pulled out of it's parking spot and went speeding by.

Joey jumped up and ran toward the curb, waving for Larry, who was standing close by, to follow him. Crouching down behind the parked cars, Joey and Larry ran along the curb to the end of the block, exposing themselves only when they reached the corner.

"Fuck," Joey cursed. "He's too far away. I can't see his license plate. Don't forget that Buick," he said to Larry. "If you see it again, get the license number; that might be our man."

* * *

Later that evening, Marco, Sarah and Donna, surrounded by their bodyguards, sat around the dining room table.

"Do you think he saw you?" Marco asked Joey, as he poured another round of coffee.

"I don't think so," Joey said, as he turned his cup around in his hands. "The kid . . . what's his name? . . . Ricky watched the guy until he was out of sight. He said he never turned his head."

"If we could only trust the police," Donna lamented. "What about the retired commander Chris knows? He helped us trace the gun used to kill Mike."

"We need someone who's inside. Someone who doesn't attract attention with his presence. Someone who can use the resources and Police Department records without arousing suspicion," Marco said with his elbows on the table, his chin resting in his palms. Suddenly, Marco's head jerked up.

"Walter!" he shouted, causing everyone to look up. "Walter Jerkowski," he said, looking at Sarah then at Donna. "Remember him? He helped me when I was being held at the Thirty-fifth Precinct. He was the only cop who showed me any respect or compassion."

Marco went to the hall closet and took the phone book from the shelf. "Jerkowski, Jerkowski," he said out loud, as his fingers walked through the pages. "Shit, he's not listed."

"Can't we call him at the station?" Donna suggested.

"I'd rather not, but we will if we have to."

Marco lifted his head in thought and sqeezed his eyes shut. Putting his right hand to his face, he said. "Gionetti, Gioninni, Garafolo . . . Garabaldi. That's it!" Marco opened the phone book again. "Garabaldi, G-A-R-A, here it is. Garabaldi, Stewart, Stewart, . . . here it is, Stewart Garabaldi," Marco yelled as he ran to the phone.

* * *

Walter Jerkowski had been a policeman for ninteen years. Unlike many men of his profession, his reason for joining the force was that he had a genuine desire to serve his community. Unlike many, he was accepted for his qualifications, not because he had political clout. After four years in the army, two of them in Viet Nam, he came back home and decided to put his military training and disipline to work in a field where they would be best utilized.

He beleived that his experience would make him a valuable asset. One drawback existed however;he was honest. His unwillingness to betray his oath to serve and protect made him an oddball among his fellow officers. Consequently, after almost twenty years, he never rose above the rank of patrolman. Not that his abilities weren't recognized. His superiors never hesitated to trust him to handle assignments too complicated or sensitive for those of higher rank.

His honor, and integrity, made it impossible for him to be accepted into the brotherhood. Walter never liked his circumstances, but learned to accept them. Now, with only one more year to serve before he qualified for full retirement benefits, it hardly bothered him at all.

Walter sat at his kitchen table, watching Mary, his wife of seventeen years, prepare his favorite dish, homemade pierogies and tripe.

"Now, don't eat too fast, sweetie," Mary said, as she set his plate in front of him.

Just then the phone rang.

"Why is it, every time you sit down to eat, the phone rings?" Mary said, disgustedly. Smoothing Walter's hair with her hand, she said, "I'll get it honey. Whoever it is can call back later."

Walter, not paying much attention to anything except the wonderful taste sensations going on inside his mouth, never heard a word his wife said to the caller. A minute later, Mary placed a small piece of paper beside his plate.

"Who was it?" he asked with a mouth full.

"Some guy named Mickey or Mikey or Morrie." Picking up the paper, she reviewed her note. "Oh, yes. Marco," she said. "Marco Fischer."

Walter dropped his fork into the plate, splashing juice and food particles all over his clean shirt. "Who?" he shouted incredulously.

*   *   *

Marco had barely hung up the phone when it rang.

"Hello."

"Marco? Marco Fischer?"

"Yes. Walter, is that you? I just called you ten seconds ago."

Marco briefly explained the reason for his call and how he'd gotten his number from Stewart Garabaldi. "Can you come to my place tonight?" Marco pleaded. "I'd come to you, but I don't think that would be a good idea, with my bodyguards and all."

"I'm on midnights this month. I could be there by ten o'clock. Is that okay?"

"That's fine. See you then."

Marco stood behind Dominick, who was seated at the head of the table. Placing his hands on the back of Dominick's chair, he said, "He'll be here at ten o'clock. We better decide exactly what we want him to do."

*   *   *

At nine fifty-five, Marco was on the phone again. "Send him up, Andy. Walter's here," Marco said, as he returned to the table.

Marco greeted Walter at the door and thanked him again for his help during his ordeal. He escorted him to the dining room table. After properly introducing Walter to his companions, Marco offered him a seat. Walter Jerkowski looked around at the strangest mixture of allies he had ever seen.

"How can I help?" Walter asked.

"The gun that killed Mike Nicoletti is the same gun that was stolen from the police evidence room; therefore, we're convinced that Mike's killer is a cop," Marco said. "Right now, that's all we're sure of. Joey, please tell Walter what happened today."

Joey spent the next several minutes relating the events that took place earlier that day at Sarah's school.

"I can tell you for sure it's a black Buick Roadmaster. It looked brand new, but it could be last year's model. We need to find out if a cop drives that kind of car."

"Wow," Walter said slapping his face with both hands. "There are thousands of cops on the Chicago Police Department; I wouldn't know where to start."

"You can begin at headquarters. We have reason to believe he works out of 11th and State. Does that narrow it down enough for you?"

"Quite a bit," Walter said relieved.

"Can you work on that without arousing any suspicion?" Marco asked.

"If you're not in a big hurry, I can."

"We're in a hurry, but your safety has to be our main concern at this point," Donna said, smiling warmly at Walter.

Walter got up and looked at his watch. "I have to check in before eleven-thirty; I better get going. I'll be in touch."

When Marco returned to the table after showing Walter to the door, he asked, "What do you think?"

Everyone looked around at everyone else without saying a word.

CHAPTER 20

"Before I take you, I'll take those around you, one at a time."

ALMOST TWO WEEKS had gone by since Mike Nicoletti's murder. Except for the incident involving the black Buick, there had been no reason for concern.

* * *

Tony Ruskin opened Marco's office door and leaned inside. "Five minutes," he said.

Marco, who was on the phone with Donna, ackowledged him by holding his hand up and nodding. "Gotta go, honey. I'll see you at home tonight; love you, too."

Five minutes and thirty seconds later, Marco was on the air.

"Good afternoon, ladies and gentlemen and children of all ages. Welcome to Marco's Morgue. Where's Robin Hood? Has anyone out there seen or heard from our old friend Robin Hood? Mr. Robin Hood, if you're out there, I'd like to hear from you." Marco looked down at his console. Pushing the button for line one, he said, "Caller, what's on your mind tonight?"

"What ever happened to Robin Hood? I'd like to hear from him, too."

"So would I," Marco said. "I haven't heard from him in quite a while. Line two, what do you have to say?"

"What ever happened to Elvis?"

"Haven't heard from him, either," Marco said with a laugh. "Line three."

Caller after caller wanted to know what happened to Robin Hood. About an hour into the show, Marco heard Tony's voice come through his headphones.

"Line one," he heard Tony say. He looked up; he could see Tony through the glass. The expression on his face was enough to tell him; Robin Hood was on the line.

"Is it you?" Marco asked, excitedly. "Is this Robin Hood?"

"Don't bother tracing this call, it won't do you any good."

"What makes you think we want to trace your call?"

"Don't insult me, Marco. You've already dissapointed me."

"How did I do that?"

"Don't play games with me. I know what you've been trying to do. I thought you were my friend, but you're just like all the rest of them. You can't be trusted. You betrayed me. You know what happens to people who betray me."

"What happens?" Marco asked, trying to keep Robin Hood talking.

"Maybe you should ask your friend, Mike Nicoletti. He betrayed me."

CLICK. The call was over.

After the show Marco, Tony and Dominick listened to the tape of Robin Hood's call. Dominick realized then that his job had just gotten a lot more difficult.

"This guy doesn't care any more," Dominick said.

"What do you mean, he does't care anymore?" Tony asked.

"He doesn't care. He admitted he's the killer this afternoon. We can expect this guy to get even more brazen and daring after today."

"You mean he doesn't care if he gets caught?" Marco asked.

"I don't think he thinks about getting caught. He's gotten away with several murders and nobody has a clue who he is," Dominick said.

"But isn't that what we want him to do, to become over-confident?" Tony asked.

"Yes, that's exactly what we want him to do, but we have to worry about how many more people get killed before he makes his fatal mistake. In a way, this guy Robin Hood reminds me of someone I once knew, a guy named Ceasar Ducato. He hated Ralph Bianco. When he found out Ralph was going to succeed Jimmy Antonini as boss of the Near North side, he went goofy. He thought the job should have gone to him, but the decision had been made to put Ralph in charge."

Dominick took a pack of cigarettes from his shirt pocket and tapped one out.

"The job was Ralph's, and there was nothing Ceasar could do about it. Ralph's appointment had been sanctioned by Albert DePaolo himself. Ceasar knew that, but he tried to have Ralph assassinated anyway. Even if he had succeeded, the job still wouldn't have gone to him, but he didn't care. He was a driven man. Driven by hatred and revenge."

"I seem to remember that name," Marco said. "This happened about ten years ago, didn't it? What ever happened to him, anyway?"

"I don't know. I heard they found him in a motel room with his throat cut," Dominick said, snapping his gold lighter, pulling the flame into his cigarette.

Silence filled the room for several seconds. Everyone's eyes focused on Dominick. Dominick was staring at something, then he broke his gaze and looked up. "Let's get going," he said. "The sooner we get you home, the better. It's much easier guarding you on the 23rd floor of a highrise than in a public building like this. I'll go down and get the car. I'll call you when I'm out front, then you can come down."

On the ride home, Marco kidded Tony. "How do you like being chauffeured to and from work everyday?"

"It'll be too bad when we catch this guy. I'll have to go back to driving myself."

* * *

After a hard day's work,Tony Ruskin's girlfriend, Karen Hovey, let herself into Tony's apartment. She removed her coat and draped it over one of the living room chairs and kicked off her shoes. She didn't feel like driving all the way out to the western suburbs where her parents lived. She was dead tired; tonight she would stay at Tony's place. *One of these days I'm going to tell my boss to go fuck himself*, she thought, as she let herself fall backward onto the couch. "If I could only get Tony to propose," she said out loud.

Karen closed her eyes. Her whole body ached from the tension she had endured all day. She began to fall into a restful nap when she heard a knock on the door.

"Yes, who is it?" she groaned.

"Police," a muffled voice answered.

"Is there something wrong?" she asked, becoming a bit concerned. She picked her head up off the seat cushion.

"No Miss, just checking on Mr. Ruskin. Is he home from work yet?"

"Not yet, but I expect him soon." Karen still held her head up off the cushion. Her neck muscles began to cramp, so she let her head fall back down.

"Mind if I wait?"

Karen rolled her head from side to side.

"He told me not to let anyone in if he wasn't home."

The voice from beyond the door didn't respond, so Karen closed her eyes again thinking the cop decided to leave, but then she heard him again.

"I understand, Miss, that you don't want to let me in . . . Is there a safety chain on the door?"

Karen lifted her head off the cushion again. "Yes," she answered with a questioning kind of intonation in her voice.

"Could I bother you for a couple of aspirins. I have a splitting headache. If you don't mind, you could attach the chain and leave it attached while you hand them to me."

Karen let her head fall again and stared bleary-eyed at the ceiling. "Okay, okay," she said. Karen grudgingly got up from her slumber and groped her way to the bathroom. With squinted eyes, she searched the medicine cabinet for a bottle of aspirins. She heard a squeaking sound. She stood still for a moment, then resumed her search.

After struggling with the child-proof cap, she shook three pills from a bottle. Still half asleep, she turned and started for the door, dragging her feet as she sort of waddled down the hall.

"Thank you," a voice said loud and clear. It was the same voice that had come from behind the door, but it was no longer muffled.

Karen looked up, startled. "How did you get in here?" she said, trying to shake herself to full conciousness. "What is that?" she screamed.

CHAPTER 21

"You can delay your punishment, but you will never escape it."

MARCO PULLED UP in front of Tony's apartment building and double parked. Dominick, who was riding shotgun, turned and handed him his .9mm automatic. "I'm going to take Tony upstairs. Keep the doors locked and your eyes open. I'll be right back. If anyone approaches the car, just take off. Use the gun only if it's absolutely necessary." Dominick turned to Tony, who was sitting in the back seat. "Let's go, I'll escort you to your apartment."

"That's okay," Tony insisted.

"Nothing doing, I'm going with you."

Dominick got out of the car and looked around before opening the back door.

"Come on, Tony, let's go. Marco, don't forget what I told you."

Dominick and Tony disappeared into the main entrance of the building. Marco leaned back and closed his eyes for what seemed like just a few seconds.

"Marco, Marco!"

"What? What?" Marco said, jerking his head up.

Excited and out of breath, Dominick was pulling on the door handle. Marco fingered the power door locks.

Dominick yanked the door open and said, "Get out of here, go home. I'll call you there in half an hour. Go! Go!"

"What's going on? What's wrong?" Marco asked as Dominick slammed the door shut and ran back toward the entrance.

* * *

Sarah, Joey and Larry were in the kitchen playing five card draw when Marco came crashing through the front door. "Has Dominick called yet?"

"No. Why?" Joey asked, looking up from his hand.

"Something happened at Tony's place, but he didn't say what. He said he'd call here in half an hour." Marco looked at his watch. "That was twenty-five minutes ago."

"Sit down, take my place. Your little girl is a card sharp; she's just about cleaned me out." Joey said disgustedly.

"Oooh, whats the matter, big bad bodyguard can't take it?" Sarah taunted as she collected her pot after another winning hand.

"Watch out, little girl, I have friends on the vice squad. Gambling is against the law, you know," Joey said, wagging his finger in Sarah's face.

Marco wasn't paying much attention to the kidding going on around the kitchen table. Pacing the floor in the living room, his thoughts were on Tony and Dominick.

"I can't wait any longer," Marco said, as he headed for the kitchen phone. "I'm calling Tony's place."

Before Marco could complete his mission, the phone began to ring. Before it could ring a second time, he yanked it out of it's cradle.

"Hello," he yelled.

"Bad news," Dominick said.

"Is Tony all right?" Marco asked, bracing himself.

"Tony's fine. It's his girlfriend Karen. The son of a bitch got to her. He picked the lock and caught her coming out of the bathroom. She must have had a headache or something."

"Why do you say that?"

"There were three aspirins lying on the floor next to her body. The light in the bathroom was on and the medicine cabinet was open."

"Did she suffer?" Marco asked, sadly.

"I don't think so. The arrow went right through her heart and through the bedroom door at the end of the hall. We found it stuck in the wall inside the room. He couldn't have been more than a couple of feet away when he let her have it."

"Why? Why Karen?" Marco sighed. "She had nothing to do with this."

"I'm afraid he's sending you a message, Marco. We're going to have to watch Sarah and Donna even closer. If I were you, I'd think about taking Sarah out of school until we grab this guy."

"I'll talk to her about that. It may be something I'll have to do."

"I don't think Tony should be left alone tonight," Dominick said. "If you don't mind, I'll bring him back to your place with me."

"Good idea. I'll tell Larry to pick you up and bring you back."

Donna, who had been in criminal court all day, covering the trial of the three cops who had arrested Marco, had gotten back to her office just as the reports of Karen's murder were coming in. Upon hearing the news, she became faint and almost collapsed. After several minutes of trying to revive Donna, Howie told one of her colleagues to call 911. The paramedics were sucessful in bringing her around and recommended she go home and rest. One of her coworkers called Marco and notified him of Donna's condition. "Please, ask Howie to bring her here to my place as soon as posible," Marco pleaded, his voice devulging the exhaustion that was overcoming him.

*　　*　　*

"You were right," Marco said, looking at Dominick respectfully. "You said he would become more daring and brazen. It seems like a month since you said that, but it was only a few hours ago."

Marco, Dominick, Joey and Larry sat around the dining room table, trying to come up with a strategy that could turn the tide and enable them to put Robin Hood on the defensive.

"There's a thin line between daring and recklessness. We have to find a way to get him to cross it," Larry said.

"You have to antagonize him, make him mad," Joey said, holding his head in both hands, elbows on the table.

"You mean me?" Marco said, wide-eyed.

"Yeah, you. You know how to rile people, you've been doing it for years."

"That's it, Joey my boy," Dominick said. "Right now, he feels invincable, he thinks he's a big hero. Especially with all those people asking for him on Marco's show today."

Joey looked at his watch. "It's one o'clock in the morning, boys, I'm tired. I say we get a few hours sleep and start fresh in the morning."

"Okay," Dominick said. "Me and Larry and Howie will stay here tonight. Joey, you take tomorrow off."

"Wait a minute," Joey interrupted. "What about Sarah? Who's going to be with *her*?"

"She's not going to school, at least not for the next few days," Marco said. "I don't want you to worry about Sarah, Joey; please get some rest. I have a feeling we're all going to need it." Marco hesitated for a second or two. "Joey, I want you to know I'm really grateful for what you've been doing, how you've been watching over my little girl."

"I never had any kids of my own," Joey said. "But if I did, I'd want them to be just like Sarah. She's a great kid."

"Thanks, Joey. I think you know how she feels about you."

*　*　*

By twelve o'clock noon, the dining room table was surrounded again. Joey was taking the day off and Donna was still under the influence of the sedatives she had taken the night before. Everyone else was there, including Chris Musso and Jerry Kaplan, who had stopped by to tell Tony he would personally cover for him until he felt like working again.

"I'm sorry about Karen," Jerry said. "I want you to take as much time as you need before coming back to work."

"Thanks, Jerry," Tony said, still a little groggy.

Jerry got up and said, "I have to get back to the office. See you at show time, Marco. So long, everybody. I'll let myself out."

"Tony, would you mind if we went over the scene again? If you don't want to talk about it, I'll understand," Chris said, as he removed a pencil and notebook from his inside pocket.

"It's okay, Chris. Talking about it may help me get it out of my system. Where do you want me to start?"

Tony, with some help from Dominick, related what he had found the night before.

"You say he jimmied the lock to get in?" Chris asked Dominick.

"He must have. There was no sign of forced entry. It looked as though she was in the bathroom getting aspirins from the medicine cabinet. She must have heard something and went to see what it was because the cabinet was still open and the light was on."

"So you think he picked the lock and walked in on her while she was in the bathroom?"

"That's what it looked like," Tony said, sadly.

"But how did he know?" Chris wondered out loud. "How did he know she'd be in the bathroom and not somewhere else?"

"It was probably Tony he was after. Karen wasn't even supposed to be there. It could be that he didn't expect anyone to be there. Maybe his plan was to hide somewhere in Tony's apartment and wait for him to come home. Karen was probably in the wrong place at the wrong time." Dominick shook his head. "It doesn't really make any difference now. We'll probably never know what really happened."

* * *

Jerry Kaplan hadn't produced an on-air radio show for years, but after an hour or so, his long forgotten instincts began to return. Once he felt comfortable and confident, he gave Marco the thumbs up sign, signaling his readiness to put their plan into motion. Marco returned the sign and began.

"Last night, one of my closest friends was murdered. Her name was Karen Hovey, and she was a wonderful girl. She also happened to be the girlfriend of another very close friend, Mr. Tony Ruskin. Those of you who are regular listeners know that Tony is my producer and has been for over six years. I want you all to be aware that the murderer is someone we all know, Robin Hood. That's right, you heard me, I said Robin Hood.

"If you'll remember, he made a kind of veiled threat when he called yesterday afternoon. He accused me of betraying him. Although I didn't admit it yesterday, I'm admitting it now. It's true, I've been trying to bring Robin Hood out into the open so I could trap him and turn him over to the authorities. Are you listening, Mr. Robin Hood? Did you hear me, you scum bag? I know you're responsible for the murders of Richard Casper, Partick Grogan, Sean O'Bannion, Daniel Castalano, Richard Testa, Police Captain Robert Krosel and two very good friends of mine, Karen Hovey and Mike Nicoletti.

"Until yesterday, your murderous rampage, by *your* warped standards, may have been justified. But when you snuffed out Karen's life, you proved yourself to be just another bloodthirsty killer. A madman, a vicious animal who must be stopped. Your days are numbered, slime ball. You'll make a mistake, and when you do, I'll be on you like flies on you know what. If you want me, come and get me. Unless you don't have the nerve. Unless it's just defenseless women you go after now. What is it, you worthless piece of dog excrement, are you a man or a louse?"

CHAPTER 22

"You'll be sorry for the things you said to me. I'll make you pay for those words. Your time is coming, but first I'll make your friends pay. Then I'll go after someone closer to you, someone very, very close."

CHRIS MUSSO LISTENED intently as Marco taunted and belittled Robin Hood. He'd left his office earlier than usual to listen to Marco's program in the privacy of his den. His wife was busy in the kitchen preparing dinner. For the first time in months, Chris had come home early enough to enjoy a home cooked meal. Having dinner at home with his wife, instead of in a restaurant, had become a luxury.

Since moving to one of the most exclusive highrise condos on Chicago's Magnificent Mile, Gail missed her duties as wife and mother, caring for her family in their suburban home. With the kids off to college and her husband spending more and more time at the office, she was beginning to feel useless and unneeded.

During one of the commercial breaks, Chris got up from his recliner to get himself a beer. When he opened the small refrigerator under the bar, however, he discovered it was empty.

"*Shit,*" he said to himself. *I hope there's more in the kitchen refrigerator.*

Chris rushed out of his den, not wanting to miss any of Marco's show. On his way to the kitchen, he heard the door bell chime.

"I'll get it," Gail said, passing him in the living room.

Who the hell could that be? Chris wondered. Gail pressed the talk button on the intercom.

"Thank God," Chris said, as he opened the refrigerator door and reached inside to grab a bottle. Hurryng back to his den, he passed Gail again. "Who was that?" he asked over his shoulder.

"It's one of the building maintainence men; he needs an asiprin."

"Oh," Chris said not really paying much attention to Gail's answer.

Suddenly, Gail's words registered in his brain. Chris stopped dead in his tracks, almost losing his traction on the smooth hardwood floor. "Gail, call 911! Call the police!" he yelled.

Chris reached the door just as it was being pushed open. Slamming his body into the door, he forced it shut. What he saw next made him thank God again, only this time it was for his life.

* * *

"It's Chris," Dominick said, holding the phone in his outstretched arm. "Wait till you hear this."

Marco took the phone and put it to his ear.

"Chris, what's happening?"

"The mother fucker almost got me," Chris said, laughing excitedly. "I know what happened with Karen. She didn't have a headache. He told her *he* had a headache and asked her to get him an aspirin. That's how he got her away from the door."

"How do you know?"

"Because he just tried the same trick on Gail. Thank God I was home."

"But you said he almost got you?"

"I slammed the door shut just as he was coming in. The next thing I know, an arrow comes flying through the door. He must have accidently pulled the trigger when I knocked him off balance."

"Oh God," Marco said. "First Karen, now you and Gail . . . it's all my fault."

"Don't start blaming yourself. This is not your fault."

"I can't help it; I feel responsible."

"The important thing is that we got him to make another mistake, and that is something you *are* responsible for. Keep the pressure on the way you did today; you're getting to him."

* * *

For the next several days, Marco was relentless in his humiliation of Robin Hood, but there was no response of any kind. Once more, Marco began to wonder if he would ever hear from him again. Once again, his concern was unfounded. The morning newspaper headlines made it glaringly clear:

ALDERMAN EDWARDS FOUND SLAIN.

Marco sat at his kitchen table reading the account of Robin Hood's latest execution. Donna and her bodyguard, Howie, had already left for her office after hearing about the murder on the early morning TV news reports.

Sarah was in the shower. Marco had reluctantly allowed her to return to school, even though her teachers had offered to assist her in keeping up with her studies while she remained at home. Sarah, however, didn't like the idea of being trapped in her room for an undetermined length of time, but most of all she didn't like being separated from Ricky. Though Marco suspected Sarah had a boyfriend, he and Ricky had never met. Sarah wanted the occasion of their meeting to be under more pleasant circumstances than those prevailing lately.

* * *

Alderman Andre Edwards had been convicted of bribery in a case where he was taking payoffs from contractors for bid fixing and using his influence in circumventing city codes and ordinances. Though captured on video and audio tape during meetings where he was recorded soliciting, accepting and, on one occasion, demanding money, Edwards continued to maintain his innocence. He claimed he had been entrapped by federal agents and investigators.

His constituents, in true Chicago fashion, came to his aid and defended him, claiming racisim and prejudice. The conviction, however, was just and withstood all attempts by his defense lawyers to have it overturned. Finally, after two years of appeals and legal manuvering, Edwards was scheduled to begin serving his jail term. Ever since his arrest, and all during the trial, Edwards swore he would never be locked up. Even after his appeals were denied, he still maintained he would remain free.

He was right about one thing; he would never go to jail. The day before he was supposed to surrender to the federal marshalls, Edwards was in his garage vaccuuming the carpet of his Merecdes sedan. He had decided to allow his wife to put it up for sale. The cash would help her survive while he was serving his sentence.

Someone entered his garage through the open overhead door. Edwards crawled out of the back seat with the vaccuum hose still in his hand.

"You're early. I'm not scheduled to leave till tomorrow," he said disgustedly, as he stood up straight to confront the man in uniform. "What's that? . . . What the fuck do you think you're doing?" . . . Edwards said, as Robin Hood took aim.

CLICK . . . WHOOSH.

The first shot ripped into Edwards' neck, driving him backward, pinning him to the wall. Edwards gasped, he tried to cry out, but he couldn't. Only a gurgling sound escaped his mouth as his throat filled with blood and the muscles in his neck tightened. Another shot pierced his chest, driving itself through his heart and severing his spinal cord.

Edwards was surely dead, but the killer wasn't satisfied. He loaded another arrow into his weapon and took aim again. He sent a third shot into Edwards' bowed head. The arrow entered the center of his skull and came out at the nape of his neck. Robin Hood turned and nonchalantly walked away, leaving Edwards nailed to his garage wall like a cardboard Halloween poster.

The blood soaked steel points could be seen protruding through the aluminum siding on the outside of the garage. It was these arrow heads that attracted the attention of his next door neighbor as he mowed the lawn in his back yard.

* * *

"In order for those arrows to penetrate the body and the garage wall the way they did, our friend Mr. Robin Hood had to be within just a few feet of Edwards," Dominick said, sipping his coffee thoughtfully. "He was probably in uniform. Being approached by a cop was nothing new for Edwards. Once he was close enough and got the first shot off, he just took his time and placed the others just where he wanted them. I think he enjoys mutilating his victims."

"He's one sick son-of-a bitch," Joey said, getting up to pour himself another cup of coffee.

"Do you think he killed Edwards just to make a point with me?" Marco asked sheepishly.

"No," Dominick said confidently. "I'm sure he's been planning this execution for a long time. If anything, he put off killing Edwards to devote more time toward getting you."

"I'm ready," Sarah said, removing her coat from the closet. "Come on, Joey; Larry's waiting for us in the car."

Joey got up and guzzled what coffee remained in his cup. He looked down at Marco and put his hand on his shoulder. "Don't worry," he said. "I'm going to talk to the principal and ask her if one of us could stay in the building and keep Sarah in our sights at all times."

"Thanks, Joey," Marco said, not looking up.

* * *

"That will not be a problem," the principal, Mrs. Floa Bart, said, pinning visitor's badges on Joey's and Larry's lapels. "We here at the Astor School want to do all we can to help you in protecting Ms. Fischer from any possible harm."

Mrs. Bart was a large, black woman. She was at least six feet tall and weighed well over two hundred pounds, with huge breasts that hung down to her waistline. She was large, but she was kind and gentle.

"Thank you, Mam," Joey said, finding it impossible not to feel like a school boy himself. "We'll try to be as inconspicuous as possible."

"That's quite all right, Joseph. I want you and Lawrence to feel free to do whatever you feel is necessary to perform your duty to the best of your ability, which I am sure is considerable."

Joey and Larry left Mrs. Bart's office feeling proud and confident.

* * *

Tony returned to work the day after Karen's funeral. Though obviously depressed, he did his job as always. He and Marco sat in Marco's office preparing for the show which was scheduled to begin in about two and a half hours.

"I couldn't face her parents," Tony said.

"I know the feeling," Marco said, trying to comfort Tony. "I've been there, but if anyone should feel guilty, it's me."

"No, Marco," Tony said through clenched teeth. "It's that fucking no good bastard, that son-of-a bitch Robin Hood asshole," Tony said, slamming his fist into the palm of his hand. "We have to nail that mother fucker. I want to kill him myself."

Marco was shocked. He'd never seen Tony that way. He'd never even heard him use that kind of language. He never knew Tony was capable of expressing such anger.

"We'll get him," Marco assured. "I'd like to kill him myself, too, but we'll have to be satisfied watching him squirm as they administer the lethal injection."

"That's too good for him," Tony cried. "Animals like him should be tortured to death, slowly and agonizingly."

Marco reached into his desk drawer and removed a bottle of brandy. As he poured a shot for each of them into styrofoam cups, he said, "Here, drink this, it'll calm you down."

Tony took the cup from Marco and gulped it's contents in one swallow.

"Watch Sarah and watch Donna, too." he said, as the brandy burned it's way through his esophagus. "He wants to get to you through them." Tony held his empty cup out; Marco filled it again. "He knows that if he hurts them, he hurts you."

Marco began to pace the floor behind his desk. "The car, the black Buick Joey saw at Sarah's school; it must have been him. He tried to kill Chris' wife Gail. We know he murdered Karen. Donna is the only one who he hasn't made an attempt against." Marco stopped pacing. He picked up the phone and dialed the number of WNUZ. He looked up at Tony. "Donna's next, I know it," he said, his eyes filled with rage.

"WNUZ," a voice said breathlessly.

"Donna Michaels, please."

"I'm sorry sir, but Ms. Michaels is not available at the moment."

"This is Marco Fischer. Can you tell me where she is or how to reach her?"

"Oh, yes, Mr. Fischer. I'm afraid there's been a terrible incident involving Ms. Michaels. She's been injured."

"Injured, what do you mean injured?"

* * *

Howie was in the E.R. waiting room when Marco came rushing through the doors. "Where is she?" he cried out.

Howie looked quizzically at Marco and pointed to the doors at the far end of the room on the other side of the reception area. "She's in the emergency room. Where's Dominick?"

"Is it serious? What the hell happened?"

"She'll live." Howie said with a curious smile on his face. "She only sprained her ankle. Where's Dominick?"

Marco turned his head to look directly at Howie. "Sprained her *ankle*?"

"Yeah. She tripped on a computer cable at the office. We thought it was broken at first, but the doctor said it was only a sprain. Where's Dominick?"

"That sissy in her office said there had been a terrible incident. I thought Robin Hood got to her. Oh shit," Marco said, slapping himself in the face. "Dominick was checking out the studio when I ran out."

"Hi, honey."

Marco turned at the sound of Donna's voice to see her being rolled out of the E.R. in a wheelchair.

"How did you find out what happened so soon? Did you call him?" She asked turning to Howie.

"No, he didn't call me. I called *you*. That fruitcake in your office scared the shit out of me."

"You mean Leslie? He tends to overreact. Hey, shouldn't you be at the studio? It's two thirty."

"I guess I'd better get back. That nitwit in your office could have told me it wasn't serious."

"Could it be that you were the one who overreacted?" Donna asked wagging her finger at Marco.

"Not under the circumstances."

"We can finish this discussion later. Let's get Donna home so she can relax," Howie said, pushing the wheel chair toward the exit.

Just then, the screeching of tires could be heard outside. Seconds later, Dominick came flying through the doors, almost bowling everyone over. Unable to stop on the slippery tiled floor, Dominick twirled around the corridor in a kind of weird ballet.

"Don't ever do that again!" Dominick roared. "That message could have been a ploy to get you out of the building."

"I'm sorry," Marco said, truly ashamed and embarrassed. "I wasn't thinking. I lost my head when I heard Donna was in the hospital. I won't do it again. Thank God, Donna's alright."

"Let's get back to the station," Dominick said, just as his cell phone began ringing. "Yes," Dominick said, a little agitated. "Oh, hi Joey. What's up?"

* * *

About the time Marco was busting through the hospital doors, Joey, who was stationed outside the main entrance of the Astor School, was being approached by two plain clothes police officers.

"Excuse me, sir. Would you mind telling us what you're doing here?" one of the officers asked displaying his badge and I.D.

Joey, who didn't quite know how to react in a situation where he actually didn't have any reason to be evasive with the police, said, "I'm waiting for a friend."

"Is your friend a student at this school?" the detective asked.

"Yeah, she'll be coming out any minute."

"Can I see some identification?"

As Joey gingerly reached for his wallet, careful not to expose the .9mm automatic tucked in his waist band, Larry stepped out onto the concrete stoop.

"What's this all about?" he asked speaking to no one in particular.

"Who are you?" the other detective asked.

"My name is Larry Divizio. What's the problem?"

"We got a call about a suspicous person hanging around the school."

"If you go with Larry, he'll take you to the principal's office. She will vouch for our presence here," Joey said.

"Okay, but you're coming along," the detective ordered.

"Look, I have a job to do. I can't leave my post," Joey insisted.

"I said you're coming along," the cop said in a gruff tone.

Joey didn't want to make the situation any worse than it already was, so he joined Larry, and together they escorted the two detectives to Mrs. Bart's office.

* * *

"Excuse me Mam, I'm sergeant Mike Morse, and this is my partner Detective Felix Zarlingo."

Joey looked at Larry with a silly grin on his face mouthing the name, "ZARLINGO?"

"Gentlemen, I assure you that Joseph and Lawrence are on the grounds with my full knowledge and their presence is most welcome and greatly appreciated."

Just then a bell rang signaling the end of classes for the day.

"Well, the person who called claimed to be on staff here. I hope you understand we were obligated to investigate."

"I understand entirely, and I appreciate your attention and prompt response. However, as you can see, there is no need for concern. By chance, did the person who called give you his or her name?"

"Sorry ma'am we don't have that information," Sergeant Morse said.

"Well, if you come to find out, please let me know so I can prevent this from happening again."

"I'll see what I can do," Morse said, as he and Zarlingo walked out.

Joey and Larry waited for the cops to leave before thanking Mrs. Bart and hurriedly excused themselves. Joey looked at his watch and said, "We better get outside; Sarah's last class is over."

"Hurry along, boys, don't let me stand between you and your duty," Mrs. Bart said.

Joey and Larry rushed out of the office and down the corridor toward the main entrance. The halls were deserted. Joey sped up his pace almost to a run; Larry followed close behind. Joey slammed his body into the doors, forcing them to strain their hinges. He stumbled onto the stoop and jumped the steps onto the sidewalk. Looking from side to side, he told Larry to go back inside and look for Sarah. Running half way down the block in either direction, he checked the parked cars and gangways between buildings. Perspiration ran down his face as he searched in vain for the little girl he'd grown to love as if she were his own.

"Oh, no," he said out loud, as he saw Larry exit the building alone.

"I can't find her," Larry said, running to meet Joey.

Just then, a voice came from out of nowhere.

"Are you looking for Sarah Fischer?"

The bodyguards turned to see a young girl, one they'd seen Sarah with several times.

"Yes. Do you know where she is?" Larry said, grabbing the girl by her shoulders.

"I saw her and Ricky get into a car with a policeman a few minutes ago."

"A uniformed policeman?" Joey asked. "Was it a police car, you know, a squad car or was it a regular car?"

"It was a regular car, a black car, it looked like the same kind of car my father has."

"What kind of car does your father have?" Joey closed his eyes and grimaced.

"A Buick, a Buick Roadmaster."

"How long ago did this happen?" Larry asked.

"About two minutes before you came out of the building. Are Sarah and Ricky in some kind of trouble?"

"Why do you ask?" Larry asked knowing what the answer would be."Because they were handcuffed."

CHAPTER 23

"Now you will have to face me on my terms."

EVERYONE WAS GATHERED in Marco's apartment.

"We have to call the police," Marco said, trying to hide his emotions. "He's got my little girl. We need all the help we can get. Besides, it doesn't make any difference now."

"I'm sorry," Larry said sadly. "It was pretty clever of him to have the police detain us the way he did."

Joey was visibly shaken, pacing the living room floor, pounding his fist into the palm of his hand. "He won't hurt her. I know what he wants. He's using Sarah to get to you. He's going to call and suggest some kind of meeting."

Just then the phone rang. No one said a word. There was complete silence; every head turned toward the telephone. It rang again. Marco lifted the receiver.

"Hello," he said cautiously.

"Is this Marco? It's Walter, Walter Jerkowski."

"Oh, Walter, yes, this is Marco."

"I checked every cop who works out of headquarters. Nobody, not one cop drives a black Buick Roadmaster. I'm sorry. I'm sorry I couldn't have better news."

"That's okay, Walter. I know you did your best. I appreciate it. If you come across anything in the future that you think might help, no matter how insignificant, please call. The situation has just gotten worse, a lot worse. He kidnapped my daughter from school today. I'm desperate, Walter. He's a madman."

"I'll keep my eyes and ears open. I'll let you know if I see or hear anything."

Marco hung up the phone and let his arm drop to his side. With his head bowed, he walked over to the couch where Donna was sitting, her leg resting on the coffee table cushioned by a pillow. Every eye was on Marco. Not knowing what to say, everyone remained silent and almost motionless until the phone rang again.

"Hello," Marco said, picking up the receiver before it rang a second time.

"I have your little girl," the hissing voice said. "Took her right out from under your hoodlum bodyguards' noses. Still think you can outsmart Robin Hood? Still think you can betray me and get away with it?"

"Where's my daughter, you mother fucker? Where is she?" Marco shouted his voice filled with a hate and anger he'd never felt before.

"She's in a safe place."

"Don't hurt her, you son-of-a bitch. You can have me if that's what you want."

"That's exactly what I want."

"I'll meet you anywhere you say, just don't hurt my little girl."

"You're in no position to be telling me what to do," Robin Hood hissed. I'll call you when I'm ready. First I'll let you squirm a while."

CLICK.

Marco stood there seething, the phone still in his hand. His face twisted totally out of shape. With clenched teeth and flared nostrils, he slammed the receiver into the wall, leaving an impression of the ear and mouthpiece in the plasterboard.

* * *

Sarah sat on the cold concrete floor, her hands cuffed behind her, contemplating her next move. Reliving what had happened about an hour earlier.

* * *

Sarah and Ricky had walked out of the main entrance expecting to find Joey and Larry waiting.

"Where's Joey?" Sarah asked, searching for her protectors. "I don't see Larry, either."

"Excuse me, Miss Fischer."

Sarah and Ricky turned in unison to see a uniformed policeman standing behind them. He was an average looking man, brown eyes, brown hair topped by his policeman's cap. His only distinctive feature was his blue uniform; other than that he was average in every way.

"Your friends have been called away. I've been sent here by Chris Musso to escort you home. You know Mr. Musso, don't you?"

Sarah was a little concerned at first, but when she heard Chris' name she began to relax.

"Oh yes, I know Mr. Musso."

"Good," the policeman said with a pleasant smile. "I have a car waiting just around the corner; this way please," the cop said, motioning with his arm toward the side street north of the school.

"Is it okay if my friend walks with me?"

"By all means," the policeman said agreeably.

Sarah and Ricky began to walk hand in hand in the direction the cop had suggested. When they reached the corner, Ricky stopped suddenly, tightening his grip and yanking Sarah's arm.

"What?" Sarah said, turning to look at Ricky.

Before Ricky could say a word, before he could do anything to alert Sarah, he felt something stabbing him in the back.

"Do exactly as I say. Don't do anything stupid and you won't get hurt. What you feel in your back is a gun. Put your hands behind your back. Both of you. Now."

Sarah and Ricky did as they were told. Within seconds, they were handcuffed and being forced into the back seat of the black Buick.

"Get down on the floor and stay down."

Sarah and Ricky layed silently side by side in the space between the front and rear seats for what seemed like foreever. Then they felt a bump as the car made a sharp turn. They heard a whirring, grinding sound. Suddenly it was very dark. The noise stopped with a clang, then started up again, then stopped again. The rear car door opened, and one by one they were pulled out of the car. It was dark, but Sarah could tell they were in a garage.

"Let's go," the cop said. Grabbing each of them by the neck, he pushed them toward a door. The door opened into the kitchen of a small house. Sarah was struck immediately by the cleanliness of the room. The floor, the cabinets, the sink-everything seemed to sparkle, and there was a clean smell to the place. She was reminded of her mother. When she was a little girl, her mother always told her how important it was to have a clean and orderly house.

"This way," the cop said, opening another door, revealing a stairway leading to the basement. Reaching into the doorway, the policeman switched on the light.

"Get downstairs. Be careful. One step at a time."

They reached the bottom of the stairs and entered a neatly organized room. On one side stood a washer and dryer and a countertop with cabinets above and below; on the other side, a work bench and another countertop with a cabinet below. Above the work bench hung a pegboard with tools of all types hanging on hooks and brackets. The outline of every tool was traced on the pegboard to assure they were replaced in exactly the correct place.

"This way," the cop said again, leading the teenagers to a room that had been partitioned off from the rest of the basement.

"Stop," he said, pulling a heavy steel door open. One at a time, he shoved his prisoners into their cell. Tripping over the cop's foot, Ricky fell to the floor. Unable to break his fall because of his restraints, he hit the concrete hard, scraping his left elbow and knee.

"You jerk. You didn't have to push him," Sarah snarled. Looking up, she caught sight of the back of the man's neck as he walked out of the room. She saw a red blotch that sort of resembled a fox's head.

The door slammed shut. The captives heard the dead bolt churn as their jailer twisted his key in the lock. Ricky began moaning in pain.

"Shhh," Sarah said, kneeling beside him. "Listen," she whispered.

For several minutes, the hardwood floor squeaked above them, a voice was heard.

"He's talking to someone," Sarah said softly.

"He's not talking to anyone. He's talking to himself," Ricky responded.

They listened for a long time. The sound of the man's voice could be heard between pauses of silence as though he were speaking on the telephone. The squeaking, however continued.

"What's he saying?" Sarah asked.

"I don't know, but the sound of his voice is scary," Ricky answered. "What are we going to do?"

Sarah didn't answer. Her eyes were intense; she was in deep thought. Ricky sat beside her for a long time, watching the subtle changes in her expression.

"Sarah, what are we going to *do*?" Ricky repeated, nudging Sarah out of her contemplation, bringing her back to the present.

"Shhh," Sarah said. "*Listen*."

Sarah helped Ricky slowly and quietly rise to his feet. Foot steps could still be heard above them. They heard a door open and slam closed. Then they heard the automatic garage door opener grinding as it did it's job. A car engine started and the garage door opener repeated it's task in reverse. Suddenly it was totally quiet.

Sarah stooped down, bending her knees, forcing her cuffed hands downward. She pulled them under her buttocks, allowing herself to fall backward against the wall. She slid down to a sitting position. Pivoting on her rear-end, she rolled onto her back, lifting her legs straight up. Slowly and painfully, she pushed her hands up as she pulled her legs through her arms. As her feet and hands met, she forced her shoes off, letting them fall onto the floor. With a couple of final jerks, she yanked one foot at a time past her shackled wrists.

"Yes!" she whispered, springing to her feet, slipping her shoes back on.

Ricky looked at Sarah wide-eyed. There she stood, still handcuffed, but her hands were now in front of her.

"How did you do that? Ricky asked. "Are you double jointed or something?"

Sarah began walking around the cramped room, inspecting the walls, occasionally, tapping on them as she went along.

"What are you doing?" Ricky inquired.

"Shhh," Sarah said without turning away.

Seconds later, Sarah was startled into redirecting her attention when she heard a loud noise. She turned to see Ricky preparing to slam his body into the steel door again.

"Stop that," Sarah scolded. "You'll only hurt yourself."

"We have to do something," Ricky whined.

"That's a steel door with a steel jamb," Sarah said confidently. "He probably has it framed with double 2X4's and a double 2X6 header. You're wasting your time trying to knock it down." Sarah stopped and pointed her index finger into the air. "The walls, however, are just drywall, with single 2X4 studs centered sixteen inches apart."

"What?" Ricky said with a twisted facial expression.

"My dad used to be a builder. When I was a little girl, he used to take me on his job sites. I had my own tool box and everything. You know how I want to be in radio when I graduate college? Well, when I was little, I wanted to be a contractor like my dad. I never realized it, but I learned a lot about how things are built." Sarah said as she knocked on the walls with her fists. "Plasterboard," she shrugged. "Between the sheets are 2X4's. Whoever built this room did a hell of a job with the door, but the walls are a piece of cake."

"What are you talking about?" Ricky moaned.

"Watch this," Sarah said, lifting her right foot and slamming it into the wall, leaving a deep indentation.

Ricky watched, dumbfounded. Sarah repeated her assault several times, creating a hole about the size of a basketball. With her cuffed hands, she tore away at the fractured drywall until the hole was large enough to allow a person to crawl through. The outside layer of wall board was even easier to demolish. Within seconds, a gaping hole appeared between the studs.

"Come on," Sarah said, crawling through.

"Please don't tell anybody at school about this," Ricky begged, following close behind.

* * *

Marco drew his arm back, preparing to slam the phone into the wall again, when he heard Donna's voice.

"Please honey, punching holes in the wall won't solve anything."

Donna got up from the couch and hopped over to where Marco stood. Taking the phone from his hand, she returned it to it's cradle, then put her arm around his waist.

"Come on," she said softly. "Come sit next to me on the couch."

As they turned toward the living room, the phone rang again.

"I'll get it," Dominick said.

Although he moved quickly, he wasn't quick enough. In a flash, Marco turned around and grabbed the phone.

"Hello," he growled.

"Marco?"

Recognizing the voice, Marco controlled the anger he felt and said, "yes, Walter. How you doing?"

"I don't know if this helps, but it just occurred to me that the Superintendent's car is a Buick, a black Roadmaster," Walter said hesitantly.

"*What?*"

"The Superintendent's car is a black Roadmaster."

"No, no, excuse me, Walter, I heard what you said the first time. It's just that the thought that our man could be the Superintendent of Police was a bit shocking."

"I'm not suggesting that at all. It couldn't be him anyway, he's been out of town for the last three days. He's attending some kind of conference in Seattle."

"Then what are you suggesting?"

"I'm not suggesting anything. I'm just telling you that he drives a black Buick."

"Where's the car now?"

"I don't know."

"Can you find out?"

"I guess so."

"Okay, find out and let me know what you come up with . . . Oh, Walter, thanks again. It's obvious that you're devoting a lot of time to this."

"I hope it pays off." Walter said goodbye and disconnected.

Dominick sat patiently, waiting for Marco to get off the phone. "So what did he say?"

After telling Dominick what Walter had told him, Marco turned to rejoin Donna on the couch.

"Wait a minute," Dominick shouted. "The Superintendent doesn't drive the car. He has a driver. Call Jerkowski back. Find out who the driver is."

* * *

When Sarah and Ricky crept into the living room, they found the house dark and deserted. The shades were all drawn. Through the edges, however, daylight could still be seen.

"What are we going to do now?" Ricky whispered.

"Shhh," Sarah cautioned pulling a shade aside to peek through the window. "I don't exactly recognize the neighborhood, but that doesn't matter. Let's just get out of here."

Sarah rushed to the front door and unlocked it.

"Why don't we just call the police and let them come for us?" Ricky suggested.

"And what if Robin Hood comes back in the meantime and finds us here? What do we do then?"

"Robin Hood? Do you really think it's him? Do you really think he's Robin Hood?"

"Don't be stupid. Of course it's him," Sarah scolded, pulling the door open, slowly venturing out, motioning for Ricky to follow.

Sarah and Ricky came upon a gas station after walking about two blocks. The startled attendant, an Asian who didn't speak very much English, finally caught the drift of the situation and allowed the handcuffed teenagers to call the police from his office phone. Sarah had to make the call because Ricky hands were still cuffed behind him.

* * *

Marco broke down when he got the call from headquarters. With the phone still in his hand and his back against the wall, he allowed himself to slide down to the floor. There he sat, emotionally spent, unable to control his tears. He let the receiver go; it hung suspended by it's cord, making a cracking sound each time it hit the floor.

"Marco, Marco," Donna cried, hobbling over to him, grabbing the phone.

"Hello," She said urgently.

"Who is this?" a voice asked.

"This is Donna Michaels, Mr. Fischer's friend. Is Sarah allright?"

"She's fine, Ms. Michaels. We have her at police headquarters. Her friend, a young man named Ricky Kelly, is okay, too. What about Mr. Fischer; what happened to him?"

Donna looked down at Marco. He was sobbing with his face in his hands. Dominick crouched beside him, looking up at Donna with a puzzled expression. Donna covered the mouthpiece with her hand. "She's okay," she said, trying unsuccessfully to control her own tears.

* * *

After picking up Sarah and Ricky from 11th and State, Marco, Donna, Sarah and Dominick dropped Ricky off at home. After explaining to his parents what had happened, Marco humbly apologized.

"Well, to tell you the truth, Mr. Fischer, we had no idea that our son was in any danger," Mr. Kelly said. "He often stops for a Coke after school, especially since meeting your daughter Sarah." Ricky's dad looked at Sarah and smiled. "Based on what Ricky told us on the phone from the police station, we should be very grateful to Sarah. She's obviously quite a resourceful young lady and courageous, too."

Mrs. Kelly added, "You should be very proud of her."

Marco wrapped his arm around Sarah and pulled her close. "I am," he said. "I'm very proud of her."

"Well, anyway it's all over now," Mr. Kelly said. "It all turned out for the best. This is an experience my son will never forget."

"That's true," Marco said. "But, it's not over yet. We still have to find our friend Robin Hood. He's out there someplace, and somehow I think he's more dangerous now than ever. But at least we know who he is now, thanks to my friend Walter Jerkowski. It was his investigation that uncovered the fact that the Superentendant's chauffeured car was a black Buick Roadmaster. After that, it was easy to fit all the pieces of the puzzle together and identify his driver as Robin Hood, a man named Raymond Lis."

"Then it shouldn't be long before the police have him in custody," Mrs. Kelly said.

"That's a resonable assumption, and I'm sure he will eventually be caught, but I'm not so sure it will be any time too soon. He's very clever and cunning. So far, he's outsmarted me and the police." Marco tugged Sarah closer. "My little girl has been the only one to outsmart him."

"Perhaps we should put Sarah in charge of the investigation," Mr. Kelly said with an admiring smile.

Sarah smiled an embarassed smile and turned away shyly.

CHAPTER 24

"You got lucky, you son-of-a-bitch, but that's all it was, pure luck. I'll have to change my plans a little, but your day is coming. You just bought yourself a little more time, that's all you really accomplished, a little more time."

IN A TRAILER park off Route 72 in a far western suburb, a small three-room mobile home sat inconspicously among others similarly situated on their small lots. Most were occupied by retirees who couldn't afford better, some by transient laborers, others by folks down on their luck doing their best to stay off the welfare rolls. Other mobile homes housed those without hope, living on the meager allowance provided by the Department of Aid. Inside the small trailer, a man in his early fifties, who had secretly maintained this home away from home for over twenty years, sat alone reviewing his life, the life which brought him to the existence he now endured.

He thought about his childhood, an only child who grew up on Chicago's South Side, whose parents strived to make ends meet, a serious child who spent many hours alone while his parents worked. His father worked the day shift at the steel mills. His mother worked at a local truck stop waiting tables. He learned how to care for himself. He learned early in life never to depend on others.

Even in school, he stayed to himself, never taking part in student activities such as sports or music or other curriculum that might bring him into close contact with his peers. Reading became his passion. He read everything he could get his hands on, novels of all kinds, mysteries, suspense, adventure. He would become the protagonist, the hero. He would extricate himself from the reality of his own existence and live in the fantasy world of what he was reading.

When he entered high school, he became obsessed with American history. He spent hours in the library studying the lives of the founding fathers. He studied the philosophy of those who created the Constitution and The Bill of Rights. Thomas Jefferson became his personal idol.

In his sophomore year, he inadvertantly became aware of his mother's infidelity with a trucker she'd met at the truck stop. He witnessed the pain his father experienced when his wife's betrayal became known to him, and felt deep guilt for not confronting his mother and making her discontinue the relationship. Although his parents never divorced, the incident remained an ever present source of unhappiness and pain in all their lives.

His mother's behavior caused him to vow that he would never allow himself to be hurt that way. Therefore, he never married. After high school, he joined the Marines, intending to make the military his life. Although he was a good soldier and an obedient servant to his superiors and country, he was never accepted by his fellow soldiers. Even while serving in Viet Nam, he found it impossible to make friends.

He was distrusted by others who felt he couldn't be depended on in combat when a friend was sometimes the only thing standing between you and a horrible death. He could never understand this attitude because he knew one should never depend on anyone other than himself. For that reason, he decided to forgo his dream of a military career.

After serving two tours, he returned to his beginnings with nothing to show for his years in the service, except one thing. After returning from combat and while serving out the remainder of his time in the States, he became involved in the only activity, other than reading, that ever interested him, the only activity that made close contact with others tolerable: archery.

For some reason, archery was more than just a sport. To him, it was an art, and he liked the idea that it was something he could enjoy alone. Dealing with others was only necessary while learning. He liked the fact that the sport required no special tools or modern technical devices. It was the weapon of primitive man—before gun powder, before modern weaponry—which did not necessarily require total mastery by it's user.

In time, he became an expert. Though he would surely have defeated all challengers, he never participated in tournaments or other competitions that would have demostrated his superior skill. As was his way of life, he kept it to himself. Keeping his sport a secret, he even made his own arrows rather than buy them through a sporting goods distributor.

Back home again, he wondered what he would do with the rest of his life. He considered many possibilties. He even considered leaving Chicago and finding a place somewhere in the mountains of Oregon or Washington State or the deserts of Nevada or Utah. But his mother had died while he was in the service, and his father, who had retired, was ailing and needed him at home. Without a college education, he considered returning to school. One day, however, his father showed him an ad in the newspaper stating that the Chicago Police Department was accepting applications for patrolmen.

"With your service record, it should be no problem for you to be accepted," his father suggested.

Still feeling guilty for his father's misfortune, he agreed to apply. Although he knew his experience in the service would most likely repeat itself in a para-military organization like the police department, he couldn't say no to his father.

After several months of written tests and physical examinations, Raymond Lis was accepted as a patrolman trainee and received his letter inviting him to begin his training at the Police Academy. While in training, he met the only person who ever penetrated his defenses enough to become what was as close to a friend as he would ever have. He shared the same love of American history, he also shared the same knowledge and interest in the originators of the American Dream. He was the only person Raymond could discuss his ideas with, the only person who seemed to understand and accept him for what and who he really was. His name was Mike Nicoletti.

It was Mike who suggested he apply for the position of driver for the Superintendent and offered to put a word in for him. Unlike Raymond, Mike had worked his way up to sergeant by that time and was beginning to make friends in the right places. Mike was respected and admired by everyone who knew him, even though he was known to be fiercely dedicated to his oath and therefore incorruptable. Raymond accepted Mike's help, and before long found himself in the job tailor made for his temperament and personality. When he wasn't driving his boss from one place to another, he was alone, either at home or in the car. He was on call twenty-four hours a day.

Even when in the company of the Superintendent, he was alone. His boss always sat in the back seat, on the phone or with someone else, rarely speaking to him except to inform him of their destination, or to occasionally utter some obligatory greeting or inquiry as to his health or general state of being. Raymond should have been grateful to Mike for his help in securing his new position. Instead, it was the beginning of the deterioration of their fragile relationship. Raymond didn't like the feeling of obligation. He didn't like feeling like a dependant. He didn't like the feeling at all.

He also didn't like the conversations he often overheard his boss having with other high police officials or politicians while driving them around. Conversations regarding coverups of misconduct by public servants, special deals with organized crime figures, even details of pay-offs and kickbacks were arranged in his presence. Feeling used and taken for granted, his resentment toward his boss and all public officals who abused their position of power grew until it engulfed him.

Again and again he was reminded that no one could be trusted, that he could never allow himself to become dependant on anyone else. After years of silently enduring the frustration, Raymond began to feel like the privileged one. He remembered his youthful vow to never allow himself to be hurt by others. He realized that fate had put him in a position where he was made privy to unquestioned evidence of corruption and abuse.

He had been chosen by the spirits of the founding fathers to right the wrongs of those who would defile the dream they created. He would begin a crusade to rekindle the flame of freedom. He would retake what had been taken by those who made a mockery of what others had given their lives to attain. He would become the savior of the American people.

He would set out on a mission to rid the world of all corruption. He would begin alone, but he knew that through his efforts and actions a new revolution would be born, and he would be the father of that revolution. Raymond Lis would no longer be "Mr. Average," average height, average wieght, average intelligence. From now on, he would no longer be "Mr. Anybody," he would be "Mr. Somebody." Somebody to be reckoned with.

* * *

The glow of headlights from an unseen car shone through the seams of the half open window blinds then faded as the vehicle passed. Raymond Lis looked around his small living room, realizing he had been sitting in the dark for hours. Reaching up from where he was seated, he switched on the table lamp. He looked around the now luminated room.

Deer heads mounted on wooden plaques hung on the wall. Squirrels, raccoons, even pheasant were displayed in various lifelike poses on the tables and shelves. He viewed them with pride, for each of them had been brought down by his arrow.

Even the pheasant, while in flight, could not escape the deadly shaft propelled by his crossbow, the only concession made to human technology, ancient though it was.

"Fool," he said out loud. "How could he betray me, the only friend he had?"

He reached down and picked up the crossbow that lay at his feet. Stroking it tenderly and lovingly, he spoke out loud again.

"I had to deny you the pleasure of executing Nicoletti, but I promise you, you will not be excluded in ending the treachery of Mr. Marco Fischer. He, however, is our personal enemy. First, we execute a greater enemy. An enemy of the people, one who has escaped our vengence long enough."

CHAPTER 25

"Soon, I'll send you a reminder, just to let you know I'm still around."

AROUND MARCO'S DINING room table, another regular meeting of the minds took place.

"He can't hide forever," Chris said. "We know who he is now. His picture has been on every front page and TV newscast in town. Sooner or later, someone will recognize him."

"I'm not so sure," Dominick disagreed. "Mike Nicoletti had this guy pegged. He's a nut, but he's smart and cunning. Something tells me he's prepared himself for what's happened."

"That's impossible. No one could be that smart," Chris argued.

"Perhaps," Marco said. "But so far he's avoided every effort by us and the police to nab him. Except for the bullet that was taken from Mike's body and the arrows from his other victims, not a single piece of evidence has ever been found. The police have had to come to the conclusion that the arrows are homemade, because they have not been able to match them up with any known manufacturer.

Sarah and Donna excused themselves from the table.

"Where are you going?" Marco asked.

"We're going to Sarah's room to watch television. We're sick of talking and hearing about Robin Hood, or should I say Raymond Lis," Donna answered. "We're going to fill our minds with something less depressing like the trivial, childish nonsense on TV."

Marco, Chris, Dominick and Tony continued their discussion, to what end no one knew. Somehow it felt better to talk about what could be done or what should be done. Just after ten o'clock, it was mutually agreed that the meeting had accomplished as much as it was ever going to.

"See you at the station tomorrow," Tony said, as he got up from the table. He turned toward the foyer closet and noticed Sarah and Donna coming out of Sarah's bedroom. They looked as though they had just seen a ghost. Their faces were devoid of any color whatsoever; their eyes were swollen and tearful.

Marco, Dominick and Chris turned simultaneously when they heard Tony exclaim: "What the hell happened to you two?"

"He did it again," Sarah said without expression, looking as though she were in a daze.

* * *

Superintendent of Police Rory J. Gallagher had been a cop for thirty-seven years. He started out as a patrolman, but not just any patrolman, because his father was a precinct commander. His grandfather had been a commander back in the Capone days. Rory Gallagher's clout in the department was strong, and it ran deep into the history of what was possibly the most corrupt police department in the country.

At sixty, Gallagher was proud of his accomplishments. He had run the gamut from patrolman, to detective, to commander, to the ultimate police official, "Top Cop." Throughout his ascent through the ranks, his record remained unblemished. Through the years, he'd managed to keep his name out of the news and free of any scandal or controversy that would serve to hinder or prevent his goal of surpassing the successes of his forbears. That is, until the call he received in Seattle while attending a conference of police chiefs and superintendents. He cut his trip short and returned to Chicago.

Now, two days later, he had to deal with questions not only from reporters, but from the mayor and the city council. How could he not know that his own personal driver was a murderer? They wanted answers he couldn't provide, and they knew he couldn't provide them. It wasn't really answers they wanted; Gallagher knew that, too. It was a fall guy they wanted, a scapegoat, someone to take the heat, and he was the most logical and convenient choice.

Superintendent Gallagher needed to release his frustration. He needed to relax and consider his situation. There was only one place where he could do both.

* * *

Rosa Martinez had been Gallagher's secretary for ten years and his mistress for nine of them. When it came to consoling and providing release, she had become an expert at it. On this night of the most embattled day of her lover's career, Rosa applied all her skills as she never had before.

Rosa was born in Mexico, but she looked more Spanish than Mexican. Her black hair, dark eyes and olive complexion were a definite turn on, but it was her large breasts and full red lips that Gallagher appreciated the most. At thirty-six, she was still as beautiful as she was the day their affair began.

* * *

Gallagher stood before the mirror, checking himself out before he went home to his wife of thirty-five years. Rosa laid in bed and watched as the man she loved combed his graying hair and checked his manicured finger nails. Rosa always admired the meticulous attention he paid to his appearance. Though physically he was average in every way, it was the way he carried himself, his confidence that he was in charge at all times, that made her fall in love with him. She knew she had been successful at revitalizing him when he turned and said, "I'll fight those chicken shit bastards. I'm not going down without taking a few of them with me."

Gallagher did feel renewed. He exited the small brick bungalow he had helped Rosa purchase shortly after their affair began and took in a long breath of cool crisp October air. Before descending the steps of Rosa's concrete stoop, he checked the street; it was deserted. He didn't expect to find anyone waiting. No one knew about his relationship with Rosa. No one except that little snake Raymond Lis.

Rosa heard a crash and the sound of breaking glass. She was tempted to get out of bed and investigate, but she'd put in a hard night's work and was too tired. It wouldn't have done any good anyway. Superintendent of Police Rory Gallagher was just as dead then as he was the following morning when his body was discovered on her front porch. The aluminum framed glass storm door was crushed by the force of Gallagher's body as it recoiled from the shock of two pointed shafts, one through his heart, another through his forehead. The police department was able to withhold the news of his death until later that evening. The first reports were made on the ten o'clock news.

* * *

Marco Fischer was frantic the next day as he conducted his radio show. He desperately pleaded for his one-time fan to turn himself in.

"Please, Ray, turn yourself in. It's not too late. You must know you can't run forever. Sooner or later you're going to stumble or run out of breath. We don't know what the circumstances will be when that happens. Maybe some trigger happy cop will appoint himself judge, jury and executioner. Don't take the chance. Turn yourself in now. Not so long ago, you considered me your friend, or at least an ally. Regardless of how you feel now, I'm still your friend, despite everything that's happened. You have my word that I'll do everything in my power to see that you're treated fairly. I'll even allow you time on my show to state your case. Just turn yourself in."

Marco's words reached a lot of people and resulted in many calls from his listeners, eager to join in support of Marco's pleas. There was no call from Raymond Lis. One of Marco's regular listeners, however, did call.

"He's gone, we'll never see or hear from him again."

"I recognize the voice," Marco said. "How are you, Steve? Tell me where did he go?" Marco couldn't help smiling as he anticipated the answer.

"He's been abducted by aliens who are participating in the Galactic Olympics. They've recruited him for their archery team."

"Ladies and gentlemen, that was Steve, and I'm looking forward to the day when aliens abduct *him*. May his last call to my show be from a UFO as it leaves our atmosphere at the speed of light."

Marco broke for commercials, and as usual, he took advantage of the opportunity to remove his headset, wipe his brow and massage his temples. Again, Tony had to resort to tapping on the glass to attract Marco's attention. Marco looked up. Tony was holding up two fingers. Marco looked down at his console after replacing his headset. He listened to the last few seconds of the commercial, then said, "We're back folks. We have a caller on line two. Hello caller, you're on the air."

"I hope you didn't keep me on hold all this time because you think you can trace this call. As a matter of fact, you *can* trace this call, but it won't do you any good."

"Are you calling to say you're going to turn yourself in?" Marco asked excitedly.

"I still have unfinished business to take care of."

"And what might that business be?"

"That business might be you, and as a matter of fact, it is. When my business with you is finished, perhaps I'll turn myself in, but I doubt it."

"And what is your business with me, if I may ask?"

"Did you forget? You agreed to meet with me."

"Come to the station. I'll be here till seven."

"Very funny, Marco. You think you're very clever, don't you? Well, you're not clever enough. I'm going to give you the shaft, right through the neck."

Marco wanted desperately to continue the conversation. He wanted to keep Robin Hood talking long enough for him to make a mistake, to leave a clue, something, anything that might bring this nightmare to an end.

CLICK. The call was over.

Marco let his head fall into his waiting hands. Suddenly, his feeling of defeat and disappointment turned to aggression and anger. Tony Ruskin was about to remind Marco that several seconds of silence had gone by and the audience was waiting. Then he saw Marco raise his head. His eyes were glaring. His teeth were clenched. Then, the explosion.

"Coward," he growled. "You're nothing but a coward. You call yourself an American? You are a disgrace to everything America stands for. You say you're fighting corruption, punishing those who are guilty of betraying the people. You compare yourself to the founding fathers of this country. How dare you defile the names of those great men? Those men who stood before a great and powerful enemy and looked it in the eye. That's right, they didn't hide behind the anonymity of a phone call. They faced their enemy with the greatest weapons of all—courage and conviction. Honor and the truth. That's why they won. That's why our nation is what it is today." Marco grasped the edge of his console and spat into the mouthpiece of his headset.

"How dare you put yourself in the same league with those great men? You, my friend, are a snake. You don't face those whom you consider your enemy. You sneak up on them from behind and strike your blow from concealment. Those you attack are not your enemies. They are your victims. Victims of your hate, your resentment, your feelings of inadequacy, your cowardice. You can threaten me. You can kill me, but you'll have to do it when my back is turned. You don't have the guts to face me, man to man, because you're a slimy, slithering snake. No, you're not even good enough to be a snake. You're a worm. Did you hear me? You're a slimy little worm."

CHAPTER 26

"When will you learn? You will never escape me. Do you think I'm afraid of your gangster friends? Send them after me. You'll see. Their fate will be no different than the others."

RALPH BIANCO SAT behind his desk listening as Marco Fischer lambasted the fugitive cop Raymond Lis. *This guy needs help*, he thought, as he switched off the radio and picked up the phone.

*   *   *

Dominick Cairo was sitting in Marco's office when his cell phone began to ring. "Hello," Dominick said.

"Dom, this is Ralph. I want to see you as soon as possible."

"How about tonight, after I take Marco home?"

"That'll be fine. I'll expect you about eight or eight-thirty."

*   *   *

At eight-fifteen, Dominick was being greeted at the front door of Ralph Bianco's River Forest mansion by Connie Bianco.

"He's in his office, Dom. You know where it is," Connie said, holding a portable phone to her chest.

Ralph was waiting at the doorway of his office as Dominick approached.

"How you doing?" Ralph said, embracing his enforcer and old friend, one of the few men he trusted completely.

"I'm okay, but our friend Marco is at the end of his rope."

"That's what I wanted to see you about. I heard his show today. We need to become more actively involved in this thing. I want you to use all your resources to locate this cop, this Robin Hood character. I can't afford to have my most valuable people acting as bodyguards any longer."

"I'm glad to hear you say that, Ralph. Not that I don't like Marco, but my regular duties are being neglected. Not to mention the duties of Joey, Larry and Howie."

"When I agreed to help, I didn't think we'd have to invest as much time as we have," Ralph confessed.

"When I find him, what do you want me to do?" Dominick asked, knowing what the answer would be.

"You know what has to be done, just do it," Ralph said, as he got up and walked out from behind his desk and toward the door. He draped his arm around his old friend's shoulder and said, "Let's go in the kitchen and see if we can be of any help to Connie."

"Help to Connie?" Dominick said, puzzled.

"She's on the phone with my brother Billy's wife, Eloyse. We've decided to have my niece Nicole's engagement party here in the spring. A lot of arrangements have to be made. I'm sure they'll have us running all over creation doing the grunt work."

"I wonder what's worse, being a baby sitter or an errand boy," Dominick said, shaking his head. "At least it'll be good to see Billy again."

* * *

Ralph Bianco wasn't the only one who was fed up with the Robin Hood situation. Marco was even more upset. He had been tempted several times to begin an investigation of his own, but of course Dominick would never have allowed that. He had almost given up hope of ever tracking down Robin Hood himself until the morning Dominick informed him that Howie would be taking over as his bodyguard.

"What's the matter, you getting sick of me?" Marco kidded.

"I got sick of you a long time ago," Dominick kidded back. "I have other business I have to attend to."

Marco shook Dominick's hand and embraced him affectionately. "Thanks," Marco said sincerely. "I like to think we've become friends. I hope you'll stop by and say hello now and then."

"You'll hear from me," Dominick said, as he headed for the door.

The moment Dominick closed the door behind him, Marco dashed for the foyer closet. He swung the door open and reached for the phone book on the top shelf. He headed for the dining room table, skimming through the Yellow Pages. He looked under sporting goods, then sporting equipment. After making a list of all the names and phone numbers, it occurred to him that there might be a specific listing for archery equipment. He turned to the A's, then flipped the pages to the AR's. Under the heading of Archery Equipment and Supplies there were two names: Archery World on North Elston Avenue and What's the Point Archery Supply on West Madison Street. Marco studied the names for a moment, tapping his index finger on the table top. He decided to call them in the order in which they were listed.

"Archery World," a voice announced.

"I have a couple questions about crossbows and related accessories."

"Are you a cop?"

"No, my name is Marco Fischer."

"Hey, Marco. How you doin'? I listen to your show every day."

"Thanks. I hope you find it entertaining."

"Wouldn't listen if I didn't."

"Can I ask you a question?"

"Sure."

"Why did you want to know if I was a cop?"

"Hell, I've had cops coming around here and calling on the phone for weeks now, asking questions about crossbows and arrows. Of course, they're not arrows to those of us who are involved in the sport. We call them bolts. Anyhow, they've been driving me nuts with all kinds of questions. One guy even brought in a bolt that was actually used in a real murder. He wanted me to identify it, or at least tell him who manufactured it. I looked at it, but there was no way I could tell him anything, except, it didn't look factory made to me. It looked like a do-it-yourselfer."

"You mean like homemade?"

"That's what I mean."

"How would one go about making his own arrows . . . I mean bolts?"

"There's really nothing to it. All you need are some extruded aluminum tubes, some fletching and heads or points and, of course, the knowledge of how to put them all together, and you're in business."

"Fletching, what is that?"

The feathers that go on the opposite side of the pointed end. Sometimes the fletching are made of plastic. In that case they're called vanes."

"Where would a person go to purchase these items?"

"Like I told the police, you could go anywhere where archery supplies are sold. We sell them here, but you could go to any sporting goods store. Even some discount department stores sell them. It's the kind of thing that's sold over the counter. Nobody makes a record of that kind of transaction like you would if you were selling handguns or other firearms."

"Thanks," Marco said, feeling a little deflated.

"Sorry I couldn't be of more help."

"That's okay. By the way, what's your name?"

"Glen. Glen Skony."

"Thanks again, Glen. I'll try to slip in a plug for your store sometime."

Marco hung up and sat with his elbows on the table top and his hands on his cheeks. "Shit, where do I go from here?" he thought.

* * *

Dominick also had no idea where to begin his search for Raymond Lis. The first thing he did was put the word out on the street. He notified every Outfit capo and soldier of Ralph's orders. Two weeks went by without any results. Finally, he decided on a new course of action. He would start from scratch. He would go back to where it all started. He could write a book on what he didn't know about his subject, so he decided to start with what he did know.

One important thing was where Lis lived. That would be where he launched his investigation. He knew the police had thoroughly searched Lis' residence and removed any items they considered valuable evidence. But it wouldn't be the first time the cops overlooked an important clue. Dominick drove to the address and parked a few doors away. Before getting out of his car, he watched and waited awhile to make sure the house wasn't being watched by the police. After an hour or so, he made his move.

He cautiously walked around to the rear of the garage. Placing his shoulder against the small access door, he pushed as he turned the knob. To his surprise the door opened. It wasn't locked. He removed a flashlight from his pocket and scanned the garage with the beam of light. He slowly inspected its contents. The walls were covered with the usual tools and equipment he would expect to find in millions of garages throughout the city.

He began to feel disappointed, wondering if he'd wasted his time. Then something caught his eye. He brought the light back to a corner of the garage where several tanks were piled on top of one another. He approached the objects and inspected them closely. He removed a pencil and notebook from his pocket. Holding the flashlight between his teeth, he began to write.

* * *

The sales clerk at Sam's Mobile Home supply picked up the phone on the first ring. "Sam's," he said, as he removed a blank order from his desk drawer. "How can I help you?"

"I'm just moving into a home I purchased last month. The previous owner left some propane tanks in the garage with your tags on them. They're all empty, but I thought you'd like to have them back," Dominick said, trying to sound sincere.

"Yeah, sure we would. Do you know the name of the person who lived there before you?"

"Offhand, I don't remember. I'd have to check my real estate contract."

"Well, he probably left a deposit on those tanks. Do you have the tag numbers? I can look up the customer's name in the cross file."

One by one, Dominick read off the tag numbers.

"Give me a minute," the salesman said, then put the phone down and headed for a file cabinet.

"I have it right here," the clerk said, picking up the phone again. "Where did you say you lived," He asked.

"I didn't," Dominick said.

"You did say you lived in a house, didn't you?"

"Yes I did," Dominick said, realizing he was about to get lucky.

"Well, according to my records those tanks are registered to a mobile home owned by a Mr. Raymond Jones at the Hide-A-Way Mobile Home Park on Route 72."

The clerk waited for a response, but there was none. "Hello. Hello? Are you there?" The clerk shrugged his shoulders. "Guess he hung up." he said.

Dominick called Ralph to tell him of his good fortune, but his call was answered by an answering machine. Dominick left a coded message he knew Ralph would understand. "Discovered the whereabouts of our old friend. On my way to see him now. I'll call again later," he said, then pushed the "end" button on his cell phone. He reached into his coat pocket and felt the cold steel instrument of death concealed there. He checked his other pocket. The cylinder he found there would soon be put to use to silence the target of the instrument's intended propose.

* * *

Raymond "Robin Hood" Lis sat silently in his trailer surrounded by his trophies. With his chair turned around facing the window, he watched the traffic on Route 72 as it rushed by. His main interest was only in those vehicles turning off the highway and into his trailer park. There were never many, and the few that did were always quickly identified. Every precaution, however, had to be taken if he was to remain free to complete his mission.

The hours rolled by like the headlights of the passing cars. They came and went uneventfully. Yet he continued his vigil until sleep would overtake him. The morning sun would awaken him as the light drove the darkness away. This night, however, would be different. The darkness would be driven away, not by the sun, but by the headlights of a Lincoln Town Car, the likes of which hadn't been seen in the run down trailer park for a very long time.

Raymond watched as the car rolled to a stop. Suddenly it was dark again. Raymond's eyes refocused, adjusting from bright light to moon light. He watched as a man got out of the car and looked around. The man took a flashlight from his coat pocket and walked back toward the entrance.

* * *

Dominick found the directory, listing the occupants of the park and their lot numbers. With his flashlight, he scanned the names, stopping at the "J's". There were three Jones' on the list. Dominick's eyes locked in on the names. Brenda Jones, Lot #76. Harold Jones, Lot #16. Raymond Jones, Lot #2. Dominick raised his head; looking to his left, he realized he was standing less than thirty feet from his final destination. A feeling of pride and satisfaction swelled in Dominick's chest as he returned to his Town Car. There he would decide exactly how he would carry out the final steps of his assignment.

* * *

As Dominick reached for his door handle, he heard a scratching sound. He instinctively reached for his weapon, disengaging the safety. Every muscle in his body froze, except those needed to focus and shift his eyes from side to side. For several seconds, Dominick remained motionless. *Must have been a tree branch swaying in the wind.* he thought, as he pulled the door open.

He slid behind the wheel and pulled the door closed quickly to douse the overhead interior light. He reached for the steering column to engage the ignition switch. Something caught the corner of his eye. He turned his head toward the passenger side window. Raising his arm, he pointed his .9mm automatic at a shadowy figure. His thoughts were racing through his mind at the speed of light, but outwardly everything seemed to be moving in slow motion.

He could clearly see the shaft as it penetrated the window. Particles of glass flew through the air like feathers caught in a gentle summer breeze. His brain frantically, desperately ordered him to pull the trigger, pull the trigger. But he was helpless to defend himself against the advancing projectile. "Sweet Jesus, forgive me," he cried.

* * *

Raymond Lis shoved the limp, lifeless body aside as he positioned himself behind the wheel of the Lincoln. With gloved hands, he searched the pockets of his victim. He smiled when he found the silencer in its hiding place. Pulling the dead man's overcoat open, he checked the inside pockets, smiling again as he discovered the small notebook and the propane tank tags.

He continued his search and came across an envelope. Quickly he opened it and inspected it's contents. Again, he smiled as he read the invitation to Nicole Bianco's engagement party, to be held at the residence of her aunt and uncle, Mr. and Mrs. Ralph Bianco. Raymond Lis stuffed the envelope into his jacket pocket. He started the engine, made a "U" turn and headed back toward the entrance, leaving the headlights off until just before turning onto Route 72.

CHAPTER 27

"You're not through burying your friends yet."

MARCO FISCHER AND Chris Musso couldn't believe their eyes and ears as they sorrowfully watched the TV news reports in Chris' office. They watched as the body of Marco's new friend, and in Chris' case a friend of many years, was loaded into a paddy wagon. The cameraman panned the area, stopping at Dominick's Lincoln surrounded by police technicians collecting what they hoped would be evidence that would help them solve the latest in a long line of gangland slayings. One was brushing powder on the doors, windows, dashboard and steering wheel hoping to find a carelessly deposited fingerprint.

"They're wasting their time and the taxpayers' money," Marco said, shaking his head.

"It's not like they don't know who killed him," Chris added.

"When are they going to catch this guy?" Marco cried out. "Will anyone ever be able to stop him?"

"Our friend better hope the police find him now," Chris said, glaring at the picture of Raymond Lis displayed on the television screen.

"Why do you say that?" Marco asked.

"Mr. Robin Hood now has a new enemy. This enemy is not restricted by the rules of law or evidence. This new enemy needs no warrants or formal indictments. This enemy needs only to be convinced in his own mind of the guilt or innocence of his suspect." Chris Musso turned his head away from the TV to look directly at Marco. "Mr. Robin Hood will have to answer to Ralph and Billy Bianco for this."

Marco looked Chris in the eye. "First the son-of-a-bitch has to answer to *me.*"

* * *

At Dominick's wake, Marco approached the casket where the Bianco brothers stood guard, never leaving their friend's side. Chris Musso and his wife also stood close by, greeting visitors and escorting them to view the body.

"I'm sorry, Ralph," Marco said. "Only the death of my wife left me more devastated. Dominick was a good friend. I'll never forget him."

"Thank you for the kind words, Marco. I know Dominick considered you a friend, too," Ralph said, taking Marco by the arm, leading him to where his brother stood. "Let me introduce you to my brother, Billy."

Billy turned when he heard his older brother's voice.

"Billy, this is the man I told you about; Marco Fischer, my brother, Billy Bianco."

Marco noticed the resemblance at once. Though Billy was younger, slightly taller and not nearly as muscular as Ralph, their faces, hair color and eyes were almost identical. One big difference was evident, however; Billy was more businesslike. Though he was an impressive man, his presence was not overpowering. Marco felt more relaxed with him.

After meeting Billy, the man who's power in the Chicago Outfit was second only to his older brother's, Marco felt an awkward sensation. He felt proud and privileged. He wondered what it was that made people gravitate to men like the Biancos. Was it because down deep they envied men who lived on the edge? Was it the courage and strength these men seemed to exude, or was it the power? Perhaps it was the strange relationship these men had with life and death. He didn't know, perhaps no one would ever know. What he did know was that being in the presence of these men was the most exhilarating experience of his life.

Donna and Sarah did their best to console Joey and Larry. Howie sat alone in a far corner of the funeral parlor. Months would pass before he could even begin to accept the death of his childhood friend. Sarah sat on Joey's lap with her cheek on his. Donna stood at Larry's side, their hands clasped together.

Marco turned to face Ralph again.

"I will be forever grateful for all you've done for me and my family," he said. "I want you to know that as of now, I want you to discontinue the protection you have been providing for these many weeks. I can no longer allow these men to risk their lives to protect us. We have grown to love and respect them too much. What happened to Dominick cannot be repeated. They've done enough. My station manager is making a formal request for police protection and he has hired a private security firm. The network has finally agreed that they have a responsibility to provide protection for me. If there is anything I can do to show my gratitude for all you've done, please call on me. It would be a privilege and honor to be at your service."

Ralph took Marco's hand in his and grasped it firmly. "Chris said you were an honorable man. He was right, as always. I like honorable men. I hope from now on we can be friends."

CHAPTER 28

"I'll have to lay low for a while, give you some time to think. Maybe you'll begin to think I've gone away, but down deep you'll know, I'm still watching, still waiting."

SARAH CONTINUED TO be escorted to and from school. Although she felt safe with her new bodyguards, she missed having Joey at her side. After school one day, Sarah was shocked and delighted to find Joey waiting on the concrete stoop outside the main entrance.

"How's my girl?" Joey said scooping Sarah into his arms and twirling her around.

Sarah locked her arms around his neck and kissed him several times, tightening her hold on him.

"Hey. What are you trying to do, choke me to death?" Joey said laughing.

"I should choke you for taking so long to come see me."

"I'm sorry, honey, but I had a lot of work to catch up on. Where's Ricky?"

"He'll be out soon," Sarah said, noticing the dumbfounded look on the faces of her new security team. "Oh, excuse me," she said. "This is my Uncle Joey. He was my bodyguard before you guys."

Joey didn't show it, but Sarah's words made him feel proud. Seconds later, Ricky came through the doors. He was almost as happy to see Joey as Sarah was. Ricky threw his arms around him in a masculine embrace.

"Come on," Joey said. "The Cokes are on me." Wrapping his arms around the teenagers necks, they began walking toward Joey's car. Looking over his shoulder, he called out to his replacements. "Come on, you're invited, too."

* * *

Donna had been staying at Marco's apartment ever since the murder of Mike Nicoletti. She had become a part of the family. The morning after Dominick Cairo was laid to rest in Mount Carmel Cemetery, Marco and Donna sat at the kitchen table having their coffee. "You know you're one of us now," Marco said, lifting his cup to his lips.

"Hmmm?" Donna said looking up from the morning newspaper.

"I said you're one of us, meaning me and Sarah."

"Are you bragging or complaining?" Donna kidded, squinting her eyes and nose in a mocking smile.

"I'm asking," Marco said seriously.

"Asking what?" Donna asked, looking up from her paper again.

"I'm asking you to marry me. Do you think you could break away from that rag you're reading just long enough to give me an answer?"

Marco prepared himself for another wild outburst, but there was none. Donna just sat there. She put the paper down and leaned forward, stretching her neck as far as she could. Marco did the same. They kissed. A tear rolled down Donna's face and followed the contour of their joined lips, then continued downward, dripping off Donna's chin onto the table. Donna got up from her chair and reached down for Marco's hand. Marco looked up at her. He was about to remind her that she was scheduled to be at City Hall for a news conference in two hours, but as she pulled his arm and led him toward the bedroom, he decided it could wait.

* * *

Ten days later, Marco and Donna were married. It was a simple ceremony at City Hall, the kind that doesn't usually get much notice. In this case, however, the clerk's office was jammed with reporters. Less than a year earlier, Donna Michaels was living and working in small town America. Now she found herself living and working in a great metropolis, a world class city, and married to it's most controversial citizen.

The reception was small. Only the closest friends and family members were invited. Joey, Larry and Howie were among them. Chris and Gail Musso were, of course, on the list of guests, and Tony Ruskin served as best man. Donna's best friend, Susan, drove in from Middletown, Ohio, to be the maid of honor. The media frenzy surrounding their wedding made it necessary to hold the reception at the condo, where they could more easily control the environment.

Jerry Kaplan, accompanied by his secretary, Sally Quinn, congratulated the newlyweds. "Does this mean you're going to quit working now and let Donna support you?" he kidded.

"Actually, we've discussed that possibility," Marco said. "Only the other way around. Donna and I are considering having children. If we do, Donna will be a stay-at-home mom."

"Mazel Tov," Jerry said, shaking Marco's hand and throwing his arm around Donna, kissing her on the cheek.

* * *

Sarah's wish had come true. Her father wouldn't be alone when she went away to college. Holding Ricky's hand, she approached her father and his new wife. "Donna, I just want to say that I couldn't be happier for my dad and for myself. I want to wish you and my dad all the happiness in the world."

*   *   *

All things considered, the day went very well. The black cloud that had been hovering over Marco Fischer and those closest to him had disappeared at least for the time being. Not a word had been heard from Robin Hood since Dominick's murder.

*   *   *

The following Monday afternoon, Marco and Tony relaxed in Marco's office for a few minutes before air time.

Do you think it's possible that Dominick got off a shot before he died?" Tony said. "Maybe Robin Hood went off and died someplace and no one's discovered his body yet."

"I wouldn't get too excited about that possibility," Marco said. "The police said Dominick's gun hadn't been fired. This isn't the first time Robin Hood has done this. He's disappeared before. He'll show up again."

Marco started his show as usual, reciting his monologue, recounting the events being reported in the newspapers and on the radio and television newscasts. Then he invited his audience to call in and discuss the issues of the day.

"Congratulations," one caller said. "I heard you got married over the weekend."

"Thank you," Marco said. "But my getting married is not a big deal. Let's talk about something important. We have Steve on line two. I don't know if I want to hear what he has to say. Hello, Steve."

"Congratulations, Marco, and by the way, I was talking to Elvis the other day; he sends his regards."

"I'm honored." Marco played along.

"Oh, one more thing," Steve continued. "I picked up a transmission from outer space. It seems Robin Hood is the new intergalactic archery champion."

"Thanks for the update, Steve, I hope you'll keep us posted as to his whereabouts."

Marco took several more calls from listeners congratulating him and wishing him good luck in his marriage, but, except for Steve's call which was useless, there was no mention of Robin Hood. Marco closed his program for the day and went into his office to go through his mail and clean up some paperwork before leaving for the day. He sat down at his desk and began opening his mail when Jerry Kaplan's secretary tapped her fingernails on his open door. Marco looked up and smiled at the pretty redhead.

"Excuse me, Marco," Sally said, dropping a pink message memo on his desk. "This call came in on the main telephone line while you were on the air."

Marco picked up the memo and inspected it. "Thanks, Sally," he said, as he tried to recall where he'd heard the name Glen Skony before.

* * *

Raymond "Robin Hood" Lis sat in front of his window watching the cars whiz by on Route 72. He knew it was only a matter of time before the police caught up with him. Sooner or later, someone, somewhere would recognize him. Perhaps one of his neighbors in the trailer park would connect him with the picture that had been plastered on every front page of every major newspaper in the Chicago area, not to mention all the TV news reports.

Sure, he'd taken great pains to avoid his neighbors over the years, never becoming friendly with any of them, even on the most superficial level. Sure, in the newspapers and on the TV screens, he was dressed in his blue policeman's uniform, complete with cap, white shirt and tie, but still there was always the possibility that someone would recognize him. For the past few weeks, he'd remained secluded, venturing out only to replenish his food supply or place a call to Marco's Morgue by climbing a telephone pole and tapping into some unsuspecting person's phone line with his lineman's instrument.

64-AMAT

Yes, he knew it was only a matter of time, but he hoped it wasn't any time soon. Spring had arrived, and he had a very special present for Marco Fischer and his hoodlum friends.

* * *

Glen Skony was in the process of closing out his cash register after a long and profitable day. He was busy counting out the coins he had spread on the counter top when his phone rang.

"Archery World."

"Glen?"

"Marco?"

"Yes, I just got your message."

"I wanted to thank you for the plug. Quite a few people told me they'd heard it on your show; thanks."

"No problem. I only hope it resulted in some sales."

"It did, but I called for another reason, too."

Marco felt a sensation of anticipation and excitement surge through him. "What's that?" he asked impatiently.

"Well, I don't know if it's important, but I remembered something. I considered calling the police with it, but since you were good enough to give me some free advertising, I decided to call you."

Marco wanted to yell, GET TO THE POINT, but he didn't want to offend someone who could very possibly turn out to be a valuable informant.

"Besides, the cops might get upset with me for not remembering it when they came in to question me."

"Tell me what it is," Marco broke in. "If it turns out to be something important, I'll give it to the police. They don't have to know where it came from. As a member of the media, I can tell them the information came from a confidential informant."

"Sounds good to me. Well here it is, I hope it's helpful. About two months ago, a guy who comes in here several times a year came in to buy some Broadheads. I didn't have any in stock at the time, but told him I was expecting a delivery in a couple days."

"Broadheads, what are they?"

"Broadheads are the type of point you would use for hunting large game, like deer or moose, for example."

"I see," Marco said, nodding his head. "Then what happened?"

"As I said, I didn't have any at the time, so I offered to mail them out to him when they arrived. I pinned his address on my bulletin board in my office. When I remembered about the guy, I checked my office and the slip of paper with his address on it was still there. That's when I called you."

"Let me ask you a question before you go any farther," Marco asked, crossing his fingers. "Did you happen to notice if this guy had a red blotch on the back of his neck, like a birthmark?"

"Yes . . . Now that you mention it . . . I remember now . . . I noticed it when he turned and walked away . . . Hey! Doesn't the guy the police are looking for have a mark like that?"

"Yes, but let's not jump to conclusions," Marco cautioned. "Give me the address and I'll check it out."

* * *

"Yes!" Marco exclaimed, pounding his fist on the desk, sending his letter opener flying through the air.

This was a stroke of unbelievable luck. A gift from God. It was also a dilemma that Marco found himself in. He got up and closed his office door. He had to think. He had to decide what to do with this windfall. Should he go to the police? Or should he check it out first and make sure it wasn't just another disappointing lead. After all it *was* a different address than the one the police had, and the last name was different, too. In his heart, Marco knew that Raymond Jones and Raymond Lis were one and the same, but he decided to make absolutely sure that Raymond Jones was really Robin Hood, too.

* * *

The instant Marco turned off Route 72, he saw it. The small trailer sat inconspicuously on its tiny lot. Marco saw no light coming from inside. He continued to drive past the mobile home and took the gravel road to a point where it turned and began to lead back toward the entrance. The moon was hidden behind a large white cloud. Marco checked his watch. It was eight fifty-seven. He'd called Donna before leaving the office and told her he would be late coming home. She was preoccupied with something at the time and didn't ask why or when she should expect him and he left well enough alone.

Marco followed the road until it brought him back to the main entrance. He passed the trailer again; it was still dark inside. He turned right on Route 72 and headed west. He parked his car on the shoulder of the road about three hundred feet from the entrance to the trailer court. He reached inside his glove compartment, grabbed his flashlight and shoved it into his pocket. He'd replaced the one the police tow truck driver had stolen several months earlier.

He walked back toward the trailer park. It was early spring and he was refreshed by a crisp, cool breeze. It felt good on his face. He stopped when he reached the mouth of the entrance and stared at the little trailer for a long moment. It was still dark inside. He looked around in all directions; there was no one in sight. He crept toward the trailer, and when he reached it, he ducked down under a large picture window. The horizontal slats of the Venetian blinds hanging on the inside were turned on enough of an angle to allow Marco to see inside.

Marco took the flashlight from his pocket and switched it on. He rose from his crouched position, stood on his tiptoes and squinted his eyes. The beam of light revealed a small room. He could see several stuffed animals and birds hanging on the walls and sitting on table tops and shelving. A large, worn-out upholstered chair with duct tape covering thread bare arm rests sat facing the window.

Marco stretched his neck to the left and aimed his flashlight in the same direction. He saw a small kitchen separated from the room on the right by a small knee wall with a wooden cap on it. A stuffed pheasant impaled on a rod coming out of a wooden base posed lifelike, as though it were in flight. He stretched his neck a little further to his left. He saw a closed door. He assumed it sealed off a bedroom.

Suddenly, he heard footsteps behind him, then a voice.

"Can I help you?"

Marco turned with a start and dropped his flashlight. With his back against the side of the trailer, he gasped at the sight of an old man leaning on a cane. Marco's heart was pounding. He felt perspiration seeping from every pore in his body.

"I . . . I . . . I'm looking for my friend; he lives here."

The old man lifted his walking stick and pointed toward the entrance door of the mobile home. "Wouldn't it be easier if you knocked?"

"Oh yeah . . . Well, I did . . . But there was no answer," Marco replied, bending over to pick up his flashlight.

"Can't say that I know the man. Never met him. Kind of keeps to himself. Only seen him once or twice in the last five years. He's a weird bird, if you ask me, but then, you didn't ask me."

"Can't say that I disagree," Marco said with a tentative smile, trying to compose himself.

"Well, I'll be on my way. Hope he shows up," the old man said, as he hobbled out of sight.

Marco pulled at the crotch of his trousers and the arm pits of his shirt. His clothing was saturated with nervous perspiration. He walked around to the back of the mobile home and peered down the path the old man had been treading. He was gone. Marco walked around the trailer checking the windows, but they were all locked and the blinds were shut tight. He was scared, but he was driven. He had to get inside. He had to know for sure.

He put his hand to his waist and felt his cell phone, which was clipped to his belt. *Should I call the police?* he asked himself. *No. I have to do this myself.*

Marco walked back to the picture window. On either side, there was an aluminum framed slider window. He slid his hand along the glass and tugged the one on the right. It wouldn't budge. He moved to the left side. He forced his finger tips into a groove in the channel surrounding the window pane. He felt a chill as his fingernails scratched the oxidized metal frame. He felt another chill when he heard a scraping sound. The window was unlocked, but it wouldn't slide freely. It had to be pulled from higher up.

From the position Marco was in, he was forcing the window out of square, preventing it from sliding smoothly. He had to find something to stand on so he could pull from the center of the frame. He frantically searched the area around the trailer looking for a box or an old pail or bucket, anything that would extend his reach a few more inches. He stepped away from the trailer and scanned the others. That's when he saw it. In the glow coming through the window of another mobile home, he saw a small ladder leaning against the back side of another trailer two lots down from where he was standing.

* * *

From his new position, the window gave way without objection. The ladder also made it easy to step through the open window and into the dark living room. Marco reached into his pocket, removed his flashlight and switched it on. He felt perspiration begin to flow again. The beam of light revealed no more than he was able to ascertain from outside. Then he remembered. He crept toward the closed door. Shining his light on the knob, he grasped it and twisted it to the left. The hinges squeaked as he pushed the door open. Marco raised his flashlight, the cramped room glowed. Then he froze when he heard a hissing voice.

"What the fuck . . . Who are you?"

Marco turned his beam toward the sound. A man was laying in bed, shielding his eyes from the light. He turned his head away and Marco saw it—a red blotch in the shape of a fox's head.

Marco threw his flashlight at the man, who was scrambling to get to his feet. He backed out of the room and slammed the door shut. He turned and ran for the exit. Without even attempting to open the door in the conventional fashion, he rammed his body into it, knocking it from its hinges. His momentum carried him through the opening, his feet never touching the two wooden steps leading to the entrance. He fell to the ground, scraping his head on the gravel. Half crawling and half running, he ran for his life, scratching and clawing at the dirt.

He didn't dare look back. He had no idea where he was running to, but he knew what he was running from. He ran flailing his arms wildly, stumbling, righting himself, then stumbling again. He didn't know how, but somehow he had reached the entrance to the trailer park. He wanted to stop to rest a moment to catch his breath, but he knew he couldn't. So he kept running, even though his heart was about to explode inside his aching chest.

His legs hurt terribly, and his thigh and calf muscles cramped up tighter with every stride. His left leg was especially painful. It seemed to refuse to obey the demands of the adrenaline surging though his arteries. Marco reached his car, thanking God he'd decided to leave the doors unlocked. He dove into the front seat and cried out in excruciating pain as he dragged his left leg into the car. That's when he realized what caused his pain.

Marco reached down and grasped the arrow protruding from the rear side of his upper thigh. Trying to pull it out was out of the question. So with what little strength he had left, he bent the aluminum shaft into a U shape so as to allow him to sit in the driver's seat. When he reached into his pocket for his car keys, he felt the arrow poking its head through the other side of his leg.

Marco reached for his cell phone as he sped away, cutting off another car as he turned into the oncoming traffic. His phone was gone; he must have lost it during his escape. He would have to wait until he found a hospital to call the police.

* * *

Luckily, the arrow did relatively little damage. It had torn through muscle tissue, but missed the bone. After three days in the hospital, Marco was released with orders to stay off his injured leg as much as possible and a prescription for pain pills.

Needless to say, Donna, although relieved and grateful that Marco was alive, was very angry nevertheless.

"How could you pull such a crazy stunt?" Donna scolded. "What were you thinking? How could you be so stupid?"

Marco silently and sheepishly endured Donna's angry tirades, while he proudly enjoyed his little girl's praise.

"I always knew you were a little crazy, daddy. But I never knew you were so brave and courageous and wonderful."

* * *

By the time the police raided the trailer home of the fugitive Robin Hood, was long gone. The lineman's phone and several boxes of arrow heads and aluminum shafts were found in the abandoned mobile home, but nothing to indicate Robin Hood's whereabouts.

* * *

After two more weeks of recuperation, Marco was back to work hosting Marco's Morgue. His leg still hurt, but he was able to walk without crutches and he had even discarded his cane. Tony, who had been sitting in as host of Marco's Morgue in Marco's absence, greeted his boss affectionately, and Jerry Kaplan was truly happy to see Marco alive and well again.

"I listened every day while I was recuperating. You did a hell of a job," Marco said, as he somewhat painfully lowered himself into his chair.

"Thanks, but I'm glad you're back. That guy Steve was about to drive me wacky."

"Yeah, I heard," Marco said with a laugh. "First he claimed I wasn't really in the hospital, that I had actually been abducted by aliens. Then he said I'd gone back in time to ask the real Robin Hood to assist in tracking down his impostor."

"Was there a real Robin Hood?" Tony asked scratching the top of his head.

Marco threw his head back and laughed out loud. "Thanks, I needed that."

* * *

Marco kicked off his show as usual. After a short monologue and a commercial break, he began taking calls from his listeners.

"Good to have you back," one caller said

"Good to be back."

"Hey, Marco, is that you? I was beginning to get used to Tony. Maybe you should retire and let him take over permanently."

"Not a chance. Did you forget I got married not long ago? I need this job more than ever now."

For the next three and a half hours, the calls were almost all on the same topic. Every caller was glad to have Marco back on the air. Except one.

"How's your leg Marco?"

Marco stiffened in his seat at the sound of the hissing voice. He sat momentarily stunned by the unexpected call.

"Hello. Are you there?"

"I'm here, scum bag."

"You got lucky. I stepped on your cell phone and it knocked me off balance for just an instant, but it was long enough to make me miss my target. I was aiming for the middle of your back. That arrow should have ripped through your spinal cord, but as I said, you got lucky."

"Perhaps I got lucky."

"Remember, Marco, your luck could change any time."

"That's right, and *your* luck could be running out."

CLICK . . . The call was disconnected.

* * *

The call from Robin Hood had put Marco in a very depressed mood for the remainder of the show. By the time he got home, he was thoroughly exhausted and emotionally spent. He went directly to bed and slept till the following morning.

* * *

Marco found Sarah and Donna in the kitchen. Sarah was reading a brochure she had received from the college she was considering attending in the fall. Donna was on the phone.

"Of course we'll be there," Donna said excitedly. "We wouldn't miss it for the world. We're looking forward to a wonderful time."

Donna hung up the phone and looked at Marco, who was still in his pajamas. "You sure slept like a log."

"Who was that on the phone?" Marco asked, pouring himself a cup of coffee.

"That was Joey. He wanted to make sure we were coming to the party."

"Party? What party?"

"The party, remember? At Ralph Bianco's this weekend."

"Oh, yeah," Marco remembered. "Billy's daughter's engagement party."

"Don't tell me you forgot," Sarah said, looking at her father and shaking her head.

"To tell you the truth, I did. I'm glad you reminded me. Robin Hood has been on my mind a lot lately. I need something positive to think about. I'm sure the party at the Bianco's will be the perfect diversion."

CHAPTER 29

"The day has come, traitor. Now you pay. You and all your gangster friends."

RALPH STOOD IN front of the full length mirror in his dressing room. A feeling of guilt came over him as he anticipated the happy occasion over which he was about to preside. The loss of his dear friend still weighed heavily on his mind and soul. The echo of Dominick's last words rebounded in his brain, reminding him of how he played and replayed the recorded message he found waiting for him that night. *Forgive me, my old friend,* Ralph thought. *Forgive me for taking so long to avenge your death.*

Connie's voice came from the foyer. "Come on, Ralph. Guests are beginning to arrive."

Pushing thoughts of vengeance out of his mind, Ralph finished knotting his necktie, slipped into his suit coat and rushed to join his wife.

"Oooh, you look so handsome," Connie said, as Ralph hurried down the curved staircase. "Please stay and greet the guests as they arrive until Billy and Eloyse come back from the airport. I still have a lot of loose ends to tie up with the caterer."

"Okay, honey," Ralph said, keeping his wife from her duties just long enough to kiss her cheek tenderly.

* * *

Connie had always been amazed at Ralph's willingness to be ordered around by her. Even after almost twenty years of marriage, he still bowed to her every wish in boyish capitulation. It only made her love him more.

* * *

Ralph's brother Billy could have had his daughter's engagement party in any one of the Outfit-controlled hotels in Las Vegas. He'd been the number one man in Vegas for almost two decades, but his older brother wanted to host the celebration in his River Forest mansion. Billy and Eloyse could not refuse the only man for whom Billy would always step aside.

* * *

"Hello, bro," Billy said, as he held the door open for Eloyse, Nicole, Nancy and Thomas, Nicole's husband-to-be. "I see Connie put you to work. Thanks for filling in, but you can take it easy now. Eloyse and Nicole will take over."

Eloyse, Nicole and Nancy looked more like sisters than mother and daughters. They had the same black hair and dark eyes, the same youthful figures and the same olive skin, darkened to a golden brown by the Nevada sun.

"Thank you, ladies," Ralph said, as he kissed his sister-in-law and nieces. Turning to his brother, he said, "Come on, Billy. Let's make the rounds. A lot of people have been asking for you."

With his arm around his little brother's shoulder, Ralph led Billy into the backyard toward the pool area, where he showed him off to all their friends, old and new. A lavish sweet table had been set up between two portable bars. Many guests were seated at round tables or gathered in small groups on the pool apron, concrete patio or half acre of grass beyond the pool. Waiters dressed in black slacks, white waist coats, pleated white shirts and black bow ties served hors d'oeuvres and champagne. A few guests danced to the music of a four-piece jazz combo led by Eddy Stevens, an old friend of the Biancos from their days on Rush Street.

Larry, Joey and Howie were especially happy to see their old crew leader. Many years had gone by since their early days on the streets of Chicago, the nickel and dime burglaries and penny ante heists. They had come a long way together, and the original crew had remained intact until the recent loss of Dominick Cairo, the most senior member.

Ralph and Billy continued to meet and greet the many guests who had been honored with an invitation to the most publicized social event of the year.

"Billy, I know you remember Marco Fischer, but I don't think you've met his wife and daughter." Ralph walked Billy over to where Marco and his family were standing.

"Donna and Sarah Fischer, this is my brother Billy."

"Pleased to meet you," Billy said with a slight bow. "Marco, nice to see you again, and thank you all for coming to help us celebrate."

Donna marveled at the resemblance of the two brothers as she shook Billy's hand.

"Are you twins?" Sarah asked.

"No. Actually, Ralph is two years older than me," Billy said. "Can't you tell by all that gray hair?"

"At least I have hair," Ralph said, rustling his brother's hair, taking a defensive stance as Billy faked a punch to his midsection.

"Hey, there's Joey," Sarah said, as she wildly waved her arm to attract his attention.

Joey came over and put his arm around Sarah. "How's my girl?" he asked.

"I'm fine, Uncle Joe. Aren't you going to buy me a drink?"

"That's a very good idea. Let's go; I have some friends I want you to meet at the bar."

"Uncle Joe?" Billy asked, raising his eyebrows.

"I'm afraid my daughter has adopted him. She loves him very much," Marco said.

"She could do a lot worse," Ralph said. "Joey cares very much for your little girl. He must have reminded my wife a hundred times not to forget to include her in the guest list. Joey always wanted children, but his wife suffered a serious injury a couple years ago and lost the child she was carrying. She's been taking a new drug that may make it possible for her to conceive again. We're all hoping for the best. Sarah may have adopted him, but I think he's adopted her, too."

* * *

By three o'clock in the afternoon, all those who had received an invitation had arrived or had been accounted for. The iron gates at the mouth of the driveway were closed, creating a continuous barrier with the steel fence which surrounded the heavily wooded property on all sides of the River Forest mansion. The party was sealed off from the rest of the world. Armed guards consisting of young soldiers of the Chicago Outfit were stationed at two hundred foot intervals for added insurance of total privacy for the celebrants.

* * *

The warm afternoon sun beat down on Paulie Grazziano's head as he took a white handkerchief from his rear pocket and wiped the perspiration from his neck and forehead. He wondered how long it would take him to work his way up to a position of privilege where he would be one of the invited guests. Suddenly, he was startled by a strange noise, then the barely audible sound of a human voice.

He removed the two-way radio he had clipped to his waist band and brought it to his mouth. It would be the last act of his

64-AMAT

short life. The first arrow pierced his throat, rendering him unable to cry out. The second punctured his chest, driving itself through his heart, ending his life instantly.

Raymond Lis peered through the iron bars. Satisfied his prey was lifeless, he hoisted himself onto the horizontal channel connecting the bars. Avoiding the spear points at the top of each bar, he carefully pivoted his body and jumped down. Reaching through the bars, he retrieved his weapon and stroked it lovingly. Remembering his military training and experience as a combat soldier in the jungles of Viet Nam, he crouched in the brush beside his victim and surveyed his surroundings. Paulie's radio crackled, then it began to talk.

"Paulie, are you there?" it said.

Raymond picked up Paulie's handkerchief, shook the dirt and twigs from it then placed it over the mouthpiece. "Yeah," he said, deliberately straining his voice.

"Where's Tony? He doesn't answer," a voice said.

"I think he's sick. He's taking a dump in the bushes."

"You tell that asshole we're supposed to use the toilets in the cabana."

"You tell him; he won't listen to me."

"I'll be right there."

Carmie D'Onofrio cleared his radio and turned to his companion. "I'll be right back; I have to go kick some ass."

* * *

Joey was busy introducing Sarah to his beautiful wife, Bogusia, a Polish immigrant he'd met on a trip to Europe, and his many friends who had come to help the Biancos celebrate. Marco and Donna were seated at Ralph's table, enjoying the company and the beautiful spring day. Nicole's husband-to-be was seated between Ralph and Billy, his future uncle and father-in-law. On the table, a beautifully decorated carton in the shape of a mailbox, hand-crafted by Nicole's younger sister, Nancy, symbolized it's intended purpose. One by one, friends and family deposited the symbol of their best wishes. Thomas looked at Ralph appreciatively. "Thank you, Uncle Ralph. This is more than anyone could have expected."

"That's okay, kid. Just remember, this is only one of the advantages that comes with being a member of our family."

Ralph's words should have sent a thrill through Thomas, but somehow he felt a chill instead. Thomas owed everything to the Bianco's. Before meeting Nicole at a party hosted by a mutual friend, he didn't have much going for him. Though college educated, he was having a hard time finding steady work.

When Nicole informed her father that she was in love with Thomas and hoped that one day they would be married, Billy made one phone call which solved Thomas' employment problems forever. Within twenty-four hours, he was working in the accounting department of the Starlight Hotel and Casino, one of the many Las Vegas establishments controlled by the Chicago Outfit.

Thomas sat silent, momentarily unaware of those around him. Then he heard a voice; it had the sound of urgency.

"Excuse me, Mr. Bianco."

Ralph and Billy turned in unison to see Bobby Meccia standing beside them. "What's up?" Ralph asked.

"It's Carmie, sir. He went to check on Paulie and Tony. I haven't seen him since."

"Did you try to reach him on the radio?" Ralph asked.

"Yes, sir. Nobody answers."

Ralph looked at his brother, then he turned his attention back to Bobby. "I want you to locate Joey, Howie and Larry. Tell them to come here. Then I want you to check the rest of the men guarding the perimeter."

Marco sat up in his seat when he heard Ralph's words, but it was his tone that made him feel a strange sensation in his gut. He sensed that something was about to happen, and he wanted to be a part of it.

Bobby turned away. "Wait a minute," Ralph said. "Give me your radio."

Bobby did as he was told, then left to carry out his orders.

* * *

"Something's going on," Ralph said, as his crew gathered around him.

Billy felt an excitement he hadn't experienced in a long time. The old crew was together again. It's leader was in charge, calling the shots, just like the old days.

"Larry, go to my office, get us some firepower," Ralph said, handing Larry his keys.

"What's going on, Ralphie?" Howie asked, as he pulled his automatic from his waistband, injecting a round into the barrel and activating the safety.

"Always prepared, as usual," Billy said with a smile.

Thomas got up, wide eyed. "M . . . Maybe . . . I . . . I . . . should go find Nicole," he stammered.

"Good idea, Tommy," Billy agreed. "But don't let on that anything is wrong. It may turn out to be nothing after all."

"Y . . . Yes sir, I . . . I won't say anything."

Billy turned to Marco and said, "I think it would be best if you joined Tommy."

Marco stood up and helped Donna to her feet. "You go, honey."

"What's going on? Is something wrong?" she asked.

"Please, Donna, find Sarah and Chris and Gail Musso and stay with them. I'll join you in a few minutes." Marco turned toward Billy. "I have a feeling that what's happening concerns me more than anybody. If you don't mind, I'd like to stay."

Just then, Larry rejoined the crew, handing each one of them a weapon taken from the wall safe in Ralph's office. Ralph took one for himself. Since Howie had his own, Ralph took the one intended for him as well.

Ralph's radio crackled; a stressed voice came over the air waves. It was Bobby Meccia. "Mr. Bianco, they're all dead, everybody."

Ralph turned to the wooded area Bobby had disappeared into just moments earlier. Screams and gasps came from everywhere as Bobby came staggering out of the foliage into the sunlight, an arrow protruding from his back.

"Everyone in the house! Now!" Ralph yelled. Waving his arm in a circular motion, he ordered his crew to get everyone inside and stay with them. "No police!" he shouted, pointing at Joey. "Don't let anyone call the cops." Turning to his brother, who was at his side, he said, "This mother fucker is mine. I promised Dominick I would avenge him personally."

Marco placed his hand on Ralph's arm. Ralph turned with a jerk. "Please, Ralph, I want to help. This is the son-of-a-bitch who kidnapped my daughter and murdered my producer's girlfriend, and don't forget, Dominick was my friend, too."

Ralph glared at Marco, not in anger, but in amazement. He shook his head as he reached into his pocket and handed Marco the extra gun. "You know how to use this?"

"I've taken a few lessons."

Ralph smiled. "If you get an arrow through the head, don't come crying to me," he said, turning his attention back toward the action.

* * *

Bobby had fallen to his knees. One of the waiters dropped his tray and went to his aid. As he bent over the wounded man, two more arrows came out of the trees in quick succession, one striking the waiter, severing his spinal cord, sending him head first into the pool. The second caught Bobby between the shoulder blades, the steel point ripping his throat open as it tore through his body. Ralph watched as his young apprentice toppled over, his life expended.

Ralph picked up a cocktail table by it's base and signaled

for Marco to do the same. Using the tables as shields, they advanced on the sniper.

Ralph heard his name being called.

"Ralph, Ralph."

It was Billy on the opposite side of the pool. He was crouched behind one of the portable bars, pushing it on the concrete patio toward the darkness of the wooded area. Ralph waved his arm in a sort of half-circle motion. Billy understood. He pushed his mobile barricade off the patio and onto the dirt. The large bicycle-type wheels rolled easily on the uneven surface and made it possible for him to position himself at the mouth of the woods which were now deep in shadow from the late afternoon sun.

Out of nowhere, an arrow pierced Ralph's shield, the point barely visible on the underside of the table top. Ralph saw another shaft leave the woods headed for Marco. "Look out!" he yelled.

Startled by Ralph's warning, Marco looked up just in time to see the arrow and reposition his shield to intercept it. The deadly shaft wasn't all he saw. The figure of a man was briefly visible as it ducked back into the leafy branches of an old oak tree.

"There he is!" Marco shouted, pointing upward. "He's in the tree."

Shots rang out from behind the rolling barricade. Leaves and branches went flying in all directions. The whirring, whooshing sound of arrows shooting through the air answered the explosion of gun fire.

* * *

Inside the sprawling mansion, the rooms were crammed with shivering guests laying prostrate on the carpeted floors. Larry and Joey stood guard, nervously peeking through the windows and French doors trying to determine the position of their embattled comrades. Howie wove through the frightened crowd, constantly reminding them to stay down.

Crawling like a combat soldier under fire, Sarah squirmed her way to Joey's side. Rising to a kneeling position, she asked, "Can you see anything?"

"No, your dad and Ralph went into the woods. I can't see them anymore. Stay back, there are bullets and arrows flying everywhere," Joey said, as he placed his hand on Sarah's shoulder and pushed her down.

* * *

With three arrows stuck in each of their tables, Marco and Ralph crept toward the old oak tree. From his position about seventy-five feet to the right of his brother, Ralph could see the portable bar Billy was hiding behind; it looked like a covered wagon in an old John Wayne movie. There were at least six arrows stuck in the side facing the oak tree. Two were shot through the spokes of the wheels, making it impossible to roll it any closer. Ralph felt a terrible sensation when he realized Billy was nowhere in sight. The gun shots coming from Billy's direction had ceased, which served to add to Ralph's fear that his brother had been lost. Then something dawned on him; the arrows had also ceased.

* * *

Stroking his mechanical bow, Raymond Lis lamented, "Sorry, old friend."

Having spent his supply of arrows, he set his crossbow into the crook of a branch. Reaching into his pocket, he retrieved one of the two .38 revolvers he took from the bodies of the dead guards. He placed the gun between his teeth. After tightening the straps on his tree climbing spikes, he wrapped his arms around the trunk of the tree. Slowly, he lowered himself from his perch.

Through the shadows, Marco could see two hands alternately moving down the side of the tree. He could also make out the

64-AMAT

crossbow resting in the branches. Jumping out from behind his shield, he ran toward the tree.

"Marco! Marco!" Ralph cried out, as he witnessed him make his move.

* * *

Joey hit the floor when he heard shots. BANG, BANG, BANG, BANG, BANG, BANG—six shots in rapid succession. BANG, BANG, BANG, BANG, BANG, BANG—six more shots. A voice could be heard. Loud, angry, desperate shouts could be ascertained, the actual words unidentifiable. Then four more shots. Then silence.

* * *

The voice Joey heard was Ralph's. He was crying out as he saw Marco ducking bullets shot from the pistols the crazed sniper now held in each hand.

Ralph advanced, firing on Robin Hood, forcing him to abandon his attack on Marco. Ducking behind the oak, Raymond Lis fired his weapons without taking aim, wasting what ammunition remained, except for one round, which struck Ralph's thigh, spinning him around and knocking him to the ground.

Recklessly disregarding any thought for his own safety, Marco rushed to Ralph's side.

"I'm okay," Ralph said, grimacing in pain. "Here's your chance; take him out. He's out of ammo."

Ralph's face took on the look of solid granite, his eyes glared like hot coals. "Come on, you mother fucker. It's time to pay for Dominick," he snarled through his clenched teeth.

Raymond Lis stepped out from behind the tree. Suddenly, he let out a wail, like that of a wounded wild animal. Marco rose to his feet, took careful aim at the charging lunatic and fired just as Robin Hood lost his footing, tripped up by his own tree climbing spikes. The bullet whizzed by Robin Hood's left ear as he pitched forward and grabbed Marco around the waist with his outstretched arms. As Ralph watched helplessly Robin Hood flung Marco to the ground like a rag doll, jarring the gun from his hand.

Using his superior strength and military training in hand-to-hand combat, Raymond Lis easily overpowered his weaker and much less experienced opponent. Pinning him to the ground, Robin Hood knelt astride Marco and grasped his neck, squeezing tight, cutting off his air supply. Marco frantically clawed at Robin Hood's hands, trying helplessly to break his grip.

"I warned you not to betray me." Raymond Lis growled. "Now you die. Now you die."

Marco fought with all his strength, but with no success, and was about to surrender his life when he heard Ralph's strained voice.

"His eyes! His eyes!"

Marco raised his arms and began to claw at Robin Hood's eyes. Backing away from Marco's attack, Robin Hood loosened his hold on Marco's throat, allowing Marco to take in a deep breath. Oxygen filled Marco's lungs and brought strength to his limbs. He began kicking his legs and bucking his lower body like a bronco trying to throw off an unwanted rider.

"His eyes! His eyes!"

From somewhere deep inside, Marco found the strength to dig his thumbs into the corners of Robin Hood's eyes. He turned his own eyes away when he heard a popping sound as Robin Hood's eyes were forced from their sockets.

Wailing maniacally, Robin Hood released his grasp on Marco's neck. Clutching at his bloodied face, he fell backward, allowing Marco to roll out from beneath him. Marco lay on his back for several seconds, taking in huge gulps of air, while Robin Hood struggled to his feet, groping and clawing wildly.

"I'm not through with you yet, you son-of-a-bitch," Marco snarled through belabored breaths. Rising to his feet, renewed by the oxygen rich blood that now flowed through his veins, Marco taunted the helpless Raymond Lis. "How does it feel not knowing where your enemy will strike from?"

Robin Hood, still screaming in agony and blinded, flailed around madly toward the direction of Marco's voice. Planting his feet firmly, Marco clenched his fist and landed a powerful blow. Raymond Lis staggered and collapsed to one knee. Suddenly, Marco felt an animal instinct swell inside him.

Before Lis could right himself, Marco buried the heel of his shoe into the middle of his bloody face. Barely conscious, Robin Hood keeled over with his left leg bent under his body. He groaned in excruciating pain. Marco felt euphoric as he kicked and stomped the limp figure beneath him. Like a heroin addict, he craved more, more, but it was not the drug he desired, it was blood. Then he heard Ralph's voice.

"Put him out of his misery."

Marco stopped abruptly. He turned to look at his wounded friend. Ralph had dragged himself to the spot where Marco had dropped his gun. Marco grasped the .38 Ralph held in his outstretched hand.

* * *

Chris Musso waited, wondering what would come next. The shrilling of human voices filled the air. Then muffled unintelligible sounds could be heard. There was silence again. Chris raised his head, straining his neck to peer through the window. He ducked down again when he heard three shots in rapid succession. Then silence again, except for the sirens somewhere in the distance.

"There they are!" Larry shouted, as he swung the door open and ran out onto the patio. Larry rushed toward Ralph and Marco. When he reached them, he could see the blood streaming from Ralph's leg wound. He could also see three teeth embedded in the knuckles of Marco's fist.

Joey, who was close behind, stopped when he saw Billy dragging himself out of the foliage, groaning in pain from two arrows protruding from his right leg.

Chris Musso left the safety of the house to join his friends. The sirens were no longer distant. Within seconds, the grounds would be swarming with cops.

Neighbors who at first thought the explosions were caused by fireworks eventually realized they were gun shots. By the time the police were notified, however, it was too late for the would-be Robin Hood.

Epilogue

After leaving Ralph and Billy in the care of their wives, Connie and Eloyse, who would care for them until the ambulance arrived, Marco and Chris walked back toward the old oak. They passed the body of Bobby Meccia. The dead waiter was still floating face down in the pool. They knew there were others yet to be found, victims of the insane Raymond Lis.

They stepped off the concrete onto the grass. Twenty feet in the distance stood the ancient oak tree. They heard one of the cops holler out,"Over here!" The bodies of Ralph's soldiers were beginning to be discovered, but Robin Hood's body had not yet been found.

"Come on," Marco said, quickening his pace. "He's over here."

Chris followed Marco to the battlefield out of morbid curiosity.

There, face up, with lifeless eyes dangling from their sockets by strands of bloody tissue, mouth agape, lay the dead man. Three surprisingly small entry wounds about an inch apart could be detected in his forehead. The ground under his head was saturated with blood.

"It's over," Chris said. "It's finally over."

"Yeah. You know, he revealed himself to me twice. Once in the underground parking lot of my office building, and again outside the courtroom the day Judge Rios dismissed the charges against me. Perhaps I could have stopped him then if I had only known," Marco said, unable to take his eyes off the grotesque face of death. "What is it they say Ralph always says?" Marco asked, removing his torn, blood-splattered, sport coat, placing it over Robin Hood's head.

Chris turned to look at Marco; he felt a chill when he noticed a revolver tucked in Marco's waistband.

Marco was still staring at the dead man when he asked again, "What is it that Ralph always says?"

Chris reached out for Marco and protectively draped his arm around his shoulders. "Three shots to the head does it every time. Come on," he said, hastily leading Marco back toward the house. "Let's get out of here."

90000
9 780738 829906